Three Novel Nymphs

Three Novel Nymphs

A XANTH NOVEL

Piers Anthony

OPEN ROAD
INTEGRATED MEDIA
NEW YORK

Copyright © 2025 by Piers Anthony

ISBN: 978-1-5040-9043-8

Published in 2025 by Open Road Integrated Media, Inc.
180 Maiden Lane
New York, NY 10038
www.openroadmedia.com

Three Novel Nymphs

Chapter 1

ONLY ONE THING

It was a typical day at the Faun & Nymph Retreat. The nude fauns and nymphs were at their usual business, the fauns chasing the nymphs, who did not flee very hard, and celebrating, as they put it, when they came together. A standard episode lasted about five minutes. Then on to the next chase and catch, changing partners. Passers-by who spied the Retreat were normally intrigued, as nothing was concealed. Until they realized that there was no real variety; the script never changed. It was like watching a Mundane show that was locked on repeat. Only largely empty-headed creatures would do that all day. The fauns and nymphs were that.

In fact, the denizens were good for only one thing, by definition. Even that could get boring in time. This was one reason the memories of all who lived there were wiped every night: so they didn't have the retention to realize how dull it really was. It took them approximately a day to catch on, about the time they ran out of new partners, and then it was night. They retired to their separate barracks and slept, to wake with no memories of the prior days. Thus their innocence was restored, and they were happy. This day was mostly used up; shadows were emboldened by the tiring sun and were growing in size and reaching out from behind trees and rocks to touch careless people. Few folk realize how sneaky shadows are. It was the shade's ambition to take over the scene and rule in darkness.

But this day something went mildly wrong. A nymph screamed cutely to get the attention of the nearest faun, flung her lustrous tresses about so that they played hide-and-seek with her shapely upper torso, and kicked one foot head-high so that everything and a bit more flashed in his direction. That signaled the faun to begin the chase, which he gladly did. So far, so good. But because this nymph remembered the myriad incidents of the day, she was beginning to think about maybe possibly perchance catching on to the larger picture. Also, she happened to be perilously close to the border, and she saw something outside.

It was a gully that happened to have wandered into sight before moving on, and in the gully was a nymph with a wild tangle of green hair. The color wasn't the problem; hair came in all colors including plaid, paisley, rainbow, barber-pole, checkerboard, polka-dot, and odd. That was in fact about the only way to tell one faun or nymph from another, as their faces and bodies were alike. Each one's hair was a different color or shade, unique to her. This pausing nymph's hair was iridescent. The problem with the gully nymph was the tangle. Nymphs were supposed to have thigh-length tresses that swung appealingly when they moved. The tangle blocked that, making the hair thunk awkwardly about her shoulders and fail to properly hide and flash her midsection. She badly needed restyling.

The tangle-hair nymph saw her and called. "Help!"

The iridescent nymph discovered that she cared. That, too, had slowly grown in her as the day passed and spot memories accumulated. True, the memories were all of the same act with different fauns, and seeing other nymphs doing the same, but they were at least kindred spirits. A sister nymph was in trouble, and she wanted to help. But it wasn't safe to leave the Retreat, which had a spell to protect its occupants. Outside, spells were as likely to be hostile as friendly, and external creatures could be dangerous to the defenseless Retreat denizens. Tangle Hair needed spot support. "Join me!" Iridescent called to the closest other nymph she saw, who was being chased by her own lusty faun. She had sky blue hair.

Blue Hair opened her mouth to say no, but encountered a problem. Nymphs never said no. She tried to shake her head, but it morphed into a nod. She, too, was coming to care about others. Selfishness and caring warred almost visibly within her. So Blue Hair reluctantly changed course to join Iridescent as she stepped across the boundary line. Iridescent felt a slight tingle as she did, and knew she was exposing herself to the risks and rigors of the outer realm. That made her passingly nervous.

The two fauns screeched to a halt just short of the line. The males were less subject to inconvenient attacks of caring, being more interested in endlessly celebrating. They were not about to risk the most fearful thing that was the Unknown.

"Be careful," the green-haired nymph called. "It's slippery."

"Okay," Iridescent called back. "We're watching out."

Side by side, Iridescent and Blue walked toward Tangle. Suddenly the gully caught them by the feet, and they slid down the bank to the base, legs waving in the air as the two fauns watched, fascinated by perhaps more than the gully. It was indeed slippery.

Irritated, Iridescent righted herself and stood, brushing off her shapely flank. She was unharmed, merely smudged. "Let's go back before night catches us outside."

But when she tried to walk back up the gully slope, she couldn't. It was too slippery. The same was true for Blue.

"That's how I got caught," Tangle said. "I veered too close to the border, stepped across, and slid on down."

"Bleep!" Iridescent swore. That at least she could do, this late in the day. She was coming to realize that it was a euphemism, though she had no idea what it was hiding. It simply meant she was annoyed, a rare emotion for her kind.

The fauns had spied other nymphs flashing their familiar assets, and hoofed off in pursuit, the outside nymphs forgotten. "Bleep," Iridescent repeated, annoyed by the loss of their lecherous attention despite beginning to tire of it.

"That's what I think," Tangle said, joining them. "We need to get back into the Retreat before darkness strikes."

"We do," Blue agreed. "The dark is dangerous."

"Maybe we can follow this furrow until we find a way around the slippery slope," Iridescent said. But as she looked, the gully just got deeper and worser the farther it went. They were unlikely to get free of it before the darkness caught them. "Bleep." The bad word seemed to help, in its fashion. Words did have magic.

There was a swirl of smoke before her, as if a miniature fire had ignited in midair. "Did somebody custard?" it asked.

They stared at it. "A talking cloud?" Iridescent asked, bemused.

"That's not the protocol," the cloud said, darkening angrily. "You're supposed to ask, 'Did somebody *what*?'"

Oh. Nymphs were nothing if not obliging. "Did somebody *what*?"

"Pudding, dessert, treat, sweet, delicacy . . . Oh, beans, they're all wrong."

Iridescent suffered a bright flash of comprehension. 'Beans' sounded almost like 'bleep,' so must be a bad word. Custard started out like a bad word that lost its way and got eaten by a larger word. "Cuss?"

"Whatever," the cloud agreed petulantly. "Was somebody swearing?"

"We're nymphs. We don't know how to swear, except maybe toward the end of the day, and then it's not much."

"What are you?" Blue asked. "Clouds don't talk."

The cloud expanded. It extended two columns toward the ground. These became aesthetic humanoid legs. Feet grew from their ends. Then two more extensions emerged, becoming arms. Hands grew from their ends. The main blob shaped into a torso with firmly projecting buttocks and breasts. The whole assembly shaped into a naked female form whose exaggerated proportions would have freaked out the fauns. "I am Metria. I check into anything interesting."

"Haven't you forgotten something?" Iridescent asked.

The shape considered. "Oh, double beans. I'm not a nymph. I'm a lower-case demoness. Real people wear habiliment."

"Wear what?" Blue asked.

"Shoes, socks, shirts, pants, underwear—"

"Clothing?"

"Whatever." A gorgeous dress formed around the torso, tight in key places to emphasize rather than conceal the suggestive bulges beneath.

"That wasn't what I meant," Iridescent said. "You don't have a head."

"Ooops!" the demoness exclaimed with a full three O's. A new projection swelled from the top, becoming a neck and then a head with a remarkably sexy face. "Details, details," the fresh mouth complained as the lips reddened brightly.

"We've never seen a demoness before, as far as we know," Blue said.

"Well, I'm banned from the Retreat," Metria said. "The anonymous proprietors seem to think I might be a bad influence." She inhaled, stretching her low decolletage until some threads started snapping. "Can't think why. You nymphs are doing it all the time."

"Doing what?"

The demoness laughed, the sides of her tight dress splitting so as to show a fair amount of what the material had covered. "You don't even know, do you! Because you're true innocents. What are your names?"

"We have no names," Iridescent said. "We go by the colors of our hair."

Metria shook her head. "That won't do. You need real names."

"Why? We'll only forget them by morning."

"Because that's what's interesting about you," the demoness said firmly. "I know the Retreat makes you forget everything every night. But you're not going back there. You won't forget."

"But we have to," Iridescent protested. "We're nymphs."

"Not any more."

"Why?"

"Because you are the new protagonist and early companions for a recorded adventure. That's why I came here: to see what was up. I am magically attracted to anything naughty or interesting. A nymph's never been one before."

"What's a pro . . . pro—whatever?" Blue asked.

"Protagonist. The main character of a story."

"Me?" Iridescent asked, astonished. "How do you know?"

"Because I spied the Baton of Protagonism coming here, and I followed it."

The three nymphs stared at her blankly.

"Oh, fudge and panties!" Metria swore. "Do I have to explain it step by step?"

"Yes," Iridescent said, and the others nodded.

The demoness gritted her teeth so hard that small sparks flew out. "I keep forgetting that you nymphs are so innocent that you might as well be children, despite your nefarious daily activity. That's why my villainous curses come out like blobs of candy. The bleeping Adult Conspiracy is taking hold. So I really must explain in a simplistic manner."

"Yes," they agreed again.

Metria sighed a cloud of purple smoke. "Back in the last story, titled *Apoca Lips*, there was a man whose talent was to see the imaginary. He saw a winged baton hovering near him. It looked like this." She briefly assumed the form of a floating wand with wings. "He learned that it was the conveyor of protagonism. That whoever it hovered near and tapped on the shoulder was the main character of the current story. When I learned of this, I studied that wand and learned to see it too. It's imaginary, true, but so am I, in my better moments, so I could do it. Now I follow it to see where the action is going to be. And it is here. You are the main character, you with the glossy hair. That's why you need a name. All main characters have names."

"But I'm nobody. I don't know anything about being a main character," Iridescent protested.

"Nor do you need to know. Protagonism has hold of you, and you are stuck with it. There are advantages."

"There are?"

"The main character always survives, no matter how frightful the adventure becomes. And there will indeed be an adventure. That's what interests me. You may even save Xanth from some awful peril. Probably also get a romance. Make the Xanth character list. So let's name you now. I will look in the Book of Names."

"Book?"

The demoness breathed out a new cloud of smoke. It formed into a floating book with the word NAMES on the cover. It opened and the pages riffed, emanating the dust of long disuse. Metria looked. "You're from the Faun & Nymph Retreat. That's a kind of refuge. So let's call you Nydia, which means refuge. Nydia Nymph."

The nymph opened her mouth to protest, but got caught by the nymphly stricture against ever saying no. Instead she accepted it. "Nydia," she agreed, discovering to her surprise that she liked having a name. It gave her a feeling of identity.

Metria turned to Blue. "You were reluctant to join Nydia. You are an unwilling lady. Therefore, you can assume the name of unwillingness. Noletta."

That nymph tried to protest, but as before, her negative effort became positive. "I am Noletta," she agreed.

And the tangle-haired one. "You look like a messy sea nymph, so we'll call you—" She peered into the book. "Nerine."

The third nymph nodded, her hair bumping. "Nerine." She, too, evidently liked it.

The demoness clapped her hands in a gesture of accomplishment. "Done." The book turned smoky and drifted away.

Nydia summoned all the negative force she could muster. "I'm not doing it. I would just mess it up. I'm going back to the Retreat where I belong."

"You can't. Once you are the Protagonist, you're stuck with it until you complete the novel."

"The what?" Noletta asked.

"Fresh, new, original, daring, narrative—"

Nydia caught on. "The story?"

"Whatever," Metria agreed impatiently. "A novel is a long story. You can't even try to escape it. Its borders are too distant and vague."

Nydia nerved herself. "Well, I'm going to—"

"To what?"

And she found she couldn't. She was indeed stuck for it. "To get on with the adventure."

"Precisely. Now go gather about four more Companions and get on with your fabulous adventure."

"But we have no idea how to handle an Adventure," Nydia said.

"Then get somebody competent to advise you. Maybe one of the Companions you recruit."

Nydia wasn't smart; no nymph was. Nymphs were all body and little mind. But she got a glimmer. "I can choose anyone I want?"

"Yes. Or they choose you. Sometimes it just happens."

"Then I choose you, demoness Metria, to be my Companion and adviser. Because you know how to do it."

Metria was clearly startled. "Me? Nobody wants me! I'm just a nuisance."

"But you know so much more than we do."

"That's the problem. I know a scant myriad of things that would toast your delicate little ears. I am not a suitable Companion."

"But you said I could choose."

The demoness considered. "Actually, I would like to participate in an adventure. It's been a long time. But I'm notorious and would surely mess up up your narrative. But maybe there's a way."

"A way," Nydia agreed.

"I see I must explain, again. A long time ago I got stepped on by a sphinx. That fractured me into three identities: Metria, who is slightly naughty, Mentia, who is slightly crazy, and Woe Betide, who is slightly childish. I have been concerned for her because she can grow and mature only when she is in control of the essence. She hasn't yet learned how to pop in and out as I do." She faded to a wisp of smoke, then reappeared. "I would like her to get some life experience. This might be a way. But I must warn you that in her presence the Adult Conspiracy has full force. No bad words, no Adult concepts. And she has to sleep a lot. She's a sweet creature, but may be a burden at times."

"We can't use bad words anyway," Nydia said. "Does she know the general lay of the land? Because we have no idea where anything is, outside the Retreat."

"She knows the general gist of Xanth. But she has little experience of it. When she's in control, I can watch and listen, but I can't act. The Conspiracy forbids it." She grimaced. "I would be a bad influence."

"But if you are all three parts of the same person . . ."

"We are three people, able to use the host body just one at a time. Only the one in control can give it up. It's complicated."

It surely was beyond the comprehension of mere nymphs, Nydia realized. Best to leave it alone.

Nydia glanced at Noletta and Nerine. They nodded obligingly. "We'll take her."

"Done!" The demoness clapped her hands again and dissolved into smoke. After three quarters of a moment, it formed into a little child about four years old. She smiled timidly at the nymphs. "Hi." But she looked nervous, on the verge of tearful. She had curly red hair, demon fire eyes, a red dress, red slippers, and a sparkling red gem in her hair, the shape of a tesseract. Overall, she was impossibly cute.

Nydia felt a new urge. She squatted, extended her arms, and hugged the child. "You're with us now. We're three nymphs going on an adventure."

Woe Betide was pleased. "Gee."

It was amazing how much that pleased Nydia in return. As far as she knew, she had never hugged a child before. The feeling was quite different from hugging a faun, whose main interest was in holding her tight enough in place to efficiently complete the celebration. She felt supportive and protective, which as far as she knew were new emotions.

"We are the nymphs Nydia, Noletta, and Nerine," she told the child. "We will try to take care of you, and you can help us find our way, wherever we're going."

"Gee," the child repeated, kissing her cheek. That sent a surprising surge of rapture through her.

"Now, Woe, we need to find our way out of this slippery gully," Nydia said. "Before we get caught by the darkness."

The child started to tear up again. "I'm afraid of the dark."

Nydia felt a chill. So was she. So were all fauns and nymphs. That was why they broke off their chases and hurried to the male and female barracks before it could trap them outside for some unimaginable horror. But she couldn't say that. It would scare the child worse. "There's nothing to be afraid of." She hoped. "But we'll try to get safely indoors before it catches us." She really hoped.

"That's good," Woe said, reassured.

Nydia stood and took her hand. "Do you happen to know where this gully ends?" Metria had said the child knew the general gist, but what was gist? It sounded like a bad taste in the mouth.

"It goes into the Gap Chasm. We don't want to go there."

Nydia strained her inadequate nymphly brain and discovered that she did have a vague notion of the Gap Chasm. It was a mile deep (whatever a mile was) cleft crossing the slender waist of the Land of Xanth. A six-legged land dragon patrolled it, gobbling up folk who got caught there. "Yes, we won't go there. Maybe we should follow the gully the other direction."

"That goes to Castle Zombie."

And she knew of that too. It was where most of the zombies lived, or whatever it was they did instead of living. Zombies were truly weird creatures with rotting bodies and brains, yet somehow able to function in their fashion. "I think we don't want that either."

"When zombies fall in love, it's necromance," Woe remarked with a naughty grin.

But the shadows of small trees in the gully were growing dangerously, testing their strength. Soon they would become unavoidable. The nymphly party could not afford to dither long.

Worse, the slanting sunlight was getting in Nydia's eyes. She spied some cap-growing plants and was about to pick a cap to use. But Woe shook her head. "Those are gas caps. Wear one of those and it drenches you in gasoline."

So the dangers of the outside weren't limited to monsters.

There was a dreadful howl not far distant, as of a hungry creature looking for dinner. Nymphs were said to be quite tasty; their flesh was firm and flexible throughout, spiced by their constant celebration. Then the outline of a giant bird passed overhead, maybe a roc; fortunately, it did not spy them. This time. Heavy breathing came from one side of the gully, as of an approaching beast. There was a booming sound in the near distance, as of an ogre beating his massive chest. Indeed, they could not afford even a token dither.

"Somewhere in between," Nydia said urgently. "Somewhere safe."

Woe focused. "There's a cave, maybe. It's supposed to be safe for travelers." She pointed out the direction. "It even has a spell warning off monsters."

"We'll take it," Nydia said, relieved. Monster was another unclassified threat they surely needed to avoid.

They set off down the gully, wee-wawing back and forth to avoid the reaching shadows. Nydia could tell the shadows were annoyed by the close escape of their prey. Soon they came to the cave. The entrance glowed faintly from the light of magic mushrooms, and there was a plaque saying CAVEAT. Below it, in smaller print, CAUTION. NO MONSTERS ALLOWED. The child's knowledge was good. That was reassuring.

They entered, discovering a comfortable chamber with cushions lying against the walls. Folk had been here before. To one side was an empty ram's horn resting in a basket. Print on the horn said HORN and on the basket said PLENTY. At the center of the chamber was a large stone cup filled with clear water. Print on its side said EIN STEIN.

"I don't trust that," Noletta said, ever the unwilling lady as she eyed the cup. "I think I heard of a Mundane with a name like that who was dangerously smart."

Nerine nodded. Nymphs generally were wary of smart folk. There was no telling what ideas they might come up with. They might even try to engage in philosophy instead of the One Thing. Awkward indeed.

But suddenly Nydia was excessively thirsty. She hadn't had a drink since leaving the Retreat. Impulsively, she let go of Woe Betide's hand, went to the big cup, picked it up, and gulped down the water. It was delicious. She felt it suffusing her body, seeming to radiate out of her stomach and into her limbs and head. When it hit her brain there was a soft explosion of knowledge. She stood there, wavering as it manifested.

"Are you all right?" Nerine asked worriedly.

"I am fine," Nydia said. "In fact, better than ever."

"I'm tired," Woe said. She went to a cushion, lay down on it, and was instantly asleep. Apparently, that was a childish talent.

"Are you sure?" Noletta asked. "The river water in the Retreat is safe to drink. But this is Outside. There's no telling what magic might infect it."

"It's Genius water," Nydia said. "Akin to Healing water and Love Spring water. Suddenly I feel ten times as smart as I ever was before. Do you want a sip?" She held the cup out.

Noletta shrank back, alarmed. "Nooo! It could infect me too."

Infect her? Well, maybe smarts were like an ailment to a nymph. Certainly they were not needed for constant celebration with urgent fauns. In fact, she realized that they could be a detriment. Smart folk were not inclined to do the same simple One Thing over and over.

"You?" Nydia asked Nerine.

"Not unless it untangles hair."

Nydia almost smiled. Humor was another largely unfamiliar emotion, and Nerine wasn't actually joking. She set the cup down near a wall where it couldn't get accidentally knocked over. "All it does is amplify intellect. I feel it working on mine."

"We'll try the horn," Nerine said. "It looks interesting." She and Noletta went to the basket and studied the item. Nerine picked it up. "I wish . . ." Suddenly a stream of chocolates flowed from it.

"That's a miniature Horn of Plenty," Nydia said, recognizing it. "Think of what you want to eat, and it will come out."

"How can you know that?" Noletta asked.

"I am now much smarter than I was. Exploring the crevices of my own mind, I realize that there is a template from which the Stork Works prints the original minds of all humanoid babies. It surely saves them time and effort. Start with the prepared model and add details to match the family lines. That serves as the basis for the discovery of useful abilities like talking, reading, and learning. We nymphs never went to school as children.

In fact, we never *were* children. But we can talk and read just fine. Most folk don't really use such abilities. Some prints are flawed and don't make the cut for normal human beings. These are relegated to other creatures, like the ogres, who hardly care for human qualities anyway. Some are sent to the Faun & Nymph Retreat, where they are given nice mature bodies. These ones are good for only One Thing, by definition: celebration. The fauns are there to enable the nymphs to practice it constantly, so they will be ready when a real man comes on the scene. Apparently real men are constantly short of celebration. But now we have escaped that stricture, and can become good for two, three, or even more things. We have only to take advantage of what is hidden in our templates."

The others were staring at her. "Are you crazy?" Noletta asked.

"Hardly. I am, for perhaps the first time in my limited life, fully sane."

"Weird," Nerine said.

Nydia didn't argue. That would be pointless, considering Nerine was a nymph. She was reminded yet again that nymphs were mostly body, hardly any mind. Just as she herself had been, prior to drinking from the Stein. "Now the question is why?"

"Why?" Noletta repeated blankly. She was of course also a nymph.

"Why make an anonymous nymph, a largely empty-headed creature, the protagonist of a significant story? She doesn't even have a magic talent, as they don't get assigned to nymphs. The only talent a nymph needs is to be appealing to a male for five minutes, often less. There are surely hundreds of other folk more worthy of the honor of being the main character in a novel, and far more capable of handling it. Why waste such an important role on a nymph?"

Nerine and Noletta exchanged most of a blank glance. They didn't follow Nydia's question.

"I'm not even very good at being appealing," Nerine said sadly. "When a faun gets a good look at my hair, he turns away and goes looking for another nymph. One with properly swinging hair. Only when it's thickly foggy, or I get caught in a shadow, so they can't see me well, or there are no other nymphs in easy range, do the fauns want to celebrate with me. Even then they usually close their eyes so they can pretend I'm someone attractive. I have tried many times to fix it, but it just tangles again. It's a curse."

"But what's the point in celebrating at all?" Nydia asked. "The same thing over and over."

"It's what we do. We know nothing else." Evidently they were satisfied with that. They were truly nymphs.

Nydia was already exploring another nuance of the template: background history. "The Good Magician exists to answer questions. He doesn't like to be bothered, so he makes his castle hard to get into, but when a person does, he has to answer. He makes them serve a year for it, but usually it's worth it. So the sensible thing to do is go ask him."

"Ask him what?" Noletta asked.

Nydia reminded herself that the others had not drunk from the Stein. They were normal nymphs, not very smart. She had not realized until the present scene how limiting that was. "Ask him 'Why? Why me?'"

"Oh," Noletta said, not really following.

"So we'll rest here overnight, then head out to the Good Magician's castle in the morning."

"Okay," Nerine said amenably. "Maybe he'll know how to fix my hair."

Now Nydia joined the others in eating candy and little bottles of sweet tsoda pop from the Horn. There was something subtly different about it. Suddenly she figured it out.

"Nutrition! These are not the usual empty calories that taste good but don't really feed."

"New what?" Noletta asked.

"Nutrition. What we eat and drink in the Retreat has none of that. It just tastes nice and fades out, not getting digested. We don't really need to take in anything; we are sustained by the magic of the premises." It was coming clear as she spoke, researching in her newly exposed template. "Because we're not real people, merely mock-ups to entertain the eye and touch of passing men who have little or no interest in mind or character. But now that we're outside the Retreat, we don't have that convenience of inherent sustenance. Now we have to eat and drink for real." She paused, chewing on the implications. "That will lead to consequences."

"Cons what?"

"Consequences. We are going to have natural functions, the way real people do."

The other two remained blank. Well, nature would take care of it in due course.

Sure enough, after they had gorged on candy and pop that had some actual substance, they began to feel funny in their bellies. Nydia took them to a private crevice in the back of the cave whose odor suggested its use, and showed them how to natural function. She gave them the real poop, as it were. They were amazed and not entirely pleased. Eating was fun, but this was messy. The liquid splashed on the floor and the solids stank. They needed to wash themselves off after. This ugh had been inside them?

"We won't speak of this elsewhere," Nydia said. "Real folk don't."

"We won't," they agreed, no longer as eager to eat or drink. Certainly not to natural function.

"Which reminds me. Real folk wear clothing. We must now do the same."

"We must?" one of them asked.

"Real folk are embarrassed to expose their bare bodies in public. We need to be mistaken for them, so folk don't assume we are still good for only the One Thing."

"Weird," Nerine said again. But she was evidently picking up on the need, maybe even feeling the first tinges of shame. What other real-folk complications lurked?

They foraged in the recesses of the cave and found a kind of closet with a collection of items. It was almost as if this Caveat Cave were here for their use. A literary device. That made her feel caution. She was coming to be wary of things that were too convenient. But was there a choice? She doubted she would ever again care to settle for being a creature good for only one thing. The Stein had spoiled her for that.

Nydia had to research further in the template to discover the nature and purpose of the bra and panty. They existed to hold the more fleshy sections of the body in place so that the outer clothing fit properly. Also, she discovered, to freak out any men who peeked, temporarily stunning them until the threatened girl escaped. It was complicated, being a real woman. Over these hidden garments the three of them put on blouses and skirts or pants, finishing off with socks and slippers and even cute little hats.

A section of the wall was shiny. It reflected their images. There stood three surprisingly normal-looking maidens. Nerine was garbed in green, matching her hair and eyes, and her hat concealed much of her tangle. She obviously liked that hat. Noletta was in a blue blouse and blue jeans, her nymphly proportions standing out impressively. Nydia was in an iridescent outfit which sparkled as she moved. She even had reflective earrings.

"We look just like real folk!" Noletta said, amazed.

"I believe we are becoming real folk," Nydia said. "We should even have memories in the morning, now that we are beyond the range of the nightly Retreat memory-wipe." But now she knew that real folk had souls, while nymphs didn't. It was all pretense. That bothered her.

"Weird," Noletta said.

"I'm tired," Nerine said, much as Woe Betide had.

They rejoined the soundly sleeping Woe Betide, gathered cushions, and settled down for the night.

Even sleeping, Nydia discovered a new phenomenon: dreaming. A genuine night mare visited her, trotting right into the cave, bringing a dream of a terrible storm, the kind that the Retreat surely protected them from. The raging winds were chasing her, determined to blow her into oblivion. Plants, rocks, small animals, and trees were flying. She screamed, terrified, and woke shuddering. More novel experiences. The template indicated that dreams had meaning, but what could this mean? Then she found that some dreams predicted the future, something she had never before been concerned with. This was in her future? She decided not to tell the others.

In the morning, they woke, rose, ate some crackers and cheese from the horn, and returned to the function section for more efficient performance as they gained experience. Little Woe, it seemed, did not have such needs, being a demoness.

Nydia was glad to feel the burgeoning intelligence in her head. So it was permanent; sleep had not erased it. That should certainly help. Mere nymph intellects could hardly handle the rigors of the Outside.

"We have decided to go see the Good Magician," Nydia told the child. "Do you know the way there?"

"Sure. Just follow the magic path."

She had answered the question literally. That was evidently another aspect of childhood. It seemed that nuances required time and experience to assimilate.

"Please show us the way to the magic path," Nydia said patiently.

"Follow the crib." And a child's bed formed around her. It floated off the cave floor and then made its way toward the entrance. Woe, satisfied, went back to sleep.

Nydia was not completely certain about this, but decided not to question it. She and the nymphs followed the crib outside.

They emerged into dawn daylight. There were no signs of the monsters of the night. That was a comfort. But was it really safe? Her new intelligence warned her that this might be deceptive. Xanth had half a myriad dangers, and more around the edges.

However, the crib contained the demoness Woe Betide and surely knew a safe route. Nydia's research in the Template suggested that the demoness Metria was extremely protective of her three aspects and did not take unwarranted risks. The landscape might be risky, but not the crib. They should be fine as long as they stayed near it.

The crib moved briefly along the base of the gully, then started sailing up the side. It of course was not hindered by the slippery slope. Nydia got a flash of inspiration that lighted the region. Escape! She leaped forward and grabbed the back panel. "Noletta! Nerine!" she called. "Grab on!"

They were a bit slow to understand, so she reached back to catch Noletta's hand. Nerine caught Noletta's other hand so they formed a chain of three. The crib hauled them all neatly to the top. Once there, they let go of it and each other. They were back on the surface.

It was beautiful. The landscape rambled down to a pleasant forest near a field of flowers. Beyond was a lazily meandering river with white birds by its bank. What a delight it would be to go swim there!

But the crib was moving purposefully onward, avoiding the idyllic scenery. That was surely best.

In a surprisingly short time it led them to a path across the landscape, clearly marked by yellow bricks. There was a sign staying ENCHANTED PATH, SAFE THROUGHOUT. Exactly what they wanted. They stepped onto it, following the crib, and the tension of danger faded.

The path went both forward and backward. Which way should they go? No need to ponder; the crib was already heading forward at a comfortable velocity. They followed.

Soon they came to a pause. A sign said STOP. PAY TROLL. There was an arrow pointing to the side, where an ugly troll sat. Beside him was a sign saying A TALENT FOR A KISS. The crib paused.

"I don't trust this," Noletta said. "He just wants to lure us off the safe path so he can ravish us or eat us or both."

Ravish. Another new concept. That could not happen inside the Retreat because all nymphs were endlessly willing, and they could not be attacked as prey. But the rules were different here. Ugly things could occur.

"Exactly," Nydia agreed. "The Template says the enchanted paths are safe, but rife with come-ons to trick unwary travelers."

"But it would be nice to have a magic talent," Nerine said wistfully. "We're not really real people without talents."

That struck home. They might look like people, but they weren't. Nydia realized now that talents were often attached to the souls. What else were they missing?

Woe Betide woke. "Oh, there's Trader Troll. He's fun."

"You know him?" Nydia asked, surprised.

"Sure. He trades for kisses. That's how I got this neat crib." The crib puffed into smoke, not needed at the moment.

"But don't trolls eat luscious maidens?" Noletta asked. "And children?" Her own template was registering.

"Sure. Some trolls do. But they're not all the same. Trader's okay." She raised her voice by floating upward. "Hi, Trader! Remember me?"

The troll looked. "Hi, Woe! I see you made some friends."

"They're nymphs on a mission. I'm showing the way."

"Hello, nymphs!" the troll called. "Come trade for a talent."

"Bleep!" Noletta swore. "I want a talent."

Nydia gave Woe a hard look. "The truth, child. Can she safely make that trade?"

"Sure. I'll show you." The little demon skipped across the line and went up to the troll. "Give me a nice one," she said, and floated up to plant a solid kiss on him. A tiny heart flew out.

"Here you are," he told her, making a gesture. "The ability to conjure eye scream."

"Gee." Woe gestured, and a big cone appeared with a triple scoop of chocolate ice cream.

"But remember, my talents aren't worth much," Trader warned her. "You can conjure each flavor only once. Then it's gone."

"I know," Woe said, avidly slurping. "But I can think of lots of flavors."

"I may regret this," Noletta said. "But I'm going to do it." She strode up to the troll. "Give me a useful talent." She kissed him with such passion that three little hearts spun out wildly.

"I haven't had a kiss like that since I visited the Faun & Nymph Retreat," Trader said dizzily.

"Maybe I was the one who did it," Noletta said. "I don't remember."

"And here is your talent: the ability to see a day into the future." He gestured. "But remember, it's limited. You can see only one day hence, ongoing, not the intervening time or context. It will take some work to make it truly useful. I'm sorry I can't give you a better one."

Noletta closed her eyes, focusing. "I'm in a bedroom somewhere, lying on a bed, looking up at the ceiling. There's no man there. Does that make sense?"

So the talent was working, Nydia thought. That meant it was not attached to a soul, as she had no soul. Too bad there was not a deal to get souls.

"It surely does make sense, once you understand it. If you track it for a while it may clarify. Probably you have found shelter with a nice bed so you can safely rest. Just don't focus on it so hard you stumble into a nickelpede nest in the present."

Nickelpedes. Another threat. Centipedes were harmless, but nickelpedes could be vicious. They had five scents, and could sniff out any prey nearby.

Trader looked around. "Anyone else?"

Nydia opened her mouth to tell him to go dunk his head in a privy, but what came out was an agreement of sorts. "I don't want a talent. I want information. Why is a nymph a main character in a book-length story?" Because if she could get the answer here, they might not need to go to the Good Magician, sparing themselves a fair hassle.

"I don't know the answer, but maybe there's a way to get a line on it. Have you considered asking Com Pewter?"

"Asking what?" But then the Template kicked in and she remembered that this was an irascible machine with an enormous amount of information.

"Don't mess with Pewter," Woe Betide said. "It's got a smart phone that makes nothing but smart remarks."

"It does," Trader agreed. "Better to do your own research. Books usually have chapters that indicate their activity. Maybe if you glimpse the chapter title for yours, or the title of the book itself, that will help."

She was intrigued. "How can I do that?"

"With the talent of glimpsing." The troll focused. "Oops, I see I am out of that one. Maybe this one: the talent of seeing the path to the Dwarf Demon of Titles, who should have the book in front of him."

Nydia was alarmed. "That's a capital D? Super-Demon?"

"The Dwarves are not nearly as important as the full Demons. They handle incidental things, like talents and titles."

That seemed reasonable. Maybe it would work. "Very well." She approached the troll and gave him a kiss that would have made a regular man float. A cluster of little hearts flew out, swirling around their heads before sailing blissfully into the sky to play tag with the watching sun.

"And that one shames the prior one," Trader said, stunned. "Here is your talent. Remember, it will fade after you reach the Demon. I regret I can't give permanent talents, but I'd have to be a Demon to do that. The ones I have are minor ones not wanted elsewhere." He made a gesture.

She felt the talent land. It seemed to add half a dimension to her mind. She focused, and saw the bypath. It started at her feet and wound away through the landscape.

"This way," she said to the others. "And thank you, Trader Troll."

"Thank *you*." He smacked his lips as if savoring the kiss.

They followed the path through field and forest, mountain and valley, yon, hither, and obscure. It led to a hidden house in a bit of jungle, and on inside to where a glowing presence was snoozing. The Dwarf Demon of Titles had fallen asleep on the job. Nydia put a finger to her lips to signal silence. It was surely best to let sleeping Demons lie.

Before him was a large book. Nydia quietly opened it to Chapter 1: "Only One Thing." That was what a nymph was good for. That was accurate but not useful for her purpose. She turned the pages back to the Title Page, which said "Three Ugly Nymphs." Not only was that not helpful, she didn't like it. They weren't ugly, they were just different.

There was a pen beside the book. She picked it up and used it to cross out the word *Ugly* and write in *Novel,* as in new, fresh, unusual, original, extraordinary, not to mention a book-length narrative. For some reason, an image of demoness Metria crossed her mind. That word more properly described them as they chose to be known. Now the title read *Three ~~Ugly~~ Novel Nymphs.* Would that work? She didn't know, but it was worth a try. With luck the proprietor would not notice when he woke.

The Dwarf Demon of Titles still snoozed. Nydia signaled the others. *Let's get out of here.*

They quietly made their way back along the bypath to Trader Troll. "Did you find out?" he inquired. He had turned out to be a pretty good guy. It seemed that trolls, like regular people, varied in type. She realized that she actually liked him a bit.

"No. But we may have accomplished something better. We'll get the answer from the Good Magician."

"I wish you the best. He is said to be grumpy even on his good days."

Her template verified that. But they were stuck with it. "Thank you, Trader Troll," Nydia said, smiling.

He smiled back. "Anytime."

They got back on the enchanted path and walked on. Soon there was a fork. The right path was marked TO THE GOOD MAGICIAN'S CASTLE. The left path was marked DON'T BOTHER.

They took the right one, not bothering with the other. Before long they came to a several-turreted castle surrounded by a moat complete with glaring moat monster. The sign said GOOD MAGICIAN'S CASTLE. GO AWAY. This was evidently the place. Even the sign was grumpy.

Chapter 2

GOOD MAGICIAN

They gazed at the castle, slightly daunted. Did they really want to tackle it? Did they have a choice?

"Just so you know," Nydia said, "it is not supposed to be easy to reach the castle. There are always three Challenges barring the way, and if we mess up on any of them, we wash out. It's not dangerous physically; we may be threatened, but we won't actually get hurt. But neither will we get the answer to why a nymph is the protagonist of a significant story and other nymphs should be her Companions. We may just have to return to the Retreat and do what nymphs do."

"Not while I'm along," Woe Betide said. "You can't do adult things in my presence."

"You'd revert to Metria and go to seek something interesting elsewhere," Nydia retorted. "Metria revels in adult things."

"Blip," the child swore, refuted.

"Not that what we do is a bad thing," Noletta said, "but doing it all day? Nothing else? Losing our memories every night? Now that I have retention, I'd rather explore the world outside, dangerous as it may be. At least there should be some variety."

"And I'd like to get my hair untangled," Nerine said.

They looked at Woe. "Do you have any further input?" Nydia inquired.

"I don't know much about the adult realm, by definition," the child replied. "But I do know that Metria is banned from the Good Magician's Castle, just as she is from the F&N Retreat. That makes me super curious to know what's in it. I'm afraid that if I don't find out, Metria will be mad at me. She may even have had this in mind when she yielded the body to me. She loves to snoop into what doesn't concern her."

Nydia nodded. "I think the vote is for trying it, and if we fail, well, we tried."

"Go for it," Nerine agreed.

But before they could act, a handsome young man approached from the side. "Hello, pretty girls," he called. "Are you going to tackle the Challenges?"

Nydia reminded herself that they no longer looked very nymphly. He thought they were real people.

"You have a problem with that?" Noletta demanded.

"Not at all. I'm trying to decide whether to do it myself."

"We have a Question we think only the Good Magician can answer," Nydia said. "What about you?"

"My name is Trade. Folk in my village all make fun of it, calling me Mark as if I'm from Mundania. My talent is that when I pick up any book, it is blank except for the last chapter, so I can never be surprised by the ending. They ridicule that too. So I want to travel far away where nobody knows me. But I don't want to do it alone. I need a girlfriend who likes traveling, but none of the local girls want to leave the village. So I am trying to decide whether to ask the Good Magician where a suitable girl is." He glanced at Noletta as if mentally undressing her. In fact, her blouse started to fade before she frowned down at it. "I don't suppose you'd be interested?"

"I'm a nymph," Noletta said.

He was taken aback. "But a nymph is good for—"

"Only One Thing," Noletta said. "And that's not traveling."

"Sorry I asked," he said, and walked on.

"That is the problem," Noletta said sadly. "He'd have liked a night with me, but in the morning he'd be on his way alone." She was evidently catching on to the nature of outside males, which was similar to that of inside males. Their interests barely extended beyond that One Thing.

Which only deepened the mystery of why they were here. Trade seemed like a good man. He hadn't lied to try to get that night, but he did have more than one thing on his mind. He might indeed have to ask the Good Magician.

They found a path leading toward the castle. The moment their feet touched it, something changed. "Uh-oh," Nydia said. "My smarts just went."

"I can't see a day ahead," Noletta said.

"The Magician knows I'm here," Woe said. "And he's not pleased."

"My tangle just went!" Nerine exclaimed. Indeed, now her hair hung loosely about her shoulders in a green cascade. It looked much better.

Then Nydia caught on. "No special magic is allowed in the Challenges, as it is considered an unfair advantage. We've all lost ours, such as it is. But it should return once we get through."

"*If* we get through," Noletta said, negative as always.

"So we're in it," Nydia said. "We'll just have to forge on through."

Noletta looked resigned. "And hope to avoid the worst."

They forged on. It was exciting to be doing this, even if they were destined to fail.

They rounded a turn and almost collided with a family going the other way, a man, a woman, and a child reasonably older than Woe. All three nymphs tried not to stare, as they were now extremely interested in what real people looked like, and this was their first close contact. "Oh, are you other folk trying to get into the castle?" Nydia asked.

"Not exactly," the man replied. Oddly, he did not seem to be mentally undressing her; her dress remained completely intact. He was moderately tall, muscular, with blue eyes, pale skin, curly red hair, and a full beard. "We're doing our year's service for our Answer. I'm Pat, and this is my wife Colleen, and our granddaughter Quintessa." Colleen was an attractive woman at least twice the nymphs' apparent age, with slightly curly dark brown hair, green eyes, pale skin, and light freckles. Quintessa was about six years old, with almost luminescent pale skin tinged peachy pink, curly medium-length blond hair, deep blue eyes, dimples, slight freckles across her nose, and a friendly smile. None of them were cast from the same mold in the manner of the nymphs; their features were completely different.

"Oh." Nydia wished she had her intelligence back so she could make a smart response. As it was, she would just have to bumble along. "We're three nymphs and a child, hoping the Good Magician will tell us what we're doing here." Which these folk probably already knew. "What were your Question and Answer?" Even as she spoke, she knew she was messing it up. She had no business poking into their business. They would set her straight in a hurry.

But Pat smiled. "You're Nymphs? From the Retreat? So you don't have much experience with Xanth proper."

Why was he being so polite? Was this some sort of trap? She lacked the wit to know. So she blabbed foolishly on. "Yes. Somehow we became characters in a narrative, and we don't know why. Nymphs are good for only one thing, and that's not handling a meaningful story. There must be some reason."

"There surely is. We sympathize. We're Mundanes who managed to find a secret avenue into Xanth. We Asked the Good Magician how we could achieve immortality, and he Answered that physical immortality is not possible for Mundanes, but a trace of literary immortality could be had merely by staying here. So we're here, hoping to stay a while."

Nydia was discovering that she liked him. He did understand what it felt like to be an outsider. "I hope you succeed. We'd better get out of your way."

Pat laughed. "We're going nowhere. We are here to try to prevent you from getting past us."

"Oh, blip!" Woe said. "And they seemed so nice. They're the enemy."

"By no means," Pat said. "Consider it more like a game where we are opponents. We will each do our best to defeat the other side, but outside of the Challenge we can be friends."

Nydia was taken aback. "You are telling us you are trying to stop us?"

"Yes. And we wish you success in getting past us. But from here on be wary, because we are in the Game. It has stopped every person who encountered it so far."

The Game? Maybe he meant Challenge. "Uh, I suppose. What are the rules?"

"There are only two rules. We are not allowed to tell them to you directly. But we will write them out for you." Pat glanced at Colleen, who carefully wrote words on a piece of paper. She pressed the paper between her hands, then handed the paper to Quintessa, who took them to Woe Betide.

Woe dropped the paper on the ground. "It's hot!"

"It'll cool," Pat said. "It's just hot from the press."

Nydia suspected there was some kind of pun there, with something figurative becoming literal, but she lacked the smarts to figure it out. That was maddening after her brief experience with intelligence.

"Now it's cool," Colleen said.

Nerine picked it up, folded it in half without reading it, and brought it to Nydia.

"I don't trust this," Noletta said.

Nor did Nydia, even in her unsmart stage. "We'll play that game another time," she decided. "Thank you, Family. I'm sure we'll like it when we have time to play it." She tucked the folded paper into a pocket.

"You're not even going to look at the rules?" Pat asked.

Her memory of being smart enabled her to fake it. "If we did that, we'd want to play it, and right now we have other business." She glanced at the others. "Let's get on with it." She might be making a calamitous mistake, but what could she do? She was a stupid nymph, good for only one thing, and sensible thought was not that thing any more than handling a significant story.

They walked on down the path a few steps.

"You have crossed the line," Pat called after them.

"What line?" Nydia called back, not even trying to seem smart.

"The line separating Challenges. Congratulations. You have won this one."

"But we haven't even played the Game!"

"Let me explain," Pat said, coming to rejoin them. "You won by not playing."

Nydia shook her head. "I'm just a stupid nymph. This makes no sense to me."

"Here is the thing. The rules are: One, you must not think about the Game, as that means you have lost."

"How can I think about it when I don't even know what it is?"

"Precisely. You can't. So you won."

Nydia looked at the others in her party. They looked as blank as she felt.

"Rule Two is that when you lose, you must announce it loudly and publicly, causing others who hear you to lose it too."

Nydia was feeling really stupid. "How could anyone win a game like that? Just knowing the rules makes them lose."

"Exactly. You won by not learning the rules. We're glad. You seem like nice people."

Nydia lacked intelligence, but caught another faint glimmer. "You seem like nice people too. I gather you're not prejudiced against nymphs."

Colleen pursed her lips but did not speak. Possibly she felt that nymphs were all right in their place, but she did not want one getting too close to her husband.

"Nymphs are like the Game," Pat said. "They don't know any better so they're all right."

"Our ignorance helps us?"

"It's like the Mundane Bible story. Adam and Eve couldn't sin because they had no knowledge of sin. Only when they ate the apple from the Tree of the Knowledge of Good and Evil did they catch on, and then it was too late. They were booted from the Garden of Eden, and their descendants have been sinning ever since. Your ignorance of the Game prevented you from losing it."

Nydia's head felt as if it were spinning. This was way too complicated for her. "So we lucked out?"

"Yes. And we are glad for you. We'd have hated to be the cause of your failure to see the Good Magician."

He seemed to be sincere. "Thank you, I guess."

Noletta and Nerine had been chatting with Colleen. Now they bid her farewell. Woe and Quintessa hugged. Then they moved on.

"That was not what I expected," Noletta said. "They were actually on our side."

"Weird," Nerine agreed.

The path wound through a grove of pretty poplar trees, followed by ugly unpopular trees. They passed a big bed with a head at one end and two huge solid feet at the other. Did the Good Magician think they were going to lie down on it and sleep?

But a little warning voice whispered in Nydia's head. Everything was here for a reason. What was the reason for this one?

She couldn't be bothered at this stage. There was surely danger lurking nearby.

There before them, suddenly, was a giant insect. No, it was, well, a girl, maybe. It had both human and insectoid features, and leg spurs like porcupine quills. It looked formidable. And hungry.

They paused. The monster stood right astride the path; they could not get around it. So this was a Challenge. They had to get past it without getting their heads bitten off.

Their heads? That gave her the clue. "It's a praying mantis!" Nydia exclaimed, horrified. "They eat folk, including their heads." For now she also saw the huge angled pincers of the forelegs.

"Yes," the Mantis Girl answered. "I am Orchard Mantis, most fearful of monsters. I even practice kung fu. And you look tasty indeed."

"Run!" Nydia cried, properly terrified. She had no idea what kung fu was, but it sounded dangerous. Maybe threats were not real here, but they could be scary as bleep.

They ran back up the path. But the mantis girl followed, taking much bigger strides than they could manage. Soon she would catch them.

Then they were up against the bed. They ran around it, trying to keep it between them and Orchard Mantis, but she was about to reach over it and nab them anyway.

Nerine dropped to her knees beside one of the feet of the bed. "What are you doing?!" Nydia asked, managing to invoke two punctuation marks at once.

"I'm praying," Nerine said. "It's the only way to save my feeble hide."

The only way? It was no way at all! Mundania had gods folk could pray to, but Xanth was something else. No deity would rescue her. The monster would pluck her still form, crush her into juicy pulp with its pincers, and gobble her down in two or three pieces.

"She's right," Noletta said, dropping to her knees at another foot. "We must pray for deliverance."

Woe Betide began to cry. The monster couldn't really hurt her, but she might not fully understand that at her age.

This was crazy! Nydia was appalled as well as frightened. But what else was there to do but give up? They were lost anyway. So she dropped to her knees between them. Woe Betide floated beside her, whimpering. At least they would all go together.

The monster loomed over them. Her giant pincers clacked menacingly. Then she got down on the other side of the bed, no longer chasing them.

And Nydia suffered a revelation. Orchard was a praying mantis. Of course she had to join the prayer!

"I'm glad you caught on," Orchard murmured. "You wouldn't have tasted very good, all stressed out." She rose and walked away.

They had survived the second Challenge as much by blind luck as reasoning. But what about the third? Could sheer chance get them through one more time? Nydia doubted it. But, again, what choice did they have?

There was nothing to do but get on with it. They walked warily down the path and crossed the line between Challenges.

There was a girl. Not a horrendous creature, just a faintly pretty brown-haired young woman sitting on what appeared to be a ramp. Could this be the dreaded Third Challenge?

"Hello," Nydia called hesitantly.

The girl glanced their way. "Oh. Hello. You must be the new Challengees."

"Yes. Are you the Challenge?"

"Maybe. I don't know. It's my job to maintain this ramp."

She didn't know? Why else could she be here?

"Let's talk," Nydia said. "We are three nymphs and a child hoping to ask the Good Magician a Question. Who are you?"

"I am Corona. My name means glowing circle, though I don't glow and I'm not circular. I get endlessly teased about it. My talent is to make invisible print appear. They ridicule that too. I asked the Good Magician how I could find a really good and understanding boyfriend. I'd like to travel some, see the rest of Xanth, but the boys in my village just want, well, nymphs, not girls with minds. They sneak out to the F&N Retreat all the time. The nymphs there never say no." She glanced questioningly at them. "You're nymphs? You're pretty, but you seem more like real folk."

"We're trying to be," Noletta said. "But it's complicated."

Nydia got a glimmer. "And the Good Magician told you that the right man would be waiting for you when you finished your Service and left here."

"Yes. How did you know?"

"A lucky guess. Do you have much of your Service left?"

"No. This is the last day of my year. I have maintained this ramp throughout, but have no idea what it's good for." Her lips quirked. "Not even one thing, maybe."

Nydia studied the ramp. It led right to the edge of the castle environment and broke off. There was nothing beyond except empty land. Anyone who walked it would fall off and land outside, not inside the castle. Obviously that was not for them.

Then she saw the glowing sun, low in the sky, as it was near the end of the day. The sun always ducked behind the horizon so as not to get caught by the looming darkness of night. But there was something wrong with it. There was a sore on its surface. "What's wrong with the sun?"

"It's got a virus on its outer circle," Corona said.

"A corona virus."

"Yes, like my name. I hope I didn't infect it. I hate to see it suffer."

Nydia summoned another memory of her smart phase. There had to be a connection. She peered at the sun as it passed below the ramp. "I think I've got it! You must run up the ramp and jump on the sun as it sinks beneath the end."

"But wouldn't I get burned? The sun's hot."

"I think not. You are at the end of your Service. You are about to get ejected from the Good Magician's property. Your name is Corona. You will give the sun a coronal injection which will cure it. It won't burn you; it will be grateful."

"Are you sure?"

"I'm not sure. But it seems very likely. Otherwise, all this is beyond coincidence."

"There's someone walking outside," Noletta said. "I think it's Trade."

"Right on schedule. He is the man for you, Corona. Quick, run up that ramp and jump! You won't regret it."

She spoke with such authority that the girl obeyed. She ran up the ramp and jumped right onto the sun. She bounced off it, unhurt, and Trade was there to catch her. He set her down carefully as they talked. Then they kissed. Little hearts flew out. Both of them waved to the nymphs.

And the sun glowed brightly as it sank below the horizon. Contact with Corona's ejection injection had cured it.

They had somehow navigated the Third Challenge.

Now the path led straight to the bridge across the moat. The moat monster eyed them but made no hostile move as they crossed. It evidently knew they had won admission.

As they reached the castle, a door opened. A middle-aged woman stood there. "Welcome to the Castle, Nydia, Noletta, and Nerine," she said. She frowned. "Woe Betide is not welcomed but tolerated as long as she stays in that form and keeps her mouth shut. I am Wira, the Good Magician's daughter-in-law. I handle household incidentals. I will conduct you to the Wife of the Month, who is Sofia Socksorter."

They were silent. Wira obviously knew all about them. They followed her into the Castle, down a hall, and to a workroom where a Mundane lady sat sorting through an immense pile of socks.

"They are here, Sofia," Wira said, and faded out.

Startled, Sofia looked up. "My apologies, all. I lost track of the time. I swear the socks accumulate faster than they can be sorted. Humfrey married me so he could catch up on them, but I just assumed my wifely turn yesterday and there's a five-month backlog. I need to clear the floor."

Nydia suffered two revelations. First, that her intelligence was back. Second, that Sofia needed help. "What can we do?"

The woman didn't protest. "Sort them into piles by color and type. If any cling to you, save them out. They will be yours."

Even smarts did not help here. "Ours?"

"Humfrey instructed me to get you socks that are resistant to hazards of fire, water, air, and earth. I don't know why."

"But aren't socks merely cushioning for the feet?"

"Let me explain. Humfrey is the Magician of Information, but over the course of centuries the magic has smeared somewhat and verges into some physical properties. Among these are resistance to the elements."

"Centuries?" Noletta asked.

"He's getting on toward two centuries old. He takes Youth Elixir to keep his physical age at about one hundred. The magic of his presence is absorbed by the socks he wears. Some have hardly any magic, but others are potent, especially in the smell. I wash them, but the magic won't wash out. Anyway, some protect not only the feet, but the whole rest of the body from damage by the elements. Those are the ones for you."

And she didn't know why. This story had started out odd and was becoming downright strange. It almost seemed to be about more than just nymphs.

Then she suffered another flash: it hadn't been sheer luck that got them through the Challenges. The Good Magician had *wanted* them to reach him.

But still the Question: why? The Good Magician had his quirks, but foolishness was not among them. This was still not making much sense.

They sat cross-legged on the floor around the pile and got to work sorting the socks, except for Woe Betide. She tried to pick one up, but it hissed like an angry insect and wriggled out of her hand. Indeed, she was not welcome here. She started to cloud up.

Nydia gave her a reassuring hug. "You can supervise," she said. "Just watch the rest of us work and make sure we do it right."

"Gee," she agreed, comforted.

"You've got the touch, Nydia," Sofia said approvingly. "Someday you will make your own child very happy."

Nydia opened her mouth to protest, but stifled it, realizing that if they actually managed to become real people, the storks would no longer ignore their signals and she could get a delivery. What a change that would be! The other nymphs looked thoughtful, sharing similar musings.

Soon there were several growing piles of different colored socks. "Wira said you are the Wife of the Month," Noletta said. "I thought a man kept the same wife from month to month. Did I hear it wrong?"

Sofia laughed. "No, you heard right. Over the decades, Humfrey outlived his wives, including me. When they died, they went to Hell, which is not actually a bad place, merely uncomfortable. Then when his last wife, the Gorgon, died, he had had enough. He got a hand basket and rode it to Hell to demand her return. The proprietor obliged, but with a caveat." She smiled. "Yes, I know you encountered a cave by that name. It's a useful term. In this case, he got back all five and a half wives at once. Since this is against the normal protocol, we make do by alternating. One of us joins him each month. This is my month. Actually, he's so grumpy that we're glad for the relief."

"Half a wife?" Nerine asked.

"That's MareAnn, his first love. They were only fifteen, still naive. Her talent is summoning equines. She was afraid that if she married him and learned the secrets of the Adult Conspiracy, she would lose her innocence and no longer be able to summon unicorns. So she declined, though she loved him. But after experiencing Hell she concluded that marriage couldn't be much worse on innocence than that, so she married him in a very small ceremony. So it only counted for half. She's a nice girl, and we all like her."

Nydia set an iridescent sock down to start a new pile. It clung to her hand. She used her other hand to pull it off, but then it stuck to the other. "Bleep," she muttered.

"Oh, you found one," Sofia said. "Put it on."

Oh. Her protective sock. Nydia pulled off one slipper and sock and pulled on the new one, then replaced the slipper. The sock fit perfectly and was completely comfortable.

Soon the others found their socks and put them on. Nydia found her second sock. They were dressed, as it were.

Except for Nerine. "I have three," she said somewhat plaintively.

"Keep it," Sofia said. "Carry it in a pocket. Sometimes a sock gets a hole, or lost. You will have a spare."

"Oh." The nymph tucked the sock into a pocket.

Nydia wondered about that. The socks had really selected themselves. Why had an extra one oriented on Nerine?

Wira appeared. "Himself is ready."

"Who?" Nydia asked.

"Another explanation," Sofia said. "One of the wives started referring to Humfrey, the Good Magician, as Himself, perhaps because she regarded him as full of himself, because of his knowledge and grumpiness. Soon it spread, and now we all use it." She shrugged. "Don't get us wrong. We're glad to be his wives, and we know he means well, but at times we do get a smidgen impatient. We are by no means rivals, but rather compatriots in arms, as it were."

Oh, again. They got up. This was, after all, what they had come for.

"Perhaps, for this, the child should stay with me," Sofia said.

So she wouldn't be right in the Good Magician's face. Even Woe nodded. Why push her luck?

The three followed Wira up a winding flight of steps to a cubbyhole of a room mainly filled by a giant open book on the table beneath. This was of course the Book of Answers. Behind it sat a gnome of a man who looked about a century old.

"Sir, the nymphs are here," Wira said, and faded again. This time Nydia watched to catch it, and saw that she merely departed quietly. No magic, merely stepping out of the central focus.

The gnome looked up. "You've got the socks on," he grumped.

Nydia had had enough. "Yes, Sofia told us to don them. Why are we here?" she demanded.

The ancient face focused on her. "Why are you suspicious, nymph?"

Nydia knew this was foolish, but her temper was chomping at the bit. "None of this was coincidence. The way that slippery gully veered too close to the Retreat border, catching Nerine when she stumbled across, trapping her and then we other two when we tried to help her. The way the nosy demoness happened by just at that moment with the news that I was the new protagonist of a novel story. The way that Caveat Cave was so convenient, with that Ein Stein set right in the center to arouse my thirst and make me smart. The clothing right there so we wouldn't be naked any more. Trader Troll, with his talents for kisses. The way the Challenges seemed to luck out in our favor so we made it through them all when we should have washed out on the first one, or been eaten by the Mantis, or let Corona finish her term and depart without curing the sun, so that we lost by default. Finally, the socks, to protect us from what? What horrendous mission have you selected us for, that needs such security? Are we chosen to be sacrifices to some impossible cause we know nothing about? Because we are expendable?"

"Yes."

She was startled. "You admit it? Then tell us why? Why stupid, talentless nymphs who are supposed to be good for only one thing?" The other two were silent, letting her carry the dialog. She knew they agreed with her, now that they were becoming real, but lacked her Stein-enhanced mode of expression.

"Because ordinary Xanth folk can be tracked by their magic, which manifests mainly as their talents, great and small, attached to their souls. Nymphs lack talents and souls, so can't be tracked."

"What about Noletta, who was given the talent of twenty-four-hour vision?"

"That is on loan from the incidental collection of Trader Troll. Tracking that will reveal only that collection, not any soul or person. So your party remains essentially anonymous." He glanced gruffly at Noletta. "You do have a talent, minor as it is, nymph. Use it."

"But it shows only a few seconds, not the context," Noletta protested. "That's like a single jigsaw puzzle piece out of place, almost useless to see the big picture."

"True. You need to ascertain how to make it more useful."

Noletta was silent, not satisfied but not knowing how to make anything of it.

"Let me see if I have this straight," Nydia said grimly, hardly half a wit mollified. "You want a soulless, talentless protagonist, so she can be anonymous?"

"Exactly. I'm glad to see that the Stein is working, providing you at least a token bit of wit."

Was that an insult or merely his normal arrogance? "Anonymous from *what*?"

"The perpetrator."

"The perpetrator of what?"

"Some background," the Magician said. "Recently there has been a plague of the elements. Fires are raging, waters are flooding, storms are blowing away whole villages, and the ground is quaking so violently in some areas that forests are being decimated. Something is angering the elements, and that something has to be a capital D Demon, proof against my talent of Information. We are allied with the Demon Chaos, who is more than capable of nullifying any other influence, including that of a Demon, but he can't act when the Demon is unknown. Your job, should you elect to accept it, is to locate that identity."

Had she misheard? "We have a choice?"

"You do. This requires your active support. There may be danger."

"Suppose we decline?"

"Then you will be free to return to the Retreat."

"And be good for only one thing!"

"True. Most nymphs are satisfied with that. So are their consorts. Once you return there, you will have no memory of this visit or this operation."

Nydia shuddered. Now at last she understood Why. There was horrendous mischief in Xanth, that maybe only they were equipped to handle because they were beneath notice. Get that understanding Wiped? Let

Xanth suffer because they lacked the incentive to tackle the problem? Because it fell outside what they were supposed to be good for? That notion was painful. "We have glimpsed the outer realm of Xanth. We don't want to go back to lascivious ignorance."

"But I'm not at all sure I want to tackle the challenges of greater Xanth," Noletta said. "There are all kinds of dangers we don't face in the Retreat."

"You are ugly nymphs," Humfrey told them bluntly. "Surreptitiously changing the title of your story does not change the reality."

So he knew about that. He truly was the Magician of Information.

"We're not ugly," Noletta argued. "We're made in the image of all nymphs, which is lovely."

"One of you now has high intelligence," he said. "That's a potent no-no for a nymph, making her attitude ugly." Nydia froze; he was scoring on her. "Another has magically messed hair; since hair is the only quick way to tell nymphs apart, that makes her ugly." Nerine froze, similarly scored on. "The third has a magic talent. No proper nymph has one. That makes her ugly in her nature." And Noletta froze.

"Are you determined to insult us?" Nydia demanded.

"By no means. I am establishing that you are no longer qualified as nymphs. But you can be beautiful as real people. For example, intelligence can be a significant asset to an appealing woman."

Nydia glanced at the others. It was clear that none of them wanted to continue as nymphs. "You have made your point, Magician," she said tightly.

He didn't even bother to look at her. His gaze was on the giant book, which was evidently more interesting than mere nymphs could ever be. "Then you are ready for the mission."

"Ready to attempt it, at any rate. What do we get if we succeed?"

"Souls and real lives."

Nydia froze again, as did the others. Suddenly they knew that this was the ultimate reward. Ordinary existence as real people, complete with souls! Oh, yes, they wanted it, now that they knew it was an option.

But that was in the future. There were intervening details. "We don't even know where all the mischief is."

"That is why you will need another Companion."

"How can another Companion help? What we need is Information."

"Her name is Wyvinia, but she goes by Vinia. She is Prince Ion's fiancee. She is fourteen years old."

"She's a child? I thought you said she is a prince's fiancee."

"When she comes of age, they will marry. She was the protagonist two
novels ago, and a significant character in the last one. She is experienced,
as you three are not, and she is not a suppressed demoness. She has two
talents."

"Two? I never heard of that!"

He didn't bother to grimace. "Of course you haven't. You have lived a
sheltered, ignorant life."

Nydia was beginning to appreciate why his wives called him Himself. He lacked certain social graces that even sheltered, ignorant nymphs
could appreciate. But that was neither here nor there, though it was tanta-
lizingly close. "What two talents?"

"Contact telekinesis is the open one. Among other things, she helps
her boyfriend walk by moving his nonfunctional legs for him. The more
important hidden one is to see the paths of the near future."

Nydia knew those abilities could be potent. "Where do we find this
two-talented prodigy?"

"At the Queendom of Thanx."

"The what?"

"Most countries are kingdoms, organized and run by men. This one,
which is really Xanth spelled backward to the extent feasible, is run by
women, with the men merely supportive. The child Woe Betide knows
its location."

There was something about that Queendom that Nydia liked. The women
were in charge! This adventure was already becoming more interesting.

"We will go there tomorrow," Nydia decided, as night had closed in
about the castle. The setting of the sun had warned them that the end of
the day was nigh. It always knew. Maybe because nigh was just one letter
away from night.

Wira reappeared. "Your room is ready." Woe Betide was with her, looking satisfied. Evidently Sofia had known how to entertain a child. Could
she have actually made sock sorting interesting?

Just like that, they were guests of the castle? Nydia saw that the Good
Magician had already tuned them out as he contemplated the book.

They followed Wira out and down a hall to what turned out to be a pleasant suite. It had three beds and a small child's crib, and there was a private room for the dread natural functions.

"Oh!" Noletta exclaimed as she entered.

Uh-oh. "You have a problem?"

"This is the room I saw in my vision of the future. I recognize the furniture."

Oh. "That does make sense. It's good to confirm that your talent is accurate, minor as it may be."

There was a sound as of a low canine howl. They looked, and there was no animal, merely an alcove with windows looking out over the exterior landscape. Then Nydia got the pun: "A bay window." They groaned, coming to appreciate puns as the inferior humor they were.

A nearby picture on the wall smiled. The image turned out to be of Good Magician Humfrey when he was a young man, a quarter way handsome. He was evidently amused by their discovery of the baying window. Surely harmless, but Nydia wondered why there should be an animated picture here. Vanity, or to spy on guests?

Nydia thought of something. "Have you checked your talent recently?" she asked Noletta.

"I've been so distracted by what's happening now, I haven't thought of it. I can't afford to tune in on the future when the present is so busy. But I'll check it now." She focused. "Oh my ever-bleeping life! That can't be."

Nerine was curious. "What can't be?"

"We are kissing a woman! Not incidentally. It's maybe romantic."

Nydia had a problem with this. "We may be good for only One Thing, but that's just with a man."

"Maybe we can change it with a decision."

But Nydia was cautious. "Kissing a woman won't kill us. Maybe it's the only way she communicates. We don't want to change our future whimsically. We've got enough on our minds without pointlessly complicating it. Let's find out what's going on when we get there. If we don't like it, then we can change it."

"Okay," Noletta said uncertainly.

Nydia hoped there would be some reasonable explanation. Certainly she would never voluntarily do the One Thing with a woman.

They returned to their appreciation of the room, putting the disquieting vision of the future as far from their minds as possible.

They had hardly settled in before Wira reappeared. Nydia had not been paying attention as she faded out. "Dinner is served," she announced. "You will join Sofia and me, as Humfrey is busy elsewhere tonight."

Suddenly Nydia was hungry. That seemed to be a consequence of becoming real: they had to eat often, even though it led to functions. Obviously real life was far from perfect.

The meal turned out to be sumptuous, with assorted pot pies in the shape of iron pots, boot rear to drink, and eye scream in the form of screaming eyeballs for dessert. The demon child loved that, even though she didn't need to eat.

"Are you going to tell us your history?" Woe Betide asked Wira.

"If you wish." She glanced at the nymphs, who nodded together. They knew so little about outer Xanth that they were glad to hear anyone's history.

"It is simple enough. I was delivered in the year 1052. It is now 1124, so chronologically I am seventy-two years old. I was a burden on my family, so was put to sleep at age sixteen, in 1068, until Humfrey's son Hugo woke me in 1090. Then I was youthened twenty-two years, so as to be younger than Hugo, and married him. I have been helping around the castle ever since."

"She gives the castle continuity," Sofia said. "We wives come and go, but Wira remains. Humfrey really depends on her."

"Why isn't Hugo here?" Noletta asked.

Wira smiled sadly. "He has become a background character. If he is ever needed in the foreground, he will reappear. I miss him."

Nydia realized that being real could have its liabilities beyond functions. Was that destined to be their own fate, even if they made it to reality? To become essentially nothing?

"Perhaps you misunderstand," Sofia said. "Background characters still exist. They have their own minor adventures. They simply are not summoned to appear in the recorded stories unless there is some reason. Many of them prefer it that way. Being a Protagonist or a Companion can get stressful."

Nydia was coming to appreciate that too.

In due course they returned to their room. They were tired, another complication of reality, and soon were in their beds and sound asleep.

In the morning, as they stirred into wakefulness, a wandering thought landed on Nydia. Thoughts did that, yet another aspect of her becoming real. "We followed an enchanted path to get here," she said. "But I'm not sure there'll be one leading to Thanx. There could be danger along the way."

"There sure could be," Woe agreed. "Monsters love the waypaths. Metria likes to tease them, pretending to be a delicious helpless maiden, then disappearing just as their teeth close on her so that they strike sparks. It makes them so mad!"

"But we really are delicious maidens."

The child nodded. "I guess you'll have to be careful."

"Very careful," Nerine said. "Not just of monsters, I think. Of men who see us as nymphs."

"Excellent point," Nydia agreed. "We now have better things to do than be constantly chased and celebrated by men."

"But how do we stop them?" Noletta asked. "Aren't men pretty much like fauns, wanting only one thing?"

Nydia spot researched in her template. "Pretty much, for the most part. But we have a defense: our new panties. We can flash them to freak out any pushy men."

"Can we? I'd like to verify that."

Noletta's natural skepticism seemed warranted. "We should test our panties," Nydia agreed.

"How? I don't want to be ravished by a passing man before I discover my panties don't work."

That was a problem. They needed to verify panties before putting themselves at risk. But how, with no ordinary men on the premises?

Then she got a flash inspiration that briefly lighted the room. "The picture!"

"The what?" Nerine asked.

Nydia walked to the picture of Young Humfrey. Its eyes tracked her approach with a certain faun-like interest. "Take a good glimpse of this," she told it. Then she turned around, hoisted her skirt, and flashed it with her iridescent panties.

"Wow," Noletta breathed.

Nydia looked. The face on the picture was frozen, the eyes no longer tracking anything. They were two patches of iridescence. It had freaked out. "It seems they do work."

"Maybe when I'm grown," Woe said, "I'll understand why just seeing cloth makes a man freak. I find it boring."

"It's special magic," Nerine explained.

"In fact, this whole castle is boring, except for Sofia. I don't know why Metria is so interested in it."

"Adults lead dull lives," Nerine said, with the gist of a smile.

Nydia remembered something else. She looked at Noletta, who was now trying on a new dress from the clothes closet. "Have you checked a day ahead? The Good Magician told you to use your talent."

"Yes. I saw us kissing a woman, remember?"

"But the future can change, even with a thought."

"That's right! I forgot that aspect. I'll look again." She concentrated— and screamed. "EEEEEEEEEE!!" It was no cute teasing sound to tempt a faun. It had so many E's in it they could hardly be counted, and they were all capitals. This was utter horror.

"What is it?" Nydia asked, alarmed.

"There's nothing!" the nymph exclaimed breathlessly. "Nothing at all!"

"Have you lost your talent?"

"No! I have it. But the other end is blank. There's nothing there."

Nydia focused her intelligence. "This answers the description of a termination somewhere between here and there. As if a monster ate you."

"Yes," Noletta agreed shudderingly.

"And if you're gone, chances are the rest of us are too."

"Yes," Nerine said, tuning in on the horror.

Nydia battened down her burgeoning panic. "Let me try an experiment. Let's say we are traveling a path, and come to a fork. We take the right-side path. That leads us to the hungry monster, and we are doomed. Now let's make a decision: when we come to that fork, we will take the left-side path. What do you see?"

Noletta's face shifted into wonder. "The picture's back! We're in another bedroom like this one, but more feminine."

"A bedroom in the Queendom of Thanx."

"It must be."

"That means we made it safely there," Nerine said, relieved.

"Because we changed our route," Nydia agreed. "Suddenly I'm seeing that this supposedly minor talent she won from the troll may be far more useful than we thought. The Good Magician told her to use it. He wasn't fooling. The scene is in the future. We're here in the present. We can change it! That may have just saved our lives."

"Wow," Noletta said faintly.

"Let's zero in on it. We want to be sure to make the best use of it. Let's try something else. Like returning to the Retreat."

"But we don't want to do that," Noletta protested.

"Indeed we don't. But this is just practice. A thought experiment. Let's go back there."

"I guess," Nerine agreed uncertainly.

"There's our decision. Noletta, what do you see now?"

The nymph focused. "I'm there. A faun has just caught me. He's throwing me down on the ground. I'm screaming cutely, egging him on. He—" She hesitated. "The picture just went blank. I mean, it's there, but there are no details, just grayed out sections."

"Because a child is listening," Nydia said. "The Adult Conspiracy is bleeping it out."

"Blip!" Woe Betide swore. She had of course hoped to get a glimpse.

"One more," Nydia said. "Let's follow the enchanted paths to go visit Castle Roogna."

"Okay." Noletta focused. "We're still on the trail, in the morning. I'm washing up in the nearby pond, my clothing on the bank. There are cherry pie plants growing beside the water, and fresh milkweed bottles. I see something at the farthest corner of my eye. A furtive motion. I think a man is hiding in the brush nearby, trying to sneak a peek."

"They do," Woe said wisely. "They like to glimpse bare women. Can't think why. Metria would moon him, but he wouldn't mind."

"No, it would just bring him in for a bleeped out session."

"And she would dissipate into smoke just as he took hold of her," Noletta said with a certain private satisfaction. Her independence was almost visibly expanding.

"I think we've verified the talent," Nydia said. "The left fork it is."

Then it was time for breakfast, before they set out for the Queendom. Nydia was increasingly satisfied. Now they knew how to proceed safely, proof against both monsters and men. That was a phenomenal comfort.

Chapter 3

QUEST

They exited the castle, nodded to the moat monster, walked across the bridge spanning the moat, and found a pleasant avenue leading to the enchanted path network. Woe Betide's crib floated beside them as she napped. A sign said CASTLE ROOGNA with an arrow. That was the capital of Xanth, not anything they wanted to mess with now. Another sign said ZOMBIE CASTLE with a similar arrow in the opposite direction. No, they weren't into zombies! A third said GAP CHASM. With its awful dragon? No thank you. A fourth said GOOD MAGICIAN'S CASTLE. They laughed; the arrow pointed back the way they had come.

The arrows finally gave up teasing them. The fifth said QUEENDOM OF THANX. That was the one. "Thank you," Nydia said. A shadow flickered across the sign as if it were nodding.

They had hardly gotten fairly started when another sign accosted them. DETOUR: PATH UNDER CONSTRUCTION. SAFETY SPELL IN ABEYANCE. The main path was blocked by a rough stone wall, and they could see ogres working in the distance, twisting bordering tree trunks into pretzels and squeezing the juice from stray stones. It seemed that the Queendom was a more recent development, and not all its paths had been completed yet. They did not want to mess with ogres, either, even tame ones.

"Bleep," Noletta muttered. "That means we'll have to be alert."

Nydia was caught by a passing thought. Thoughts did that, apparently drifting randomly around until one collided with a receptive head. "Maybe it's for the best. We need to test our socks and your talent. We won't always be on safe paths, and we need to be prepared."

Noletta nodded. "Let's do it." Now that she had learned more about the larger realm of Xanth, and kept her memory, she was committed.

They stepped onto the bypass, which was a crude trail through the jungle, maybe hacked by the ogres. Nydia was hyper-alert, remembering how Noletta's talent had shown them extinct at one point. "Stay tuned," she told Noletta.

"Oh, yes! So far we're fine."

The trail meandered down to a passing stream just deep enough to soak their slippers. But the tumbled stones of the channel looked sharp, so bare feet were not the answer. Then Nydia remembered. "The socks! They should keep us dry and whole."

"If they work," Noletta said dubiously.

"I'm not afraid of water," Nerine said, and waded in. And paused midstream, taken aback. "It's dry! Even the slippers, I think."

Oh? Nydia strode in. Indeed, it was as if there were no water, except that she could feel its slight resistance to the motion of her legs. She reached down to touch her slippers, and not only were they dry, so was her hand. The magic of the hosiery was not limited to the feet. "I think the socks are working."

Noletta joined them. "They do work," she said, surprised in her turn. "But this is water. What about fire?"

The crib floated blithely across, unconcerned.

They walked on. Soon Noletta sniffed the air. "I smell smoke."

It turned out to be a fire salamander chasing insects, leaving a thin, smoldering trail behind. Nydia got down and blew on a likely section, evoking a small flame. She gritted her teeth and touched it with a finger. And felt—

"Nothing," she said. "I do not feel the heat at all. The socks are working for this too."

The others tried it, and confirmed that the fire was harmless to them. The socks were proving out, not at all limited to feet. That was a relief.

They walked on. "Uh-oh," Noletta said. "My vision just flickered. We must be in danger."

"More smoke," Nerine said.

Nydia looked to the sides. The jungle was impenetrable, and some of the trees looked hungry. Tangle trees, surely, that grabbed and ate any creatures with edible flesh. Like tasty nymphs. The trail was the only avenue anywhere. "We'll just have to be careful."

They rounded a curve and spied a blazing fire in the middle of the trail. They paused.

"Haa!" a loud voice came from behind. "Fresh meat!"

It was a troll, and not a friendly one. He blocked the trail behind.

"Uh-oh," Noletta repeated. "A worse blink."

They had walked into a trap. "Remember," Nydia warned, "not all trolls are like Trader. Most are vicious."

Now other trolls appeared, skirting the fire to close in on the nymphs. "Dibs on the blue one," one said. "I want to use her before I roast and eat her."

That was Noletta. For a moment she froze, checking into her future vision. Then she made a decision, surely guided by that.

"I got the shiny one," another troll said, stalking Nydia.

"The green one's mine," a third one said, eyeing Nerine. "I don't care how messy her hair is; her body is good. At least for this one thing."

He meant two things, the second being roasting and eating her.

The crib floated on, ignored, as Woe Betide slept. The trolls surely knew better than to try to eat a demon. All they'd get was a foul taste before she dissipated into smoke.

Nydia was for the moment stunned, unable to come up with a viable escape plan. It was Noletta who acted. "You want a piece of me?" she demanded of the one who clearly did want exactly that. She strode toward the bonfire as the troll pursued her. She reached in and took hold of a blazing stick. She held it up, the fire not touching her. "Come and get me, foul-face!"

The troll paused, not certain if what he was seeing and hearing was real. Nymphs were supposed to scream cutely and fling their hair about. Not carry a burning stick bare-handed!

"You deaf?" Noletta demanded. "Or just hungry? Then take a taste of this. Open your ugly mouth." She advanced on him, brandishing the torch. "Eat this, imbecile!" She shoved the brand right at his face.

The troll, astonished, fell backward. Noletta pursued him as he landed on the ground. "Come on, bleep-face!" Her language was getting worse as she jammed the fire at his open mouth.

The troll screamed in pain. He scooted away on his back, then got up and ran.

But Noletta wasn't through. She whirled on the one orienting on Nydia. "You hungry for tender flesh, too, bleep for brains? Here's your meal!" She swung the stick at his head. "You like roast? Chomp down on this."

The troll retreated, cowed. Noletta focused on the one stalking Nerine. He, marginally smarter than the others, bent away and averted his face.

"Oh, you're hiding your ugly part?" she demanded. "Then I'll serve your pretty part." She jammed the stick at his exposed bare rear.

"Oooooo!" he howled, taking off as if jet-propelled.

But the remaining trolls were reorganizing, arming themselves with damp sticks to fend off her attacks. This wasn't over yet.

Nydia came to life as she saw the way. "Grab more firebrands!" she yelled. "Drive them off!" She plunged a hand into the bonfire and got hold of a fine flaming branch. Nerine joined her. There was no pain at all. "Charge!"

They ran at the trolls who, surprised again, scattered. The siege was over.

Victorious, the trio circled the bonfire and walked on down the trail. Once they were certain there was no pursuit, they set the branches down on a clear section and moved on. They knew the trolls would not tackle such weird creatures again.

"Noletta, that performance was brilliant," Nydia said. "How did you come up with it?"

"I just did what I had to to keep the future active. Whenever it wavered, I got more aggressive until it clarified. It's clear now."

"That talent of yours is more potent than we thought."

"I'm learning how to use it," Noletta agreed, pleased.

"The socks are potent too," Nerine said.

"Indeed they are. The Good Magician gave us a real gift."

"He must really want us to succeed in our quest," Noletta said thoughtfully.

As he had from the outset, Nydia realized. From the moment Nerine got caught in the gully. Had they ever had any free will, or was that merely a pleasant illusion? Still, this was vastly better than endless celebrating in the Retreat. Even the danger, since they were handling it.

They continued walking, intrigued. Woe Betide still accompanied them, having slept through the whole fracas. They could have awakened her, but why? The trolls were hardly child's play.

They passed a field of pie plants and harvested some to eat. Nydia had apple pie, Noletta cherry, and Nerine watermelon. Woe woke long enough to grab a small chocolate pie. She didn't need to eat, but liked candy.

Then they came to a larger river. This one was too wide and deep to wade across, and there were no bridges or boats; they would have to swim. Fortunately, the template also had that ability. They mainly just had to spread their arms and kick their feet.

Except that the socks prevented it. They walked down into the deep water and seemed to be encased in bubbles of air, keeping them dry. Could they actually walk across the deep riverbed?

"No," Nerine said. "I've got to get into this." She removed her clothing, handing the wadded outfit to Nydia, then stooped to remove her socks. She was now nymphly nude.

"But you need the protection," Nydia protested. "You could drown."

"I think not." She handed Nydia the socks, then stroked with her arms and swam into the deep water.

And was transformed. Her tangled hair spread out into a luxurious shawl that played about her splendid body. She was absolutely beautiful. She dived, and seemed to have no trouble breathing; in fact, she was breathing the water. Now there seemed to be translucent webs between her fingers and toes to aid her swimming. She was plainly in her element.

"You're a nereid!" Noletta exclaimed. "A sea nymph!"

"You must have been sent to the wrong Retreat," Nydia said. "A paperwork mistake. That's why your hair fouled up. It needs to be surrounded by water to flourish."

"I never knew until I got in the water," Nerine said, gratified. She was even able to speak with her face below the surface.

Meanwhile, the other two forged across the riverbed by foot, encased in bubbles of air so they could breathe. The socks remained impressive.

They rejoined at the far bank, where Nerine recovered her clothing and her tangle. Woe Betide's crib, of course, floated placidly over the water. It seemed to keep track of them, needing no directions from the child.

Then they came to a section where nickelpedes swarmed. Nydia knew from her template that there were many kinds of bugs in Xanth, many of them harmless to human folk. Centipedes normally went about their own many-legged business, as did dimepedes. But nickelpedes and quarterpedes were vicious. They gouged out nickel or quarter-sized chunks of flesh. They were not elemental, so the socks would not protect the nymphs against this.

But the bugs were across the trail and along the sides. Even as the trees opened up into a valley, there was no way to avoid them. What were the nymphs to do? Stomping them would squish only a few before the rest scrambled up their limbs and bit them to death. Even if they escaped, they would have ugly welts in the worst place, their legs, making them unsightly. That horror was almost worse than death. There was no fire to burn the insects back, or water to drown them. Nothing but a solitary windmill placidly blowing small white clouds to and fro.

Nydia was stumped. Unless . . .

"Woe Betide," she said urgently.

The child woke, startled. "Are we there yet?"

"Not yet. Our way is blocked by nickelpedes. We can't get through. What would Metria do?"

Woe laughed. "That's easy. She'd insult that windmill."

Could this possibly be relevant? Was the child teasing her? Nydia was discovering a temper, something true nymphs lacked, but she held it in check, just in case she was missing something. "How would that help us?"

"It'll blow them away. The socks will protect you but not the 'pedes."

Nydia glanced at Noletta, who pursed her lips thoughtfully. Weird things could make sense in Xanth. The inanimate could indeed get riled up. Worse, stones could see up under skirts and sometimes make vulgar comments. Nymphs hardly cared, but they were trying to leave nymphdom behind. That was surely why the path-making ogres were squeezing stones dry. A squished stone could not look up anyone's skirt, let alone make a naughty remark.

All they could do was try it and see what happened. "Thank you, Woe."

"Sure." The child went back to sleep.

Nydia faced the windmill. She marshaled her insult ability, another part of the template. "What do you think you're doing, fan-face? Leave those poor clouds alone."

The windmill revved up angrily, orienting on her. She was scoring!

"You heard me, blades for brains. You're not supposed to be picking on innocent clouds. Stop it immediately."

Now the mill sped up furiously. A gust of wind came right at them, blowing leaves and twigs away.

"Is that the best you can do, airhead? Your name must be Zephyr."

That did it. The wind intensified. Now it blew dirt and stones from the ground.

But it did not affect the nymphs. Air was an element, and they were protected against it. They stood unmoved. That only incited the mill to further effort. But it could not touch them.

The nickelpedes, however, were not so lucky. They were blown away. She almost, but not quite, felt sorry for them.

"Good show," Nydia called to the mill as they quickly passed the section that had been buggy. Partly mollified, the blades eased off. Regardless, the nymphs were now passing out of range.

So the child's advice had been good. They had found a way to make the socks work for them indirectly. There would surely be other occasions where they could sock it to the environment, if they were just cunning enough to do it.

But further mischief lurked. A werewolf spied them. It howled the news to its pack: delicious maidens in range. In barely half a moment, the response came: two-thirds of a baker's dozen acknowledging howls. They would likely converge within seven and a half moments. Then the nymphs would be tasty dead meat. No need to roast them.

Bleep! Nydia thought. This time there was no windmill in sight, merely a small volcano resting in the distance with barely a wisp of smoke rising from its cone. No wind blowing there. "Woe," she said imperatively.

The child woke. "Insult the 'cano." She returned to sleep.

What the bleep good would that do? They were here; the volcano was there, maybe an hour away by foot. Even if it erupted, it wouldn't affect them. But what else was there? The template had a memory of when a princess had insulted a volcano, saying she had seen a better cone on eye scream. The volcano had really blown its top. The template also had a memory of Mount Pinatuba going Ooom-pah! and blowing out so much smoke and dust it cooled all Xanth by a degree. She suspected that drear Mundania had never seen anything like that. Only this was a magnitudinally inferior volcano not even looking for a quarrel.

But she had to try. She dredged the template for suitable language. "Hey, cone-nose!" Nydia called. "You're sleeping on the job!" There was an angry puff of smoke from the cone. It had heard her.

"Yeah, you, hotbox! You hardly look warm enough to heat a pot of gruel lukewarm."

More smoke belched, forming a cloud over the cone.

"What a pantywaist!" she called, though she didn't know what a panty-waist was; it was just a word in the more obscure region of the template lexicon.

Nevertheless, it had power. A torrent of smoke shot up from the cone, forming the shape of a huge mushroom in the sky. The volcano was truly insulted. But Nydia still did not see how this aerial show could save them from the werewolves.

As if on cue, the pack appeared. The leader morphed to man-form. "Wow!" he exclaimed. "These girls have nymphly proportions. We'll do some celebrating before we tear them into screaming toothsome pieces!"

Somehow males always seemed to want to celebrate before getting down to business. If only it stopped there!

In desperation, Nydia stuck out her tongue at the volcano. "Nyaa-nyaa, conic symbol! You can't get me, you pile of sludge!"

The volcano rumbled so hard its sides split open and melted rock spewed out. *Lava*, the lexicon said. But it was still over there, while the werewolves were here, leering closer.

Blazing rocks heaved out from the cone, crashing into the ground all around them. This was getting scary! Then the ground around them shook violently. It heaved up, tossing trees and werewolves into the air. The wolves howled in surprise and panic.

But there was no effect on the nymphs. Then Nydia caught on: this was the Element of Earth. It extended everywhere they walked. They were protected from it. The werewolves weren't.

Woe Betide had come through again.

They walked calmly through the carnage. It looked like the template's recording of a battlefield, with debris littered across it. Now Nydia almost felt sorry for the wolves, as she had for the nickelpedes, until she reminded herself what they had planned to do to the nymphs. Live by the sword, die by the sword: another nugget from the record.

The socks had now proved themselves four ways, protecting them from Fire, Water, Air, and Earth. There was one more element, the Void, but Nydia hoped they wouldn't have to face that.

They crested a hill, then came to a fork. Uh-oh. "Take the left trail," Nydia said. Then she wondered. "Hold on; let's try the right trail first."

"Noooo!" Noletta wailed, suddenly stricken.

"Correction. The left one."

Noletta relaxed. Her talent, too, was proving out.

They walked along the path, relaxing; this could have been horrendous without the socks and Noletta's talent. But Nydia was not about to relax completely. There were too many uncomfortable nuances.

"I wonder what's on that other fork?" Nerine asked.

Nydia was curious too, but saw no safe way to find out. "Nothing we want to mess with." All the same, she wished she knew. As a nymph, she had not been curious, but of course there had been nothing to be curious about. Fauns, nymphs, and the One Thing were the extent of it. Here in outer Xanth, everything was odd, quite apart from the danger of some of it.

In due course, just clear of an undue course, the trail rejoined the enchanted path. It looked very nice; the ogres had done good work. It seemed that ogres, like trolls, varied, with some being almost decent, hard to imagine as that was.

The day was tiring, having seen enough action to hold it. Shadows were taking advantage of that weakness to grow longer. The sun, taking notice, descended toward the safety of the horizon.

And there was a nice-looking campsite, complete with pie plants, milkweed bottles, a clear pond, and a neat cottage cheese. Their ideal place to stay the night. The enchanted paths really took care of their travelers.

They went to the cottage, opened the door, and peered inside. It did not smell cheesy at all.

"This is what I saw in the future," Noletta said, satisfied.

On a shelf were bottles labeled Moonshine, Sunshine, and Earthshine, made from distilled spirits. "I don't think we want this," Nydia decided. "They may be fine for experienced folk, but we're still new to Outside Xanth. No offense to Metria, but I don't quite trust spirits, even distilled ones."

The others accepted her judgment.

Nerine found an old mirror in a corner, its glass cracked. "Oh, you poor thing!" she exclaimed.

They settled in, harvesting pies and milk, and washing in the pond.

Then another person appeared, walking along the path. It was a girl, maybe an early teenager, kicking pebbles ahead of her. She had hair-colored hair, eye-colored eyes, and a face-like face, essentially anonymous. She spied the campsite and veered off the path toward it. This made sense, as this was a camping spot and the day was ending.

If they were going to have company for the night, they needed to get to know each other. "Hello!" Nydia called.

Evidently startled, the girl paused, gazing at her. She did not speak. Maybe she was shy.

"Are you joining us for the night?" Nydia called.

"I guess."

She was evidently not much for dialog. "I am Nydia. Who are you?"

"Ara. It means Most Able Maiden." She recited it as if it were a spot memorization.

Still not much. Nydia had an idea. "Woe," she said to the crib floating nearby.

The child woke. "Oh, that's an Autism." She returned to sleep.

Nydia spot-researched the word in the template. It referred to a type of person who was not much for communication, had a rigid personality, and was emotionally detached. That explained things somewhat. She would have to initiate most of the conversation.

"Ara, where are you going?"

"To the Queendom of Thanx." So she could respond satisfactorily to direct questions.

"That's interesting. Do you have business there?"

"No."

"Family?"

"No."

"Friends?"

"No."

Nydia couldn't think of what else to ask. Then she got a different idea. It was far-fetched, even wild, but just maybe it would work. "Nerine!" she called. "May I borrow your extra sock?"

"Sure." Nerine tossed her the sock. It landed obligingly right in her hand.

"Ara, I have something that just possibly maybe might help you get along with us. May I explain?"

The girl just looked at her, maybe not understanding, maybe not much interested.

Nydia held out the sock. "This is a magic sock. I am thinking that if you put it on your head as a cap it might help you, well, talk."

The girl continued to look at her.

Nydia was learning how to take the initiative. "Let me try it on you."

"Okay."

Nydia approached Ara and fitted the sock carefully on her head, like a cap with a topknot. It fit nicely, as the other socks did on their feet. "How does that feel?"

The girl's face lighted. "That feels wonderful! Suddenly I can speak freely. I have so much to say!"

"Say it."

"I am here because my family in effect threw me out of the house, tired of my stupidity. I am not stupid, I merely had little to say to them. They engage in what they call small talk, which I have no use for, so I ignore it. I am not yet equipped to live alone, so I decided to go to the Queendom of Thanx where they welcome girls of any type, even ant and nickelpede girls. This campsite is merely a stop along the way; I do not mean to intrude on your party. I did not know you were here until you called. I was busy counting my steps."

Counting her steps. That, too, seemed to be part of the syndrome.

"We are going to Thanx too," Nydia said. "You are welcome to join us. We expect to arrive there tomorrow."

"Thank you! I am so grateful." She paused, surprised. "I could never say that before. It is awful being emotionally isolated."

"It surely is," Nydia agreed, gratified that her idea was working so well. She was still learning how to relate to real people.

The girl touched the sock. "If I may ask, what is this headpiece you have lent me? It is doing marvels for my comprehension, let alone my sociability."

"It is a sock once worn by the Good Magician Humfrey. His magic suffuses it. It protects against damage by the elements."

"Like Earth, Air, Fire and Water? These are not oppressing me. I get along with them better than I do with people. They don't pester me with pointless dialog." She paused again. "Though now I appreciate that this is the way other folk relate to each other. They need diversionary distractions. I am not like that. I am of a different and probably superior stock. But I don't see how the elements relate to my sociability."

It was becoming wonderfully clear. "There is a Fifth Element, the Void. You suffer from a void in personal communications. This leaves you emotionally detached from other people. The sock is protecting you from that."

"The fifth Element," Ara breathed. "I knew of it, but thought it was nothing, literally. How wrong I was! It is transforming me! I will be really sorry when I have to give it back."

Nydia glanced at Nerine. "Keep it," the sea nymph said. "I have two socks; I don't need three."

"I am so grateful! I want to be your friend."

Nerine was plainly taken aback. "But I'm a nymph! Good for only one thing."

"I am too young to know what that one thing is. But does it exclude friendship? I truly understand what it is like to be limited by the opinion of others."

Nerine was suffering her own expanded appreciation. "Yes, I'll be your friend." She approached and hugged Ara.

The evening and night passed amicably enough. There were comfortable old cots for all, as was to be expected in a cot-age cheese. In the morning, they found a patch of breakfast cereals, breakfasted, washed, dressed, and returned to the enchanted path, now a party of four and a half, Woe Betide being the half. Nerine's tangle was back in her hair, but Ara clearly didn't care. The two walked side by side, chatting, handling small talk.

As the sun climbed to the very top of the sky so as to be there by noon—it being a punctual entity—they came to a sign. QUEENDOM OF THANX. MEN WELCOME AS LONG AS THEY KNOW THEIR PLACE. They laughed together. Evidently there would be no faun and nymph chases here, unless the nymphs chased the fauns. But Nydia wondered what kind of men would submit to rule by women. Would they be femaleish men? She had no personal experience with authentic men, but doubted she would want one herself who only looked male while lacking the spirit. Not that any real man would want a nymph for anything but the One Thing she was good for.

There was a girl of fourteen walking out to intercept them. She had evidently expected them. She had brown hair and brown eyes. "Hello, Nymphs!" she called. "I'm Vinia. The Good Magician called me via our magic mirror and told me to join your Quest. So today I'll show you around the Queendom and tomorrow we'll head out." She glanced at Ara. "We have a nice room for you with a roommate who likes the artistic type."

Ara frowned. "I'm not artistic. I'm autistic."

"Oops. We can get you a different girl. What kind would you like?"

Ara paused, evidently guided by the sock. "It's all right. I'm sure I can get along with her. Maybe I'll try being artistic too."

Vinia smiled. "Artists are great folk. You will like it here." She glanced at the floating crib. "And hello Woe Betide! We like you better than we do Metria."

"Gee," the child said, abashed.

"Is that all?" Noletta asked archly.

"No, of course not. Nydia, I brought another Companion for you. Meet Anthem Ant." She held up a hand. There was a red ant on it.

"That's a fire ant!" Ara exclaimed. "They burn folk!"

"Anthem is one of the few telepathic ones," Vinia explained. "We have a colony here and get along fine. The Good Magician said you'll need her. She's nice; you'll like her." She poked her hand toward Nydia. "Take her. The moment she touches you, you'll feel her mind. Ants don't have big minds, but the telepathic ones can draw on the brains of their companions to make them fully smart."

Nydia decided to gamble, as what Vinia said seemed authentic. She extended a hand. Vinia took it in hers, and the ant walked across.

Suddenly there was a whole new person in her mind. "Hello, Nydia," the ant said, not audibly but in meaning, with a musical quality.

Amazingly, Nydia already liked the ant. She was indeed a nice person; there was no doubting it, because Nydia was sharing her mind. Deceit between them was impossible. Yes, she was an ant, a dangerous one, but it seemed that ants, like trolls and ogres, differed. "Hello, Anthem."

"We'll get along," the ant said.

Indeed they did. They were lost in dialog as Vinia guided the group to their suite in the Queendom and the party got settled in for the day and night. Anthem could read the minds of any folk Nydia touched physically to make the connection. She was also musical. She shared her memories of the ethereal music of the spheres, which was transcendent.

Then Nydia remembered something. "There was some dreadful danger we managed to avoid on our way here. Had we taken a wrong turn on the path, it would have wiped us out. Do you have any idea what it could have been?"

"Oh, yes! Reading your mind, I see exactly the place. There's a rogue dragon in that area, preying on travelers who aren't protected by the usual path enchantment. Queen Demesne is organizing a posse to take it out."

The template lacked that name, which must therefore be recent. But as soon as Nydia realized that, the ant's mind provided it. Queen Demesne, called Mesne for short, pronounced Meen, was a demoness with a good nature and a talent for organization. She was making Thanx a worthy Queendom, able to compete with the surrounding kingdoms.

Nydia's attention wandered. She lost track of incidental events. Then they were at a dance. There must have been things happening because now the nymphs were clean from their traveling and garbed in appealing dresses, with flowers in their hair. Even Nerine had her hair done so that her tangle looked intriguing. Nydia had to break off her rapport with the ant in order to pick up on the details of the event. It seemed Thanx had regular occasions like this for the benefit of its citizens. There were men there in plenty, and Anthem assured her that their interest in girls was the same as that of the fauns, but they were far more polite about it. There was no chasing, no grabbing and wrestling for position, and they kept their clothes on.

A courtly man with plaid hair approached. "Will you dance with me, fair maiden?"

"But I have no idea how to dance," Nydia protested, though flattered by being taken for a genuine maiden. "I'm from the Faun & Nymph Retreat. I'm a nymph."

He smiled. "And I am from the Naga Kingdom. I'm a naga."

"In fact he's the Naga Prince," Anthem said. "Nolan, Queen Apoca's consort. A former Protagonist."

"He's a prince?!" Nydia exclaimed aloud. "I can't dance with a prince! Even if I could dance. I'm nobody."

"Be at ease," Nolan said. "I must admit to an ulterior motive."

"We don't do that away from the Retreat."

He laughed. "You are shapely enough to arouse that thought. But my motive is for my companion Aurora to confer with your companion Anthem while we are touching. They can do so in privacy while we dance."

"But I can't dance!"

"Yes you can," Anthem said. "I will guide you."

The music started, and suddenly she knew exactly how to do it. The ant was lending her her own ability, which she must have learned from associating with the humans when training in for this mission. She stepped confidently into the Prince's embrace.

And with that contact, she became aware of the presence of his companion Aurora. She was another fire ant, and another nice girl, quite pretty in her species. She also had a crush on Nolan, which might have been considered odd because ants and humans did not interact that way. But mind to mind, it worked. His wife Apoca did not disapprove; she understood this sort of thing.

Meanwhile, Nydia was dancing flawlessly with Nolan, every step matching his step perfectly. It could hardly be otherwise because the two ants were coordinating the two humans telepathically. They were indeed like one person.

"Hello, Nydia," Aurora said in her mind.

"Uh, hello, Aurora," Nydia said the same way. "This is all so new to me! I never interacted with a man this way before."

The ant laughed. "Human men are complicated creatures, unlike male ants or fauns. They are worth getting to know."

"I suppose so," Nydia agreed uncertainly as her body moved gracefully, independently of her mind.

"Though Nolan is not exactly a man. He's a naga with three forms: serpent, fish, and human."

Nydia hardly knew what to make of this. "Three forms!"

"Nagas are shape-changers. He even has a separate talent: he can see the imaginary."

"But imaginary things don't exist!"

"They exist on another plane," she said. "For example, he can see the Baton of Protagonism, which has no physical presence but is definitive when it comes to storytelling."

Nydia realized that it must be so. Metria had referred to the Baton, and used it to zero in on the nymphs.

"Now let's excuse the fire ants while they engage in their private dialog," Nolan said, "and we can enjoy the dance."

Nydia discovered to her surprise that she was indeed enjoying the dance. Its smooth motions and interactions were pleasant, and the music and beat animated her in a new way. Being close to a real man in this different manner was also gratifying. There was nothing effeminate about Nolan, but neither was he a male seeking Only One Thing. She saw Noletta, Nerine, and Ara dancing with other men, though not as aptly as she herself. They lacked ants to make them expert. But the men were competently showing them how. "It's fun," she confessed.

"It certainly is," he agreed.

In due course the dance ended. Nolan bid her a courtly farewell and returned to Queen Apoca, who was lovely but with outsized lips and plaid hair, matching his. It seemed that those lips could kiss a man into love slavery. She was certainly a woman of the Queendom!

Then they went on a tour of Thanx, passing the Fire Ant Nest that Anthem and Aurora had come from, as well as a horrendous Nickelpede Nest. It seemed that all types lived here, as long as they behaved themselves.

"Aurora had heavy news," Anthem said, with a somber background note. "Tackling a Demon is dangerous work."

"We don't want to cross a Demon," Nydia said. "We're just investigating."

"But the Demon does not want to be discovered. If he catches us, we could be blown to Hell, literally. Hell is not a nice place."

"If our alternative is to return to the Retreat and be good for Only One Thing, I'm ready to risk it. It's not that I object to that One Thing, I just don't want to be limited to it."

"I am supposed to guide you to a woman who conjures and shapes ectoplasm."

"Ecto what?"

"Ectoplasm. I never heard of it before either. It seems it's a kind of magic tissue that seems almost alive. She makes figurines of it that are said to be very realistic, but they don't do anything."

"I am having trouble seeing how this relates to the mischief of the Elements."

"As I understand it, the Elements will animate the figurines so we can talk with them."

"Elements talk?" Nydia asked, surprised. "Fire, Water, Air, Earth? Whatever could they have to say?"

"Who is stirring them up."

Now Nydia saw the relevance. "And when they do, we'll be in big trouble with the Demon."

"Big trouble," the ant agreed. Now the background music was threatening.

Then Vinia reappeared. "A path has opened up," she said. "I must lead you to Apoca."

"But we just saw her at the dance," Nydia said. "Is she mad that I danced with her husband?"

"No, she understands about that. This is something else."

Nydia shrugged, another human gesture she had picked up recently. "Lead on, though I can't say I really understand about paths. Something about the near future?"

"Yes, actually," Vinia said as she led the way and the nymphs and Woe Betide followed. "They are colored, with green being the best. I always follow the green paths if I can. But sometimes they get tangled. That's when there aren't any good choices. But mostly it's clear enough." She smiled. "Apoca really showed me how to use them. We're friends."

"Is it true she can kiss a man into love slavery?" Noletta asked.

"More than that. But she doesn't do it casually, only when necessary. One reason the Queendom has no problems with men is that Apoca or one of her tribe kisses any that misbehave, and they never do again." Then the girl pointed ahead. "There she is now, in her privacy room."

In barely two and a half moments they were there with the Queen. Nydia realized with surprise that the woman's hair had changed color. Now it was green. "My paths led us to you," Vinia told Apoca. "Here are the nymphs."

"Her hair changes colors with her moods," Anthem explained. "Green is positive."

"Oh my!" Noletta breathed. "She's the one!"

Apoca glanced at her, her hair turning yellow. "Do I know you? I believe I saw you at the dance."

"I'm Noletta. My talent is to see the future exactly one day ahead. Yesterday when I looked, I saw us kissing you. But we nymphs never kiss women, only men."

The hair turned green again. "Ah, yes, of course. Let me explain about my kisses. I am a Lips woman. Our talent is to kiss men into love slavery. We all have it, though our romantic interest is in independent men. But I also have a second talent, which is to reverse it. I can kiss a man out of slavery, or a woman out of submissiveness. You nymphs are about to embark on an extremely challenging mission where you will encounter several dominating male spirits. You will need protection against that."

"But we're *nymphs*," Nydia protested. "Submitting to males is our nature. It's the One Thing we are good at."

Apoca's hair turned yellow. "Not anymore. You must become fully independent women, good for anything you truly want to be, using that One Thing to control men, not be controlled by them. You will not be able to kiss them into love slavery, but you can fascinate them into doing your will if you manage your assets properly. You will pacify the Elements so that they no longer ravage the countryside. My kiss will enable you to do that."

Nydia shook her head. "We are barely learning how to get along in regular Xanth. We can't control men, let alone these formidable Elements."

Apoca's hair turned green again. "You will by first intriguing them, then captivating them. My power is merely an exaggeration of what every mature woman has. Never underestimate the power of a kiss! It can transform a relationship, especially when it generates little hearts. When the alien child Squid kissed the Demon Chaos, it gave him reason to spare the Universe. When I kissed him, it transformed me. The Elements will have had no experience with it, and will be vulnerable. For them, you will be like me. But I can't be sure exactly how potent it will be, as they are not normal males. You may have to marry them to complete your control."

"Marry them!" Nydia exclaimed. "We're nymphs! We don't marry, we merely oblige."

"As I said, not anymore," Apoca said. "The Good Magician messaged me by the magic mirror to make sure you were up to the task. I will do that by kissing you. Then you will understand."

"Trust her," Anthem said. "She's an honorable woman who truly means to help you succeed in your Quest."

"Trust her," Vinia murmured, perhaps knowing what the ant was telling her.

Nydia was already coming to understand, thanks to her intelligence and the advice of her companions. She looked at the other nymphs. "It's to help us, to make us stronger," she said. "We'd better do it."

"Yes," Vinia agreed. "The green is all around her."

Nydia felt a qualm. She drove it away with a fierce denial. She stepped up to the Queen. "Then do it."

Apoca embraced her and kissed her firmly on the mouth. The contact was not romantic so much as fulfilling. She felt the power of the Queen infusing her, banishing her former submissiveness, forging her into an amazingly assertive woman. Yes, she could kiss an Element and make it count! Indeed, she was no longer exactly a nymph!

Nydia stepped back and Noletta stepped forward. Apoca kissed her, too, and her stance straightened as she strode into fulfillment. Then Nerine, with a similar response. They had all been transformed. They felt like complete females, even without souls.

"Hey, what about me?" Woe Betide demanded.

Apoca smiled, her hair flashing yellow-green with humor. "What, indeed? Come here, child."

Woe came, and the Queen kissed her as she had the others. The child fuzzed around the edges, turned smoky, and finally managed to firm back into place. "Nobody's going to push *me* around!" she declared.

"True, Woe," Apoca agreed, her hair now plaid. That, Nydia realized with Anthem's assistance, signaled mixed emotions. Kissing a demon was bound to be chancy.

Then another thought caught up to Nydia. "Something doesn't mesh. Noletta saw the kissing before seeing the bedroom, but the bedroom actually occurred first. Her visions of the future are fixed at exactly one day ahead. So it can't be."

Apoca smiled, her hair rippling colors. "Rest your concern, dear. Your futures are constantly developing. Even a thought can do it. You must have changed your thoughts along the way, and unknowingly altered timelines. Times can change as well as events. What counts is that you made it safely through."

"She is making confusing sense," Noletta said. "We did change our futures, and saved our lives. This is minor."

Nydia's head felt halfway knotted inside. "I suppose so."

Apoca smiled again. "Time magic is especially tricky because of lurking paradox. Keep practicing until you get used to it."

"We will," Nydia agreed uncertainly.

Then it was time to go their own ways. "Thank you so much, Apoca," Nydia said more confidently.

"Welcome, all of you," Apoca said. "But wait, I just remembered there is more." Her hair flashed gray on the way to green. "You will be encountering fierce and powerful spirits. You will need to negotiate with them to get them to behave. To do that requires them to assume human form so you can have a dialog. That means you will need two things. One is human-shaped forms for them to occupy. The best such figurines are made by a woman named Ecstasy who will be glad to cooperate if you show her any appreciation. The other is the magic wand of a long-gone Magician that can summon spirits and transfer them to objects. The only one who knows where that wand is is his ghostly assistant Wanda, who endures indefinitely because she is not alive. Unfortunately, she is not interested in telling anyone where the wand is. Persuading her to tell will be one of your early challenges. Vinia's paths will lead you to both women." Apoca smiled. "This is very much a woman's challenge, which does seem fitting for a party based in the Queendom of Thanx."

"Couldn't a man do it?" Nerine asked.

A blue flash of hair. "No, for two reasons. Men tend to be hard-headed dominant types relying ultimately on force of one kind or another, and the Elements can't be dominated or forced. Also, there are subtle qualities of perception and adaptation women possess that should enable them to be sufficiently persuasive."

"But we're not women, we're—" Nydia broke off. They were no longer mere nymphs. Apoca's kisses had indeed converted them to something beyond. "Inexperienced," she concluded.

"By the time you complete this Quest, you will be thoroughly experienced."

Nydia hoped it was so. But she had a question. "You were a Protagonist last time. Can you give me any advice now about that?"

"Of course, dear. Remember, Vinia was a Protagonist too. You already know that Protagonists are bound to have great adventures, which they are almost guaranteed to survive. They also generally have Romances. What you need to do is to try to conduct yourself in such manner that any other woman who learns your story will seriously want to emulate you. That is the best guide I can give you."

"But I'm only—"

"A dawning woman," Apoca finished for her. "When the Quest is complete, you and Noletta and Nerine will stop by the adjunct to the Stork Works to pick up the souls you have earned. Then you will indeed be complete."

"Uh, yes," Nydia agreed hesitantly.

"Vinia will have some tools from Prince Ion and Princess Hilda that you should find useful. Then you will be ready for your Quest." Her hair returned to green.

"Uh, yes," Nydia repeated faintly.

"That went well," Anthem said.

Then they were on their way back to their room. Nydia knew that the other ~~nymphs~~, or rather, females, were as confused as she was.

"And here they are," Vinia said. "A package of vials of elixirs from my fiance Prince Ion, such as Love Potion, Healing Elixir, and Fear Factor. Plus a bottomless bag from Princess Hilda containing an expandable magic carpet she sewed especially for you." She opened the bag and brought out a small square carpet that was several times as big as the bag. "They want you to succeed too."

"Uh, tell them thanks," Nydia said as faintly as before.

Then the routine was upon them. They needed to get a good night's sleep to be ready for the morrow.

Naturally Nydia found it hard to sleep because of the distractions of the Quest.

"I can help," Anthem said. "I can send you sleep vibes." There was a background of glorious music.

"That would be wonderful! Can you help Noletta and Nerine too?"

"Take me to them."

She did. The moment she touched Noletta's hand, the ~~nymph~~ female sank into sleep. Then they did the same for Nerine. And finally for herself, back on her own bed, floating on melody.

The day was finally done. What an experience day it had been!

Chapter 4

FIRE

They set out second thing in the morning, after trying for the first thing and not quite catching it, as a party of six: three nymphs, a demon child, a human teen girl, and a fire ant. "First Ecstasy, the ectoplasm conjurer," Nydia said. As Protagonist, she was responsible for making most key decisions. She was working on beginning to get used to it.

"There's a nice green path," Vinia said, and set off walking. They now had a magic carpet, but Nydia didn't want to use it for routine things. Only Vinia could see the path, but they trusted her to have it right.

"She can show you the path, if you want," Anthem said.

That provoked Nydia's curiosity. "Okay."

"Ask her."

"May I see the path?" Nydia asked the girl.

Vinia smiled. "Take my hand."

Nydia took it. Suddenly she saw half a welter of paths radiating out from the girl. They were of several colors. She realized that Anthem was enabling her to see them through Vinia's mind. Green was best, blue was negative, red was danger, yellow was mystery, gray was neutral, and black was likely death. "Like Apoca's hair!" she exclaimed, belatedly making the connection.

"Yes, Poca and I are parallel, mostly," the girl agreed. "We understand each other. She helped me discover my second talent, which I hadn't known about."

The path directly in front of her was solid green. That was indeed the one.

"Thank you for showing me," Nydia said. "That's certainly a useful talent." She let go of the girl's hand and the colors faded.

They walked to the access to the enchanted path network, with the demon child's crib floating along beside them. Nydia was relieved not to have to worry about trolls or werewolves or nickelpedes on unenchanted paths. They had handled them, but it was really more comfortable being safe. Toward mid-morning, they passed a small shelter containing a desk with several books. A sign said ENCYCLONEPEDIA.

"Isn't that misspelled?" Noletta asked. "A couple of extra letters?"

"It shouldn't be harmful, here on the enchanted path," Vinia said. "There's a yellow-red path leading to it. That means mystery and some danger, but the enchantment will stifle the danger."

"I'm curious." Noletta walked to the shelter. She opened the first book and peered at the page. "Oh my, this is really something!" she exclaimed. "A wonderful fount of information! So many words! So many concepts! I never dreamed there was anything like this! In fact, I never dreamed at all before now. True nymphs don't dream. What an experience!"

Nydia opened her mouth to ask a question, but Noletta kept on talking, not saying anything in particular, just making a storm of exclamations. She just couldn't stop.

Then Woe Betide woke and caught on. "That's a cyclone," she said. Her crib floated up, and she reached out and slammed the open book shut.

And Noletta's torrent of words cut off in mid-exclamation. She stood there, breathing hard, as if she had been running.

Relieved, Nydia inspected the shelter and table. "It's just off the path," she said. "Outside the spell. Someone must have put it there to make mischief for unwary travelers."

"I couldn't stop talking," Noletta said breathlessly.

"En-Cyclone-pedia," Nydia said, figuring it out. "A storm of words."

"Technically harmless," Nerine said. "But nevertheless a nuisance."

"I'll know better next time," Noletta said, her breath slowly returning.

"We need to get this out of here so it won't bother other travelers," Nydia said. But when she tried to push the stand away from the path, it wouldn't budge. "I'll have to step off the path to get at it."

"Don't do that!" Woe exclaimed. "That's what such traps do: lure you off the path so you can be caught by something bad. Metria likes to tease them by pretending to fall for it, then puffing into stinky smoke when the monster grabs her. Sometimes she leaves nothing but smoke-filled panties to freak them out." She paused. "Though I still don't see why panties should freak out males. There's nothing interesting there. Bags of candy would be better."

Nydia nodded, not commenting. Anthem was cluing her in on things like this. In due course the child would learn that it was the suggestion of what was inside the panties that turned males on. Males wanted to play Faun & Nymph all the time. Still, the child was proving to be useful.

"More useful than Metria would have been," Anthem agreed.

They resumed their journey, a bit wiser than before. As noon approached, Vinia paused. "The green path veers off here. But it should be safe."

Nydia looked at Noletta. "Does your vision approve?"

"Oh, I've been forgetting it." She stopped to check. "We seem to be back on the enchanted path tomorrow, so I guess it's all right."

Nydia realized that most of ordinary life was dull routine, so unless Noletta checked at exactly the right time, she wouldn't see anything significant. But her talent remained quite handy for steering them clear of mischief in a general way. When the future stopped showing, that meant trouble within a day. "Keep checking whenever you think of it."

They left the enchanted path, following the invisible green one. It led to a rundown old house with a sign saying FIGURINES FOR TRADE. This was obviously the place.

Nydia knocked on the door. "Come in," a woman's voice called.

She turned the handle and pushed the door open. The interior was mainly one big room filled with life-sized dolls or figurines, many of them quite realistic. Most were like people, but there were some ogres, trolls, elves, and, yes, fauns and nymphs. A woman was working on a robot figure, a deliberately crude imitation of a man.

"Uh, we're a party of females on a Quest," Nydia said. "We were told to meet with you. I'm Nydia."

"Hello Nydia," the woman said, glancing up from her work. "I'm Ecstasy; my parents were so thrilled to have me that they named me that. What kind of figure do you want?"

"We're not exactly sure. We need ones that can be animated by the Elements."

Ecstasy drew back from the robot and stood. She was a halfway portly, middle-aged woman with gray-brown hair and eyes that matched, as most people's in Xanth did. "I have an Element section." She gestured, and there was a set of five figures. Three were males, representing Fire, Water, and the Void; two were female, representing Air and Earth. All were dauntingly handsome or beautiful, their elemental powers evident in their stances and expressions.

"That's them," Nydia said, impressed. "We want them all."

"And what do you have to trade?"

Oops. Of course, the woman wanted something in exchange. Why hadn't they thought of that? Nydia was caught short. "Uh—"

"Be at ease, nymph. Demon Grossclout messaged me you were coming."

"Uh, who?"

"Queen Demesne's consort," Anthem said.

Oh. "I guess we didn't think it out completely."

Ecstasy smiled. "You're nymphs. You don't have much experience. Grossy had a suggestion. Suppose I join your Quest? I'd love to be a significant character for a while, see the sights, have an adventure, be remembered. As a background character I encounter little real excitement in my life. This would fix that."

"I—" Nydia started uncertainly.

"None of that, girl. Grossy said Apoca kissed you. That means you now have backbone. All you need to do is say 'yes' with conviction."

"Do it," Anthem said.

"Yes," Nydia said with simulated conviction, feeling the rightness of it as she spoke. She had for the moment forgotten her new assurance.

"He also said you have protection against the Elements."

"Yes, we are wearing some of the Good Magician's socks. Their magic prevents us from being burned, drowned, or blown away. So I can tackle the personified Elements with confidence."

"That's my girl." Ecstasy looked around. "Maybe I can craft a wagon to haul them along."

The conviction translated to practical thought. "We have a bottomless bag."

Ecstasy actually clapped her hands. "Wonderful! That's much simpler."

Nydia had the purse tucked into her waistband. She lifted it out, opened it, reached in, and hauled out the carpet and the smaller bag of vials. She tucked those into the back of her belt. The carpet seemed to weigh slightly more than nothing, which was perhaps not surprising, as it was made to float people in air.

Ecstasy lifted the Fire figure and set it in the bag. It disappeared inside despite being far larger than the bag. That was part of the beauty of such magic. It was followed by Water, Air, Earth, and the Void. She closed the bag. It was no larger than before and weighed no more.

"I will fetch my incidentals and be ready to go," Ecstasy said.

Just like that?

"When your life is as dull as mine," the woman added, "it is easy to park it for a while. I have little to lose but my boredom."

So it seemed.

Before long, they were back on the enchanted path, following Vinia's green route. Woe Betide, after being introduced to the new member of the Quest, was taking her long daily nap, floating in the crib. Nydia talked with Ecstasy, finding her interesting despite her protestations of dullness. She did have life experience, something the nymphs lacked, apart from the One Thing, and even peripheral details could be intriguing. Such as her passion for art in the form of sculpture. Ecstasy poured her very soul into her figurines, imagining them to be having adventures she wished she could share.

"But what of creatures like the trolls, who only want to catch, cook, and eat a person?" Nydia asked, omitting a detail of what trolls wanted. Why would the woman care about the One Thing? "We barely escaped their ambush."

"I made a figurine that looks like a basilisk. It can't really kill with a glance, but monsters don't know that. They skedaddle."

Neither Nydia nor Anthem were familiar with the word, but they got the general idea.

"Still, there are times when I almost wish that a troll would look at me with the same desire it would look at you. Even as a young woman I never attracted that sort of attention."

What was there to be said to that? Nydia hadn't realized that males weren't interested in ordinary women. What was dull routine to a nymph was lost fascination to Ecstasy.

Then the paths diverged, leading them to a small cabin in isolated woods, the kind of dwelling nobody would have noticed were it not for the invisible path.

Nydia knocked on the door. There was no response. It was as if the cabin were deserted, but Vinia was sure it was not. So Nydia turned the handle and pushed the door open cautiously.

Inside was a pretty young woman, black of hair and eye. The type males did like. "You must be Wanda," Nydia said.

"I must be," the girl agreed.

"We are looking for the Magician's lost wand."

"You are looking."

"And you are supposed to be the only person who knows where it is."

"I am supposed," she agreed.

"How can we get you to tell us?"

"How can you."

"There is something odd about this," Anthem said, echoing Nydia's sentiment. "She's not saying anything original. It's as if she's more of an echo than a person."

Nydia's intelligence focused on that. "She may be a creature of illusion, like the Baton of Protagonism."

"Maybe," the ant agreed. "See if you can touch her, so I can read her mind."

Nydia reached out toward Wanda, and the girl dodged aside as if magnetically repelled. But Nydia was too smart for her. She reached again, this time putting her left hand behind the girl. Sure enough, Wanda's next dodge took her right onto Nydia's left hand. Yet there was no contact.

"She has no mind!" the ant exclaimed.

"Or body. She may be illusion, but the wand isn't," Nydia said, sweeping her hand through the apparent body of the girl until it caught the generating force: the floating wand. "Gotcha!"

Wanda disappeared. All that remained of her was the wand. It had been cleverly concealed, but now she had it. The ancient Magician must have set up the illusion to protect his legacy.

Nydia tucked the wand into her belt. "Now let's go tackle Fire."

They emerged from the cabin and explained things to the others. "That was a nice ploy," Ecstasy said. "It must have hidden the wand for decades."

"Saving it for us," Nydia agreed. "Now lead us to Fire, Vinia."

The girl glanced at her paths. "This way. But be on guard; the green is mixed with other colors. I will watch for the greenest path, but it won't be perfect. We're heading into some risk."

"Maybe you are," Woe Betide said. "I'm not." She returned to sleep, bored with these routine proceedings.

"Stay alert, Noletta," Nydia said. "We need to be ready to change course before we get locked into some disaster."

"Oh, yes," the nymph agreed. "The future is flickering."

"It is fascinating watching you girls operate," Ecstasy said. "Not to mention a demon child."

This time, the way did not return to the enchanted path. It wound into the deepest wilderness.

Nerine wrinkled her nose. "I smell smoke."

"Where there is smoke, there is fire," Ecstasy said wisely. "Which reminds me of an analogy. A man was shopping for a figurine in the form of a pretty girl. I have many of those, as all species value them. I can't think what he might have wanted to do with it." Obviously she had a notion, but was bypassing it in the presence of the child. "My assistant at the time, an ordinary girl externally, was annoyed. Maybe she didn't like being bypassed in favor of prettiness, when there are so many other aspects of womankind. I do have half a notion how that is. She informed him that he should take the trouble to learn how to treat a real woman, not an imitation. When he turned to her to argue the case, she kissed him with such force that little hearts flew out and it shut him up." Ecstasy smiled reminiscently. "I lost that assistant when she married that man. I provided figurines for their wedding party."

Nydia found that interesting. It seemed that even ordinary girls had power when they chose to invoke it, just as Apoca had hinted. The nymphs had no problems with prettiness, being cast in that mold, but it was worth learning what else there could be.

The smell of smoke grew stronger. They were coming to the fire.

That made Nydia nervous. She realized that she had no idea how to perform with the wand to capture an Element, and less idea what to do once that was done.

"Ask Ecstasy," Anthem suggested. "She's had time to learn to be a woman, and must have thought about what her figurines might do."

She might indeed have information. "Ecstasy, I really don't know how to use the wand or the figurines. Do you know?"

"I can't say I know, but I have thought about it on occasion. It seems to me that the wand may require some additional instruction, such as

'Wand, conjure this Element into this figure.' If that works, then you can talk with the Element, find out what's bothering it, and maybe make it stop being so destructive."

Once she heard it, it seemed obvious. "Thank you. I'll try that and hope for the best."

"Remember, you are not about to be intimidated by any male, including Fire."

"Yes." She had to stop forgetting that, even temporarily. "But what else is there, for a woman? We nymphs have no experience other than the One Thing."

"At the risk of boring you, I will elucidate. There is indeed far more to a woman than panties, whatever the men may think." Ecstasy went into lecture mode. Boring? Hardly! Nydia was fascinated, and she could see Noletta and Nerine paying rapt attention. Indeed, there was more to a woman than her external appearance. She might use the One Thing to fetch and hold a man's attention, but it was her qualities of character that truly secured him.

Even Vinia was interested. "I will have to remember this when I come of age. Why depend on appearance, when there are so many other things to use?"

Why indeed!

They walked a fair distance, but they barely noticed, being absorbed in the lesson on the Powers of Womanhood. They weren't even magic, but they were potent.

"A woman's eyes are powerful tools to catch the attention of a man," Ecstasy continued. "There is magic in the exchange of gazes. She can also attract and hold his stare with a low neckline. If need be, she can even kiss him. Kisses have special power. If a little heart shows, she's got him. Then it is time to play the innocent, pretending not to comprehend that she has conquered him. That is a special part of the game of love that makes her all the more appealing. All part of the female arsenal."

It was a considerable education for the nymphs, who had never engaged males in dialog, just lured them into the chase, catch, and celebration. But of course, real women wore clothing, which masked their assets. That meant they had to work at it. They could make things so much easier for themselves if they simply went nude. Why didn't they?

So she inquired.

Ecstasy laughed. "Because they don't want to be limited to that One Thing. They want to be known for other things, too, like character, intelligence, and industry. If they went bare all the time, the men would never have interest in any Other Thing. Men are governed by their gonads. They want to play Faun and Nymph continuously. Also, many women prefer to restrict their intimate activities to one partner, and to be left alone by others, so they can focus on those other things. There's a convention that governs that. It's called Marriage."

This was a completely new concept to the nymphs. They questioned Ecstasy closely, gradually coming to an understanding of it. Commitment to just one man! What a novelty! But it did have its appeal. Nydia suspected that men, too, might have more than One Thing on their mind if the clothing enabled it. Maybe.

They crested a hill and saw the valley beyond. It was nice, with a fair-sized river, beyond which was a pleasant human village. And, a moderate distance away, a raging forest fire, sweeping avidly toward the village. The villagers were plainly alarmed, smelling the smoke. They would have to flee their homes, which might be burned to oblivion. They surely wouldn't like that.

Woe woke. "Wow!"

Suddenly their mission leaped to prominence. "We have to stop that fire!" Noletta exclaimed.

Indeed. But there were complications. They could cross under the river, but what about Vinia and Ecstasy?

"The carpet," Anthem reminded her.

Oh. Yes. Nydia brought it out and spread it on the ground. "We'll have to fly across, and maybe on up to the fire." And realized that she had no idea how to guide a flying carpet.

"Don't worry," Vinia said. "I know how to do it."

"Wonderful!"

They sat on the carpet, which obligingly expanded to accommodate all five of them plus Anthem. Vinia took her place front and center. "It's a mind control thing," she explained. "I just think at it, and it obeys. Don't worry; you won't fall off. Staying in place is part of the magic."

The carpet lifted smoothly, achieved a reasonable height, then flew over the water, accelerating. They were comfortably anchored to it. Vinia's and Ecstasy's hair flowed back as the breeze of their passage tugged at it. The nymphs' hair was still; they were shielded by the socks, as wind was part of the Element of Air. The crib trailed them.

They flew along the river, as it made a convenient channel through the forest. Soon they reached the fire. Smoke enveloped them, making Vinia and Ecstasy cough.

Nydia got a notion. She put a hand on Ecstasy's arm, extending the protection of the socks. Nerine did the same with Vinia. The coughing stopped. "That's a relief," Ecstasy said. "Thank you."

"I should have thought of it before. I'm still new at Protagonism."

"But you're learning. That's good."

"Should I go right into it?" Vinia asked.

"I think so. The heart of the fire must be where the Element can be summoned."

The carpet flew into the center of the blaze. They felt no heat. Apparently their contact also protected the carpet. They landed in a small clearing where the blaze was limited to the grass. "Hold my hand," Nydia told Ecstasy.

"Oh, I will!"

"This is fun!" Woe said, now awake for the action.

They stepped together off the carpet, as did Nerine and Vinia. Nydia reached into the bottomless bag and brought out the Fire Figurine. She gave it to Ecstasy to hold with her free hand. Then Nydia took the wand in her free hand and brandished it. "Fire Element, appear! Occupy this figurine so that we can talk with you." Would it work?

There was a flare of power from the wand, and it radiated, causing Nydia's skin to tingle. It caught hold of the fire, changing the flame's color from deep yellow to pale orange, molding it into a pulsing sphere. Then the sphere sailed into the Fire figurine, infusing it with a glow. Indeed, something was happening.

The figurine seemingly came to life. "What the blazes is this?" it demanded.

Nydia was thrilled. It was working! The animated figure was a handsome man clothed in flames. His hair reached up in brilliant wisps, and sinuous smoke rose into the sky. He was actually quite impressive. "Fire Element, we are here to stop you from burning up the village. Put out the forest fire immediately."

The well-favored features shaped into potent negation. He was handsome that way too. "The hellfire I will! I mean to burn everything in this valley, then go on to the next, and on until there is nothing left to burn. Who the Hades are you to tell me nay?"

Nydia was set back. She had assumed that conjuring the Element would give her control of it. Apparently not.

"He's fiery, of course," Anthem said.

Noletta stepped up. "We are three nymphs and associates on a Quest to stop the damage wrought by out-of-control Elements. Now answer, fire spirit. Why are you suddenly doing so much damage?"

Fire paused, evidently appreciating the direct challenge. "I'm not sure. I just got a sudden urge to exert my power fully, instead of letting it lie fallow. What's it to you, floozy?"

Woe tittered.

Noletta turned almost as fiery as the animated figure. She became an impressive figure herself as she caught and held his gaze. She inhaled, causing her chest to expand impressively. She seemed to be about to burst out of her blouse. "Who the blowtorch are you calling a floozy, ash-for-brains? You are burning things indiscriminately with no concern for the welfare of others!" She seemed to be as hot as he was, at least emotionally.

He angrily put his fiery face close to hers. "Listen, girl-brain! I—"

He was cut off by her ferocious kiss. It was so strong that a ball of light flared around them, the sky flickered, and a burning heart sailed up and hovered over their heads. It was plain that she was scoring.

"Metria does that," Woe said. "It gets men really hot."

"Oh, I felt that even without a physical touch," Anthem said. "There's an ambiance about him."

"Well, he *is* an Element," Nydia reminded her. "His awareness may be in the figurine, but his essence is all around us."

"In fact, now I can feel his mind. It depends on the proximity of folk like you, especially Ecstasy, because she has a soul. I may use my telepathy to tune him in better so that he is more focused."

"I think Noletta is focusing him pretty ably."

"She certainly learned my instructions well," Ecstasy said. *And Apoca's,* Nydia realized. That kiss had been like a detonating bomb.

"We nymphs aren't stupid, just ignorant," Nerine said. "We are eager to fix that. We want to become real people."

Nydia realized it was true. She had drunk from the Ein Stein, but even when the Good Magician's Challenges nullified that, she had handled things reasonably well. Nymphs had a lot of potential, if they only knew it.

The kiss broke. Fire stared at Noletta, his brightness dimming. "Oh, my," he whispered, nonplussed. "What have you done to me?"

Now Noletta played innocent, as pretty that way as she was when fiery. "I kissed you. If you want any more, rogue spirit, you will have to oblige my whims."

He flickered, waxing and waning in rapid succession. "I never felt this way before. Suddenly, I just want to please you."

"You're right," Anthem said. "She has tamed him."

Noletta relented slightly. "Get used to it, spirit. You're in love."

He shook his head, amazed, but did not argue the case. "I am at a loss how to proceed. How can I please you?"

"By doing anything I ask of you. Starting with dousing this forest fire. End it now."

The figure gestured. The surrounding fire faded. In barely half a moment all that remained of it were a few wisps of steam from cooling vegetation. "Now what?" he asked.

She fixed him again with her compelling gaze. "What do you want?"

"I want to be with you, man to woman. To kiss you constantly. To love you. But I don't know how. I've never been a man before, or been with a living woman. All I know is that now I very much want it."

"One moment, please." Noletta left him and went to Nydia and Ecstasy. "I think I want to be with him, too, and teach him how to be a man. He is handsome, and hot, ideal for a bold girl. But I don't know how, myself, as I suspect that is well beyond the One Thing. Can you teach me, Ecstasy?"

Ecstasy made a soundless whistle. "That will take time. There are nuances within nuances. Folk think that a man and woman together is all about stork summoning, but it's vastly more than that. Ask any married couple. I'd have to be right there with the two of you as you work it out." She grimaced. "That's not how it's done."

Nydia got a notion. "Suppose we bring him along in the bag, quiescent, while you explain it in detail to us, including Noletta? Would he mind waiting between times?"

Vinia spoke. "Inside the bag, time is frozen along with weight and light. To him, it would be like going in and coming right back out, no matter how much time passed outside."

"Then it could work," Noletta said, gratified.

"It could," Ecstasy agreed thoughtfully. "If he agrees to do it."

"I'll ask him." Before any of them could protest, Noletta walked back to Fire. "Here is the case: I want to be with you, too, woman to man. You're a lot of male. But I'm a nymph. I have real experience with Only One Thing, and that's not enough to make a lasting relationship. In fact, it's usually good for only five minutes. We hardly even know each other yet. So I need to learn myself before I can teach you. But if you are willing to ride timelessly in the bag while we travel, I will learn the first stage, then share it with you. Then the second stage, and the third. So that we can do it right. In time, we can go through all the stages and become a complete couple. Does that appeal?"

"Yes," he agreed without hesitation. "I want to do it right. So as to please you."

"Then we are on the way." She led him to the bag, paused to kiss him again, evoking two burning hearts that orbited each other, then stepped back. He jumped lithely into the bag, and Nydia drew it closed. The hearts, flummoxed, faded out.

"You are one swift learner," Ecstasy said. "You played him perfectly."

"My talent was guiding me. Whenever my future flickered, I changed course slightly until it firmed. I kept him by my side, one day hence."

Nydia appreciated the further power of the talent. Noletta was using it well.

"And you will teach me the first stage," Noletta said to Ecstasy. "As we travel."

"Yes, to the best of my ability."

"And Nerine and I will listen," Nydia said. "So we can all do it right when we have Elements of our own to tame." For that was plainly in their future.

"Agreed." Then Ecstasy thought of something. "But what about Vinia here? The Adult Conspiracy will prevent us from covering certain details in her presence."

"You don't need to educate them about storks," Vinia said. "Nymphs already know all about that. I am jealous of their experience. But I recognize that the Adult Conspiracy has too much power. Until we children take over and abolish it. The rest of it I need to learn too."

Ecstasy nodded. "Then I think we have a system."

Woe went back to sleep now that things were getting dull again.

"We should let that village know that the danger is over," Nydia said, "but I think it would be best not to tell them our Quest or the true nature of the Element of Fire. We don't want the other Elements to be warned if word gets out, let alone the Demon who is agitating them."

"Good strategy," Ecstasy agreed. "But we can use the village as part of our training. If we can get Fire to pass as a regular man with a special talent, we'll know we're getting there."

"Oh? How can we do that?" Noletta asked.

"We can get him to wear the semblance of clothing. I suspect he can do that, covering his central anatomy behind flames. You can introduce him as a man with the talent of fire. When he fools the villagers, you can reward him by taking him to a private place and doffing your clothes. Except for your socks."

"Why not the socks?"

"He will jet fire."

"Oh." Noletta looked momentarily pained, as if she had swallowed a ferociously hot pepper. "Yes, I will keep the socks on."

"Am I missing something?" Vinia asked. "He is made of fire. Who cares whether some escapes?"

"It might set fire to the surroundings," Ecstasy said wryly.

The girl did not look completely satisfied, but let it pass.

They walked on toward the village as Ecstasy drilled the nymphs on social protocol for enabling an Element to appear normal. Nydia noticed in passing that a patch of pie plants was now nothing but ashes and burned sticks. Too bad they couldn't have saved them. But it gave her half a notion.

Then they paused to bring the fire figurine out. "We are about to visit a local human village," Noletta said. "We want to pass you off as a regular human man with the talent of making or dousing fire. If that is successful, I will be grateful. You will like that." She touched her blouse suggestively as she inhaled. As a nymph, she was good at this type of suggestion.

"Anything to please you, Letta," he agreed, his eyes locked on the blouse. Oh yes, she had him leashed. As perhaps any woman could do with any man when she tried.

"Now all that business about One Thing is making sense to me," Anthem said with a background chord. "She's using it to enhance his desire to please her."

"That's right," Nydia said. "We nymphs may be limited to One Thing, traditionally, but we are very good at that." Then, to the Element: "We will call you Flame."

"Flame," he agreed amicably.

Nydia clarified that he should make minimal use of his firepower, so as to mask his identity. "Cute little flames, not infernos."

He glanced at Noletta, who smiled. "Little flames," he repeated.

They followed a path to the village. An old woman came out to meet them, probably the Village Elder's wife. "Who are you?" she demanded. Evidently the village men were away on business, such as fetching wagons of water in a probably vain effort to douse the coming fire, leaving her in charge.

"We are a traveling party out to tour Xanth, among other things," Nydia said. She didn't want to start telling lies, but the truth was hardly safe, and this was not a lie so much as a partial truth. "But the fire burned up the local pie plants. We would like to trade for some you may have saved, if there is anything we have that you want."

"You came through that awful fire?"

"We felt it was dangerous. Our friend Flame here has the talent of fire. He can make it or put it out. So he put it out." She turned to him. "Show them a flame, dear."

He glanced at Noletta, who nodded. He obligingly shot a small flame from his forefinger. It burned for a moment, then stopped.

"But we were too late to save the pies," Nydia finished. "They were burned to ashes."

"You stopped the fire?" the Elder asked, as if not quite believing it.

"Yes," Noletta said. "It's Flame's talent."

"But that was a huge fire!"

"He had to really focus," Nydia said. "Fortunately, he caught it at the right time." She did not clarify that any time was the right time for the Element.

"Can we see him do it?" As if they hadn't just shown her.

"Certainly," Noletta said with schooled patience. "Do any of you need a fire?"

A housewife-type woman came forward. "I can't get my cookfire to burn. It just sputters out no matter how often I light it. I don't know what's wrong with it."

Noletta smiled. "Flame, let's start her fire."

They went to the cookfire, which was just a mass of grudging smoke. Flame pointed a finger at it. It burst into vigorous flames.

"How did you do that?" the housewife asked. "I mean, I know you can make fire. But this is burning nicely. It refused to start for me. It just sputtered out."

"I can shoot fire from my finger, as I showed you," Flame said. "But this one needs something else. I believe you have a branch of Lighter Not in there. That stifles any fire you set. If it happens again, all you need to do is breathe the letter k on it. That will make it Lighter Knot, which will burn hotly."

Several women tried it with other stifled fires. They must have collected wood from a patch of Lighter Not. They were thrilled when it worked. This was magic anyone could do. Soon there were more fires than they needed. Flame went to the extra ones, breathed on them, and they expired.

"Oh, I'd like to kiss you!" a pretty girl exclaimed. "You'd be so handy to have around the house."

"No!" Noletta said sharply. This, too, had been schooled: jealousy. The others laughed. They understood why she did not want that kind of competition for her handsome, talented man. Single pretty girls were a universal menace to committed ones.

"Take all the pies you want!" the Elder said. "We believe you put out that forest fire we feared."

Flame smiled. "It was a challenge, but yes."

Loaded with assorted pies, they departed the village. Woe immediately woke up, so as to share a pie.

"That worked nicely," Nydia said, pleased. "Flame passed as a regular man."

"I just did what Noletta told me."

"That, too, is typical of real men," Ecstasy said.

"Now I want to get you private," Noletta told Flame. All three nymphs had to train themselves to celebrate only privately. Outer Xanth was not the F&N Retreat, where there was no subtlety or privacy, nor any desire for it. "You did beautifully. But I don't see a convenient private place."

"Maybe a housefire," Ecstasy said. "Or a firehouse."

Flame gestured. A wall of fire appeared. He walked around it, making other walls, then a fiery roof. It was indeed a housefire, complete with a chimney issuing cloudy smoke. Obviously the Element could do what he wanted with fire.

Flame opened the door, and the two of them entered the house. "And that is how a woman manages a man," Ecstasy said.

"I feel the explosive ambiance," Anthem said. "That passion could set fire to a bed of rock."

Ecstasy smiled. *Bed rock.* "I think burning rock is the province of the Element of Earth."

"But how far can we trust him?" Nydia asked. "He's not a real person, he's an Element, an impersonal force of nature."

"Not anymore. We can trust him as far as we can trust Noletta," Ecstasy said. "She is training him into shape. I'm so glad that my ectoplasm figurine is able to perform in that manner! I wasn't quite sure it would, though I make them all anatomically correct as far as possible. It will be the same for the other Elements."

Nydia realized that making figurines with male and female anatomy did not guarantee that they could perform in the manner of living folk. The spirit of the Element must have made that possible. That augured well for the other figurines and Elements. If it so happened that she herself chose to get intimate with an Element, she wanted the One Thing to be feasible. Not being limited to it was one thing, no pun intended; abolishing it was quite another.

"Also, he doesn't know how to lie," Anthem said. "It's not in his nature."

"So let's not teach him that," Nydia said.

"And maybe it's better to have the Elements actively on our side, with full understanding," Nerine said. "Because we really don't know what we're up against."

That made sense to Nydia. "He should be mellow, as the fauns are, after a celebration. We'll talk to him when they emerge."

"I wish I knew what is supposed to be so great about all that kissing they must be doing," Vinia said. "I like kissing, too, but it's not better than chocolate cake."

"You got that right," Woe said.

No one clarified the reference.

In due course, or maybe undue course, the firehouse door opened and the couple emerged. Flame looked dazed; this was evidently his first direct experience with the Faun & Nymph routine, and it clearly wowed him. That, too, was typical of males, once they came of age.

The firehouse collapsed into a glowing pile of ashes.

Noletta, too, was changed. She put a hand on Nydia's arm so that she could borrow the ant's telepathy to communicate privately, so as not to be censored by the Adult Conspiracy in Vinia's presence. "I never before had such a sincere appreciation. The fauns do it all the time, and are maybe jaded, but to Flame it was a psyche-changing experience. I like it better that way. It's not at all routine." Her mouth quirked. "But I'm glad I kept the socks on. I would have been burned like those pies, from the inside out."

Vinia and Woe exchanged a glance, not getting it.

"We need to talk," Ecstasy said to Flame.

"Whatever Noletta wants," he agreed, clearly still distracted by his introduction to the physical expression of love.

"What about?" Noletta asked.

"We have decided to acquaint Flame with our Quest."

"Okay. I don't want to keep anything from him anyway." She turned to the Element. "Pay attention to Nydia, and I don't mean her nymphly proportions. She has something special to say that you need to understand."

"Okay."

"But he is aware of your proportions," Anthem said. "Don't blame him; he's male. But he knows it would displease Noletta if he tried to get his hot hands on them."

Just so. "Flame, we have covered this before. We're not just wandering nymphs," Nydia said to him as they resumed their walk along the path between villages. "We have an important mission to accomplish. It's called a Quest. We have to find out what's stirring up the Elements."

"I don't know," he said. "It's just an urge to go wild."

"Exactly. It has to be caused by a Demon. We need to find out who he is so he can be stopped. We must operate pretty much in secret so he doesn't catch on that we're looking. We'd like to have you and the other Elements join our search."

"I'll do whatever Noletta wants."

"That's fine. But we want you to understand and agree in principle apart from that. To become, in effect, part of the Quest."

"I don't care about your Quest. Only about Noletta."

"We think you should care. Because something is interfering with your nature. Instead of just handling fire when you choose, something is causing you to do it flat-out, regardless of your wish."

Flame considered. "That's true. Now that I think about it, I am annoyed. I don't want anyone messing with my nature." He paused, glancing at Noletta. "Except you, my dear."

"I want you as you are," she said fondly. "Not changed by someone else."

They came together and kissed. More little burning hearts appeared, circling their heads before spinning off to see the rest of the scene.

Woe made a face. "Sappy stuff."

"So I am with you," Flame concluded. "I will help as I can."

"Oops, I need a moment of privacy," Noletta said. "Even from you. It's a natural function thing. Those village pies are catching up with me. I want to be lean and trim outside and inside for our next romantic session."

"Go behind a bush," Ecstasy suggested. "We'll wait."

Noletta walked to the bush.

"What is this thing called natural function?" Flame asked.

"Living folk can't draw on the natural power of the elements," Ecstasy explained. "We have to eat and drink to sustain our bodies. That means we digest food, which in turn means we have to get rid of the residues from it. It's not romantic, so we don't talk about it much and don't do it in public. You can just ignore it, as you don't have such needs, and let Letta have her private moments. This is the way it is among living folk."

"Oh. I will let her be."

Noletta emerged from behind the bush, pulling up her pants. She started walking toward them—just as an ogre appeared from the forest, perhaps looking for more saplings to tie in knots or young dragons to educate on the nature of fear.

"Me see she," he exclaimed. He reached down to grab her by the hair. He effortlessly hoisted her up to his head height, which was twice hers. "Twirl girl." He flicked her with a ham finger, making her spin in place.

"Put me down, you brute!" she screamed.

Nydia was unable to think of an appropriate course of action. All the nymphs together couldn't budge an ogre.

"Ask Flame," Anthem said. "I'll enhance his understanding."

Oh, of course. "She needs your help, Flame," Nydia said urgently. "Don't burn him to a cinder, just make him go away. So folk don't see your real power."

"Got it." Flame strode rapidly toward the ogre, now that he had been told what to do. "Unhand that damsel, varlet!" he called. He seemed to have a good vocabulary.

The ogre heard him and turned as he arrived. He did not set Noletta down, letting her dangle by her hair. "Who you?"

"I am this woman's friend. Now set her down and scram, or I will toast your toes."

"Ha, ha." The ogre swung his free hamhand out and clasped his hamfingers around Flame's neck. Then he screamed in pain because he was not wearing magic socks. There was a fierce sizzle as the fire scorched through his fingers, leaving ash and bone amid a cloud of foul smoke.

He dropped the nymph, who landed lightly on her feet and ran clear.

"Go!" Flame called, sending jets of flame toward the ogre's feet. "Or I'll make you dance." That had to be Anthem's prompting.

Ogres were justifiably proud of their stupidity, but this was registering. He turned and lumbered away.

Flame sent a bolt after him, scoring on his backside. "Ooo-ooo!" the ogre howled as he accelerated.

"My hero!" Noletta flung herself at Flame, hugging him fervently. More little hearts spun out.

"It occurs to me that an Element is good protection for a nymph," Nydia said, gratified. The others nodded.

Chapter 5

WATER

They rejoined the enchanted path and walked along it, explaining how the path worked to Flame as they went. He was surprised. "So that's why I could never burn it! The magic protects it."

"Yes," Ecstasy said. "The enchanted path network is secure from hazards so that travelers can safely reach their destinations. But that's only for traveling; the rest of Xanth still has its perils." She smiled thinly. "Such as rampaging Elements."

"Noletta cured me of that."

Noletta smiled. "Any time you need further curing, let me know." He opened his mouth, but she closed it with a gesture. "Not yet." Now the others smiled. She had him thoroughly leashed.

As the day declined, they came to a camp. "These, too, are enchanted to be safe," Noletta said. "But I think you can protect me from the threats of the night, Flame. So if you prefer to camp with me apart from the others, we can do that."

He was perplexed. "Why apart?"

Ecstasy stepped into the dialog. "Normal living humans prefer to keep some things private. In fact, the dread Adult Conspiracy enforces privacy relating to details of romance, at least in the presence of children. Nymphs are completely open about it, but this is taken as a sign of their incompleteness. These ones are learning how to be real people, so they honor the strictures too. Hugging and kissing is about the limit."

"Until we children stage our revolution and abolish the ridiculous Conspiracy," Vinia said. "It's been messing us up far too long." Woe Betide nodded in agreement.

"Thank you for explaining that," Flame said. "I am finding human culture fascinating, even in its peculiar quirks." He turned to Noletta. "I do want to be with you. But first I'd like to learn more. When you pass for a woman, I'd like to pass for a man."

Noletta grinned. "We'll do it together."

"The template helps," Nydia said. "But there are nuances."

"Template?"

Nydia realized that he needed to understand about that too. "We nymphs are based on a template, which is a sort of fundamental pattern that specifies everything about us. Our appearance, our minds, our emotions, our ability to speak and read and to understand others. Then, as we spend time in life, we acquire experience and memory, which gradually make us become individual people, instead of identical copies except for the colors of our hair."

"I wish I had a template."

A quirk hovered near Noletta's mouth. "Then you would be a faun. I like you better as you are. You value me for more than Only One Thing."

"You are my Everything," he said sincerely.

Noletta drew him close and kissed him. "Thank you."

"But we can share, to an extent," Nydia said before this could become a distraction. "My companion Anthem Ant is contact-telepathic. Touch my hand and meet her."

He extended his fiery hand and she took it, the socks protecting her from the heat. "Hello, Flame!"

"You're a fire ant!"

"Yes. We should get along."

Nydia remained silent, except for murmuring the ant's words so that the unconnected members of the party could follow along, letting them talk. Of course they would be compatible!

"Anthem," he said. "Can you show me this template?"

"Yes. It is right here, hidden in every cell of her body and brain. It's small but powerful. It looks like this."

"The Mundanes call it DNA," Ecstasy said. "I think that stands for Do Not Amend."

Flame frowned. He was learning human expressions. "It's too complicated for me, but I can find out in time. This spot of it is different. What is it?"

Anthem focused, analyzing it. "That's the date stamp. This model was made two years ago."

This was news to Nydia. "I'm only two years old?"

"What difference does it make," Ecstasy asked, "when you are crafted complete, with no childhood, and have no memory in the Retreat?"

That set Nydia back. Until recently, she might as well have been only one day old. Even if she could remember, what would there be except endless repetitions of that One Thing? The fauns might like it, having no wider horizons, but she would perish of boredom.

"How old is mine?" Noletta asked, extending her hand. Nydia took it with her free hand, so the ant could connect.

Anthem checked. "A year and a half." She made a mental smile. "You nymphs are newly minted, like ants."

"Mints are delicious," Noletta agreed.

"And me," Nerine said, extending her hand. Nydia let Noletta's hand go and took Nerine's.

"One thousand years, give or take a few seconds," Anthem said.

A stifling silence landed on them all. Finally, Ecstasy fought free of it. "How's that again? Did you slip a few decimals?"

"That's the date," the ant insisted. "She's older than she looks."

"By nine hundred and eighty-three years, give or take a few seconds?"

"Yes."

"I had no idea," Nerine said, awed.

"We need more information," Ecstasy said. "There has to be a background story. First you discovered that she's a water nymph, misplaced in the Retreat. Now this. It can't be coincidence."

"Could she have been hiding from something?" Vinia asked.

"With no memory, until recently? More likely she was being hidden, even from herself. Who would think to look for a lost person in the Retreat?"

Nydia got an idea. "If the templates are dated, do they have other features, such as maybe personal histories? We nymphs have none, but a real person might."

"But a real person should have a soul," Ecstasy said. "Where is hers?"

"A soul!" Nerine exclaimed. "Now I feel the loss. I did have one!"

"Look for her history in the template," Ecstasy said. "There wouldn't be any after she came to the Retreat, but before that there could be."

Nydia and Anthem looked. There was a subsection labeled PERSONAL HISTORY. Nydia's own was blank, but Nerine's had content. Voila!

"My future is flashing," Noletta said. "That signals danger."

"There may be mischief here," Ecstasy said. "Suppose she was hidden a thousand years ago, and we find out why, and it's a dangerous enemy who then comes after us? We need to be careful."

"I have an idea," Vinia said. "Suppose we link together as a party, using Anthem's telepathy, and explore her history together? I might be able to use the paths to make sure we don't get in trouble."

"This sounds crazy," Ecstasy said. "But this is Xanth, where craziness is almost a way of life. Maybe it would work."

Nydia's smarts came into play. "If we did that, we could be sitting here unconscious, completely tuned out of this situation and into the thousand-year-old one. Suppose someone else came? We'd have trouble explaining ourselves."

"Maybe more trouble than that," Ecstasy said grimly. "If half a passel of males came upon three unconscious nymphs, there's no telling what they would do."

Noletta glanced at Flame. "Can you help?"

"Yes. I can set a low, controlled burn, a ring of fire around the cabin that would scorch anyone who tried to pass it. We would hear their screams as they got hot feet."

A glance circled around, finally returning to Nydia. "Let's do it."

"Let's eat and natural function first," Noletta said. "And sleep. In case it takes time."

Vinia laughed. "Less than a thousand years."

They went about the routine. Then in the morning they gathered together, the cabin surrounded by the faint ring of fire, and made a ring of their own, holding hands. There was a throbbing background chord as Anthem Ant borrowed from all their brains, becoming immensely greater than ever in her natural state, and made a scene where they seemed to be in a craft resembling a large, curled leaf floating down through a complicated network of paths. It was the template, by whatever name. They landed before a closed door marked PERSONAL HISTORY. This was the place.

Nydia turned to the others. "Are we ready?" Her voice seemed normal, though it was mental, as they were all in the scene together.

"The path is green," Vinia said. "Right through that door."

So the paths functioned even in this state. Magic was wonderful!

Nerine pulled the door open. Beyond it was a wall of water. She stepped into it, her hair spreading out luxuriously as it had before. It seemed almost alive in its own right.

The others followed, neither afoot nor swimming. They were like ghosts, visible only when focused on. "Remember," Nydia said. "This is a memory we are watching. We're not really here. It's like reading a book or seeing a magic mirror show. Only Nerine is real for this scene, and even she can't actually change anything."

"Fascinating," Flame said. "I've never been in another Element like this."

Nydia realized that this would indeed be a novel experience for the Element of Fire, surrounded by water yet not being put out.

"I know you're as hot as ever, inside," Noletta said fondly.

"This is a deep freshwater lake," Nerine said. "Ancient Ogre-Chobee, to be specific. I am actually a naiad, a freshwater nymph, though Metria in her ignorance gave me the name of a nereid, a sea nymph."

"How could she know?" Woe Betide asked, frowning.

"It doesn't matter. It may even keep me anonymous."

Nydia found that interesting. She hadn't realized that there were freshwater and seawater nymphs as well as assorted land nymphs. But they were there in the template, once she thought to look.

They were passing through what seemed to be a seaweed forest, with tall treelike plants, some of which bore strange fruit. An orchard, perhaps.

"Your hair is beautiful," Noletta said.

"It's actually borderline prehensile. It smooths out the currents around me when I swim, facilitating my progress. It warms me when the water is cool and cools me when it's too warm. It frames my face, covering blemishes, making it prettier. It's mainly cosmetic, but I keep it secret, except from my closest friends, as naiads normally don't have talents. I never wanted to be different from my siblings."

Nerine swam toward an elaborate underwater palace in the distance, her green hair rippling as she moved. She was utterly lovely in her nudity. The water prevented any part of her from even thinking about sagging.

The only thing she wore was a small green crown set on her head, above the main mass of hair.

Crown?

The triton guard at the palace gate saluted as Nerine approached. He was a handsome figure of a man above the waist, with an equally handsome fish tail below it. "Welcome home, Princess," he said by rippling the gills of his neck.

Princess? Nydia was sure the others were as surprised as she was.

Nerine rippled her own gills. "Thank you, Tris."

She had gills? These had never been evident before.

"Now we are within a kind of protective magic bubble that surrounds the palace," Nerine explained to her invisible audience. "It surely will electrify any hostile intruders. Only those it knows and accepts can pass harmlessly, as I did." She swam through and on up to her own royal chamber, which overlooked the stately royal garden.

"You're a princess?" Nydia asked.

"Yes. Princess Naiadia, one of several here, my sisters. At this stage we don't know which of us will eventually ascend to the throne. Naiads are theoretically immortal, unless we get killed. Something else must have happened to me."

So they could talk freely with each other, here in the memory. But it would have no effect on the ancient reality.

They approached a barred turret window surrounded by pretty sea flowers. Nerine touched it, and it swung open, recognizing her. She entered a nice apartment chamber, with royal feminine touches, like rippling curtains that made their fish pictures seem alive. She picked up a piece of seashell candy and nibbled on it, relaxing.

"Princess!"

Nerine looked. The voice was from outside the window. There was a naiad there. "What is it, dear?" she called.

"I'm Neoma. My name means 'From the light of the new moon,' though I can see the moon only when I swim to the surface. I'm in trouble. I need your help."

Nerine, as Naiadia, clearly had boundless sympathy for distressed girls, and this was surely generally known. Some might try to take advantage of it. But what could she do except follow her nature? "Come in." She opened the window.

Relieved, Neoma swam into the room, and Nerine closed the bars behind her. Soon she was telling her problem. "Prince Norward is after me."

"Norward!" Nerine obviously knew the name. "Wasn't he banned from recruiting here?"

"Yes. But he has ways. He approached me as I worked in the wider palace garden, and I did not recognize him, as he wore a mask. I thought he was a local man, a worker. Then I was temporarily stunned. Before I knew it, he had his compelling lasso around me and was hauling me away. I could not even try to escape."

"You poor girl," Nerine said. "How did you escape him?"

"He kissed me. I was plainly unwilling, but I could not resist his awful caress, having no command of my body. Then his hand snagged on the lasso, which was across my bottom as he goosed me, and jarred it loose. For the moment, I was able to move, though he still had hold of me. I bit him on the shoulder, hard. 'You female dogfish!' he swore as he involuntarily let go. I launched myself clear and fled. He pursued me, but I dived through the magic bubble, feeling only a tingle because it knows me, while it electrified him. He fell back, swearing so savagely that bubbles of roiling smoke floated up. Then he went to brace the triton guard, and I knew he would soon be through, by crook or hook or bribe. He'll be here momentarily. Princess, you have to help me!"

"He should be arrested."

"Princess, please. You know they won't do that. He's a prince, while I'm only a lowly naiad without influence. He'll haul me to his garden of horrors as an exhibit for his collection. Fate only knows what revolting things he'll do to me there. Theoretically the frozen naiads are works of art decorating the garden, but I've heard stories that sicken me."

"So have I," Nerine said. Then, to her memory audience: "We naiads are very free with our favors, but there are limits, and Norward made a practice of transgressing them. But somehow, he escaped any reckoning. Even the authorities feared him."

Nydia knew from the template that some males were like that. They were barred from the Retreat because they could ruin nymphs in ways even memory wiping couldn't fix. She did not know what could do that, and did not care to know, but was sure that it was true. This was outside the Retreat, where there was less security.

"I can protect you," Nerine said to Neoma. "But there are cautions. I can send you to the Secret Garden as a worker. But you will be unable to return to your former life. It's a one-way journey."

"So I have heard," the naiad said. "But I'll never be safe from Norward if I remain here. I am ready to go."

"It's not a bad life, and the plants are magical. But you can't leave it."

"I know. But it's vastly better than what I would suffer here."

"Then come this way." Nerine led Neoma out the rear door of her suite and down a slanting tunnel that led to the palace basement. No stairways were needed, since they swam wherever they went. Down below was an oubliette which it seemed no one frequented. A strong current of water was pouring into it from a vent in a wall. "This leads to the Secret Garden," Nerine said. "The current will carry you there. When you arrive, the garden mistress will assign you to a section, and that will be that. You will be completely protected against villains like Norward. You'll soon make friends with other workers, male and female, in your time off. It's a good existence. Just not the same as here."

"I understand." Without further dialog, the naiad plunged into the oubliette and was gone.

"But I wish we could be forever rid of ilk like Norward," Nerine muttered as she swam back to her suite. "She should not have to give up her life here because of him."

She entered her suite.

"Hello, princess."

She was startled. "What?"

A man was hovering just outside her access window. "You sent the naiad away."

"Prince Norward!"

"The same."

"How did you get here?"

"I bribed the triton."

They had feared that. "Get out of here! I want nothing to do with you."

He smiled cruelly. "Not so fast, princess. You owe me a conquest."

"I owe you nothing! You are a blot on the depths of the lake. If I had my way, you'd be executed!"

"Now, is that a nice way to address your future master?"

"You are a master of ordure!"

He nudged close to the bars. "You are lovely when you're mad."

"I'm calling the guards!"

Again the smile. "I think not."

She opened her mouth to curse him—and froze in place. She couldn't move. What was happening?

"It's a useful elixir, parallel to the lasso," he said. "You can act only as I direct you to. The effect is temporary, but it suffices. Now open the window."

It turned out that she could move after all, but only at his direction. Numbly she opened the window, letting him in. Then he looped the lasso over her, drawing it snug about her waist. She was unable to resist.

"As I said, you owe me a conquest. You are a fine-looking creature, especially that wavy hair. First, I'll have my will of you. Then I will take you away to my garden. You should provide me with what I lost when you stole away the pretty naiad. Everything and more. No one else will know what happened to you. You will be my passion slave."

She tried to protest, but could neither move nor speak. She was his captive.

"Of course you are a princess, so I shall have to be careful. I will stuff you in a bag so one sees you. After I ravish you, of course. Remain quiet and enjoy it." He put his arms about her and drew her in close. His inquisitive hand grasped her rear.

Still, she could not fight him. The elixir had worn off, but power of the lasso was absolute. She might as well have been a doll.

But as he took his time nastily teasing her, her hair came quietly alive. It seemed it was not affected by the lasso, and not charmed by his attitude. It subtly circled his throat. As he pressed in close, the strands of it slowly tightened.

"Wha?" he exclaimed, surprised. That was all, as the hair constricted just below his gills. Soon, he was silently gagging, unable to breathe. He might have clutched at the strands and ripped them off, but he didn't understand what was happening.

Nerine could not do anything about it, and would not have cared to anyway. The foul man was getting what he deserved: execution.

In due course, the prince was still, his life expired. The body drifted away from her as the hair slid away from his neck, but the lasso remained in place, preventing her from moving. Time passed.

Then the palace guards were there, discovering the scene. "He's dead!" one exclaimed.

"She's not," another said. "She's pacified by the lasso."

"He's been throttled. Who did it?"

A third guard laughed. "Not her, obviously. She's helpless. Someone else must have come in and killed him in a jealous rage."

They freed Nerine from the lasso. "What happened, princess?"

"He was going to—to—" Then, rather than continue, she burst into tears. It wasn't lying, exactly, merely avoiding the key aspect. It was better that they did not know.

Soon the authorities were there. "Prince Norward was a disreputable man," Nerine's father said. "But he was a royal from a rival kingdom and had formidable connections. I am furious at what he evidently tried to do to my daughter, but it would be awkward trying to explain what happened to him when we don't know it ourselves. His folk will assume we murdered him. There could be war. It would be better to disappear him without explanation."

"And her," her mother said. "Folk will assume that they eloped and are hiding together."

"Chubby chance," Nerine muttered to her Quest companions.

"A cunning ploy," her father agreed admiringly. "She was always my favorite child because of her beauteous hair. There's just something about it."

Nerine did not comment. He surely knew her hair's real nature, and suspected what it had done, but had the wit to avoid that aspect. Especially in the presence of the guards, who could gossip about secrets.

"We certainly don't want to hurt her, but we shall need to hide her where she will never be found, at least until this washes over." Her mother was supremely practical when it came to complications. She, too, was staying clear of mentioning the hair. That secret had to be kept.

"We'll feed the body to the pet sharks, so there will be no trace. As for her—" He gazed at Nerine, considering. "We can hide her, but her soul can be tracked. The only way to truly protect her is to separate her soul, cruel as that may seem, until this crisis passes."

Nerine realized that he was right. It was an awful thing, but it was necessary to protect her from vengeance-minded enemies. She nodded acceptance.

"I know a soul collector," her mother said. "He truly values every soul he gets. He owes me a favor. He will make the deal." The parents exchanged a glance. She was a beautiful woman, and ready to do what was necessary to make key deals. Her father knew better than anyone how persuasive she could be, and approved it. They understood each other perfectly. Diplomatic expedience took priority over private romance.

And so it came to be that Nerine spent a thousand years as an anonymous, soulless, one-day-at-a-time nymph in the Retreat. Maybe she had been hidden too well. Surely the crisis had passed in months or a few years. What could have happened in the interim?

"Wow!" Vinia said as they came out of the memory. "What a history you had! But what was the foul prince planning to do with you? And how did your mother make the deal with the soul collector? No, don't try to answer; I know it will be censored out by the Conspiracy." She clearly had two thirds of a notion, but pretended ignorance.

"Close enough," Nerine agreed. It was a horrible memory, but she was, she said, perversely glad to have it back.

They looked around. The cabin was undisturbed, and Flame's fire still circled it. The whole thing felt rather like a dream. But there were cautions.

"I lost my talent," Nerine said forlornly. "It must have been attached to my soul."

"Which perhaps explains why your hair tangles," Noletta said. "It's the remnant of your talent, cut off at the knees."

"Now that makes sense," Nerine agreed. "My talent is annoyed. I'd be annoyed, too, if most of me were gone. In fact, I *am* annoyed. I was a compassionate princess, and all it did was get me in trouble!"

"Now we know your history," Nydia said. "And an amazing story it is! But I think we need to know more. I don't like to imagine a threat to you could last a thousand years, but there is that chance. We need to research before we act."

"I want my soul back," Nerine said with feeling.

"And your recovery of it could be the trigger for a trap. Remember, souls can be tracked."

Nerine winced, knowing it was true.

"We can recover her soul and put it in the bag," Ecstasy suggested. "Where it will remain untrackable but available."

"Brilliant," Nydia agreed. "Now how do we track it down?"

"I can do it," Vinia said. "The paths will lead me to it."

"Good enough. Tomorrow."

They settled down for the night. Nydia was sure she was not the only one amazed by what they had discovered. Who could ever have thought that an ordinary nymph could have such a background?

But the remaining mysteries were disturbing. A thousand years! Why had Nerine never been released from the Retreat and her soul returned to her? Her parents surely would have rescued her the moment it was safe. Was there indeed danger awaiting them, even after a thousand years? They needed to be excruciatingly careful.

At last, almost reluctantly, Nydia slept. So did the others. Sleep had been carefree in the Retreat because the nymphs had no worries. Yet this discomfort was probably better, overall.

In the morning, they went about their routines as usual, except that Noletta took a walk with Flame to see the sights, as she put it. She would likely be doing more showing than looking. Now that she had a genuine boyfriend, she was making the most of it.

"First things first," Nydia said when they were ready to go. "Nerine's soul." She glanced at Vinia.

"On our way," the girl agreed. She focused for two and a half instants, then pointed south. "That way."

When they came to an intersection, they took the enchanted path south. In another day, they came to Lake Ogre-Chobee, where ogres and chobees lived in reasonable compatibility. It looked wide and shallow, but Nydia knew that was deceptive.

They left the path and went to the edge of the lake. "Under there," Vinia said, pointing.

"There may be a problem," Ecstasy said. "You three nymphs can go anywhere, thanks to your socks. But Vinia and I can't. I'm not sure about Flame. The figurine can handle water, but might now be too hot for it."

"I won't need the socks underwater," Nerine said. "I will share mine with you and Vinia. I think one sock each will do it." She sat down, lifted her legs in a manner that would have freaked out any normal male, and drew off her socks. She handed one to each of the two live folk, who put them on their right and left feet respectively, under their shoes.

"What about Flame?" Nydia asked. "He can travel in the bag, of course, but I think he would rather be with Noletta, and she with him."

"I would," Flame agreed. "I can tone it down, here in the figurine. My wider self is out with the elsewhere in the countryside fires."

"Can you?" Ecstasy asked shrewdly. "We should test it."

They tested it. Flame squatted beside the water and touched the surface with a finger. A gout of steam surged up. He tried again with no better result. He could not entirely douse his nature, even in the figurine.

"I will share with you, hot stuff," Noletta said fondly. She drew off one sock and gave it to him.

Flame donned the sock on his right foot, then touched the water again. There was no burst of steam, merely the thin film of air that enabled regular folk to breathe. He moved on into the water, bemused. "I'm an Element protected from an Element!"

"And still hot inside," Noletta said, smiling.

He smiled back. A little burning heart sailed across to her. She caught it and tucked it in her hair, which changed from blue to bright red in that vicinity.

"Yuck," Woe Betide muttered. She knew mush when she saw it.

They removed their clothing, as it would only get in the way in the water, and put it in the bag. They were reasonably ready.

Vinia led the way into the water, followed by Nerine. Soon they were walking along the bottom while Nerine swam beside them, her gills now visible, and Woe floated nearby, as it were. Fish swam by, unconcerned. There were natural paths through the water plants.

The invisible path led to an underwater cave. There was no sign of any other person; Nydia was watching closely. The cave was tall enough that they could walk upright. After a few serpentine turns, it opened into a somber chamber.

They paused, surprised. There was a circle of about fifty candles, their flames different colors.

"Candles burning underwater?" Ecstasy asked dubiously.

Nydia checked the closest one. It turned out not to be a candle exactly, but a miniature pedestal with a starlike glowing ball hovering close above. "It's a soul!"

"The soul collector's acquisitions," Noletta said. "Mine must be one of these."

"This way." Vinia circled the ring, stopping at one with a flickering blue gleam. "Here."

Nerine went to it. She touched it with one finger. Her hair flared like a miniature nova, its talent returning. Her body seemed to come doubly alive. Indeed, this was the one.

"But you can't wear it," Nydia reminded her. "Lest you be tracked, and get us all in trouble. It must go in the bag."

"I hate to confine it there." Then she brightened. "Unless I can loan it to Flame? He's an Element; if somebody tracks it, all they'll see is fire."

Could that work? All they could do was try it and hope for the best.

"Take it," Noletta said to Flame.

He reached out and cupped the little ball of light in one hand. In half a moment, it disappeared into the hand.

"Awesome!" he said. "Suddenly I care about more than you, Noletta. I want to be a good person and do decent things." He paused. "I love you, Noletta. But I also love Nerine, in a brotherly manner."

Nerine smiled. "Consider me your soul sister. We'll get along."

"What next?" Nydia asked, discovering that she had not thought beyond this point.

"I would really like to know what happened during my absence," Nerine said. "If by some miracle I retain some royal privilege, I might be in a better position to recruit the Element of Water. A princess should have more clout than an anonymous nymph." That was a considerable understatement, given how nymphs were regarded.

There was an indefinite silence. They were waiting for Nydia to make a decision.

"That makes sense to me," Ecstasy said, interrupting the silence before it could really get started. Annoyed, it departed.

"And to me," Nydia agreed. "But how can we learn the intervening history? It's not in our template. I think the assumption is that history would be wasted on nymphs."

"A historian should know it," Ecstasy said.

"This way," Vinia said, observing her paths.

They followed her. Those paths were indeed proving to be useful.

They came to an underwater village of mermaids and tritons, who ignored the nymphs as not being their type. Down here, legs were not nearly as efficient as tails. Tritons surely preferred nice pieces of tail.

Vinia's path led to what appeared to be the slum section. There, in a shack formed from part of the hull of a sunken ship, was a triton hovering near a desk. The path led right to him.

Nydia put on her best positive expression, uncertain of the protocol here. "Hello, triton. I am Nydia Nymph in search of what may be an obscure bit of history. Can you help us?"

The triton gazed at her upper section, perhaps embarrassed by the awkwardness of her lower section. Tailless creatures had to be rare here, and not very interesting either in the faunly manner or personally. "That depends on the obscurity. I am Clovis Cleric, an undistinguished incidental historian. What are you looking for?"

A historian. Good enough. "Nerine here will explain it. It's her business."

Nerine came forward, her hair lovely even without the enhancement of her talent. She named the ancient kingdom and the mystery of the princess who had disappeared.

"Ah, *that* history. I know it, but am unable to resolve the mystery, as the lost princess was never found. Her disappearance, together with that of a hostile prince, was not taken well by his kingdom. They suspected that she had somehow ensorcelled him, as he was not one to take his conquests seriously. There was war, which so depleted both kingdoms that a third one was able to take over both their territories and forcibly retire their royalties. Their history stopped there."

A tear rolled down Nerine's cheek, which was a good trick in water, but she managed it. "I am that lost princess. I was hidden in a Faun & Nymph Retreat and never released until now, mostly by accident. I am so sorry to learn of my family's misfortune."

Now the triton's interest intensified. "If you can document that, I can write a codicil that will make me fractionally famous among cleric historians. Do tell me more."

She did, and he avidly made notes. She was, in effect, paying for the information he had provided.

"Now we know," Ecstasy said as they waited for the dialog to conclude. "I feel somewhat sorry for her, though it does free her for the rest of the Quest."

"She was not likely to return to her former life after a thousand years anyway," Nydia said. "I wonder what the fauns would have thought had they known the nymph they ridiculed because of her tangled hair was actually a princess?"

"Assuming they even knew what a princess is." They laughed together. Fauns had become the ridiculed symbol of the life the nymphs had left behind.

In due course, the dialog completed its course and expired. Nerine returned to the group. "My feelings are so jumbled. I'm glad to know the rest of it, but sorry my background is gone."

"At least you have a history, as we do not," Noletta said. "You're not a nothing nymph."

Nerine shook her head. "None of us are nothing anymore. We're friends."

"And we're on a Quest," Nydia added. "That's not nothing."

"I'm so glad!" Nerine reached out to embrace them both together. They hugged her back. Three little hearts flew out and orbited them.

Astonished, they stared. Hearts?

"Don't be so surprised," Ecstasy said. "The hearts signal love. It doesn't have to be romantic."

"It's nice," Nerine said as they separated and the hearts faded.

"We're jealous," Vinia said, standing beside Flame.

"I have half, maybe even three quarters of a notion how it is," Flame said. "Thanks to the soul."

It was time to get on with things. "Where can we find the Element of Water?" Nydia asked Vinia.

The girl focused. "This way."

It turned out not to be far. They swam to the deepest depth of the lake, where there was an ancient cathedral braced by a massive scaly rope on either side, north to south. The structure needed to be held down?

Vinia's path led right to it and into it. "My future just flickered," Noletta said.

Flame moved closer to her. "You are in danger? I'll scorch it!"

"Not that straightforward, dear. It means we could make a wrong decision and get in serious trouble. We just need to be careful. We have navigated threats before."

He let it be, though plainly on guard.

They entered the cathedral and paused. There was a monstrous serpent head, as tall as they were, and considerably longer, with its teeth biting firmly on its own tail.

"What is this?" Nydia asked.

"I think it's the biggest snake ever," Nerine said. "Those cables coming to this place must be its body. Who knows how far it reaches?"

"I believe this is Ouroborus," Ecstasy said, awed. "The serpent who circles Xanth, holding it together so it doesn't split apart at the Gap Chasm and drift off as two pieces."

"Ouroborus!" Flame said. "Now I recognize him." He moved close to the giant head. "Hello, Tailchomp!"

The answer came in their minds, a powerful thought. "Hello, Fire Head."

The enormous serpent is telepathic, Nydia thought. That surely facilitated communication when its mouth was occupied.

"It does, nymph." The thought startled her, coming directly to her mind.

"I haven't seen you in a while," Flame said.

"My body is hidden so that the birds don't poop on it. I am still holding things together. But it does get dull, in the course of eons. So I converse here with the Element of Water to pass the time. He has been around even longer than I have."

So they had come to the right place. "True, nymph," Ouroborus answered her thought.

"I am here to recruit the Element to our Quest," Nerine said. "There is a problem we need to resolve."

"What problem is this?"

"There are rivers in torrents and floods galore. Whole villages are getting drowned. Only the Element can stop them."

"He hardly cares about the convenience of villagers. He won't talk to you."

"He will after I kiss him."

Ouroborus laughed mentally. "You think that the puny kiss of a mere nymph will influence an Element? Don't make me laugh physically. It would shake the world."

Nerine eyed him. "You are one big phallic symbol. If there's one symbol a nymph is not afraid of, it is that. We tame them many times a day. Who are you to laugh?"

"I am more than a symbol. I am the serpent who seduced the first woman into eating of the fruit of the Tree of Knowledge of Good and Evil and inciting in her and her man's simple mortal hearts the endless yearning for more knowledge, especially the forbidden kind. The two of them became so persistent about poking into what didn't concern them that the Deity got fed up and kicked them out of the Garden of Eden. Then they set about populating the planet with their kind, ruining it, and venerating me as the representation of Wisdom, though I never claimed to be wise. I am the Teutonic Midgard Serpent and the Hindu Asootee, the eternal path of the sun. I signify that good and bad, perfection and inferiority, are bound together in matter, like day and night. I also symbolize the Four Elements."

"Four?" Nydia asked sharply. "But there are five."

"The Void doesn't count," Ouroborus replied. "He's empty."

"We'll see." But Nydia was shaken. Now that she thought about it, she had to ask: how could emptiness be considered an Element? Were they on an impossible mission?

"Enough of this chitchat," Nerine said impatiently. "We're going on to Water."

"Only if you can get by me," Ouroborus said. "He doesn't want to be bothered by silly nymphs."

"Silly?" Nerine asked. "Do I have to pacify you on the way to him?"

The serpent eyed her with contempt. "I could swallow you in a tiny fraction of a gulp, you arrogant piece of fluff."

"You're bluffing, Oro. You are not about to let go of your tail and let Xanth fly apart. Then you'd have nothing to do, no justification for your existence. Here's a sample of my power. I am going to kiss you."

"You wouldn't dare!"

She laughed. "Try me, Symbol of Wisdom."

"How are you ever going to manage it, tiny cutie?" The disdain was as big as the body.

"Like this." Nerine marched up, leaned forward, and kissed a section of his lip where it was up against his tail. The section was as big as she was, but the impact was apparent. A little heart formed by a miniature serpent with its tail in its mouth flew out. A visible current ran down along the mighty head, neck, and body. Steam bubbled up where it passed, and the lake floor quaked with the force of the serpent's involuntary squeeze.

"It's a good thing I'm not human," Ouroborus said dazedly. "And that you could not deliver the full force of your smooch. As it is, I will dream of you."

"Do that, Oro," she said, satisfied. "You will not forget me."

"I should have warned you, Oro," Flame said. "These creatures possess the Power of Love. There is nothing else like it. Now you know."

"Now I know," the serpent echoed, and sank into a turmoil of bliss.

They swam over the body and entered the inner chamber of the cathedral. The invisible presence of the Element was subtly tangible. Nydia brought out the water figurine and the wand. She waved the latter. "Element of Water, enter this figure," she said.

There was a swirl, and the figurine came to life. "I heard," Water said. "Your companion's kiss won't compel me."

"We shall see." Nerine caught hold of him, oriented him to face her, and firmly kissed him. This time, a heart in the shape of a quivering water bomb flew out.

"Then again, I could be wrong," he said, shaken. "I suspect I underestimated the Power of Love. Does it come with privileges?"

"Yes, when I deem them appropriate."

"I anticipate that deeming with joy."

"You are learning," Flame remarked. "As I did." He smiled. "It's not a bad thing."

"Not bad at all," Ouroborus's thought came from the other chamber.

"Come with me," Nerine said. "Read my mind for the necessary background. We have a job to do."

"I'm not telepathic. That's Ouroborus."

"Oh." She pondered half a moment, then looked at Nydia. "May we borrow Anthem?"

Nydia took her hand, and the fire ant crossed over. Then Nerine took the figurine's hand. They were connected.

"You were a princess," he said, surprised. "I remember your ancient kingdom. No wonder authority comes so naturally to you."

"I think I am not a princess anymore. My kingdom no longer exists."

"You are still my queen."

She laughed. "Thank you."

They bid Ouroborus farewell, exited the cathedral, and swam to the surface of the lake, Nerine and the Element communicating all the while. They decided to call him Flood. They waded to the bank.

Where a smoker dragon happened to be drinking. "Out of our way, sootsnoot," Flood said impatiently.

The dragon swelled up, taking in air for a phenomenal blast of smoke. Many folk did not realize that smoke killed more people than fire, suffocating them. But a cloud of water bombs appeared, pelting the dragon mercilessly. Enraged, it opened its mouth wide—and a huge water bomb sailed in, splashing inside its throat. The dragon went into a coughing fit, balls of smoke flying from its ears. Realizing it was over-matched, it retreated.

They walked back to the enchanted path. Now Flame strolled beside Flood, and they chatted, comparing notes.

They spied a passing valley that had become a lake. "What made you do that?" Nerine asked.

"I don't know," he said, surprised. "I don't usually bother incidental bits of scenery." He raised an arm and waved. The water level dropped. In a few minutes the valley was clear, with only a normal river running through it.

"That's the way it is with me," Flame said. "Something is making me get all stirred up. I don't like being interfered with."

"Me neither," Flood agreed. "I'll stop the damage."

This Element, too, was handy to have around.

Chapter 6

AIR

"I need a sock back," Nerine said. She glanced at Flood. "Now that we're out of our element."

Immediately, both Ecstasy and Vinia reached down toward their socks, about to take them off.

"Wait," Nydia said. "Both of you may still need protection as we approach other Elements. You should keep your socks, just in case."

"I don't need mine," Flame said. "That was just to mask me so that we could go into the lake without evaporating the water or disturbing the natives." He lifted his foot and pulled off the sock. He presented it to Nerine. "I have your soul; you are welcome to my sock."

Nerine laughed, accepting it. "Fair trade, hot stuff. So now I will wear Noletta's sock."

"Don't mistreat it," Noletta said, forcing a frown that endured barely half an instant before being obliterated by a smile.

"What's our next element?" Nydia asked.

There was a roll of thunder in the distance. A storm was building.

"I think we have our answer," Ecstasy said. "We can be sure that's no ordinary storm. We need to stop it before it blows away a village or two."

"Air," Nydia agreed, though she distrusted the coincidence. Was the Element of Air aware of them and their Quest, and wanted to be included?

"It's coincidence," Anthem said. "There have been storms in the distance all along, but we haven't been paying attention."

"Air can be erratic," Flame said.

"We all can be," Flood said. "I am increasingly curious who or what is messing with us."

"We hope to find out soon," Nydia said.

"But a caution," Ecstasy said. "A potent female kiss won't suffice this time. I crafted the figurine of Air to be as my insight indicated. Female. Sightly."

"She is that," Flame agreed. "With a temper to match."

"What are you implying, soulkeeper?" Noletta demanded, bridling.

He laughed. "That she's like you, you beguiling bundle of ever-changing moods. I love that in you. You constantly stoke my fire. What a time I could have had with Air, were we Elements not like siblings, socially. I have no romantic interest in Air. But I'm sure she could use a man. Too bad there's not a handsome, robust, macho male in this Quest."

"True," Flood said. "My water helps power her storms, as does your heat. She's alluring, but not for us."

Nydia realized that they had a problem. Men did not have the kissing power women did, as far as she knew. They were the objects rather than the forces, though they might see it the other way around. Few men realized that women were the secret mistresses of Xanth, Mundania, and points between. It was the Female Conspiracy. How were they going to pacify this wild Element without that kiss power, even if they got her in a figurine? They had been able to focus the other two Elements, but Air was everywhere and nowhere. They needed her cooperation.

"We need a man," Ecstasy said. "A special one. The right men do have their unsubtle appeal."

The other females nodded, knowing their power. The two Elements looked blank, not really aware of the nature of their appeal. Just so. It was best that men remain ignorant, lest they become even more difficult than usual.

Then Nydia suffered a realization. Air was everywhere, seeing, hearing, and feeling everything no matter how private or intimate. But she had no solid body to experience it personally, no brain to understand it. She might be curious as to what she was missing, but unable to satisfy that curiosity despite how much information she acquired. She might be extremely frustrated.

They could help her, via the figurine and their dialog. But how could Air ever come to know the kind of emotional interaction Noletta and Nerine had with their boyfriends? Nydia herself had no personal acquaintance with it despite her experience in the Retreat, and intelligence thereafter. Fauns were no substitute for a real relationship with a man. If she thought about it too much, she would work herself into a siege of jealousy. She wanted a man, too, even if it was only an animated ectoplasmic figurine.

Better to change the subject. Nydia looked at Vinia. "Do your paths lead to any prospects?"

The girl focused. "Not here on land or in the sea. In the sky, maybe."

That was not much help. What was in the sky but wind and clouds?

"The moon!" Woe Betide exclaimed. "The Man in the Moon! Even I know how intriguing he is, always out of reach."

A look circled, its adult aspect passing over the child's head. Could this crazy notion actually be viable?

Ecstasy was practical. "How would we get there to recruit him, assuming it could be done?"

"The magic of perspective," Nydia said, remembering how that had been useful when addressing the sun. "Catch the moon when it is near the horizon. Get on it and search him out, following Vinia's paths."

"Get Air into a figurine and take her along," Nerine said. "Then she can fascinate him and be satisfied herself." She glanced sidelong at Flood, ready to do both with him soon.

Maybe that made sense.

"Very well," Nydia said, though she was not at all sure it was even a trifle well. "We'll walk into the storm and clamor for her attention."

"No," Noletta and Vinia said almost together.

The others looked at them.

"The paths are scrambled, with no clear green one," Vinia said.

"My future flickered," Noletta said. "It reeked of disappointment."

This was interesting. "Can the two of you work together to find a clear and safe path to success?" Nydia asked. "Maybe if we use our magic properly, it will guide us."

"Try making decisions," Ecstasy suggested, "while watching the changes only you can see."

"The storm's no good," Vinia said. "But where else can we go to find her?"

Noletta looked around. "Back the way we came? No."

"To the nearest village?" Vinia asked. "No."

"That low hill," Noletta said, glancing to the side. "I got a flicker and I think it's positive."

"A green path is forming, but it's obscure."

"That is nevertheless progress," Ecstasy said. "Try variations."

"We climb the hill and do something," Noletta said. "Another flicker."

"Do what?" Vinia asked. "Put on a show?"

Then both of them paused as if something impressive had made an appearance.

"I saw the Air figurine already come to life, tomorrow," Noletta said. "Beautiful and sexy. Maybe it happens today. She was beside Flame and Flood, and smiling."

"And the path to the hill flashed bright green."

Before long they worked it out. Flame and Flood would stand at the top of the hill and make a show of fire and water to impress Air, demonstrating that they really were part of this party. And it seemed that Air would be affected and elect to join them, at least to the extent of animating the figurine so they could talk with her. Then Nydia would make the pitch for trying to recruit the Man in the Moon.

They marched up the hill and made their show, knowing Air was watching without understanding. The key was to intrigue her enough to join the game. Flame made a fire, then let his figurine image sag as if empty. Nydia waved the wand and the fire moved to the figure, which came to life. Then Noletta stepped up and kissed it. A fiery little heart flew out. They walked away, hand in hand. A capsule romance. Would it interest the Element? She had surely seen romances galore, right down to any details air touched; did they mystify her so that she wanted to know more?

Flood stood by a hollow in the ground and gestured, filling it with water. His figure went inert. Nydia waved the wand, and the puddle floated up and doused the figurine, which woke back up. Then Nerine kissed it, generating mini water-bomb hearts, and they held hands. Another spot romance. The difference between these and others Air had seen was that they involved Elements. Would she care?

Finally, Ecstasy got out the Air figurine, which was a wild and lovely form. She held it up, as it was obviously vacant. Nydia waved the wand. Was the essence of the Element close enough to animate it? Only if she chose to be.

The figurine twitched. Its sky-blue hair flung out. Its matching blue eyes opened. Air was there! She was a beauty, with a shape rivaling that of a nymph. Ecstasy had outdone herself fashioning this one. But did Air even care about appearance?

Nydia spoke to her immediately, improvising. "Hello, Air! We'll call you Aery. Welcome to our Quest. The magic of the figurines enables you to understand our speech and to respond in kind. We regret we do not have a man for you to kiss and fascinate, but we're working on it. If you cooperate with us, not only will you come to understand what we are up to, you will have a chance to experience a kind of fulfillment you may not have had before. You are welcome to talk with your sibling Elements Fire and Water, who are working with us by choice."

"Talk?" Aery asked, as if trying out the verbal mechanism. Yes, it worked.

"Talk and act," Nydia reassured her. "You can indulge in the full range of life. You will finally know the meaning of what you have only observed before."

"I don't know. This is so strange."

Flame stepped forward. "I am Fire. You know me by my heat and smoke. Trust me, parallel Element, you will enjoy this experience." He beckoned to Noletta. "You will know passion. There is nothing else like it." He kissed the nymph, who of course cooperated fully, generating another heart. "Perhaps even love. That is something we Elements never knew before."

"Love," Aery repeated somewhat blankly.

Flood joined them. "You will know it when you find it." He kissed Nerine. "I am Water. Together we can discover who or what has been messing with us, and set it right. And we Elements can get to know each other better. We have been interacting for millennia as virtual strangers. It is past time to become friends."

"Friends," Aery repeated. This was evidently another foreign concept.

The other members of the Quest introduced themselves and explained how their group had formed.

"Something has been agitating the Elements," Nydia said. "We feel this is rank interference in the natural order and needs to be stopped. So we are trying to organize the Elements by making them part of our Quest, and hope you agree and join us."

Now Aery began to connect. "So some outside party has been making me stormy. I don't mind being tempestuous, but I want it to be my own decision, not someone else's."

"Exactly," Flame and Flood said almost together.

Aery turned to Nydia. "You mentioned finding a man for me to fascinate. Who?"

"We were thinking of the Man in the Moon."

"I know of him! He's been watching me for eons, the voyeur. Now that I have a mind, I am making sense of some of my memories."

"We really don't know his nature, but thought he might find you interesting."

Aery frowned. She was rapidly learning common expressions. "I want any relationship between us to be my choice, not his."

There spoke a like-minded woman, Nydia thought with a certain muted pride. "We all do."

Flame and Flood exchanged a glance, but didn't comment. The problems of male and female interaction seemed to extend well beyond species, or even type. They might or might not figure it out in due course.

"So I need to learn how to kiss with power."

Naturally, she had had no experience, without a body. She would need to learn.

They tried to decide how to teach her. But the males knew better how to receive a kiss than how to deliver it, and of course they were like brothers to her. It had to be the women.

"Women kissing women," Noletta said. "That's not my style."

"Nor mine," Nerine agreed. "Nymphs never kissed nymphs in the Retreat."

"I'm too young," Vinia said. "I've kissed Ion, but we're betrothed."

"I'm younger," Woe Betide said. "Metria really knows how to do it, but that's different. She's a messy part of the Adult Conspiracy, shame on her." She grimaced cutely. "And our third personality, Mentia, is worse. She's crazy. She can drive a man bonkers with a kiss."

"And leave me out of it," Ecstasy said. "I never aspired to be a siren." But she looked a smidgen sad.

"Well, we did kiss Apoca," Nydia said. The others nodded; the nymphs could kiss women when there was reason.

So it was up to them. "I'll start," Nerine said. "I kissed men when I was a princess. Of course, that was a while ago."

"A thousand years," Woe said, laughing. "You'll be rusty."

Nerine faced Aery. "I will pretend you are a man I want to impress. Then you can imitate that and kiss me back, pretending I'm the man."

"This is all new to me." The Element looked confused but determined.

New to all of us, Nydia thought, and Anthem agreed. But what else could they do? Aery needed this tool.

Nerine kissed Aery firmly on the mouth. No little hearts showed. Then Aery kissed her back. "Little or no magic there," Nerine said regretfully. The Element sadly agreed.

Then Noletta kissed her, evincing some fiery passion, and she kissed Noletta back. "Some there, I think," Noletta reported. "For half an instant, I felt a whiff."

"That was my air stirring. Maybe I'm learning."

Finally, Nydia took her place. She visualized the Air Element as a handsome man, maybe like Prince Nolan, and kissed the figurine as passionately as she could.

"Hoo!" Aery breathed. "That had force." Then she kissed Nydia back. The kiss had impact.

"I think you're getting it," Nydia said, surprised.

"You showed me how."

"Where did you learn to kiss like that?" Ecstasy asked. "I could see the power of it."

"I have no idea. Maybe I was copying Apoca." Certainly she had never kissed a faun like that, and she didn't see how the Stein could have contributed.

"The thing to do is put feeling into it," Ecstasy told Aery. "Passion can make up for inexperience."

"I'll try," Aery said uncertainly.

"Now we have to go corral the moon man," Nydia said, evincing more decisiveness than she felt. It was evident that being a leader meant faking significant parts of it. "The day is getting on. We should be able to catch the moon near the horizon soon."

"Let's get on it," Noletta said.

Sure enough, the moon was low in the sky, full and bright. At least they wouldn't have to wrestle with the points of a crescent. She didn't see the face of the Man in the Moon, but knew it didn't always show. He might be taking a potty break.

"Problem," Ecstasy said. "The moon is canny. You can't just run up to it and jump on. It will set elsewhere, avoiding you."

Oops. Nydia realized she was right. She focused her Stein intellect on the problem—and came up with a possible answer. "We'll hide in a tree, then use the flying carpet to get above the moon when it passes, and jump down, catching it by surprise."

She brought out the carpet and spread it flat, and they piled on, all nine of them neatly fitting. That seemed to be part of its magic. Nydia found herself sitting next to Aery, which was fine. Vinia took over the steering, and the carpet flew in a wide circle to a spreading acorn tree close to where the moon was heading.

"Now the magic of perspective makes big distant things appear small and close," Nydia explained, drawing on the information in the template as interpreted by the Stein. "The moon may look small, but it's actually pretty big. We'll have to catch it just right. When I say 'Jump!' we'll all hop off the carpet and down on it. If this works the way it's supposed to, we'll be there, with it full size. Then all we'll have to do is find the Man in the Moon."

"My paths will lead us there," Vinia said.

They peeked through the foliage, watching the approaching moon. It seemed to be about the size of a Mundane basketball, slanting slowly down through the air toward them. Could it really be big enough to land on safely, or would their weight push it down into the ground, ruining everything? Their jump was going to be a leap of faith.

Nydia remembered a detail. She caught hold of a stray thread of the carpet and tied it around her wrist. She didn't want to lose it when they jumped.

The moon finally came touchingly close to the ground, about to go out of sight of any distant viewers. Its surface consisted of ridges of green cheese and dark seas. No surprises there; everyone knew the moon was made of green cheese. "Now," Nydia whispered to Vinia.

"I know," the girl whispered back. "There's green ahead." Was that a joke?

The carpet lurched up out of the tree and sailed over the moon, which was surprised and froze in place for a moment. "Jump!" Nydia called loudly, and leaped.

For a moment, two things nervoused her. The first was whether the others would jump at her command or hold back, messing up the transfer. The second was whether the little ball that was the moon would actually support them. The third was whether the thread she held would haul the carpet back into the bag so they wouldn't lose it.

"A third?" Anthem asked as they dropped. "You said there were only two."

"I miscounted."

Suddenly, the moon was vastly larger than it had been. Nydia plopped into a pile of, yes, soft green cheese. Around her, the others landed similarly, *plop, plop . . . plop*! Eight in all. The smell of cheese was almost overpowering.

They were on the moon. It was indeed larger than it had looked. And the carpet yarn tied to her wrist was threading into the bottomless bag, hauling the carpet with it. Even the improperly counted concern had worked.

They stood on the cheese and looked around. The ground was spongy, of course, just soft enough to break their fall without bruising them, but firm enough to walk on, with cheese bushes and trees spotting it. Nearby was the shore of a great dark sea, which seemed to be formed of liquid cheese. Beside it was a sign: MARE IMBRIUM. Nydia recognized that from the template; it was where the night mare Imbri came from, her home pasture, as it were. The night mares brought bad dreams to deserving sleepers, punishing them for their waking transgressions. It was a useful service to keep bad folk in line. Mare Imbri had even been the Protagonist of a story; she was famous. Of course, she wasn't here now; she would be on bad dream duty. No, Nydia remembered, she had retired, taking up with a tree faun after losing her body in the Void.

The Void. That gave her a chill. It was the last of the Elements, and likely the one Nydia herself would have to recruit. She had no idea how she would manage that. Would the others do their parts, only to have her foul it up and maybe get them swallowed by the Void? She shuddered.

Something charged across the surface toward them. It looked like a giant box of cheese crackers. Flame stepped up to toast it, but it stopped just out of range. The box opened and disgorged a cracker. The cracker sprouted little legs and fled toward a nearby cracker barrel. Then the box departed.

"A moonster!" Noletta said. "Instead of gobbling prey, it spits out crackers."

So it seemed. Nydia was relieved it hadn't attacked them. Flame would have burned it up.

"The green path goes right into the sea," Vinia said. "Good thing we have those socks."

"Socks?" Aery asked.

"We got them from the Good Magician," Noletta explained. "They protect us from the Elements. Even other Elements can use them, when they have to."

Oops. "There are not enough to go around," Nydia said. "We'd better avoid the sea. It would be pretty messy to walk under it, and how would we get clean again?"

"We could sail across it," Nerine said. "I remember seeing many boats on the surface when I lived underwater."

"If we had a boat," Noletta said. Oops again.

"Maybe we could use the carpet," Ecstasy suggested.

Nydia reached into the bag and caught hold of the carpet. It resisted coming out, and she was cautious about yanking it, lest it unravel. "Either it's tired from flying so many folk at once, or it doesn't want to mess with gooey cheese."

"Or maybe we could *make* a boat," Ecstasy said.

That seemed to make sense. They cast about and found the old, tough rind of a long-since hardened giant cheese. Flood washed it out with a conjured blast of water, and Flame dried it with fire heat. The two Elements were working well together. They found a solid cheese pole left from twisted strands of ancient string cheese and some cheesecloth. Soon, they had their boat, floating on the edge of the sea. They piled in, with Nydia sitting beside Aery again.

But there was no wind.

"We need paddles," Ecstasy said. "Maybe fashioned from fragments of rind."

"No, I'll handle that aspect," Aery said.

Wind formed, filling the sail and propelling the craft across the sea. Vinia steered it using the rudder they had made from a flake of rind, guiding it along the path she saw. The smell of the breeze was cheesy, but bearable.

Something appeared on the horizon. It seemed to be a flying moonster. "Um," Noletta said, "that's no Gouda."

"That's a cheesy pun," Nerine said.

"Thank you. That intrusion is an Edam shame."

Vinia and Woe tittered, knowing that it sounded like proscribed cursing without quite getting there. They loved to see the Conspiracy get teased before they grew up and abolished it. The adults were quiet, knowing that throughout history children had had the same intention, but then meekly joined it when they came of age.

The object seemed to be a cheesy blimp. It belched out a cloud of yellow vapor.

Ecstasy wrinkled her nose. "Eau de Limburger."

"What a stench," Vinia said.

"Too high in the sky for me to burn," Flame said. "And my fire would just make it smell worse. Smoked Limburger."

"I can't wash it out from here," Flood said.

"I can blow it away," Aery said. "But that would make a storm because I am already directing one wind in this area, for the sail, and that would complicate the local weather."

The cheese blimp belched another cloud of fetor. They all grimaced. "Blow it away!" Vinia gasped. "Better a storm than a cheesy stink." The others agreed. Indeed, the odor was horrendous. Even the three Elements were having trouble with it. It was clear that the moon really knew how to cut cheese.

"As you wish." There was a howl as the wind around them picked up.

In about two and a half moments, it developed into a raging storm. It caught hold of the blimp and blew it away, tumbling end over end and looking not at all pleased. But it also generated a shower of sticky cheese bits that made ready to pelt them and the boat unmercifully.

"The sail!" Nydia cried. "Take it down and use it as a shield!"

They quickly did so, and huddled under it as the bits splatted down.

Then the storm faded, no longer needed. They dumped the sheetful of odoriferous bits into the brine, which seemed to like them well enough. They bubbled merrily as they dissolved, generating puffs of reeking cloudlets. "Honey sheet," Noletta muttered, evoking more titters. She was playing to an audience. Nydia was impressed by the social expertise she was developing—and the alternate vocabulary. Indeed, the Nymphs were becoming real people.

"If things conclude as I would like," Flame said, "you will be good with our children."

Noletta froze an instant over a moment, absorbing that. Had he just asked her to marry him? Was she ready to go that route? He was an Element, no more a real person than the Nymphs were, but he was learning too.

"Why not?" Nerine asked. "You'll never get cold, Letta."

Noletta nodded. "Maybe it could work."

Had she just accepted? Not that Nymphs had any fear of the Conspiracy.

The others stayed out of it, but Nerine and Flood looked thoughtful. How serious a relationship were the two pondering?

The pelted sheet back in place as the sail and the moderate breeze again blowing, they resumed traveling.

Other flying moonsters appeared on the horizon, but they stayed clear, evidently having gotten the message.

Soon the boat reached the far shore. They disembarked, anchored it to a cheese boulder, and walked on, still following Vinia's path. They were now curving around the moon into territory not normally visible from Xanth. They could see that parts of the curve were actually quite sharp. The moon was really like a dish.

The cheese landscape turned blue. Clumps of azure mold grew all around, and music sounded.

"That's blues music," Anthem said, surprised. She, of course, was familiar with all types of melody. "It will have its effect."

Sure enough, a pall of depression enfolded them. Was their mission here really worthwhile? It was starting to seem pointless. Would they even find the Man in the Moon, let alone recruit him? Nydia could see the dejection forming in her companions.

"Don't be discouraged," she told them. "We are crossing Blue Cheese geography. It makes us sad. It has nothing to do with our natural feelings. Just ignore the music and keep going."

Reluctantly, they obeyed. But it wasn't easy. Nydia was coming to appreciate that depression was not something that could be ignored; it clung to them with grim tenacity. It would not be abolished by mere smiles.

Then they came to a Red Cheese section, and the gloom was replaced by ire. Why was this spot mission taking so long? They had better things to do than waste time here.

"My kind of territory," Flame said with satisfaction.

"Oh?" Noletta said. "You like fighting?"

"You kissed me when we argued. I've liked you ever since, you hot-blooded creature."

"Well, I'm not sure that makes sense."

"If you don't shut up, I'll kiss you again."

"You think that would stop me?" she demanded angrily.

"I'm not saying *where* I'll kiss you."

She froze in horror. "You wouldn't dare!"

"Wouldn't I, hotbox?" He grabbed her and kissed her passionately. She met him two-thirds of the way.

But they were laughing. They were putting on another show, and not just for the children. Nydia couldn't help feeling a tinge of envy. She had never had a relationship with a male other than a faun, which hardly counted, and wasn't sure she ever would. She saw a similar expression hovering near Ecstasy.

After that came a Yellow Cheese section. Now they were afraid of every shadow, even though they knew Flame could readily protect them from any moonsters.

Then on through a Black Cheese section, fearing doom. And White Cheese, feeling foolishly positive.

They spied something ahead. Could it be?

"That's a cow!" Vinia said.

Sure enough, it was a white cow with black spots that looked like small moon craters. She was grazing on something, maybe moon dust.

"Actually, that makes sense," Ecstasy said. "Where else is the milk going to come from to make all that cheese?"

"It must be the cow that jumped over the moon," Noletta said. "And she didn't quite clear it, so she got stuck here."

"At least she is giving milk here," Vinia said. "So she's not an udder failure."

The cow lifted her head and saw them. *"Mooooon!"*

"And she's lonely," Nydia said. "No bull."

The others sent her a groaning look. Oops! She had inadvertently punned.

They moved on. At last they came to a Plaid Cheese Section.

Plaid? They paused uncertainly.

"I don't know which way to go," Vinia said. "The paths are tangled. I can't see which color goes where."

Then Nydia remembered. "Apoca! When she's in doubt, or changing her mind, her hair turns plaid. It must be the same with the cheese. It's in transition, maybe not yet selected for a type. It doesn't know whether it's going to be Brie, or Mozzarella, or Parmesan, or Swiss, or whatever. We'll just have to find our own way through this one."

"I suppose," Vinia agreed doubtfully.

"Look around," Nydia told the group. "Find any path through."

They looked. This region had odd geography. The ground was not level, but contorted into ridges and channels. Paths went every which way, some of them ending abruptly, others making sharp turns and exploring new directions. It was like a giant maze.

"A puzzle!" Nydia exclaimed as an idea flashed brightly. "We have to solve it."

So it seemed. They spread out, investigating. There had to be a path to somewhere.

"I found a hole!" Woe Betide called. "Down into the ground."

The others made their convoluted ways to her. There was the path, leading down below the surface. It was big enough for them to walk upright and illuminated by glowing moonshine.

Nydia considered. "We *are* looking for the Man in the Moon. It stands to reason that he's in it, not on it, because that's part of the definition." Actually, she wasn't sure, but needed to seem confident. "We had better look."

"Now the path is untangling," Vinia said. "This *is* the way."

They followed her into the depth of the moon. Here, the plaid cheese hardened into seeming stone, with bands of color throughout. It was actually quite pretty. The path corkscrewed in a spiral as if trying to confuse them, but finally descended into a colorful cave.

There, focused on a board game on a table, was a man, so absorbed in the game that he was not even aware of them. Was he the one?

Nydia glanced at Vinia. The girl nodded, seeing the green. They had found him.

Aery stepped forth. "Hello."

The man looked up, startled. "Who are you?"

"I am Aery, the Element of Air, in figurine form. And who are you?"

"I am Moonroe, relaxing in my off-duty hours. You are disturbing my game of Moonopoly. I was about to make a huge pile of play mooney." He indicated a stack of plaid-colored paper bills. "It's most of what I have to divert me from terminal boredom."

She frowned prettily. She had learned how to do that too. "Disturbing you? Look who's talking! You've been mooning me for eons!"

"That was my face, airhead! The telescopic lens I use to observe Xanth magnifies it, being two-way, but you should be able to tell the difference."

She considered, her eyes flicking from his face to his backside. "I doubt there's much."

"If you took the trouble to sharpen the eyes of your cyclones, you'd have no trouble telling top from bottom."

"You're loony!"

"You're a tempest in a teapot."

"I'll tempest you, you mooning voyeur."

"I'd like to see you try, stormy."

Nydia was alarmed. Was this blowing up before it ever got started? She opened her mouth to intervene. But Noletta cautioned her with a glance. Oh. It was a show? Was that possible?

Then Aery kissed Moonroe. Little hearts exploded outward, splatting into the cavern walls like soft cheeses. Nydia knew now that Aery had indeed learned how to do it.

When the kiss ended, Moonroe leaned back in his chair, almost floating, and Aery sat on his lap. "I think I have always loved you, Air Element," he said. "With your marvelous patterns and storms, constantly changing. But I thought you were hopelessly out of my reach."

She gazed into his face. "Not anymore, Moony. I found a body to borrow. It's made out of ectoplasm, but it functions in essential respects."

"I love this body!" He patted it there and here.

"So do I." They kissed again. More hearts erupted. It was definitely love. Mundania lacked the magic of First Sight, but it governed.

He looked at her while the hearts cleared. "Who is stirring the leaves and rippling the waters during your absence from Xanth?"

"I am," she said. "This body is merely my focus so I can interact with solid folk. The rest of me is still quivering trees and making air waves as usual. I assure you I can do anything that might interest you."

He hugged her to him. "That notion intrigues me. I'd like to return to Xanth with you, but I'm not sure it's safe."

"Why not?"

"It's a brief, dull story. I was a lowly official who loved a princess and she loved me, but her father intended her for a political marriage, so he got me out of the way by having the court sorcerer conjure me to the moon. I have been here ever since, my age remaining as it was when I got here because the cheese does not allow anything else on the moon to age. I fear that if I should return to Xanth, it would trigger a magic curse that would rend me limb from limb."

Nerine was interested. "I come from history myself. How long ago was this?"

"About half an eon, give or take—"

"Ten seconds," she finished, smiling. "That should have expired by now."

"Not necessarily," Ecstasy said. "Some curses are open-ended."

"We need to find out," Nydia said. "Maybe there's a reference in the template, as it should be ancient enough for that."

They got on the template with Anthem's help. Vinia focused, finding the path to a record of a long-term curse lurking for a banished courtier. The kingdom and its denizens were long gone, but not the curse. It was stored in an obscure mountain grotto, unvisited for several centuries, but still active.

"We can handle that," Flame said. He made a potent shielded firebomb and put it inside a water bomb Flood created. When the water splashed, the fire would be explosively released. Moonroe knew where there were old doga- and cata-pults stored by long-ago alien visitors of the canine and feline persuasions; they used one to hurl the bomb to Xanth, where Aery made a wind that blew it right into the grotto. They watched via Moonroe's lenses as the explosion blew the top off the mountain, destroying whatever it contained, leaving only a mushroom-shaped cloud. The locals would think it was a new volcano.

The curse was no more.

"I think I'm going to like you Elements," Moonroe said. "And not just because one of you kissed me."

"Oh?" Aery asked, as if mystified. "Which one was that?"

"I think it was the stormy one with the swirling contours. It almost blew me away." They kissed again, generating a curvaceous windblown heart.

Ecstasy nodded. She, of course, was glad that her Air Element figurine would get good use.

Nydia wondered how well a figurine would work for the fearsome Void. It was another handsome ectoplasm man, but the Void itself was something else. Could it actually animate substance?

Now all they had to do was get back to Xanth. The 'pults were too crude for that. They would need to catch Xanth by the magic of perspective, when it was on the moon's horizon. Because the moon did not spin the way Xanth did, that meant traveling to the edge and jumping.

The trek was not difficult because Moonroe knew the way. They avoided the main hazards and came to stand at the flat edge of the disk of the moon, overlooking Xanth. It was a peninsula-shaped land surrounded by assorted seas.

Moonroe had a bag similar to Nydia's. He opened it and brought out soft cheese cushions to pad their landing.

They hid in a Ricotta tree, sitting on the carpet, until the Xanth world forgot they were there and remained in one spot for a good five moments. Then they leaped, taking care to hold the cushions close.

The land expanded as they fell toward it. Then *splash!* They landed in water near a beach, the cushions shielding them from the concussion and wetness. But they had to get their feet wet as they waded to the beach. Nydia could see that it was a very small island featuring a ring of land surrounding a lagoon. They had missed the Xanth mainland.

There was a sign. THIS IS THE EYE SOLATED SOUTH SEE EYE LAND OF LITTLE ATOLL, FAR FROM ANYWHERE. YOU CAN'T GET THERE FROM HERE. Another sign said BEWARE THE GORGON.

"The gorgon!" Noletta exclaimed. "Doesn't its mere gaze strike others dead?"

"Turns them to stone," Ecstasy said. "But only if you meet its gaze."

"Didn't the Good Magician marry a gorgon?" Vinia asked.

"Yes. But she's a good one who masks her gaze with a veil so as not to stone anyone by accident. Others are vicious."

"What does it do if you don't meet its gaze?" Nerine asked.

Ecstasy considered. "I'm not sure. But I believe they like to eat the flesh of regular folk before it gets stoned. Tastes better that way."

"I hope it doesn't come here," Nerine said.

"Too late," Nydia said. "It heard our splash."

Indeed, there was an ugly winged woman flying crookedly toward them. Her hair consisted of hissing vipers. But it was her great shining eyes that scared them. They dared not look at those orbs. But how could they stop the creature if they couldn't even look at it?

"That's an awful dress," Ecstasy said. "Horribly out of style." Evidently she know how to look without meeting a gaze.

But if the gorgon really meant to eat them . . .

"I can handle this," Moonroe said. "I brought some cheese."

"Cheese!" Noletta exclaimed. "What good will that do? Make her laugh herself to death?"

"Watch." He approached the gorgon, who was just landing on the edge of the beach, not looking directly into her face. "Try this, spook," he said, and held up a gob of cheese.

"Oooo-O!" she exclaimed, and her hair-snakes made a frenzy of hisses. She snatched the gob from him, turned about, and spread her wings. She launched aloft. In hardly a moment and a half, she was gone.

"What was that?" Ecstasy asked, impressed.

"Gorgon Zola. It does for gorgons what catnip does for cats. She won't bother us again; she'll be happily freaked out by the cheese."

It occurred to Nydia that Moonroe, too, was a worthy addition to the group.

"Now that we're halfway safe," Noletta said, "How do we get to Xanth?"

"We fly there on the carpet," Nydia said. She brought it out.

But the cloth now had a tag attached. LOW ON MAGIC. USE AT OWN RISK.

Oops! It was running out of fuel. The moon excursion must have depleted it, maybe because moon magic was not the same as Xanth magic. That might explain why it had been reluctant before. It probably needed to get to the peninsula and rest, recharging with the right grade of magic. This eye land of Little Atoll was probably too small to have enough magic. But how could they get the carpet to the mainland without using it? "We have a problem. The carpet is too low on magic to get us there."

"We could walk," Nerine said. "But it may be a long way, and we don't have enough socks."

"Or we could build another boat," Noletta said. "But it's still a long way."

Vinia closed her eyes, focusing. "The strongest green path goes due west from here."

"West!" Moonroe exclaimed. "Xanth is north. I've seen the geography. There's nothing west but water."

"True," Flood said.

"My paths don't lie," Vinia said. "It's our best route."

They considered, but the issue remained in doubt. Nydia would have to make the decision. "Vinia's paths have been accurate before," she said. "I confess I don't see the sense of it, but I'm inclined to trust her green vision. We'll fly west as far as the carpet will take us, hoping for the best."

There was no argument, but she could tell that the others were not at ease with it. Yet what else was there? The Quest would wash out if they just stayed here and waited indefinitely. There seemed to be no food on the atoll. How long would Moonroe's cheese last?

They ate some of the cheese Moonroe provided, saw to natural functions, and boarded the carpet. "Disaster, here we come!" Woe Betide said brightly.

Vinia steered the carpet west. It functioned well enough, but Nydia could see that it was gradually nudging closer to the sea surface as its energy faded. They were going to get dunked before long. As if anticipating that, loan sharks appeared, eager to take an arm and a leg the moment any limbs came in reach. Sure, Flame could burn them back, but it still wasn't very encouraging.

Then something appeared ahead. It was a ship! A tourist cruise ship, with piled-up decks looking like sugar wafers. The name on its prow said WET TURTLE TOURS. "That suggests it is based in the Wet Turtle islands south of Xanth," Ecstasy said.

"I have seen them," Moonroe agreed.

A tourist ship! Exactly what they needed now. Except they might need to buy tickets. Did they have anything that would do?

Flame smiled. "We can put on a show to entertain them." He held up one hand and a puff of fire appeared.

Flood held up a hand and a water bomb appeared.

Aery's hand generated a miniature tornado. It caught hold of the fire and water bomb and whirled them around. "I can also do a weather dance." She spun around, her skirt flaring. Moonroe looked appreciatively of course. So did Flame and Flood, evoking faint frowns from Noletta and Nerine. The Elements might be like siblings, but not entirely.

Moonroe fished in his bag and brought out assorted cheeses. "Snacks for the audience."

"I can turn smokey and fade out," Woe said.

"I think we have the makings of a show," Nydia said. "Let's see if they're interested." She was pretty sure they would be.

They approached the ship and landed on the deck as the carpet sputtered out. Vinia's path had been correct, but they had barely made it. They stood in a group as a handsome older man with a name tag saying CAPTAIN CRUISE walked up. "Welcome to Wet Turtle Tours," he said. "Who are you?"

Nydia stepped up to face him. She put on her best artificial smile and breathed deeply, not ashamed to employ nymphly tactics in this moment of need. "Our carpet ran out of magic, stranding us. We are three novel nymphs on a Quest for the Good Magician, along with our companions. We hope you will give us a ride to mainland Xanth."

He nodded. "How will you pay for your tickets?" Obviously he wasn't in this business for pleasure.

The tourists had spied them and were gathering. Men, women, and children in holiday outfits.

"We will entertain your passengers. We have some amusing skills." She signaled the Elements.

Flame made his fireball. Flood made his water bomb. Aery blew them around. Then she did her twirl, showing her nice legs just far enough up to pop some eyeballs. They heard the pops. Oh, yes, the male tourists were interested.

"Our Air Show includes a Peep Show," Nydia explained. "We'll show a Road, too, in due course." Maybe they could paint a road on the floor to serve as their stage. She knew the show must go on, and the road would suggest where.

Captain Cruise nodded, his own eyeballs slightly glazed. "It will do. We will assign you rooms." He indicated a row of little cabins on the deck. "Your first show will be at twenty-two hundred hours tonight." He walked away as an attendant approached.

A tourist approached Moonroe. "Have we met somewhere? You look vaguely familiar."

Nydia realized it was because he had seen the face of the Man in the Moon.

"Perhaps," Moonroe replied. "Have a cheese nugget."

They were home safe, as it were. They would work out a more complete show in the interim. Nydia was sure she wasn't the only one who was relieved.

Chapter 7

EARTH

Back on Xanth three days later, and on the enchanted path, they held a meeting of ten—three nymphs, three Elements, three humans, plus an ant—to discuss strategy. "We have two more Elements to recruit," Nydia said. "Which one is next? Earth or the Void?"

"Earth," Ecstasy said. "Maybe if we're lucky we won't need the Void."

Nydia was glad to agree. She feared the Void, as did they all. It was the challenge of no return. "Earth is everywhere, right under our feet. But where can we reach her spirit, which could be anywhere?"

"She hangs out at Mount Pinatuba," Aery said. "I see her there often in my natural guise. She likes its vigor." She smiled thinly. "It is also a giant breast symbol, proving she is female."

The Conspiracy tried to erase that, but had been caught off guard. There really weren't any bad words to delete. Vinia had the wit to keep her face straight. She was close to comprehending what it was all about.

Flame and Flood nodded. They knew where their fellow Element was.

"Pinatuba . . ." Ecstasy said thoughtfully. "Isn't that the one that got mad and went Ooom-pah! and blew out so much smoke and dust that it cooled all Xanth by a degree?"

"Ooom-pah!" Anthem echoed appreciatively, playing a chord. "A mighty note."

"That's the one," Aery agreed. "Fouled up my upper region for a year. I couldn't blow that dust away because it was everywhere. I just had to wait for it to settle out."

"So that's where we'll go," Nydia said. "And hope that our Quest doesn't annoy it into another blowout."

But Ecstasy had a caution. "Isn't Earth the strongest of the Elements, apart from the Void? I have a figurine for her, of course, and it evinces power. Suppose she blows her top rather than joining?"

"Not to worry," Flame said. "She's not a hothead like me. She's a hot belly. And she knows we're coming."

Nydia was surprised. "She does? Then why do we have to travel all the way to her island to recruit her?"

"She's female," Flood said. "She likes to be asked."

"Oh, you think all females are passive creatures, waiting on males to motivate them?" Noletta asked archly.

"Stop flirting with Water," Nerine said. "You've got your own Element to pacify."

"Oh, I don't mind," Flood said. "A little superficial firewater can be fun."

"Is that so?" Noletta demanded indignantly. "You deserve a drenching."

Flood smiled. "That's my job, not yours. Care to join me in a shower?"

"No, she doesn't," Nerine snapped.

There was two thirds of a titter. The children were enjoying the show again.

"But seriously," Ecstasy said. "The Element of Earth is nothing to mess with."

"Which is why we need her on our side," Nydia said.

"She'll join," Aery said. "She wants a man of her own to play with." She blew a windy look at Moonroe. They had had several nights of play, and seemed to like it.

They got moving. The next path intersection had an arrow and sign saying MOUNT PINATUBA—FAR FAR AWAY.

"We'd better use the carpet," Nydia said, bemused by the way the signs picked up on their needs. "Now that it has had time to recharge." It was brought out, smelling faintly of cheese.

They boarded, the three Elements beside their companions, Vinia at the helm, and Ecstasy and Nydia left over. "There's a Mundane song," Ecstasy murmured. "'Brown's Ferry Blues.' One of its lines goes 'Two old maids sitting on the sand, each one wishing the other was a man.'"

Nydia felt a pang. "You are scoring."

"You'll get one. You're a nymph, able to catch the eye of any man you choose. But what about an old bag of potatoes like me?"

"But your talent with the figurines is remarkable!" Nydia protested. "You're an artist."

Ecstasy grimaced. "That and a pie plant will give you a pie."

There really wasn't anything Nydia could say to that. Middle-aged women were sadly not much in demand, regardless of their abilities. Certainly not the way nymphs were.

The carpet took off, heading westward. Soon they were flying above the land, with its variegated patterns and colors; then above the sea, with its green waves and islands. Nydia remembered that sightings of Pinatuba had been reported in various places over the decades. Either they were erroneous or the mountain could travel. Did it matter?

A tall, conic mountain peak appeared on the horizon, closing in on them. Above it was a sign made of clouds: DO NOT RILE THE CONE. This was the place.

They cautiously crested the giant crater, discovering a flat floor inside. "The lava is liquid when it's hot," Aery explained. "Then it cools in place, becoming a plain. I have seen it many times."

"But wasn't it smoke and dust that blew out?" Nydia asked. "Not lava?"

"Yes, at first. But beneath them rose the lava, which was left when they were gone. The hot lava really powers the eruption."

"Suppose more lava surges up while we're here?" Vinia asked anxiously.

"We'll fly away in a hurry," Ecstasy said with a grim smile.

"But it's not surging now," Aery said. "She wants to meet us."

"Yet don't rile the cone," Flame said. They all laughed, though it wasn't funny. They didn't want to encounter boiling liquid rock.

They landed on the floor, which wasn't hot. Vinia looked blank for a moment, orienting on her paths. "That way," she said, facing a mound in the center.

They walked toward the mound, which was venting wisps of steam. There was also a sound.

"Tuba music, of course," Flood said. "This is Pinatuba."

"Earth herself is musical!" Anthem said. She sounded a friendly chord that resonated in Nydia's mind.

The mound responded with a deep smoky chord that caused the rock-ground to reverberate. Anthem sounded another, and the mound matched it. In barely a moment and a quarter, they were in a sonorous duet, with side notes from the steam vents.

"The fire ant comes through, of course," Flame said.

"I think they're going to get along," Ecstasy murmured.

Nydia brought out the Earth figurine and the wand. Ecstasy held the figurine upright while Nydia waved the wand and uttered the conjuration.

The figurine animated. "What are you calling me?" she asked.

Nydia hadn't thought of that. "Uh, Eartha."

"Hello, Eartha!" Flame, Flood, and Aery said in unison.

"Hello, fellow Elements," Eartha responded. "And Questers." Then she turned back to Nydia. "Now tell me. What's this all about?"

"Something is disturbing the Elements," Nydia said. "We are trying to find out what."

"I have felt it. Sometimes I shake the ground for no reason." The cone's floor rumbled, reminding them of her power. "Next question: have you found me a male to associate with?" She eyed Moonroe.

Nydia knew she should have thought of this before, but somehow in the distraction of events it had slipped by her. What man would want to be with a woman as powerful as the ground itself, and with a volcanic temper? No ordinary one could measure up.

"Ouroborus!" Nerine exclaimed.

Eartha considered. "I know him. We've been in touch a long time. In fact, he holds me together. But he's not human."

"Neither are you," Nerine said. "You'd both be borrowing human bodies made of ectoplasm, where you can interact off the record."

"Off the record," Eartha repeated thoughtfully. "But if he gets conjured into a figurine, what will prevent my globe from flying apart?"

Now Nydia got into it. "It's not exactly a physical transformation. It's a spiritual one. Your main awareness is here talking with us, but your essence is everywhere, as you showed by rumbling the ground just now. His snake body would remain clasping yours, while his human figurine talked with yours." She glanced at Ecstasy. "You can make a figurine for him? One that is tough enough to handle a strong woman?"

"Oh, yes. Ectoplasm is infinitely malleable and almost indestructible." The woman reached into the sky and hauled in a cloud of ectoplasm from apparently nowhere, which she began shaping into a lean, muscular, serpentine figure. Colors appeared as she worked, the hair and eyes turning greenish, the skin tan. She did not omit any detail; he was indeed a man.

Eartha licked her lips, eyeing the handsome form. "That will do."

Nydia was silent. The Element of Earth was satisfied, but would they be able to persuade the giant serpent Ouroborus to do it? Suppose he was turned off? Making the figurine was one thing; convincing a monstrous snake to play house with an Element in human form was quite another.

"Remember, he's telepathic," Nerine said. "He can read the importance of the mission in our minds. He wouldn't want to slither away from that."

Nydia hoped that was the case. She was not absolutely sure which side the serpent was on. If it turned out to be the wrong side, disaster was in the making.

They discussed details with Eartha. Then she joined them on the carpet as they flew toward Lake Ogre-Chobee and their rendezvous with Ouroborus.

"Call him Rob," Vinia suggested as she steered.

For the accented syllable. That made sense.

Eartha looked around. "This is fun, seeing my landscape from this perspective."

Flame nodded. "I could spread my fires far more effectively using this map."

"And I could flood without wasting much water," Flood agreed.

"And I could blow whole villages away," Aery said. "Using these eyes and this brain to organize what was largely haphazard before."

Nydia hoped they were teasing.

In due course, they reached the land, then the lake. Nydia put away the carpet.

Now it was time to redistribute the socks. Flood and Aery manipulated the water around the Elements to protect them, so the extras went to Ecstasy, Vinia, and Moonroe. They waded into the lake, protected by the enclosing bubbles of air. They descended to the bottom and marched to Ouroborus's spot. They entered the pavilion.

"Hello, Rob!" Nydia called mentally. "We have brought you a companion. Read our minds."

The serpent did. "This is interesting. But why should I agree to inhabit an inferior foreign body just to forward a Quest that does not relate to me?"

Now Eartha spoke, mentally. "It does relate to you, tailbite. Remember when that alien influence threatened to blow me apart, and you saved me and Xanth by wrapping around and holding us together? I smell the same influence now. Read my mind for that odor. We balked it then, but it has returned. This time we need to abolish it. We need your help. We also might have some foolish human fun during the pauses, as the other Elements are doing. Read my hot-bellied mind." The sea floor quivered with racy anticipation.

The serpent considered. "You do make a case, rock-head."

"If we are successful, you will no longer have to hold things together. You will be free, as you were before." The floor made another quiver.

"That does appeal." An eye flicked in Nydia's direction. "Very well, nymph, wave your wand."

Nydia didn't hesitate. She propped the completed figurine up against a wall and conjured the spirit of Ouroborus into it.

The huge serpent did not change; it still chomped its tail. But the figurine animated. "Hello, Quest."

"Hello, Rob," they chorused.

He turned to face the huge head. "Hello, self. Keep holding on."

There was no response. The awareness was now all in the figurine.

"Weird," he muttered.

Nydia had to agree.

Rob turned back to face the others. "Before we go further, we shall need to review some history."

"History?" Nydia asked.

"Things have happened over the eons. Now that I have more of a mind, for all that it is made of ectoplasm, I am coming to understand events better. This may be more of a challenge than you reckoned on."

"It is already that," Nydia said.

"One of you is telepathic."

"That's me," Anthem said, sounding a chord.

"Ah, the fire ant. Join me in making the scenes I remember."

"Gladly." It was plain that the two telepaths understood each other almost perfectly, unsurprisingly.

They made themselves comfortable in the chamber, and tuned in on the scene.

It was a garden, a kind of island on a larger plane, like an oasis, glorious in its luxury of exotic plants. Sweet-smelling flowers were all around, and the memory image enabled scent. Trees bore flowers and fruits like none seen elsewhere. Inviting paths circulated conveniently, showing off the land's features. Hills and glades decorated it. A river flowed through it, forming sparkling pools and gentle rapids and waterfalls. Friendly bees buzzed as they harvested pollen for delicious honey. Tame deer grazed, and in one nook, a lion lay down compatibly with a lamb, resting. It was at peace.

"This is what some Mundanes call the Garden of Eden," Rob said for their minds only as he slithered up to the verge of the flora in ordinary serpent form, not the globe-encompassing one. "I am the symbol of wisdom, and the wheel of eternal life, and my white and black colors represent the connection of Good and Evil, which are not really opposites but interpretations. In my explorations of the newly formed ancestral world, I discovered a hostile alien force intending to destroy it. The evil was masked from the Proprietor, but I was able to observe it while hidden in the grass. I knew I had to do something. But I was banned from the Garden, as the Proprietor assumed without justification that I had evil intentions. I had to sneak in, and it was chancy."

Now he slithered on into the vegetation, his sinuous body largely hidden by the grass and foliage. He was clearly good at sneaking. "There were two inhabitants," he continued. "A man and a woman, set there as exhibits by the Proprietor. They had complete freedom of the Garden, but in their innocence lacked the wit to take real advantage of it. They had minds, but used them only for routine things, like finding new kinds of sweet fruit to eat. They were forbidden to eat the fruit of only one tree, the Tree of the Knowledge of Good and Evil. They did not question this or anything else. But I knew they needed to question it, to learn about the destructive force that intended to ruin everything. I could not take direct action myself, but they could, if only they knew it. How could I make them understand?"

He came to a glade in the center of the Garden, remaining hidden himself. There was a young human woman walking there, naked and pristine. She was absolutely beautiful as her dark hair swirled around her shapely torso as she walked. She smiled as she saw a baby deer, a friendly fawn, and the expression brightened the glade. She seemed to be looking for something.

"She thinks it is a new and tasty fruit to fill her belly," Rob said. "Actually, it is an awareness to fill her mind. This is the moment for me to strike. I can't tell her directly of the threat because that is part of my banning. I can't say it directly to any souled creature. But I can perhaps facilitate her discovery of it indirectly."

Then he called to the woman telepathically. "Eve! What you want is here! It is the fruit of this most special tree." He showed himself twined around a branch. "Try it and see if you like the taste." For this was the Tree of Knowledge.

"But it's forbidden," she protested.

"The Proprietor won't know if you don't tell him. Just take a tiny bite to see if you like it. Why should he care what you sample?"

She approached the tree uncertainly. She had no fear of the serpent, only of violating a stricture. Compliance warred with temptation.

"Pick a fruit," Rob urged. "Bite into it a little bit." The fruit was of no currently known variety, perhaps a knowl, for knowl-ege, but looked and smelled delicious. "If you don't, you will always wonder whether you missed out on a great experience."

Eve hesitated, then took hold of the fruit. She ate a tiny nibble. Her face lighted. "Oh!"

Oops! Was she regretting it already?

"Suddenly, I yearn for more knowledge," she said. "No mere taste can match that."

Rob was relieved. The thirst for knowledge, once invoked, was exhilarating and unquenchable. Also addictive.

Eve took a larger bite. "Oh, there's so much more I want to know! I must share this with Adam!" She hurried back the way she had come, carrying the partly eaten fruit. The serpent quietly followed.

She paused. "Oh! I am unclothed. Nude. Naked, in fact. That's not right." She hastily harvested several big fig leaves and a vine, and made herself a skirt that covered her midsection partially while enhancing its appeal.

Adam was a handsome man playing a game of toss-and-catch-a-stone with himself. He stared at Eve's short skirt, intrigued. "What's this?"

"It's a new kind of fruit," Eve said, misunderstanding. "There's nothing else like it. Try a bite!" She held it forth.

Bemused, he humored her and took a bite. His eyes went wide. "I'm bare!" He quickly fashioned a fig leaf loin cloth.

Rob quietly slithered away. He had accomplished his purpose, or at least started the process.

"But when the Proprietor saw them clothed," Rob said to the group, "He threw a fit. He had worked so hard to keep them sheltered and innocent, and now it was ruined. They had acquired a thirst for knowledge that would never be completely quenched. He also did not like the way Adam looked at Eve now." In the scene, the man licked his lips as he stared at the woman's short skirt. "He kicked them out of the Garden so that they had to struggle continuously to survive and prosper. That was such a chronic distraction that they never did learn about the outside threat. Even their children had problems. When the first two quarreled, and one man killed the other, he was banished to the Land of Nod, which was east of Eden and not nearly as nice. In fact, it was mostly a dream realm. I watched them over the years and decades. When the surviving brother, Cain, arrived in Nod, he encountered a marvelously fetching girl."

The memory scene shifted. The young man was chopping wood to make a fire for the night, to fend off dangerous creatures of the darkness, when the girl approached him. "Who are you?" he asked, as she was the first woman he had seen, other than his mother.

She adjusted her shapely fig leaf skirt and blouse to become even more so. "I am the Daughter of Nod," she replied. "You may call me Lilith." Her skirt moved slightly, causing shadows to show, outlining her evocative thighs.

The scene froze as Rob paused the memory narration to clarify an aspect. "Lilith is special. She is an ancient demoness who was Adam's first wife and taught him all about the pleasures of the flesh. The Proprietor asked her to serve as Adam's companion and teacher, educating and supporting him, making a man of him in every sense. But then she got a notion of the external threat and tried to warn Adam, who was alarmed. The Proprietor was annoyed, and banished her from the Garden and cleansed Adam's mind of any memory of her or their activities together. He took a rib from Adam and expanded it into a new woman, Eve, who was innocent as the demoness was not. Lilith had known better than to try to approach Adam once he was expelled from the Garden, but she regarded his son as fair game. Indeed, she gave him a better time than he deserved, and he was quite satisfied to remain in the Land of Nod all his life."

The memory scene faded. "But the distant threat remained," Rob continued. "I saw it lurking throughout the history of the humans, waiting its chance. Finally I came to Xanth, tired of drear Mundania. When the threat acted to blow Xanth apart, and the Gap Chasm opened, I had to act immediately. I circled the land, clamping my teeth upon my own tail to hold it together, foiling the grievous plot. The evil force somehow spread rumors about me, causing the people kind to fear and hate my kind. But if I ever let go to defend myself and my reputation, all would be lost."

"So that's why you are doing it," Nydia said.

"Yes. The people here are far from perfect, but they don't deserve explosive extinction."

"It seems we owe you much," Ecstasy said.

"I do what I feel is right, even if it is not appreciated. I always have."

"So do I," a woman said, appearing before them, having no apparent trouble with the water. Her voluminous hair was bright red, her eyes lambent blue. She was remarkably well formed, her scant outfit barely concealing the details. Nydia had never seen her before.

"Lilith!" Rob said. "I thought you'd departed for Mundania or worse."

"I'm through with Mundania. The folk there don't believe in demons anymore, or even in magic. They are hopelessly blind to the mythical reality, thinking it is just stories. Xanth is much better."

Nydia wrestled down her surprise. "I thought you were a creature of mythology. Why are you meeting with us?"

"I *am* a creature of mythology. The ancient Sumerians and later Babylonians were well familiar with me, especially their menfolk." She quirked a quarter smile. "So are the denizens of Xanth. Universal currency, you know." She glanced at Woe Betide. "You recognize me, don't you, Woe?"

"Yes. I've seen you around, over the centuries. You're like Metria," Woe said. "Maybe as bad."

"I am a demoness, yes, as is she and your third component, slightly crazy Mentia. I like men, the way Metria and Mentia do, and can have a fair amount of fun with them. But I am not into pointless mischief the way your alter ego is. I am seriously trying to save Xanth from destruction."

"That's what I'm doing," Rob said.

"Indeed, and I applaud you for it, you phenomenal reptile." She eyed his figurine up and down. "Your humanoid format is certainly handsome."

There was a warning rumble in the ground. Nydia was alarmed. An earthquake was building!

"Oh, don't be concerned, Earth Element," Lilith said. "I'm just window shopping, not buying." She returned her attention to Nydia. "What you are doing is admirable. But this Quest needs more help than you can provide."

"Help?" Nydia asked, uncertain about this.

The demoness gave her a straight look, for half a moment showing her age of millennia. "For example, you will soon need to enter the Void. That is easy enough to do. The challenge is exiting it. I can pop safely in and out, and take you with me. That is the help you need at the moment. There may be other occasions in the future."

It was indeed needed help! Nydia feared the Void for exactly that reason. Still, she did not completely trust this. The template had bits about this nefarious demoness. "But why?"

"You are on a larger Quest than you know. It's not just to quell inconvenient perturbations in the Elements, who in this regard are effects rather than causes. It is to save Xanth itself from destruction."

Lilith was impressing Nydia despite her caution, but she still did not have confidence in the demoness. "Why?" she asked again. "If Xanth explodes, you can pop off to Mundania, even if they don't believe in you there, or anywhere else you choose. You can make it with any man you choose, in any locale. What do you care about the welfare of Xanth?"

"I don't have any particular concern for Xanth. It's that it's not right to let it be pointlessly destroyed, or to let evil win without even a fight. Your Quest seems to be the most promising avenue to prevent that termination from happening."

Nydia was further impressed, however reluctantly. She looked at Woe. "You know this demoness. Can she be trusted?"

The child smiled. "Oh, sure. She does naughty things with men, with the details fogged out for me, and she makes kings and queens mad sometimes

by telling them the facts their yes-men won't, but she never betrayed anyone. Metria was curious and checked her out. She's a foreign demoness, one
of the oldest, who takes herself seriously. That means she's honest. The bad
stories about her are mostly false, spread by folk who don't much like being
faced with inconvenient truths. You can trust her, but you may not like her."

That seemed like an excellent recommendation to Nydia. "You think
she should join this Quest?"

"Sure."

It was time for an Act of Leadership. Nydia turned to face the members of the Quest. "Lilith says she can help us, and I believe her. But she
is in most respects a stranger to us. I feel we should learn more about her
before inviting her to join the Quest. How do the rest of you feel?"

"I had a fair history before I joined," Nerine said, "though I didn't know
it. Yes, it is safer to learn hers first."

Nydia got a notion. "Noletta, check how we are a day hence, with her
and without her."

Noletta focused. "Without her we seem to be sort of aimless. With her
we've got Void in figurine form."

Nydia glanced at Ecstasy. "Your perspective?"

"It's always better to act on information rather than ignorance."

"Vinia?"

"The paths around her are mostly green."

"Elements?"

The four of them nodded. The two males were looking openly at the
demoness's flexing midsection; the two females squinted, preferring to
shut it out.

"Moonroe?"

He, too, was looking. "Get her story."

"Rob?"

He wasn't looking, surely aware of Eartha beside him. "I know much of
it already, from observation. I'd like to have her take on it."

"Anthem?"

There was a positive chord.

Nydia smiled. "Tell us your story, please, Lilith. We have two telepaths
in our number, so you can think it if you prefer, and they will make the
scene."

"Gladly. Make yourselves comfortable. I will edit it down substantially, but there's a fair amount." She glanced at Woe. "Suitably edited for a child."

"Oh, blip!" Woe swore. "I hoped you'd forget that part. I hate the spot fog."

"It's dull anyway, as the Good for One Thing nymphs know."

The nymphs nodded. They had been trying to get beyond the One Thing ever since escaping the Retreat.

"The story of the Beginning starts really dull, but in due course it gets into the interesting parts. Bear with it; it is necessary background."

They resigned themselves to the dullness.

Then the history started.

In the beginning was the fabric of nothingness. The universe was without form and void, a monstrous blankness. Then there was a blip, with the emptiness erupting into quantum flux, tearing apart into positive and negative energy that explosively repelled one another. A picture formed of two rapidly expanding clouds, illuminated by the aspect of energy called light.

In time, the positive radiation got twisted at the edges and curled into specks called atoms, which possessed some of each form of energy, positive protons and negative electrons, clumped together to form matter. The same happened with the negative radiation, only with the pro-tons being con-tons in nuclei orbited by positrons. Thus came to be two complementary universes, exactly even in energy and matter, with gravity dominating one and magic the other. When examined too closely, the marvelous probabilities of each collapsed into dullness. So it was best simply to take things on ignorant faith.

The Mundane universe came to be governed by several underlying forces like the strong and weak nuclear forces, the electromagnetic force, and gravity, while the mythic universe was governed by magic, similarly applied. Each universe was peripherally aware of the other, though they could not touch directly without mutual destruction. Together they amounted to nothing, so for the sake of continued existence they had to remain apart, only eyeing each other wistfully, like a man and a woman who could love from afar but never embrace.

The Mundane universe came to manifest the marvels of technology like paperclips, television, and the outernet. Now there was a box with talking pictures on its face and vehicles that generated much pollution and some motion. The mythic universe formed the demons, both capped and uncapped, the former infinitely more powerful than the latter. The Mundanes worked with science, the mythics with magic, the positive and negative aspects of the same phenomenon.

"That accounts for our present situation," Lilith concluded. "We are creatures of the mythic universe. The spirits formed from vast clouds of magic dust, the powerful ones becoming Demons, like Xanth, the leftover bits becoming incidental demons like me or Metria. Other bits became ghosts."

The presentation paused. "Are you still with me?" Lilith inquired.

"Barely," Ecstasy answered. "It's like foul-tasting medicine, awful but necessary." The others nodded agreement.

"Good. The worst is over."

The picture resumed, this time showing Lilith as a blob of animated vapor. She formed an eyeball, looked about, and spied the Proprietor fashioning the Garden in his own private realm, a minor section of the larger reality. Curious, she watched as he laid out all manner of plants and trees, set up hills and vales, and coursed a river through it. Then he made the animals, including the first man, Adam. And looked about. Something was missing. He spied Lilith. That was it! The man needed a companion, a woman, so he wouldn't get bored.

So he hired Lilith, who was satisfied to have something to do. She entered the Garden, took the form of a female of Adam's species, becoming a lovely humanoid woman, and took over the practical instruction of the man, who really knew nothing. She became his wife, running his life as women were to do with men ever after. Until she proved to be too good at it, producing dozens of children who ran all over the Garden, throwing fruits about, peeing on flowers, stepping on bugs, messing it up. The din of their laughter, crying, and games gave the Proprietor a headache. But her real problem was when she saw the nebulous mischief coming from afar, and tried to warn Adam of it. That was not what she was supposed to be there for, but she persisted. Then the Proprietor, who regarded such information as manifestations of Hell, expelled her from the Garden, eliminated the bothersome children, took a rib from Adam, and fashioned it into a more obedient woman. Lilith was out.

Until she took up with Cain and generated many more offspring, the children of Nod. When Cain died of old age, as mortals did, she moved on to one of the cultures that had formed in the interim, the Sumerians. They were in need of temple mistresses, so she took that position, disappearing into comfortable anonymity, generating no children; she could turn that aspect off at will, and actually the Proprietor had a point about their nuisance value. The demoness was very popular with the visitors; in fact, she converted multitudes to that sect. One of the other sects did not like the competition, so tried to make this sort of activity into a sin. That hardly slowed the action, but did generate quite a number of sinners and copious guilt. Why not? It was a convenient way to discipline errant folk.

But her covert activity in Sumeria was intellectual. Lilith studied with the clerics, who were vulnerable to her persuasion just as other men were, and learned their most secret lore. Their knowledge was never written, in part because writing did not then exist, but it was potent. They did not share it with the laity, but in time, she became a cleric and acquired it. Thus she learned of the source of the mischief she had been wary of before. But still she was unable to do anything about it. That was extremely frustrating. But one day, she swore she would find a way.

Eventually, the cultures warred and changed, and she found herself out of a job again. So she went to Xanth, pleasing any men she encountered. They thought she was good for Only One Thing, and she was outstandingly good at that, and protected her anonymity by encouraging them to see her that way. But she remained aware of the threat, which was slowly coming closer. She had to let someone know. Someone who might be able to do something about it. Kings and queens were out; their main interest was in maintaining their power. Magicians and sorceresses were out because their magic could not address it.

· When the threat tried to rip Xanth apart, Ouroborus slithered in and circled the land and held it together, though that deprived him of his freedom of motion. She admired that act of sacrifice on his part. But still the threat was unknown to anyone who might be able to do anything about it. Only the Good Magician had any inkling, and his ways were barely scrutable. What could she do?

"And so I come to you," Lilith concluded. "To help you accomplish the necessary, if you will accept my help."

Nydia glanced around at the others. "Welcome to the Quest," she said. "But there is a condition: you must not interfere with any of the existing relationships. No flirting with any of our men. No One Thing here. If you want a man for yourself, he must come from outside this group."

"Done," the demoness agreed. "Seduction is my tool to manage men and punish women who try to interfere with me, not my passion. I can turn it off." And, remarkably, her radiating sexuality faded, and she became just an incidental person. She looked the same as ever, but somehow it was neutral.

Nydia was relieved that it was working out, not least because she did want help getting in and out of the Void. But there was one more thing. "You spoke of the great threat to Xanth that we may be about to address. Exactly what is that, and why hasn't anyone else except Rob picked up on it?"

Lilith took a breath that was just air, not enhancing her bosom. "Just a bit more background. I had time to study details in Sumeria, and learned interesting and alarming things. The universes not only formed atoms, they developed elements, not the same as the Elements you know, but unique accumulations of matter. These in turn clumped together in combinations to form objects, which collected to form planets, stars, and galaxies. We are in a galaxy the Mundanes call the Milky Way. Another is called Andromeda. The two galaxies are orbiting each other, gradually coming closer together. Eventually they will crash, forming one giant black hole, wiping out everything in both of them. We don't want that, and neither does the spirit of the other galaxy, the Demoness Andromeda. Her solution seems to be to destroy us so there will be nothing for her to crash into. That may work well for her, not so much for us. She has been investigating, looking for a way to obliterate us. Over the eons, she has tried different things. None have worked. The last was to blow us apart, planet by planet, but Rob stopped that by clamping Xanth together. He locked that mechanism in place so she has been unable to do it to other planets, to her frustration. Now she is trying to stir the Elements into wiping out the folk here, including Rob, so that they can't stop the explosion. That explosion will trigger other explosions, in a process called nuclear fission that will rapidly blow up everything. That's why they have been so agitated. It will only get worse unless we stop not only this ploy, but Andromeda herself."

Nydia froze in horror. "But—"

"Exactly. Andromeda is a Demoness. Specifically of the force of Flux, or Change. The foreign galaxy is only her residence. The Sumerians knew. We as ordinary folk cannot hope to oppose her directly. That's why the Good Magician arranged to set up a Quest run by soulless nymphs no one would suspect of tackling any ordinary task, let alone foiling a Demoness."

Nydia gazed at the others, aghast. "But—"

"Exactly," Lilith repeated. "We have, as the Mundanes say, our work cut out for us."

"And—and if we fail—"

"Our entire galaxy is gone."

"Let's consider," Nydia said. "My template indicates that the ratio of a Demon to a demon is about that of a galaxy to a grain of sand."

"Correct."

"So we are a few grains of sand going up against a galaxy."

Lilith smiled grimly. "I see that you do appreciate the odds."

"We shall have to strategize." She looked around. "Any ideas?"

Eartha glanced at Rob. "You surely suspected this, as I did. Have you thought about it?"

"Yes. It occurs to me that there could be something in the Void. I never had the nerve to enter the Void, but with Lilith's help we may be able to look there. Even if it is only an idea of how to proceed, it might help."

"I already have an idea," Eartha said. "Another place to look is Galaxy Andromeda itself. We should perhaps travel there, quietly."

"Travel there!" Nydia exclaimed. "It was all we could do to make it to the moon and back. How could we ever get to a foreign galaxy?"

"There is a mortal with the talent of making holes, including between planets. He might make us a hole from here to Andromeda."

"Santo," Lilith said. "With a Magician-level talent. I know of him. He intrigues me."

"He is gay," Eartha said.

"That's why he intrigues me. As a challenge." For the better part of a moment, her allure returned, causing male eyes to swivel.

"That in turn intrigues me," Eartha said. "You think you could seduce a man who has no interest in women?"

"I believe I mentioned the challenge."

A look circulated. This could get interesting.

"What could we do in Andromeda Galaxy," Noletta asked, "other than walk into the web of the enemy?"

Moonroe laughed. "Excellent question! But since the alternative is for us all to be destroyed, it may be worth considering."

A silence hovered near. Nydia intercepted it before it could get established. "Perhaps the Void has something that would serve."

"Lilith could help one person enter and depart the Void," Ecstasy said. "But the whole Quest?"

"I could move a number of people," the demoness said. "One at a time."

Nydia spoke. "My thought is to conjure the spirit of the Void into a figurine, then talk with him. He might then be willing to let the other members of the Quest in and out."

"You?" Eartha asked.

Nydia nodded. "It is, I think, my turn." She glanced at Lilith. "You would take me?"

"I would take you," the demoness agreed. "I could assume the semblance of a flower in your hair, so as not to intrude on the dialog."

"If this should work," Flood said, "and the rest of us are allowed to visit the Void, what would we do there?"

"We would search for that object or idea that we need to accomplish our Quest," Nerine said. "If it exists, that is where it is most likely to be."

"Then I think we have our mission," Nydia said. "I suggest we relax today and tackle it tomorrow—with renewed vigor."

No one argued. Just digesting the information they had received was a job, let alone acting on it.

They walked away from Ouroborus's material body, still clenching its tail, and ascended to the land, where those who needed to harvested fruits and pies for dinner. The Elements, of course, did not need to eat. They drew their energy from their aspects of the environment.

Rob looked about. "It has been some time since I have seen this, other than via my lesser surrogates." He meant ordinary snakes, with whom he was in telepathic contact.

"I have more to show you," Eartha said. "Let's leave these folk to their devices for a few hours while we explore more fundamental interaction in some private place. We have been touchingly close for a while, but not as close as we can be now via these proxies."

"This promises to be interesting," Rob agreed. "I have had little experience with the human form, but discover it has its impulses."

"Indeed. So does this figurine of mine." Eartha indicated a pair of rounded mountains on the horizon that resembled nothing so much as the bare bosom of a giant woman, lying on her back. Adjacent hills resembled head, arms, and legs. "I believe there will do. I like its contours." They walked away together.

"Blip," Woe repeated. "That cursed privacy again."

The others set about making a camp, with several temporary shelters for the respective couples. The children Vinia and Woe Betide shared one, Lilith was single, and Nydia shared one with Ecstasy. "I think I know exactly how you feel," Nydia said.

"Unfulfilled," Ecstasy agreed. "They must be getting to it about now."

The ground shook with a mounting series of quakes. Then a ring of volcanoes erupted, illuminating the night sky, followed by a gradual relaxation.

"I suspect they are making it," Nydia said.

"Did I mention jealousy? Bleep! I am experiencing it." Ecstasy laughed without humor. "The irony is that they are both using figurines I crafted. I am envying my own artistry."

"We need to find a good man for you. One who appreciates your artistry with the figurines."

"That's not the kind of artistry I am thinking of at the moment. But what man would ever desire a lumpy middle-aged woman?"

"There must be one. We just need to find him." But Nydia had doubt. So she changed the subject slightly. "You craft the figurines with inanimate ectoplasm. How can they perform like living creatures?"

"Ectoplasm is special. When fallow, it resembles inactive mist or dust, but it is actually solidified magic. My talent is to shape it, as if it was merely a type of clay, but its properties are way beyond that. When it is animated by a soul or Element or even just a living plant or creature, it conforms to the functioning of that thing, only better, as it is inherently healthy. It enhances the ideal. Most folk would be better off with plasm bodies."

"So couples really are experiencing the wonders of the Adult Conspiracy?"

"They really are, probably with better performance and feeling than fleshly living folk. That's not my doing, it's the plasm. I liken it to a bottle of love or healing elixir: I merely make the bottle."

Nydia shook her head. "You make remarkable bottles."

"Thank you," Ecstasy said sadly.

Chapter 8

VOID

In the morning, as a party of fourteen—four Elements with their four partners, two regular single humans, two demons, one ant, and one unattached nymph—they walked the enchanted path to the next intersection. Sure enough, there was an arrow pointed north. ELEMENT VOID. CAUTION. Vinia could have followed a green path there, but this represented a more general confirmation.

"Next question," Nydia said. "Do we want to walk there, following the arrows, seeing the sights along the way, or fly directly there on the carpet?"

"We can see the sights better from above," Vinia pointed out. "And the carpet will be faster." The others nodded.

Faster. That was what bothered Nydia. She was in no hurry to tackle the dread Fifth Element. It might be the last thing she ever did. But she couldn't show hesitation, let alone fear; she was the leader. "Carpet it is," she agreed, hoping her racing pulse didn't show. She hadn't known until this moment that nymphs even had pulses. She realized that it was fear that stalked her, and she wasn't used to it. Yet it was better than the largely mindless oblivion of the Retreat. At least now her limited life had some suggestion of purpose.

She brought the carpet out and unrolled it. They took their places, the material spreading to accommodate them flawlessly, the fabric firmly anchoring them in place. They could probably fly it upside down without falling off, not that they would care to try. Vinia took the helm, and the carpet sailed grandly up into the sky.

"This is interesting," Rob said as he sat beside Eartha. "I would have liked to view the night's pyrotechnics of the volcanoes from this vantage. I have hitherto been limited to ground level scenery."

"You were bored with the personal interaction?" Her face was straight, but her tone quirked.

He laughed. "By no means. I just would have liked to see the remarkable external show."

"There will be other chances," Eartha said, nudging a knee. She seemed more than satisfied with their association. It was surely fun playing at romance in foreign bodies, as they could never manage it in their original forms.

"We have no business being jealous," Ecstasy murmured.

Nydia understood perfectly. "We just have to hope our turns will come." Yet what were the prospects, realistically? Nydia might be steering into her doom.

A monstrous cleft in the ground came into sight. "Is that the—?" Rob asked.

"Yes, that is the Gap Chasm," Eartha answered. "You are invisibly preventing it from becoming a slice through the entire Land of Xanth. More power to you. A cosmic break might be inconvenient."

"It's nice to be appreciated."

"I am coming to appreciate you in other ways now."

They were flirting. Nydia and Ecstasy kept their mouths tightly shut. So did Vinia, who could also overhear the dialog. Woe Betide pretended to be asleep.

North of the Gap Chasm were ordinary human villages. Then came the home regions of the Elements. All of them studied their own sections closely. Of course, they weren't limited to them, any more than ordinary folk were limited to their houses or villages; they were just intrigued by the sight from outside.

Then the Void, which, not oddly, had no display. It was just a vague dark patch. They glided down toward its edge.

"What is that?" Moonroe asked.

Aery looked. "I think it's a person. A woman. Looking for something."

They all looked. What was a woman doing so close to the dangerous Void?

"And a big dog," Flame said.

"No, a wolf," Aery said.

"In fact, a werewolf," Eartha said. "They are subtly different from animal wolves."

The carpet angled down to land at the fringe, and they debarked. They stood before a blank wall.

The woman saw them and came close. "Hello! I'm Jenny Elf, and this is my steed wolf, Wolfram." The wolf changed briefly into manform, showing that he was indeed a werewolf.

"Oh, you're a wolf rider," Ecstasy said.

Now Nydia found it in the template: Jenny Elf had come from a foreign land and married the leader of the pack. She was actually a queen, or the equivalent. Evidently, she preferred to be anonymous in that respect.

"Yes," Jenny said. "I was taking a shortcut home to the pack when there was a flux in the Void perimeter that almost caught us. We bounded into the brush to avoid it. A branch caught my wrist and ripped off my amulet." She held up her hand, showing four fingers, including the thumb. "I lost my treasured trophy medal. We were searching for it when you came."

"A flux," Flood said. "That figures."

"We are a Quest," Nydia said. "I am Nydia Nymph, and these are my companions. We are trying to find out why the Elements are acting up. You evidently ran afoul of mischief at the verge of the Void."

"Yes. I will be heartbroken if I lose my medal. It's a miniature of the infamous Catastrophe sculpture. You know, the rear end of a cat."

"Cat ass trophy," Ecstasy said through a groan. The others made silent groans.

"My favorite cat was Sammy, who could find anything but home. He finally went his own way, but I kept the medal in memory of him. Now it's gone, and I can't find it anywhere. If it flew into the Void, it's doomed. I've looked and looked, but I only found someone's lost abacuss, and all it did was cuss at me."

Nydia got a notion. "We are about to enter the Void on business, as we have a way out again. Why don't you join us, so you can search inside?"

That paused the woman. "Is that safe? Nothing leaves the Void, except—"

"Anything can enter the Void," Lilith said. "Hardly anything can leave it. Only ghosts, night mares, demons, spooks, and the like. Creatures without permanent mortal substance. I am the demoness Lilith. I can navigate it." She looked around, addressing Jenny and the others. "I know you won't want to risk it until I demonstrate—that's not exactly a pun, demon straight—that I really can convey you out." She turned to Nydia. "Are you ready?"

As if she would ever be really ready! "Yes," she said tightly.

The demoness addressed the group again. "Nydia and I are about to demonstrate how to pop in and out of the Void. Do not be alarmed; we will soon return. Meanwhile, the rest of you can get to know each other better."

"She means it," Rob said, reading her mind. "All we have to do is watch and wait."

Eartha smiled. "I am finding another reason to value you. Your telepathy."

He smiled back. "So I am good for Two Things."

"Three, counting your holding Xanth together."

They were still flirting. Nydia suppressed yet another shapely tinge of envy. She wanted so much to have a romantic relationship with a worthy man, but all she faced was likely oblivion in the Void. Her mind kept coming back to that. She wished it would stop.

Lilith returned her attention to Nydia. "I will assume the form of a passion flower and tuck into your hair so that you seem to be alone, unless you wish me to show myself as nominally human."

"That's fine," Nydia said through forcefully unclenched teeth. It wasn't association with the demoness that bothered her, but fear that the departure would mess up and she would be forever stuck in the Void. Having escaped the Retreat, she did not want to be captive elsewhere.

Lilith puffed into smoke, reformed as a pretty flower, and floated to Nydia's hair. "Hello, Anthem Ant," she said mentally, picking up on her contact telepathy.

Anthem played a chord. "Hello, Lilith."

"I love your music." Then back to Nydia mentally: "Now for a sample excursion. Steady, Nydia; there will be a wrench as we move. I can do it smoothly alone, but your body is solid. There will be a pop as you vacate this spot and a minor explosion as you displace the air in the new location. You won't be hurt, but you may feel briefly strange."

"So there's a reason demons turn smoky as they travel," Anthem said.

"Indeed. We integrate with the air, between the molecules, so that the displacement is easier, saving energy." She oriented on Nydia. "Ready?"

"I am ready," Nydia replied silently, hoping it was true.

Then came the wrench. Suddenly she was in the center of an explosion, the air heating as it puffed outward. Then it cleared.

They were standing on a gentle green slope. Colorful bushes and trees dotted it. This was the dread Void?

"It is indeed the Void," Lilith said. "Seeds blow through the perimeter, discover the fertile soil, and grow readily enough. Sufficient sunlight filters through to sustain them. Plants don't travel the way animals do, so are satisfied to remain in a single spot indefinitely."

"It seems, well, just like normal terrain."

"It is not. Try walking."

Nydia walked. There was no problem. She went around a bush, down the slope.

"Now try to go uphill."

She turned about and took a step back the way she had come. And got nowhere. Her feet moved, yet her body remained where it was. Alarmed, she tried harder, but still did not get anywhere. "This is weird."

"The Void is three-way. You can go forward or sideways in either direction, but not back. The safest thing is to stand still."

"Weird," Nydia repeated.

"Actually, if you concentrate you can go back a step or two, but that's the limit. It gets harder, and you tend to slide back to your original spot."

Nydia concentrated and finally managed to take a step up-slope. But it was difficult and tiring and she knew it was a lost effort. "I am satisfied that this is the Void," she gasped.

"Now for the return." There was another wrench and hot puff of air. Then she was back where she had been, facing the other members of the Quest. They looked surprised and concerned.

"I'm all right," Nydia said, though slightly flustered. "It's just a green slope."

"Not a dark gulf?" Noletta asked.

"No, just a hillside. But I couldn't step back up-slope. It's three-way travel: left, right, forward. Not back." She forced a smile. "Anyone else?"

Jenny visibly nerved herself. "I will join you for this. Wolfram will be satisfied to wait outside. Don't worry; he doesn't eat people."

"We don't have to use the demoness," Eartha said. "We can simply march through the wall as a group and see for ourselves. And come back one at a time, courtesy of Lilith."

"That seems apt," Moonroe said. "But perhaps one person, or couple, should remain outside, just in case. Then if there's a glitch, they can return to the Queendom of Thanx and report."

So Aery had told him about the Queendom. "That seems sensible," Nydia agreed. "So who should it be?"

"We volunteer," Nerine said, and Flood did not differ. Maybe they wanted more alone time together. Or to learn about the tame werewolf.

"We'll send someone back to report every so often," Nydia said. Then, as much to shore herself up as the others, she faced the wall. "Forward march." Before any of them, especially her, lost their nerve.

They walked together through the wall. This time there was no wrenching, merely a faint tingling; this was not conjuration. They emerged at the top of the slope, the scene spreading out below.

"Interesting in its ordinariness," Noletta said. She took a few steps down the hill, then tried to return. And made no progress.

Soon the others were doing it, Elements and companions alike. They could walk forward, left or right, but not back up the slope more than two or three feet, and that against intangible resistance. Jenny was meanwhile eyeing the ground, looking for her lost medal, but there was no sign of it.

"Who wants to make the first report, back outside?" Nydia asked.

"I will," Noletta said.

The flower floated from Nydia's iridescent hair to Noletta's blue hair. Then the nymph vanished, leaving a popping implosion of air. Flame looked nervous without her.

In two and a half moments, she was back, this time the air briefly exploding, hitting them all with the passing puff. "Report made," she announced. "They were relieved, Wolfram too." The flower floated from her back to Nydia.

"I am oddly reassured," Jenny said.

"So are the rest of us," Ecstasy said.

They proceeded carefully down the slope, which led to a small and perfectly ordinary forest of nutty acorn trees, sad pining trees, and assorted aromatic pie trees. No one had to be hungry here. They passed through it to find a field of flowers of many kinds. In it was a sort of sidewise house fashioned of woven sticks and hay, all width and no depth.

"People!" someone called. A girl of about eighteen appeared, running along the path in front of the house. "Hello!"

"Hello," Nydia responded, taken aback. There were residents here? "We are exploring the Void."

"By choice?" the girl asked. "Don't you know you can't leave it?"

"We have a way," Nydia explained. "We have a demoness."

"One and a half demonesses," Woe Betide said.

The girl's mouth opened cutely. "Oh! Let me tell my sisters!" She ran off, her short skirt flouncing in the manner teen garments did. Nydia made a mental note to adjust her own skirt, in due course.

In three moments they were back. "I am Sweetie," the first girl said. "This is Sourie, and Saltie." Indeed, the first looked sweet, while the second frowned, and the third seemed to have a mixed taste in her mouth. All three were nevertheless reasonably cute in their skirtlets, young legs, and blouses. Their tresses were respectively blond, brunette, and salt gray, waving enticingly as they moved.

"How did you get here?" Noletta asked. "Didn't you know it was dangerous?"

Sourie laughed sourly, of course. "We were young and careless. We were warned to stay away, so naturally we came to explore, thinking it was an old wives' tale." She grimaced. "We were fools." Her sisters nodded agreement.

"We'll help you escape," Nydia said. "Do you have things you want to take with you? This will necessarily be a one-way trip."

"Not even our memories," Saltie said wryly.

"Except maybe how we flashed our panties at the man next door and made him freak out," Sweetie said. "That was fun."

"For you or for him?" Noletta asked. Nymphs lacked panty experience, normally being nude. They were still not completely accustomed to clothing.

Sweetie giggled. "For both, we hope. It's a mutual thing, display and audience, especially when there's nothing else to do."

"We have been here some time, but don't seem to have aged," Saltie said. "It gets dull."

"No aging," Anthem said to Nydia. "They must be in a kind of suspended animation. Conscious, active, but in limbo as far as life goes."

"Everything must be in a kind of stasis here," Lilith said, manifesting in her human form. "Who first?"

"Me," Sourie said. "I'm a fatalist anyway."

So they were anxious, despite their girlish manner.

Lilith became the flower and floated to the girl's brown hair. After a generous moment, both vanished with the implosive pop.

"I hope this works," Saltie said nervously.

"It works," Nydia reassured her. Then, to change the subject: "You say you were flashing a man?"

"He lives the next rung down," Sweetie said. "He can't join us, and we can't join him unless we are prepared to go even deeper into the Void. So we can see each other, but not talk; sound doesn't cross upward, only sight."

"He seems to be a decent sort," Saltie said. "But too old for us. At least forty."

Then Lilith reappeared, alone. "Next?"

Saltie stepped up. "Me."

The demoness became the flower and floated to her gray hair. There was the pop of implosion as they disappeared.

"This neighbor man is a generation older?" Nydia asked Sweetie.

"Yes. But still halfway handsome. I wouldn't have wanted to waste any flashes on an ugly man."

"So it's a kind of flirtation," Anthem said privately. "Showing a man what is being offered without actually risking commitment."

"It's a bleeping tease," Nydia answered her. Then to Sweetie: "If you liked him despite his age, why didn't you cross to his level and join him?"

"I considered it. But then he stopped freaking."

Which ended that, it seemed. Only freakable men need apply. The perspectives of youth were evidently limited.

Lilith returned. "Next."

Sweetie nodded. The demoness became the flower, and in a generous moment, they were gone.

"This house is interesting," Ecstasy said, examining it. "Constructed all on one plane so sideways motion is feasible. They couldn't go back, and refused to go forward."

"Which was sensible," Noletta said. "If dull."

Lilith appeared. "They are on their merry way home," she reported. "But they may have a bit of trouble adjusting. My impression is that they were here at least a decade. Their original teen boyfriends will be married and familied."

"Extended youth never hurt a woman," Ecstasy said. "They will make good use of their panties."

There was an open space in the center of the structure. They stepped into it and saw the next house down, similar to this one but better constructed. Within it stood a man of about forty, gazing up at them.

"We are visitors," Nydia called. Could he hear them? He should, being downslope. "Nod if you hear and understand."

The man nodded.

Good enough. "We would like to talk with you," Nydia continued. "May we approach?"

The man nodded again.

They walked slowly down toward him. "We are a party of fourteen, no, fifteen." Because Jenny Elf was with them for now. "We are on a Quest to discover why the Elements are being disturbed, and to deal with it if we can. Four of our members actually are Elements, animating human figurines. One is a telepathic ant. Two are demonesses. Three are nymphs. Three are human, one is elf, one is of serpent stock. We will introduce ourselves more formally if you are interested. Who are you, what is your talent, and how did you come to be here?" For now they were coming into audible range.

"I am Oakley," the man said. He was brown-haired and eyed, and indeed handsome for his age. "I was hiking, exploring new territory, and did not recognize the event horizon in time."

"The what?"

He smiled. "The event horizon. It surrounds a black hole, which is really what the Void is. It is the line of no return."

Oh. This hinted at how smart he was. "Thank you for that clarification. I'm a nymph from the Faun & Nymph Retreat, and haven't had opportunity to learn a lot about the realm beyond the Retreat. And actually, we can return because we have the cooperation of the demoness, Lilith."

Lilith materialized, her allure turned on. "Hello, Oakley. Doesn't your name mean 'From the Oak Tree Meadow'?"

"It does. Just as yours means 'wife.' I don't suppose you are any relation to the demoness who was Adam's first wife?"

Her low decolletage dropped a notch lower. "The same. But I took my assignment too seriously and got fired."

"The same," he said appreciatively. "You are famous, or perhaps infamous."

Lilith's skirt lifted shorter. "My reputation among mortals is not stellar, but I get along well enough." Her bosom swelled slightly as her waist cinched tighter. "Because I deliver."

"I'm sure you do." His gaze returned to Nydia. "To complete my answer to your question, my talent is to see the obvious that others don't see."

Nydia was impressed by two things. First, that he was so readily able to shift his gaze away from Lilith when she was in flirtation mode. This was a man with amazing self-control. Second, he had an interesting talent, dependent on the context of his companions to be properly expressed. But was it of any real use? "Suppose I introduce you to the rest of our party?"

"By all means. I note you have a few handsome men and a number of sightly ladies. My recent experience of the latter has been limited to three. But all they seemed to want to do was flash me, so finally I turned my reaction off."

He could do that? No wonder the demoness hadn't mesmerized him.

The introductions proceeded, with each member of the Quest chatting briefly with Oakley. The one he seemed most interested in, oddly, was Ecstasy. He questioned her closely about her manikin art. She answered, clearly flattered by his attention, but not letting herself dream of any further relationship. Art was one thing; romance something else, especially for older folk.

He was also interested in Jenny. "Aren't you the wolf rider from another realm? In fact, didn't you marry a werewolf prince?"

"Yes," she agreed, taken aback by his recognition.

"Why are you here in the Void?"

"I lost my little cat trophy medal, and the Questers are helping me look for it. But it seems to be permanently lost."

He smiled. "This is, after all, the place of lost things. Tell me the details of the loss."

She did. Oakley frowned. "I believe we can find it. Check your hair."

"My hair?" she asked, surprised.

"Humor me. My talent suggests it may be there."

Jenny caught hold of her hair and brought it around to her face. There, snagged at the end of her hair, formerly concealed by the tresses surrounding it, was a small coin-like disc. "That's it!" she cried, pulling it free. "Oh, thank you so much! It's such a relief."

He made a gesture of unimportance. "I am glad to have helped."

"But how—when none of us thought—" Then she laughed. "You did tell us of your talent. It must have caught on my hair when it blew across my face. Obvious, in retrospect."

"Your medal didn't want to be lost any more than you wanted to lose it. It grabbed on to what offered."

"How ever can I thank you?"

"Your pleasure is thanks enough."

Jenny turned to Nydia. "Is it all right if I go now? The pack will worry if I'm away too long without explanation."

"We understand," Nydia said.

Lilith became the flower and floated to Jenny. There was a pop as they vanished.

Oakley turned back to Ecstasy. "I believe I would like to join this Quest, and not simply to escape the Void. Would you do me a favor?"

"A favor?" she asked blankly.

"Would you make the loveliest lady manikin you can, complete with removable habiliment?"

"Oh, you want a pretty companion doll?"

"Yes. I'm impressed by the examples I have seen here, such as Aery and Eartha. I may be of middle age, but I still like the look and feel of young women. That's why I was for a time vulnerable to the next-door trio. I believe you could make the perfect one."

Bemused, Ecstasy drew ectoplasm from the air and started sculpting it. It seemed that the Void had brought in some of that, along with everything else. Soon she had a ravishingly beauteous form that made even the nymphs and other figurines look plain in comparison. She completed it by fashioning separate underwear and outer clothing, and putting them on appropriately. It was indeed one gorgeous doll.

"Perfect," Oakley said. "Just one more detail. It needs to be animated." He paused half a moment. "By you, if you are amenable."

"Me?" she asked, astonished. "But I'm a baggy middle-aged spinster."

"Not anymore, if you agree. You have missed the obvious: using your remarkable art for your own benefit. You already have the maturity and experience I need in a woman. I have had a fair amount of time to reflect on what I truly want in a partner. I thought it to be an impossible dream, a foolish fancy. Now I'd like to see you in the body I like. That will make you my perfect companion, if you will have me." He smiled again. "Is it not obvious?"

Ecstasy was unable to speak; her jaw had fallen too far.

The others nodded. They had missed it too. It was indeed obvious in retrospect. She was suddenly all she could be. He was perfect for her, being smart, talented, and of her generation. Not to mention handsome and genuinely interested in her.

Nydia stepped forward, bringing out the wand. She waved it, speaking the words. The figurine animated as Ecstasy sank to the ground, unconscious. Flame and Flood caught her just in time and propped her up, then sat her in a chair.

Now the figurine inhaled spectacularly and spoke. Inanimate, she had been a stunning doll. Now she was an outstanding woman. "What about my original body? That is the real me. This manikin, as you put it, is only a, well, a temporary costume. If my body perishes, so do I."

"Store it in the bag," Oakley said. "It will be safe there, and timeless, until you need it back."

Now it was Nydia's jaw that dropped, figuratively. Store the body in the bag! Obvious, again, now that it had been spoken.

Oakley smiled, taking Ecstasy by the shoulders and staring into her face. "And I do want you out of costume, too, in due course. The real world is not make-believe."

They put the body carefully in the bag, while the new woman felt herself with her hands without moving her face. Then Ecstasy-Figurine spoke again. "This is amazing! I feel so real. And alive. And robust. Is it too soon to—?"

He slowly brought his face down to hers, so she could change her mind if she wanted to. She did not turn aside. They kissed. Little hearts exploded, some colliding with some of the watching folk. One hit Nydia, infusing her with a jolt of love. If only she could have discovered such a partner! But of course, she was not the woman Ecstasy was. She was only a nymph, a form without real substance.

"Oh, my," Ecstasy breathed as it concluded. "What about—?"

"As it happens, I have an open-face room." He glanced about. "If the others will excuse us."

"Excused!" Nydia said for them all. "Let's hold a conference to consider what's next."

They walked single file to the side, then paused, considering.

"Well, that was a surprise," Noletta said. "But I'm glad for Ecstasy. She certainly deserves it."

"She does," Nydia said. "Now I'm the last one left. I confess I'm a bit jealous."

Lilith appeared, laughing. "Me too. I thought he was going to be interested in me, and I would have obliged him, but he found a better way."

"Obviously," the others chorused.

"Green was all around them," Vinia said. "Bleep, I want to grow up and find out what it's all about."

"Me too," Woe Betide said. "Eventually."

Lilith opened her mouth, but nothing emerged. She was unable to make a raunchy comment. It seemed the Adult Conspiracy still governed here.

"So what *is* next?" Nerine asked.

"I think we should continue down-slope," Nydia said. Then she reconsidered. "But, really, I am the only one who needs to do that. I have to confront the Void, and animate him, and try to recruit him. It will be safer if the rest of you, except for Lilith and Anthem, depart. We will rejoin you in due course." If she survived.

"Let's remain together a little more," Moonroe said. "We can see the sights, proffering moral support, then leave you to the finale, which we can't share." The others nodded.

Nydia was relieved for that much. "Thank you."

Oakley and Ecstasy returned. Both were radiant. Ecstasy, especially, seemed fulfilled. She looked at Nydia. "You're next."

Nydia hoped so. But how could a mere nymph ever win over the dreadful power of the Void? All she had going for her was One Thing, and that was hardly enough for more than a few minutes. She felt horribly inadequate. She didn't even have a soul.

They proceeded down-slope. Now the ground was littered with lost things. There were plates and spoons, combs and hairbands, gloves, and piles of lost socks.

Then something odd: a faint whirling shadow. "What is that?" Rob asked.

"I have seen it before," Aery said. "I believe it is a wraith. A drifting spirit."

"Wits," Oakley said. "Someone lost their wits."

They passed dozens of shiny coins mixed with lovely, faceted gemstones. Lost wealth. Then something much larger: a ship. The crew was still on board, evidently afraid to leave it. They did not approach it closely, as sailors were notorious for wanting that One Thing.

"How did a ship get overland to the Void?" Noletta asked.

"I can answer that," Oakley said. "The Void is not limited to this site, any more than the other Elements are limited to their sites. Anything ever truly lost comes here. It phases through reality until it settles here."

That seemed to make sense.

Then came something else: a marching column of soldiers led by a general. They must have gone seriously astray. It might have been better to avoid them, but the local terrain made that awkward.

Nydia went forward to meet the vanguard. "I am Nydia Nymph, on a mission to try to save Xanth. May I ask your identity?"

"You're a nymph!" the general said. "We are the Lost Legion. You are, of course, good for Only One Thing, but that is exactly what we are missing. Take off your clothes."

Nydia suppressed her annoyance. The general obviously didn't know any better. "My group is otherwise occupied. Go your way and we will go ours."

"Not so fast, tart. You can depart after we finish with you, if you can still walk." He reached out and grabbed her by an arm before she could jerk it away.

Nydia clung desperately to her politeness. "Please let go of me. I am not your plaything."

He laughed cruelly. "That's what you think. I'll take you first, then pass you down the line to the terminal grunt. We've been a long time without nookie. Now get your clothes off."

A whirlwind of fire appeared not far distant, consuming everything in its path. A nearby river they hadn't seen before overflowed its banks, advancing toward them. A twisting wind stirred, forming an expanding cone. The ground rumbled warningly. A volcano fired a shower of burning rocks into the sky. The Elements, perhaps prodded by their companions, were not too subtly expressing their annoyance.

Then Ecstasy spoke. "I will handle this." She strode forward, now clothed in a hooded cloak that concealed her face and form. Even so, she was beautiful beyond belief. "General, the lady asked you nicely. Now turn her loose or suffer the consequence."

The stirrings of the Elements subsided. They were letting her manage it her way for now, just in case she knew what she was doing. Nydia was surprised; this was a side of the woman she had not seen before.

The general did not let go. His gaze flicked sidelong. "And who the bleep are you, hussy?"

Ecstasy drew back her hood to reveal her lustrous face. Her searing gaze made his eyelashes and whiskers curl and smoke. A terrible beauty was manifesting. "I am a fair-minded woman trying to make allowances for your time away from civilization, thug. Now I ask you again: release my friend and go your way with your contingent. I do not want to embarrass you unnecessarily." Nydia was impressed, but what was Ecstasy up to?

"*Ha HA!*" the general laughed without humor as he shook the ashes off his face. "You'll be next, trollop. Get your clothing off."

Ecstasy frowned, and the air before her face crystallized and dropped to the ground as sleet. She shrugged out of her cloak to reveal her clothed torso. Now the general reacted, amazed by the scintillating outline. Mere cloth could not conceal the phenomenal perfection of the covered form. "Once more," she said evenly.

"What a shape!" He raised his voice to call to his subordinate officers. "Grab this creature! She's prime meat."

"These nymphs without souls are more decent, have shown more courage, and have already done more good than anyone else I have encountered," Ecstasy said severely. "You in contrast are nothing but a brute. You should be ashamed. Your soul is wasted on you."

Indeed, Nydia thought, *possession of a soul obviously did not guarantee good character*. Maybe army life degraded some of those with souls so that they were indeed no better than vicious animals.

"Strip her carefully," the general called. "So we don't have to mess with damaged goods. We want to savor the best bodies."

There was another rumbling of the Elements. They were not about to let Ecstasy be ravished.

"It seems I must do the necessary," Ecstasy said calmly. She caught hold of her dress and drew it down across her left shoulder, exposing that side of her bra. "Give over and get out, you ludicrous excuse for a biped." She twitched her shoulder, making the bra move slightly.

That did it. The general saw the fabric and froze in place. He had freaked out. Nydia was able to free herself from his slack grasp.

Then she saw that the four officers coming toward Ecstasy were also frozen. They, too, had freaked out. Not only that, the entire front line of the army had similarly freaked. Every man looking at the stunning creature had been smitten. Ecstasy hadn't even shown her panties; she had done it with half a bra. That had to be some kind of record.

"Now that's a performance like none other," Oakley said. "I never heard of the like. You are a woman among women."

"I am a crafted figurine," she replied. "Calculated to appeal to the male eye, per your directive. It's all artificial. You know that."

"I was referring to your manner and poise."

She pulled her dress back over her bra, becoming slightly less compelling. Her lovely lips quirked. "To be sure." Then they both laughed.

Nydia had to agree with Oakley. Ecstasy had demonstrated remarkable presence of mind and control, quite apart from the scintillating beauty of the figurine. She had vanquished the Lost Legion without violence or injury, except for a few face hairs, in a way no other woman could have.

They left the Legion frozen in place. There were other troops behind the officers. They would soon enough snap the leaders out of it, surely to their great embarrassment. Would they have learned their lesson? Probably not. But it had been well worth doing.

They resumed their walk, wending ever downward toward the dread center of the Void. They passed every imaginable kind of thing. It seemed that losses had been constant throughout the history of Xanth. There were more of the swirling mists that suggested lost wits or maybe lost loves.

Then they came to what seemed to be a kind of storm in the sky. "Not anything of mine," Aery said.

Pictures appeared, of children, women, couples, animals, fading in and out. They couldn't make sense of it.

"Lost memories," Oakley said. "I have seen some drifting by on occasion. This must be the main repository."

Of course. Suddenly it was obvious. Memories were constantly being made, too many to keep, so some were inevitably lost. Also, what happened to the ones whose folk died? The really important ones were better organized and not lost.

"You're so smart," Ecstasy said, squeezing his arm.

"Do you believe that, or are you just trying to flatter me?"

"Yes." Then they kissed, and a little heart sailed up to join the show, making the pictures waver.

"Are you confused, or pointlessly jealous?" Anthem asked Nydia with a suggestive background melody.

"Yes."

The next section had subtly different pictures. Not exactly memories, but somehow related. Nydia was not the only one curious about this, but their nature remained obscure.

"Lost dreams," Oakley said.

There was almost a common groan. Obvious!

"Let's each focus on a different dream," Nerine suggested. "That way we can examine several at once. Then we all can share the best ones."

They agreed and faced in slightly different directions, looking at particular dreams. Nydia focused on a young man who was evidently a prince because he had a crown. He was dreaming of achieving the position of a king. But then his elder brother took it, and the dream sank into the Void. So much for that. She tried another, a young woman dreaming of being swept off her feet by a handsome virile man, a marvelous romance, only to lose him to a prettier sister. Another loss.

"I found a piquant one," Moonroe said. "It leaves my feelings mixed."

They all focused on the dream in front of him. It was of a dull-looking man sitting at a desk with a clean scroll on it. He was writing, using a large bird feather whose stem he dipped into a bottle of ink every few words. What was he up to? Nydia glanced at other faces, but they were blank. None of them saw the point of this dream.

"An aspiring author, probably Mundane," Oakley said, and suddenly it was obvious. Of course! Mundanes were notorious for their determined dullness. They didn't even believe in magic! What was there for a truly dull person except imagination? So he was invoking it by writing a story or maybe even a novel. An exercise in Let's Pretend. Regular folk had better things to do, of course.

From the scrawl on the page rose an image that clarified as it expanded. This was the story being written, surely more interesting than the author. It was his forming dream. It was evidently a Romance, but, his muttered commentary made clear, no ordinary one. This was to be the most strikingly original romantic tale ever told. In stark summary it was Boy meets Girl, Boy loses Girl, Boy regains Girl. It was bound to wow the editor, get promptly published, and amaze the readers into a delirium of sheer delight. It would win awards galore and make the author rich, famous, and desirable. A figure of literary history. What a dream!

He completed it and sent it off to the most prestigious publisher extant. Then he waited for the inevitable exclamations of wonder and pleasure.

Instead, there came a slip. That was all.

His magnum opus had been rejected! How could any publisher possibly be that stupid? They had been publishing tedious reworkings of hoary old ideas for centuries. Now they had a chance for rare originality and they bounced it?! What was the matter with them?

But what could he do, except move on to some other line of more prestigious work, like ditch-digging or sewer-dredging? The universe was simply not ready for quality fiction.

Thus the dream was lost, sadly.

"But there is a codicil," Oakley said. "A footnote."

"Dreams have footnotes?" Vinia asked.

"It seems it is no ordinary dream," he said, perusing the small print. "That slip was not paper, it was silk. In fact, it was not a rejection at all, but a garment worn by the sightly lady editor. She had taken it off and sent it to the author, whose sheer originality had so impressed her that she saw herself in the role of the Girl. All he had to do was carry it back and claim her as his prize. Boy wins Girl, as well as fame and fortune." He grimaced. "Instead, he threw it away, forfeiting his dream."

"Ouch," Vinia said.

Could that be true? Nydia wasn't sure, but she agreed with Moonroe: her feelings were mixed. She knew that Mundane editors were notorious for their literary ignorance, at least among writers, but this seemed a bit too fanciful. Maybe it was actually part of the dream.

"Let's move on," Rob said. "We have a dream of our own to achieve."

He was making sense. They resumed their travel downslope, ignoring the remaining dreams. But Nydia was privately impressed by the quantity and variety of lost things here, physical, mental, and emotional. This was a realm in itself, the realm of whatever Xanth no longer had.

They finally came to the lowest place in the region. Lost items and debris had been cleared, leaving a bare spot of rock in the center. That was all.

"This is it?" Noletta asked.

"I feel the flow," Aery said. "This is the Element."

"But it's nothing!"

Aery just looked at her. Oh, of course. The Void was nothing. Obviously.

"I think this is it," Nydia said to the others. "I must conjure the spirit of the Void into the figurine, talk with it, and hope for the best." Phenomenally faint as that hope might be.

"So you must," Ecstasy agreed. "We will wait for you at the rim."

"The event horizon," Nydia agreed, feeling the chill again.

Lilith joined the members of the group one by one, conveying them out. Nydia was glad that they were escaping the Void, but with each departure she felt more alone. Was *she* ever going to leave here? Or would she be Voided into nothingness? She was too nervous even to be properly afraid.

At last, only Nydia and Anthem were left. Nydia reached into the bag, felt the original Ecstasy's hair, turned it loose, and found the final figurine. She brought it out and propped it up against the closest rock near the center. It wasn't ideal, but would have to do. The figurine was dourly handsome, befitting its subject.

Lilith reappeared. "All outside," she reported. "They pretend nonchalance, but they are seriously concerned for you."

"Ditto here." As if admitting it could cure it.

"Do you want me in your hair or on the periphery?"

Nydia pondered briefly. "Periphery. I don't know how he would react to a demoness."

"Done." Lilith stood back. "I will report on the outcome, regardless."

"Thank you." Then she thought of something else. "Anthem, how about you? You don't have to take this risk either. Lilith can take you out to join the others."

"Without you, I am nothing," the ant said, a sad chord in the background. "I prefer to remain close."

Nydia felt a wash of emotion. She would not be entirely alone. "Thank you. I think I love you."

"We are friends." That said it all.

Nydia nerved herself for what might be a painful final ordeal—if she even survived it. She brought out the wand. She stepped close to the central swirl, next to the figurine.

"Void, I conjure you into this figurine." She waved the wand. "If you care to oblige me. So we can talk, and maybe work together." She desperately hoped.

There was a pause. Then the figurine animated. It stood up straight. "I am here. What do you want of me?"

It had worked! But it was only the beginning. "I am Nydia Nymph, here to recruit you to join a Quest to discover and maybe handle whatever is agitating the Elements, you included. The other four Elements have joined, but we are incomplete without you. I hope you will want to participate." It sounded so puny, now that she was actually saying it. But what else was there?

The figure considered, assimilating the properties of the figurine, which included a brain. "I am the Void. All lost things come to me, including treasures, memories, ideas, dreams, and power. I am the richest and mightiest entity on the planet, except for the Demon Xanth himself."

"You surely are," she agreed, shivering. "I am relatively nothing, a mere nymph. Yet for the good of Xanth, I am asking you to join our effort. I will give you whatever you demand, if it is in my feeble power to provide, if you will only join. It may come to nothing anyway, but without you it will surely fail." She was conscious as she spoke of a kind of pun, "coming to nothing" when he was the virtual god of nothing, but it could not be helped. "Please, please, I beg you, help us."

"I know my power," he said. "It is virtually limitless. I am a black hole. All others fear me, as they should, even the other Elements."

"They do," she agreed. This was not looking promising. "And so do I. But we need you. Please."

Then came the sheer hunger. "I'm so lonely."

She knew this was significant. It required immediate attention and action. But what? Her mind was for the moment, well, blank.

What would Ecstasy do? She was the only complete adult woman in their group. The one with a functioning soul.

And suddenly Nydia understood. All her brief life, her existence, her mission coalesced to a single kernel of meaning. She knew why she was here, and what the rest of her being was to be. "Oh, my!" Anthem said, with a magnificent chord in the background as she read Nydia's mind. "You have found it."

"Yes, I have."

Nydia went to the Void figurine and enfolded him in her warm embrace. She spoke the two words that were to change everything. He was lonely? "Not anymore." Then she held him close while he sobbed into her iridescent hair. He had everything and nothing. Material things and power, even dreams, were ultimately meaningless without companionship, understanding, and love. She was bringing him that meaning. She was filling the emptiness that even a black hole could not. She needed him for the Quest, yes. But he also needed her, for meaning. She was molding his essence, making him human, doing everything a woman could do for a man, which was infinitely more than One Thing. She would never let him down in that respect.

"You have become a woman," Anthem said, awed, playing a chord of accomplishment.

Nydia realized that was true. She was transforming the Void while transforming herself. She was indeed a woman.

Chapter 9

THANX

In due course, they separated slightly and talked. Void seemed comfortable as long as he was close to Nydia. She understood why: she was the end of his abiding, eons-long loneliness. She knew him for what he was, and accepted him, something no other woman could do. He was also the end of her own isolation, though she hadn't known it until now. If she was still good for Only One Thing, it was sustaining him and herself. That was worthy.

"We shall call you Vol, rather than Void," Lilith said as they prepared to rejoin the Quest. She had stayed discreetly out of sight until the two of them came to terms. Anthem, too, had stayed clear. "Short for Volney. The name means 'Most Popular,' perhaps a misnomer, but it will do. You don't want to reveal your nature except when you specifically choose to."

Void looked at Nydia. "She is making sense," Nydia said. "Folk will be afraid of you if they realize your identity before they come to know you as a person. It is better to be largely anonymous, normally. I will speak for you until you become familiar with our folk and our ways." As if she hadn't just been learning them herself since escaping the Retreat.

"Vol," he agreed.

"My small companion is Anthem Ant. She will be your friend. When you touch me you will feel her musical mind."

He touched her hand, making the acquaintance via the contact telepathy. "I thought that was *your* music, Nydia."

"No, I am merely an obscure nymph without any such talent."

"Not anymore," Anthem said with a resounding chord.

Lilith laughed, picking up on it, and even Vol smiled. Indeed, Nydia had inadvertently vaulted to future prominence. She had become the companion of the most powerful of the five Elements. In effect, a queen consort.

"Now let's go meet the others," Nydia said. "They all need to know you personally, and you need to know them. All members of the Quest must feel at ease with one another, trust each other. We face a monstrous challenge, and need to know that we can depend on one another no matter how difficult it gets. Most of them are partnered, as you and I are now."

"Through her you can now have friends," Lilith said. "I have had some experience with being apart from normal society. Friends are better."

And Nydia realized that the demoness was lonely too. That was probably one reason she had elected to join the Quest: for the companionship, temporary as it might be. "You may flash him if you choose," she told Lilith. "I am not the jealous type, and besides you have no chance to win him."

"I wouldn't think of flashing him," Lilith said, her dress fading to a provocative bra and panties for half a moment.

Vol looked blank.

"A woman's underwear is considered sexy," Nydia explained. "Ordinary men can freak out merely glimpsing it. You will have to fake it if some young woman tries it on you. Just freeze in place until I snap my fingers."

Vol froze. Nydia snapped. He reanimated. "Perfect!" Lilith said, laughing.

"It's one of a number of social conventions," Nydia said. "I understand that some women freak out at tight trunks on a handsome man."

"I will pop you out," Lilith said, changing to the flower form.

"No need," Vol said. He took Nydia's hand. His touch was light, but she felt the immense negative power behind it. Only the fact that he was now animating a positive energy body made him safe to touch. She was holding hands with an Element.

They walked up the slope without difficulty. She was surprised, until she realized that of course it would be this way. He was the personification of the Void, and it answered to his touch, just as the other Elements did for their personifications. Each could nullify as well as enhance.

Soon they emerged from the perimeter, the so-called event horizon. There were the others.

Lilith reappeared. "All, this is Vol, the personification of the Void. He is now one of us."

"True," Nydia agreed.

Ecstasy stared at her. "You have become a woman!"

How did she know? Was there a sign on her? "Yes," she said simply.

"There's an intangible aura," Oakley said. "You now carry yourself with the assurance of personal legitimacy. You wear your female power." He smiled. "And you carry it well."

"I'm jealous," Noletta said. "I'm the only nymph left. Nerine was only ever a pretend nymph."

"No, you're getting there too," Ecstasy said. She turned back to the couple. "Welcome to the Quest, Vol."

Vol was silent, not knowing what to say. Nydia spoke for him. "He appreciates your welcome. He has had no interpersonal contact for eons, so is cautious about reactions. We will all be helping him become acclimatized. We'll treat him exactly as an equal, though we are of entirely different frames."

Lilith performed the introductions, identifying each Element and his or her partner. She concluded with Vinia. "She has two talents, contact telekinesis and seeing the colored paths of the future. We depend on the latter."

"What color is my path?" Vol asked her. Nydia was privately surprised. He was interested!

"All colors surround you, including some I haven't seen before; I think they must have gotten lost in the past, which I guess is why they came to you, but the side of you nearest Nydia is bright green. That's good."

"Without her I am nothing."

Vinia smiled. "Like Squid with Chaos. The right companion means everything."

"Now I think our roster is complete," Nydia said.

Vinia frowned. "Not quite. There's one more path."

"One more? We already have sixteen people!"

Vinia focused. "I think it leads to Santo and his friend."

"Who?"

Vinia smiled. "I forgot you came on the scene later. Santo is a Magician-class young man, about age twenty. He's gay, but he has a girlfriend, sort of. Her name is Noe."

Now she remembered. Lilith had mentioned Santo and his powerful talent. Nydia said thoughtfully, "Doesn't he prefer to have a romance with another man?"

"Exactly."

"Then why—?"

"In Mundania they call it a beard. It means to have a girlfriend so others think that's the way it is. A cover. Because gay folk get discriminated against, and it's a hassle they can do without. It got complicated when they discovered new gender-changing technology. Now he can be a woman, and she can be a man. There's a whole village of transgender people, each finding out what the other kind is like. It also means Noe can be a boy for Santo now, and she's willing to do it, because she loves him any which way. They're quite a couple."

"They must be," Nydia agreed. "But what does this have to do with us? We're on a mission to save Xanth from rampaging Elements, or whatever is behind that."

"And to do that, we may have to go to the Galaxy Andromeda."

"Exactly. So why mess with this odd couple?"

"That's the thing. How do we get there?"

A pause smote Nydia in the face. How, indeed! Again she had forgotten, in the press of other activities.

Vinia banished the pause. "I said Santo has Magician-class talent. It is making holes."

"Holes?" Vol asked.

"Any size, anywhere. He can make a pinhole through a pin, or a big hole that connects two planets. Maybe even two galaxies. The holes are short inside, but each end is another planet or whatever. The Mundanes call them wormholes. That makes travel easy."

"Now it registers," Nydia said. "We do need that talent."

"We do."

"Next question: I have no idea where Santo is, let alone whether he would have any interest in joining the Quest. We can ask him if we find him. But how do we contact him?"

Lilith appeared. "I can do that with Vinia's help. She can point the direction, and I can pop over to intercept him."

Nydia looked around. "Does this seem viable?"

"Find him," Ecstasy said. "Ask him." The others nodded.

"Let's see how well we can coordinate," Lilith told Vinia. "You tell me which direction and how far, and I'll pop us there. It may take several jumps, but we should be able to do it."

The demoness became the flower, and settled on the girl's hair. They paused for a generous moment, then the air imploded where they had been. They were on their way.

Nydia turned to Vol. "This is a convenient example of how we work together. We trust each other, coordinate, and get things done."

"I am impressed." She suspected not by the talents, but by the interaction of a girl and a demoness.

"Let's find a convenient place to settle down and get to know each other better while we wait." Nydia looked around. "Maybe that glade."

They walked to the glade. "Uh-oh," Moonroe said. "We may have blundered into a nickelpede nest."

So it seemed. The nest was beside the path, but hidden by foliage. They had walked innocently past it. Now the nickelpedes were spreading out across the path behind them, cutting off their escape.

"This is a rogue nest," Anthem said with warning music. "Not tame, the way the ones in the Queendom are. This is mischief."

"I will burn them," Flame said as a ball of fire appeared.

"I will wash them out," Flood said as a nearby puddle swelled out of its banks.

"I will blow them away," Aery said as a conic swirl of wind formed.

"I will bury them," Eartha said as the ground shook.

Nydia nudged Vol as Anthem communicated her thought: to make a demonstration.

"Let me handle this," Vol said. He gestured and the nest, along with the surrounding nickelpedes, silently disappeared, leaving a hole in the ground. They had been banished to the Void.

The others nodded. Vol had made his demonstration.

They spent the next hour comfortably chatting about that and this, with Nydia explaining things to Vol as necessary. He was smart enough, merely ignorant of conventions. Things like teen girls or lost legions had not clarified some aspects.

The day was waning. "I think we had better get where we are going," Ecstasy said. "If only to shelter for the night." Nydia was not yet used to

her awesome beauty, which at times threatened to freak out women as
well as men. Yes, Ecstasy was using a figurine she herself had crafted, but
she animated it perfectly and seemed completely personal.

"There's plenty of shelter at the Queendom," Vinia said. "We can get
there within an hour by carpet."

Oops! She was back. Nydia hadn't noticed her return. "What about
that Magician?"

"Santo and Noe will meet us there."

"Who?"

She laughed. "Noe." She pronounced it NO-ee. "His girlfriend, sometimes boyfriend."

Oh. That was another thing that might take time to get used to. "Then
we'd better get moving."

She brought out the carpet and spread it on the ground. They took
their places, with Nydia this time beside Vol, holding his hand, while
Ecstasy sat beside Oakley. They were no longer the two leftovers. Nydia
was sure that Ecstasy, too, was more than pleased with that aspect.

The carpet sailed up over the landscape. While they traveled, Nydia
explained about the Queendom of Thanx to Vol. "Most of the nations of
Xanth are kingdoms, governed by men. This one is governed by women.
The name is really Xanth spelled backward, acknowledging the reversal
of the supposedly natural order. When it formed, the male kingdoms surrounding it invaded, but they were defeated, as the women had prepared
carefully, had allies, and were ready for them. Now they get along okay.
The queen is a demoness called Demesne, de-MEEN. She's a good and
fair-minded person."

Lilith appeared. "I know her. She has a talent for organization."

"Which is why she is Queen. Her consort is the Demon Grossclout,
former professor at the School of Magic, whose talent is Intimidation. He
really terrified the students. I understand that she has mellowed him."

"She sure has," Vinia said as she steered the carpet. "She was in his
classes, but now she's the boss. He's almost nice these days."

Oakley shook his head. "Women do have that effect on men, unfortunately."

"Unfortunately?" Ecstasy asked, firing a scintillating sidelong glance
that trimmed some threads off his shirt.

He shook the shirt clear of the debris. "Oh come on. Would you want a milquetoast for your very own?"

"Bleep," she muttered cutely. "Got me there." Even the expurgated expressions she made were now aesthetic.

A cloud loomed ahead. "That's Fracto," Vinia said. "He must have run out of parades to rain on, so he's intercepting us."

"I'll blow him away," Aery said, and did so. The cloud looked startled as a stiff wind blew him tumbling through the sky.

Then a passing roc bird spied them and swerved, looking for a snack. It was bigger than the whole loaded carpet. Flame sent a firebomb that singed its feathers warningly, and it changed its mind. Rocs were big but not stupid.

"What is that sound?" Vol asked.

"Rock music," Nydia said. "It must have been humming it. They love that kind."

Finally, the turrets of the Queendom showed on the horizon. They angled down to the landing field. As they landed, a queenly figure appeared. "It's Demesne!" Vinia exclaimed, surprised.

"Hello, Quest!" the Queen called.

"Why are you here, Meen?" Vinia asked. "I mean, you're the Queen. You don't have to do chores yourself."

Meen? The two evidently knew each other well.

Demesne laughed. "Two answers. A queen can do chores if she chooses, and I choose to make myself useful. Second, your Quest is crucial, deserving my direct attention."

"Oh. Of course." Then the girl thought of something else. "How did you know we were coming in now?"

"Santo told us you were on the way."

"How did he get here ahead of us?" Nydia asked.

"He made a tunnel here," Demesne explained. "He can travel faster than anyone." She eyed the carpetful. "I see you now have a full complement."

"Pretty much," Nydia agreed. Then she set about introducing all the newcomers.

"I am impressed," Demesne said. "I have allocated an apartment complex for you. You will be feted tonight at dinner. I know your mission is vitally important." She glanced at Nydia. "You have changed."

"She has achieved womanhood," Ecstasy explained.

"That is surely an interesting story." She gestured. "This way, please." She floated just above the ground, and moved her legs so that it looked as if she were walking. Her hips even tilted appropriately, attracting the gaze of the males. Nydia made a mental note: with a woman, walking was only incidentally to get somewhere geographically. Its main object was emphasizing femininity.

They followed her into the complex.

Nydia found herself seeing it with new eyes. She had been here before, but the new additions to the Quest had not. It was impressive, with an external wall manned—or perhaps more properly, womanned—by Amazons. The entrances were open now, but could clearly be closed at need. This was a fortress: the female version of a fort.

Demesne delivered them, then popped off on other business. Lilith joined her, probably to update her on incidentals. They were, after all, both demonesses.

The apartment complex seemed, like the carpet, to have expanded to just the right size to accommodate them all. Almost. There were seven suites facing a central court when they needed eight. "I'll go to be with Prince Ion tonight," Vinia said, catching Nydia's thought. "He is, after all, my fiance."

Oh, of course. They were young, but committed to each other. The Adult Conspiracy was probably strained in their vicinity.

They had hardly settled in when a young couple arrived. The man approached Nydia. "I am Santo. This is my companion, Noe. Shall we talk? Be candid."

Candor was surely best. But how much of it? "Uh, yes. But first things first. Do you care to join the Quest?"

"Yes. You need me, and it should be interesting. But Noe and I need to clarify our relationship for your group, in case any object."

"No one objects," Nydia said firmly.

He smiled warily. "Best to make sure of that." He had clearly had experience with folk whose tolerance was superficial.

Nydia shrugged. "As you choose. But I must warn you privately that demoness Lilith has her eye on you, as a challenge. That could be awkward."

"Let her flash all she wants to," Noe said. "He's not interested."

Nydia focused on her. She was a moderately pretty girl, fair of hair and eye, with a nice shape, but not spectacular. "I confess to being somewhat at a loss of understanding why you care to associate with a man who, well, is not your type." Was that too much candor?

"Santo is not only Magician-class talented, he is the smartest person I know, and sensible too. He deserves better treatment than he gets from some ilk. I try to shield him from the worst of it. I am noe the smartest, prettiest, most athletic girl extant, in fact I am noe much of anything, but this much I can do. But apart from that, I love him."

There was a "but" Nydia needed to utter, but she couldn't get it out.

"And I love her," Santo said. "As a friend, associate, and companion. I know her well, and I trust her. There is no one I'd rather have at my side when complications occur. But I am not romantically inclined toward her, as she knows and accepts. That's part of what I like about her. She knows we have no long-term future together, and accepts that too. She is a good person. We will in time go our separate ways, still friends. Except—"

"Let me change," Noe said. She went to a closet and shut the door behind her.

Nydia looked at Santo. "Change?"

"She has a portable portal, but prefers not to use it in public."

"Portal?"

The door opened. A young man emerged. He wore the same clothing Noe had, adjusted for the male outline. "Yes, I am Noe," he said. He walked to Santo and kissed him. "He likes me better this way."

"I do," Santo agreed. "Though I know his essential nature, and that limits our association to a temporary one. But it will do."

Noe glanced at Vol. "I understand you are nothing. My name means nothing, maybe in a different way."

"So it does," Vol agreed, interested. The two were soon in a separate dialog, clearly intrigued by each other in that minor manner. Nydia glanced at Santo, who glanced back. Nothing had become something.

Queen Demesne appeared. "I trust we will see all of you at the dance tonight. The citizens very much want to meet the Elements."

Nydia was surprised. "They know?"

"They know, and they support your Quest completely. They just want to interact with you before you depart." She glanced about. "Our tailors will see to your outfitting for the event. Communal dinner is in one hour." She popped out.

Nydia took a deep breath. Then she raised her voice, speaking to the Quest. "The local folk very much want to interact with us. We shall have to oblige them, as we depend on their support. There will be a dinner followed by a dance. Their tailors will dress us." She glanced at Ecstasy. "I think you know more about this sort of thing than we nymphs and Elements do. I hope you can school us in the appropriate behavior."

"I can, to a degree," Ecstasy agreed. "But it would help greatly if I could borrow Rob, with his powerful telepathy. Words are not necessarily enough. Together we can, I think, make a decent presentation."

Nydia looked at Rob. "Amenable?"

"Let me share your mind," he told Ecstasy. After a third of a moment, he nodded. "Yes, we can do it."

Nydia was relieved. "Thank you."

Then the tailors arrived, male and female, and things got busy.

"I am glad to have you with me," Vol murmured. "You are a leader."

Nydia shook her head. "I am desperate. I am trying to do the right thing, but at times that gets lost in the turmoil of events."

The tailors were efficient. Within the hour, the entire party was beautifully garbed for a social event, the men in perfectly fitting suits, the women in marvelous evening gowns. Nydia was amazed how appealing they all were, Ecstasy especially. She was like a star among planets.

The dinner was elegant, with food that was more apparent than real for those who did not need to eat, so they could fake it. For the others, it was delicious.

Then came the dance. It was indoors, but framed as a forest glade, with assistants garbed as green elves. There was an orchestra, the musicians made up to resemble goblins. The ugly males beat the drums, clanged the cymbals, and honked the horns, while the lovely petite females blew delicate flutes, stroked small violins, and played the harpsichord. Some of them seemed so real that Nydia suspected that there were real elves and goblins among them. A refreshment stand was serviced by mermaids, their tails supported by small traveling water tanks. A cute little sea serpent swam in the lemonade, sweetening it. The lights were muted, but bright enough to display the ladies fetchingly.

"When Thanx does a dance, it does it right," Ecstasy murmured.

So it seemed. This wasn't Nydia's first such experience, but she was just as seriously impressed as those in the group who had never attended a Queendom ball.

The music started. Couples took to the floor, dancing slowly.

"The waltz," Ecstasy said. "Tune in on Oakley and me." Nydia saw that Rob and Eartha were sitting this one out, he focusing on Ecstasy and Oakley, receiving and sending their movements, she cluing him in on details. The other Element couples began to dance perfectly, except that they were in sync with the lead couple and each other. It evidently wasn't feasible to provide them with individual moves, unless the receiving couples could deviate enough to do it themselves. If any of the Thanx couples noticed, they were discreet about showing it.

At any rate, it was working for Nydia and Vol. She tuned in on the lady's side of the waltz, which was not complicated, and Vol responded to the man's side. They moved well enough together. They got through the first dance flawlessly.

Vinia was dancing with Prince Ion. Nydia remembered that the girl's other talent was telekinesis. She was actually making Ion's legs move so that they could dance together, despite his paralysis.

Then the mixing began. A couple cut in on them, the lady taking Vol, the man Nydia. She found she could continue doing the steps well enough, now that she had some practice in them. "I am just an anonymous worker," the man told her, "but you are a stunning creature."

"I'm a nymph," she replied. "All appearance, little substance."

He shook his head. "I know the difference. You're a woman." Evidently so.

As they danced, Nydia tried to keep an eye on Vol. He seemed to be handling it too. That was a relief. There was no loneliness here.

Then she saw Ecstasy dancing with others. She was as beautiful in motion as in person. It was as if a cloud of brilliance surrounded her. She was much in demand, and clearly enjoying it. Oakley was showing not a trace of jealousy; he had enabled her to achieve her dream of being lovely and popular by pointing out the obvious: to use a figurine herself.

And Santo with Noe, back in her girl form. They danced wonderfully together, which was perhaps no surprise, as they knew each other so well. They were putting on their normal-couple show, though the citizens knew that was the limit of it.

Until Lilith cut in. Noe yielded gracefully, having been warned. She retired to the sideline and watched, a faint smile hovering near her face.

Lilith's outfit was, of course, part of her demon substance, maybe a variation of ectoplasm, answering to her preference of the moment. It faded out where Santo touched her, so that his arm rested against her bare back. When she did a twirl, the material across her bosom flashed translucent, showing most evocative flesh beneath. Her skirt flung out, but that hardly mattered, because it, too, flashed translucent, showing marvelously formed thighs and evocatively flexing posterior. Panties flashed brightly. Nearby men started freaking out, having to be snapped back to attention by their annoyed partners, only to freak again.

Except for Santo. He danced blithely on, unaffected. Lilith was increasingly frustrated, trying wilder flashes to no effect, despite the carnage elsewhere in the hall. At one point she was completely nude, with an exaggerated shape, but she might as well have been swaddled in a thick wool coat for all the effect it had at close range. The smile caught up to Noe's mouth and prospered there as the dance finished, with the demoness looking somewhat wild-eyed and weathered, and the hall resembling a bombed city inhabited only by outraged women staring at their fallen men.

Lilith gave it up as a bad job, plainly irritated by what might have been her first seductive failure in generations. Noe resumed dancing with Santo. Now a trace of the smile touched him also. He had known what the demoness was up to, and perhaps enjoyed demonstrating his immunity to her charms. He had looked at everything and been bored. He truly was not into women as romantic or sexual objects. That made his association with Noe more significant, as he obviously valued her.

The next dance was a different type, with couples mostly facing each other, slightly apart, gyrating in place. Queen Demesne joined in with Grossclout. Then she beckoned to Lilith, who took her place. This time, she did not even try to freak out her partner, knowing infinitely better.

Neither did Grossclout try to intimidate her, ditto. A smile circulated around the women. The demoness had been put in her place.

As the dance concluded, Eartha spoke to Nydia. "Rob is picking up on something we perhaps need to know about," she murmured. "There is a deep distress in Thanx they are not telling us about."

"Our fault?" Nydia asked, alarmed.

"No. They don't want to bother us with it, so are pretending all is well. It isn't."

Noletta was near. Nydia turned to her. "Something's wrong. What does your future vision indicate?"

The nymph focused. "We are on the way to Andromeda Galaxy. We seem to be okay."

"Suppose we stay here another day?"

Noletta focused again. "There seems to be mischief. We're okay, but those around us are in panic. I can't tell why."

Nydia beckoned Vinia. "There's a problem. What do your colored paths indicate?"

The girl focused. "The whole area is turning red. We need to be out of here."

"Is there a green path?"

"Um, yes." She looked up. "It leads right to Apoca."

Who had her own powers and understanding. "Stay here, all. I will talk privately with Apoca." Nydia crossed the hall to where the Lips queen sat with her husband.

Apoca looked up as Nydia approached. Her hair turned red. "Bleep! You're catching on."

Nydia sat in the chair next to her. "Only to the fact that something is wrong. Please, tell me what. Why is it being concealed from us?"

"Your mission is essential. We don't want to delay you or distract you with something that need not concern you."

"We are already concerned. Is there anything we can do?"

Apoca sighed. "I really don't see what. That's part of why we prefer to leave you out of it."

This continued to be curious. "But there might be something?"

"There might be. But you need to be on your way."

"Tell me the essence so I can judge."

"Thanx may be destroyed."

Nydia suppressed her dismay. Their experience with the Queendom had been slight so far, but she already valued it, and was sure the others did too. Good folk were here. "Suppose we get in a private room and you tell the members of the Quest about it? Then we can decide whether to try to help, if we can, or simply get out of your hair."

The queen nodded, her hair going plaid. "That's fair." She stood and spoke to Nolan, the Prince of the Naga. "Cover for me, dear. I have to tell the Quest."

He nodded. "It would be marvelous if they could help, though I don't see how."

"This way." Apoca walked toward a door Nydia hadn't noticed before. "Don't let them make a scene. Not all citizens are aware yet. In fact, only a few of those in the know are here, deliberately."

"Got it." Nydia returned to the others. "We will gather quietly in that chamber with Queen Apoca. There is serious business afoot."

"There sure is," Vinia said. "There are red paths all around."

They filtered in, two by two, without attracting attention. Santo and Noe were nearby, but hesitated. Nydia signaled them to come along. If they were joining the Quest, they belonged.

Soon they were all seated in the room, facing Apoca. She started in without preamble, her hair flashing a welcoming green. "You may have noticed how busy Queen Demesne is, and how she lacked personnel to handle visitors, so she had to do it herself. The Queendom of Thanx is threatened with extinction, not by any attack of her neighbors, who are similarly threatened, but by an outside force." Her hair turned blue. "I must use, excuse the term, science, to explain. There are two tectonic plates to our east and west that seem to be at war with each other." She smiled grimly. "These are not exactly dinner plates. They are huge sheets of rock upon which the Land of Xanth rests. When they move, the earth shakes. They are pushing at each other, striving for competitive dominance. Unfortunately, the Queendom happens to be right between them. When they push too hard, the land will buckle, forming new mountains, as has happened elsewhere in the past, when other plates collided. Everything we have built will be destroyed. Yes, we can hastily move elsewhere, before the crisis peaks, pardon the pun, but there are complications. The rest of Xanth is mostly settled, and evacuees may not be completely welcomed. When the Queendom was established, the neighboring kingdoms immediately invaded. They won't be kind to refugees. We would have to rebuild everything. The ardors of travel will be stressful. So we prefer to remain here. But we don't know how to stop the plates. Already the tension of that pressure is causing fires to break out, floods to occur, and terrible windstorms. It's all we can do, cooperating with the kingdoms, to contain their damage." She allowed half a pause, her hair turning gray. "Any feasible suggestions are welcome."

Flame stood. "I can quell the fires, at least as long as I am here."

Flood stood. "I can abate the flooding similarly."

Aery stood. "I can still the winds."

Eartha stood. "I am the Element of Earth. I have been quelling those two juvenile plates for eons, but the moment my attention wanders, Tek and Tonik are at it again. Now that I have joined the Quest, and I am not watching as closely, they feel free to misbehave. I can stop them, but I must go to Andromeda Galaxy, and that will free them to resume their rivalry. They can't be abolished because they are the foundation of Xanth. I regret I do not have a viable suggestion." She sat back down.

Moonroe stood. "I have a question, Lips queen. You speak of plates. Are there cups, knives, forks, spoons, or other utensils?"

Apoca plainly was not amused, her hair turning orange for annoyance. "Not that we know of."

Moonroe was unfazed. "My thought is this: if the plates are male, the other meal utensils may be female. They might represent a fair distraction, so the plates would no longer feel the need to contest for land." He glanced at Aery. "I can attest that a female can distract and calm a male when she tries."

"Obviously," Oakley agreed, glancing at Ecstasy, who smiled.

Apoca was taken aback, her hair flashing assorted colors. "I happen to know that female power over males. But where would we ever find suitable tableware for such plates?"

Vol stood. "I have stores of every kind of tableware that has ever been lost. The problem is how to get it to the buried plates."

Santo stood. "I can make tunnels for them to use for access. That is my talent."

Could this actually work? That depended on the plates. Nydia was afraid it was not enough. "Knives and forks are not very expressive on their own."

"Spoons would be better," Noe said. "They are obviously female, with their curves."

"You have a wand," Oakley said to Nydia, "which can animate as a young woman. Could you prevail on her to teach the utensils how? The spoons how to spoon, as it were?"

That was so far-fetched it seemed ludicrous. But what choice did she have? She brought out the wand. "Wanda, we need your help. Please animate so we can talk." She set it down on an empty chair, uncertain that there would be a response. They had, after all, pretty much abducted her and made her perform involuntarily. She could be angry.

Wanda appeared, black of hair and eye, lovely in her disguise. "I heard everything. I can do it. What's in it for me?"

So they *could* bargain. Wanda was no longer playing the almost-echo game. "Your freedom, after the Quest is done. I can return you to the house where we found you."

"That's not enough."

"What do you want?"

"A male, one who knows my nature and accepts me as I am. Your Questers all got partners. I want one too."

"But you are illusion!"

"Conjure me into a figurine. Then I'll be physical."

"Obviously," Oakley said.

Nydia felt her jaw trying to drop. She fought it back into place. "Uh, Ecstasy?" Could she craft figurines while being a figurine herself?

"Coming up." Ecstasy reached into the air and hauled out a blob of ectoplasm. Soon she had it shaped into a duplicate of Wanda, like a twin sister. She could indeed do it, and her artistry remained excellent.

"Perfect," Wanda said. She turned to Nydia. "Now do me."

Bemused, Nydia reached into her and grasped her essence, the wand. The illusion of Wanda disappeared. "I conjure you into this host," Nydia said.

She felt the wand go. She no longer held it. Oops! Had this experiment destroyed it?

The figurine animated. "Thank you," Wanda said. "This makes me real in a manner I never was before. I can actually touch and be touched, not just wielded. I even have a brain, and can think for myself. That's awesome." She smiled. "Now let me try my power on some spoons."

"But the wand is gone," Nydia protested.

"You forget I *am* the wand."

Oh. Was this making sense?

Wanda turned to Vol. "Spoon, please."

Vol lifted one hand. An ornate spoon appeared in it, surely an antique. He handed it to Wanda.

She held it up. "Clothe yourself," she said to it.

The air around the spoon shimmered and formed into a fair woman with a small but pretty head, small bosom, narrow waist, and a large pelvis. Spoon shaped, of course. She looked down at herself, then formed classic clothing that further enhanced her proportions. It was working!

"We want you to fascinate a big plate," Wanda said to her.

"But I am good for only one thing: eating," the illusion woman protested.

All three nymphs (Nerine still counting herself as one) smiled reminiscently. How could they ever have accepted such a notion? It was sheer male propaganda. Neither was a spoon limited to utensilizing.

"He won't be interested in eating. Just let him look at you. Dance for him. Dish it out. Tease him with your silvery beauty."

The image looked at herself. "I could do that, as long as he doesn't actually touch me."

"He has no hands," Eartha said. "Just an awareness of your presence. That should suffice. Males can study females indefinitely."

"At least, they do in Mundania," Ecstasy said. "They call it pornography."

"But I don't know where he is, or how to reach him."

Wanda looked at Santo. He smiled. "One tunnel coming up." He focused and a hole appeared before him, slanting down under the floor and nearby wall. "The plate is at the other end. All you have to do is get in range and hold his attention."

"I can do that," the spoon said, wiggling her evocative midsection with a scooping motion. "I will flash panties. He'll never take his attention off me." She walked into the tunnel and soon was gone.

"Another spoon," Wanda said.

Vol produced it. They went through the same procedure, and soon another illusory lady was walking down another tunnel, toward the other plate. They followed with several more spoons for each plate so that there would be variety, as males tended to like that. The plates would never think of quarreling with each other again.

"Now," Moonroe said. "Your turn, Wanda. You want a man who understands and accepts you as you are. How about a knife?"

"A dull utensil? I can do better than that."

"I was thinking of a fancy carving knife, quite sharp. Vol surely has a fine collection."

Vol raised his hand. It held an ornate blade whose handle resembled a handsome man. "This was owned and used by a great hunter. It has surely seen much of interest."

Wanda gazed at it, impressed.

"Conjure it as you did the spoons," Moonroe said. "If you don't like it, abolish it."

She considered half a moment. Then she decided. She took the blade and held it in her hand. "Clothe yourself," she said.

A man formed around the knife. He slid from her hand and stood before her, tall and well-favored. "Well, hello, lovely lady."

Wanda was clearly impressed. "You do know my nature, and yours?"

"Of course I know. But I can't touch you, lest the illusion dissipate."

Wanda turned to Ecstasy. "Already on it," the woman said as she pulled ectoplasm from the air. Soon she had a figurine exactly emulating the knife man.

Wanda gestured. "Enter the statuette," she said.

The illusion took one step into the figurine. Then, tangible, he took hold of Wanda and kissed her. "Let's get to a more private place. I have significant things to tell you." Surely more than that!

"Yes," she breathed, clearly delighted. They departed together.

"I confess to being impressed by the incidental magic," Apoca said, "but will this ploy actually stop the plates?"

Rob gestured toward the closed door. "News on that front approaches."

There was an imperious knock. "Come in," Apoca called.

It was her husband, Prince Nolan Naga. "Word from the field. The plate pressure has eased!"

Apoca looked at Nydia. "Even more impressed!" She was gone.

Nydia sat down, impressed herself. Had they really thus simply solved the Queendom's problem? By providing pun distractions for the rogue plates? That seemed too easy. But in Xanth, the pun was king. Time would tell. Favorably, she ardently hoped.

She looked at Noletta. "What's your verdict?"

"We are on the way to Galaxy Andromeda. There seems to be no more panic."

"Most paths are green now," Vinia said.

"I believe this team is working well together," Oakley said.

"Obviously," several others replied, laughing.

They retired to their suites. "That was a nice thing you did for Wanda," Nydia told Vol. "It seems that she was another lonely person, for all that I had thought she was just a tool."

"I do understand loneliness."

She kissed him. "I mean to see that you will never again be lonely."

"It ended the moment you joined me."

"For me too." She kissed him again.

There was a tap on the door. It turned out to be Demesne. She did not need to tap, as she could have phased through the door, but she was being polite. "I believe you have saved Thanx. Apoca told me what you did."

"It was really Wanda, the personification of the magic wand I use to conjure spirits into the figurines Ecstasy makes. I didn't know it would work out that way, but I am pleased it did."

"We owe you more than I can say."

Nydia shook her head. "You helped make the Quest possible. There is no debt."

"You and your friends will always be welcome in the Queendom." Demesne faded out.

Nydia closed the door and returned to Vol. "I believe we were working our way into the One Thing a nymph is good at, unless you are bored with it."

"Never." He kissed her almost savagely.

There was another tap on the door. "One of those nights," Nydia muttered, returning to open it. Vol waited, letting her handle her business her way.

This time it was Wanda and the personalized knife. "We need to clarify something."

"The deal was your freedom and a man," Nydia said. "You did your part, and it saved the Queendom of Thanx. That's clear enough." With luck that would end it, and she could get on with what had bored her in the Retreat, but now was something she ardently desired.

"May we come in? There is more."

Nydia sighed inwardly. It really was one of those nights. "Come in," she said with forced courtesy.

They entered and sat. Nydia and Vol sat opposite them, he maintaining his silence. "Vol gave you a gift you may not have realized," Wanda said.

Nydia was perplexed. "A gift? To me?"

"My loyalty to you."

Had she misheard? "I do not understand."

"I need to explain about my companion Knight Knife. He is no ordinary instrument. He is an enchanted hero who excelled with the blade. He was favored by the gods of old, thus could not be killed, but his enemies wanted him permanently out of the picture. So when they finally captured him, suffering horrendous losses in the process, they chose another way. They transformed him into a sword and masked even that by giving it the semblance of a mere hunting knife. Then they threw it away so that it was lost."

"Lost," Nydia repeated, understanding how it had come to the Void.

"Now he is mine, and I love him and he loves me. We come from wildly different backgrounds, but we are both utilities, and because of you we have joined together."

"He was a living man? I didn't know."

"But Vol did. That's why he chose Knight to join me. It was his quiet gift to you."

Nydia looked at Vol. "That's ridicu—" But the word foundered in midair as she saw his trace nod. Maybe the terminal "lous" was now in the void.

"He wanted to please you," Wanda continued. "Without being obvious. He found a way."

Nydia shook her head ruefully. "It has been a busy day. I seem to be slow on the uptake. How was helping you a gift to me?"

"Vol knows my nature. There have been other wands, and some must have gotten lost and wound up in his domain. So he knows that a wand, like a sword, is not complete in itself. It has to be wielded by a sentient creature, like a human being, or it lacks any point in existence. That was the true punishment meted out to Knight. He was rendered lost and useless. With me he has companionship and love, and that's good, but we both still lack that point. We need to be wielded. Unlike other tools, we now have a choice in whom to be wielded by. And we choose you. Vol knew it would happen."

"Me!" Nydia exclaimed. "I'm only a nymph!"

"You're a woman and a special one. You are a good person, without selfish designs. You just want to do the right thing. We really respect that."

"But—"

"She's right," Anthem said with a background chord of conviction. "You are not only a woman, but a good one."

"And so we come to you," Wanda concluded. "We want you to be the one to wield us. We will do everything we can for you with absolute loyalty. We know you will use us appropriately, always doing the correct thing."

"But soon the Quest may end and the adventure will be over."

"Not just during the Quest," Knight said. "During your life."

"But even if I am, well, worthy, I'm no warrior. I could hardly lift a real sword, let alone wield it effectively, even if I had the nerve. Your loyalty would be wasted."

Wanda smiled. "You need to learn more about magic swords." She glanced at Knight. "Show her, dear."

Knight came to Nydia and took her right hand. He dissolved into the sword, which she now held. It was featherlight.

"But if an enemy came at me, I still would not know how to, um, wield it."

Vol smiled. In his hands appeared a full-sized mock-up of a predatory troll intent on violence, rapine, and worse. It eyed Nydia as Vol stepped back. Its teeth showed in a smile that had nothing to do with niceness.

The sword leaped forward, hauling Nydia behind it. It plunged into the center of the troll. Nydia shrieked and let go, scrambling backwards.

The troll stood there, not falling. Because the sword had passed through its body and into the wall beyond, literally pinning the supposed monster in place.

"You don't need to know how," Wanda said. "*It* knows how." She went to pull the sword out. The troll collapsed. Vol gestured and it disappeared, returned to the void. Wanda kissed the hilt of the sword and Knight reappeared. Both looked at her expectantly.

She could indeed be a warrior lass with such a weapon. And there just might come a time when she needed it, for herself or to help another member of the Quest. Yet she was only a nymph, maybe morphing into a woman, not at all a creature of violence, however she appeared.

Nydia fought off the feeling of being overwhelmed. "I think I need advice."

Wanda smiled. "Get it."

Nydia rose and went to the door. Vol remained behind. "I do not want to influence your decision," he explained. "I will talk with these folk."

She didn't argue. She went to Ecstasy's door and tapped lightly.

"Nydia!" the woman said, surprised, when she saw her. "I thought you were breaking Vol in."

"Something came up. I'm the one being broken in."

Ecstasy might look like a bombshell creature at the moment, but now the internal maturity came through. "Come in."

Oakley was there, of course, slightly disheveled. "Bleep!" Nydia swore. "I'm interrupting."

Both of them laughed. "We make out continuously when alone together," Ecstasy said. "It's impossible not to interrupt. Sometimes I revert to my real shape, which the ectoplasm enables me to do without having to fetch my original body, or I add substance and become hugely endowed, and it hardly makes a difference. Oakley likes me any which way and enjoys the variety. We are reveling in it. That activity can wait a moment or three. You need help, obviously. We are happy to provide whatever we can. We owe our acquaintance to your Quest."

Nydia quickly explained the situation. "So what is the right thing for me to do? I am not trusting my own judgment at this point."

Ecstasy pulled a skein of ectoplasm from the air and quickly fashioned it into what looked like a wide utility belt. Then she put it on Nydia, snapping its clasp shut. "There are pockets for a wand, knife, bag, and other items as necessary."

"You—you are saying I should do it?"

"Obviously," Oakley said.

Nydia's next thought seemed almost irrelevant. "Your ectoplasm makes them solid. How can they still become wand and knife?"

"Ectoplasm is marvelous stuff. It can be solid or vaporous as necessary. Ideal for them, and they know it."

So it was decided. "Uh, thank you."

They were already back making out. "Mmmph," Ecstasy said around her kiss.

Nydia returned to her own chamber. All three understood the moment they saw her. Wanda and Knight touched the belt, reverted, and fit into adjacent pockets next to the bag. Vol enfolded her, heedless of the belt. So they weren't alone, technically. It didn't matter; Wanda and Knight understood perfectly. Nydia set the belt aside, along with her clothing, and delighted in the moment.

In the morning, Nydia clarified for the others the developments of the night. Then the group went to the communal hall for breakfast before their departure for Andromeda, including those who merely kept company. They liked being together, and it continued being a learning experience for the Elements.

Demesne was there, and Apoca, together with their spouses and many of the leading citizens. "There has been no more mischief," Demesne said. "The magic mirror says that will continue. So does the Good Magician. Thanks to your intercession. We hereby award you and all of your Quest members honorary citizenship of the Queendom of Thanx. Your return to us will be welcomed." The others applauded.

Soon they were out in a field with the citizens attending. "I can make a tunnel to Andromeda," Santo said, "but that's a galaxy, and far away. I can only be sure that there will be land at the other end." He glanced at the assembled Elements. "We may need your help."

"That's why we're here," Flame said. The others nodded.

Santo gestured. A hole in the sky appeared at the top of a rise, tilting upward, large enough for people to walk through upright single or as couples.

Nydia's heart was beating almost painfully hard, but she put on her best social smile. "We shall return," she said, waving to the citizens. They waved back. Then she nerved herself and strode into the tunnel, Vol beside her. They were on their way to Andromeda Galaxy.

Chapter 10

ANDROMEDA

Nydia led the way, deliberately not looking back, implying that she had absolute confidence in the journey and the endorsement of the others. That it was almost routine to cross between galaxies. But her hand clutched Vol's with tremulous tightness, betraying her fear. He kept pace with her, firmly sustaining her fingers between his. Anthem Ant relayed his thought: "You comforted me when I was alone. Now I support you when you are afraid."

Afraid? "Not anymore," she responded gratefully. His presence and understanding, backed by his phenomenal power, made all the difference. Her fear retreated, losing the battle for her mind.

"And now you have us," Wanda said. "I will conjure what you need to animate, and Knight will make you a formidable warrior lady."

That was indeed reassuring. "Thank you both."

In fewer than a hundred steps, they reached the exit of the tunnel. It was hard to believe that they had traveled three million light years. Not that she really understood what a light year was, let alone millions of them. The tunnel opened onto a barren plain. Now she hesitated for another reason as a thought erupted. "Is—is there air?"

Moonroe and Aery stepped forward. "Now there is," Aery said, gesturing as a gust stirred dust beyond the exit.

They stepped out. Suddenly it was horrendously cold. "He-heat!" Nydia gasped.

Noletta and Flame joined them. A blast of heat warmed them. Oh yes, they needed the Elements.

The others emerged. There was still a problem: they were so light on their feet that even a little jump would send them flying.

"I could add matter to increase the gravity indirectly," Eartha said, "but that might mess up this planetoid in other ways. It's not used to heaviness. We're probably better off to bear with it briefly while Santo generates another tunnel to wherever we're going in this galaxy."

"This is the galactic periphery," Santo agreed. He smiled. "The outer edge." That was for those who lacked his vocabulary. He glanced at Vinia. "Where to next?"

The girl oriented. She pointed. "That way. I think it's near the center. That makes sense, doesn't it?"

"Absolutely," Moonroe said.

Santo nodded. "I will tunnel to it."

Something occurred to Nydia. "The old tunnel, the one we came through—what happens to it?"

"Fear not. I will leave it in place so that you can take it back, should anything happen to me."

Noe shuddered. "Please don't let anything happen to you." She loved him and didn't mind showing it, one-sided as the affection might be.

"You don't have to shut down the prior tunnels before making new ones?" Nydia asked.

"Correct. I do not, though I try not to litter the landscape with them. They could be awkward in the wrong hands." He focused and a new tunnel opened before them.

They took it of course. This one exited onto a larger planet where there was plenty of gravity, heat, and air. But it was strange in undefinable ways.

"This is curious," Rob said. "It's not like the Land of Xanth or any Mundane planet I am aware of. I think we would be best off learning more about it before we go farther." He had a certain feeling for planets, as his body was still holding Xanth together.

Eartha agreed. She, too, had special awareness, her essence being the substance of those planets. "For one thing, it seems to lack magic."

That gave Nydia a chill. She felt naked without magic.

A big book appeared in Vol's arms. "This is an atlas of the galactic cluster, lost so long ago there is no current record of it or its origin," he said. "The ancients knew things we have forgotten."

"True," Santo agreed.

"True," Lilith echoed. Santo had not humiliated her on the dance floor so much as won her respect. He really was immune to her charms.

"It should have the information we need." Vol found a waist-high stone with a flat surface and opened the book on it.

They pored over it. The atlas was amazing. It identified every star in all the galaxies of the cluster and all their myriad planets. It must have been compiled by a Demon who eventually lost interest and went on to other projects. All they had to do was focus mentally on the type of information they wanted, and the book somehow guided them to it. Soon they were looking at the planet they stood on. It was named GEH, for Galactic Event Horizon, the dread boundary of which it seemed GEH orbited just outside. It was illuminated by the massed stars of the galaxy beyond, and heated by the furnace of the compression of space itself in the vicinity. It had been deformed by the extreme stresses of gravity here and was now not a sphere but a long, flat band.

"Like my house in the Void!" Oakley exclaimed. "By no coincidence, obviously. Because the only free travel is along or beside, not above or below."

"Only this is bigger," Nydia said nervously. "Much bigger."

"Surely larger than most planets," he agreed. "We should be safe as long as we stay on it and don't step off the edge."

They all looked at the GEH edge, visible not far distant. A suppressed shudder rolled through them like the stress of an approaching earthquake. Beyond it was deadly nothing. They would stay well clear of that!

"Actually, a person stepping off that edge would not fall," Santo said. "He would be in orbit beside it. But he might have trouble ever returning."

"So it seems best to stay close," Noe said.

Nydia wondered passingly whether Noe had a special talent that would be of assistance on GEH.

Rob answered, mentally. "Her talent is to be anonymous in plain sight, not the best or worst in anything, so folk tend not to notice her. When he is close to her, Santo shares that anonymity. That can be useful."

Nydia realized that it could indeed be useful, considering the prejudice against his orientation.

They resumed their trek across the strange landscape.

"Who is that?" Noe asked.

Nydia looked. There, almost hidden by a low hillock, was a vague man-shape right at the edge. But it couldn't be a man unless the human kind had somehow colonized this galaxy. That seemed quite unlikely.

"A native, obviously," Oakley said. "Evidently about to step off."

"No!" Noe said in horror. She hurried toward the shape, heedless of any danger.

"She has a tender heart," Santo said. "Especially for anyone or anything that's different. I may have to rescue her." Yes, Noe's sympathy evidently extended to any conscious creature. Nydia was getting another inkling why Santo liked her; she was a worthy person. He followed Noe's path to the hillock.

So did Nydia and Vol. The figure turned to face them as they approached it, though it did not seem to have a face or even a front. It looked vaguely like a big snail or slug near the ground, with a vertical body formed of what looked like water and air, weird as that was. Above it hovered a flickering fire, vaguely like a head of hair.

"What is the color around it, as Vinia sees it?" Nydia asked Rob silently. "Green."

That was a relief. They had to be extremely wary of strangers or odd things here in the alien galaxy.

"Hello!" Noe called.

The figure formed an extension with a water-lens and turned it toward her. Its surface shimmered. Sound came from the shimmering torso, rising like a question. "Eeelooo?"

"Oh, we don't speak the same language, of course!" She turned to Vol. "Do you have a translator?"

A device appeared in Vol's hand. It had various bells, whistles, lights, and whatever else it thought it needed. "Yes. But it takes a while to orient on unfamiliar communication. Keep it talking."

Rob spoke, aloud this time. "I am reading its mind, but the specifics are alien. It is sapient, it means well, but is in trouble. That's why it is considering suicide. It has no future with its associates."

"We'll call these creatures Droms," Nydia decided. "For An-DROM-eda."

No one objected. They were satisfied with her seeming certainty with decisions. She was still learning leadership.

Noe turned back to the creature. "If we continue our dialog, maybe the translator will catch on to words. I am Noe and these are my friends. We're visiting from another galaxy."

Now the figure flashed and vibrated, seeming interested. "Noo-eee. Viss-ting."

"Yes, visiting," Noe said. "Because something is stirring up the Elements, and it seems to be from here."

"It is realizing that we are friendly," Rob said. "Though we are quite unlike anything it has encountered before."

"As it is to us," Oakley said. "Obviously."

There were more flashes and sounds, the colors and beeps meshing, seeming to be parts of the communication. Gradually, as they continued their interaction, some sense came. Noe needed a name for it, so she said, "I will call you by an acronym, since you seem to be made of Elements: fire, air, void, earth, and water. FAVEW. Is that okay?"

"Favew," the figure agreed, with colors augmenting it.

"Oh, pretty! I like the colors, even if I can't make them the way you do." Noe glanced at the translator. It repeated the new word, complete with colors.

The dialog continued, and the sense of it slowly increased. Once the translator had a few words, it built on that foundation, and more meaning developed. The Droms were unisexual, any one of them able to mate with any other by forming the necessary body parts, but they decided to think of Favew as male for convenience.

It took hours, even with Rob's telepathic help, but all of them were riveted to the unfolding contact. Finally, they had enough to understand that Favew was an original thinker who had been cast out of his community for expressing the opinion that there could be intelligent life in other galaxies. It was dangerous outside, and before long, the wild beasts would discover him and consume him. Rather than give them that satisfaction, he was ready to step off the edge.

"Not anymore!" Noe said firmly. "We'll help you somehow."

"Thank you," the translator said colorfully.

Yes, Noe was definitely a positive influence.

It further developed that there were factions among the Droms, which Nydia thought of as liberal and conservative, though that was likely a bad guess. The conservatives did not believe that there was any sapience anywhere else in the universe, and when they got in power, they'd made it a crime to express any contrary opinion. Thus Favew, a liberal activist, had been promptly banned. It had seemed to be his termination. That had insulated him from fear of the visitors, since he was doomed anyway.

Recently the elements had been acting up, just as in Xanth, and in this section fires were raging, coming ever closer to the settlement despite efforts to douse it. Flame nodded; this was his department.

It was Nydia's turn. She faced Favew, making it plain she was addressing him. She used more words rather than fewer to give the translator a better chance to make connections. "We are here on a special mission. I believe we can help each other. We can, I think, restore your position among your people by demonstrating both our foreign galaxy origin and our control over fire. You in turn may be able to help us find our way to the Demoness Andromeda, with whom we need to talk." Of course, Vinia's paths showed the way, but socially it was another problem. It was best to get along with the natives. They could certainly use a Drom ally.

The translator beeped and flashed, handling her words. Then Favew responded with more special effects. "Perhaps. But there is a monster between us and town. It was stalking me. It will prevent our access."

"Describe this monster," Flame said grimly.

There were more sounds and flashes. "Much larger than me. Of Drom general nature, but malicious and deadly. My void orifice I use only for eating. Its orifice is its weapon. It will take in anything in range."

Void orifice? Evidently the translator was having trouble with *mouth*.

Vol smiled. "We shall see."

Nydia was appreciating having the Elements along more and more, and not just because she was committed to one. They could handle things that normal folk could not.

There seemed to be no day or night here. The planet GEH was locked to its primary, not rotating, not changing. "Some of us need to sleep," Nydia said diplomatically. "Preferably with darkness. Is there a suitable cave nearby?" A cave had been their salvation at the start of this adventure.

"Cave, yes," the translator said. "But estivation is not safe. Monsters come."

Nydia glanced at the Elements. "We have guardians."

Favew led them to a mountain slope where the mouth of a large cave opened. There was darkness in its recesses and a crack in the floor not too wide, but reassuringly deep. An underground river formed a small waterfall into one end of the crack. "This will do for sleep, functions, and a cleansing shower," Nydia said. "But we still need food."

"On it," Vinia said, focusing. She pointed. "That way."

Nydia discovered the sword in her hand. Had she drawn it, or had Knight Knife volunteered? Regardless, it did buttress her courage. She was almost beginning to like the feel of being a warrior lass.

They followed Vinia to a patch of fern-like plants that had fruits vaguely resembling fruitcakes. Nydia plucked one and bit into it. The taste was odd but not repulsive. "Oyster soup–flavored chocolate cake," she concluded. "With green candy corn–flavored frosting and maybe just a tinge of horseradish." There were also colored water balls that turned out to be bacon-flavored drinks. She would have preferred old-fashioned boot rear, but couldn't be choosy in a foreign galaxy. The water did not splash to the ground when touched; it had a surface tension that held it together the same way Favew's water sections did. They drank by putting their lips to the surface and sucking. ·

They decided that would do. At least it was edible. Anthem Ant nibbled on some cake and liked it, sounding a chord of appreciation. "This is, I think, the oddest adventure yet."

"I think I am developing a taste for weird," Nydia said.

In due course they returned to the cave, and the ladies and men took turns performing their ablutions and settling down for the makeshift night. The five Elements stayed with their partners, though they had no need of food or sleep. They helped make tent-like enclosures for privacy, complete with fern bedding. Vinia and Noe took one together. Nydia realized that the two were becoming friends, being of similar age and not really attached to males, at least while on the Quest.

When they were alone together, Nydia stripped away her clothes and wrapped her arms about Vol. "This is the one skill I started with. Let me know if you get bored."

He clasped her with enthusiasm. "You are everything I lacked. I have not been lonely or bored since I met you."

She kissed him avidly. "Me neither." In fact, his acquaintance was fulfilling her in ways she had not imagined at the outset of the Quest. The nightly memory erasure of the Retreat was actually a mercy, making each day a new experience instead of deadly dull repetition. Now each day really was a new and wonderful experience.

If any predators approached the cave during the break, they lacked the gumption to try to enter it. That was surely just as well—for them. Nothing with any sense risked riling the Elements, regardless of the galaxy.

In the "morning," they resumed traveling. As they walked, Nydia looked around, admiring the scenery. This world might be essentially pancake-flat, but close up, it was vaguely like Xanth or Mundania, with hills and fields, forests of ferns, mountains in the background, rivers, and lakes. Natural paths wound between the sights, as if making sure they would be properly appreciated. Scenery did not like to be ignored. The sky differed, being a bright carpet of stars carefully arranged in alien constellations, but she hardly noticed it while her gaze was on the ground. There were scurries as small wildlife fauna sought cover, flashing their lenses, and jet-propelled bird-like creatures flew in the air and perched on the branches of the larger ferns. It was all very natural, in its fashion. Nydia reminded herself that it *was* natural for this galaxy and planet.

They crested a moderate mountain that put on a nice valley view beyond. Favew formed an extension and pointed. "There is Politan." That was the name they had decided to give the Drom settlement. Metro-politan.

They all looked. In the distance was a formidable stone wall, with guards spaced along it, their lenses flashing warningly. Any creature or person approaching it would soon be spied and stopped, if unapproved. Behind the wall were fern trunk houses, where the citizens could surely sleep or estivate in comfort and safety.

Then something else appeared between them and the town. It was large, with a big void-maw. It sounded a nasty note and flashed a forceful flare. The monster! It meant to intercept and consume them.

"Draw me," Knight Knife told Nydia. "I can slay it."

"But this isn't ordinary flesh," she protested. "It might suck you in and abolish you."

That made him pause. Nothingness was not an enemy he was used to.

"Let's make a demonstration," Flame said. He strode out to meet the monster, Noletta following. It reared up to face him, for all that it had no face. There was a howl of wind flying into its vacuum-void snout.

"Do you have a small telescope?" Nydia asked Vol.

He handed her one. She put it to an eye and trained it on the town beyond. Sure enough, the guards had seen the monster and were watching it. They would observe the coming action. That was part of the point.

Flame faced the monster, whose business end was taller than he was. The noise of deadly suction increased. The small ferns nearby leaned toward the void-mouth, blown by the inrush of air. Flame gestured. A ball of fire struck the snout, burning off the tip.

The monster howled in pain. At least, that was how the translator rendered its flashes. Then the orifice doubled in size. The circle of vacuum expanded. Chunks of fern flew into the hole. Noletta's blouse almost tore off her torso, flashing glimpses of her underwear. Nydia knew that this display bothered her not at all. Nymphs were made to be looked at; they had it and flaunted it. The males of the party had the sense to avert their gazes.

Flame gestured again. A much bigger and more intense ball of fire struck the snout, burning off its whole end. Ashes dropped to the ground as the wind faded.

The monster belatedly realized that it was overmatched. It retreated, sliding backwards along the ground. Flame followed, tweaking it with further jolts, prodding it along toward the wall. Nydia, watching through the telescope, saw the guards watching too, clearly impressed. This stranger was openly toying with the monster, treating it with contempt.

Finally the monster slid off to the side, abjectly fleeing. Flame goosed it once more, scorching its tail, and let it go. He turned to face the other members of the Quest. Noletta beckoned.

It was indeed time. Nydia strode forth, joined by Vol. "Let's go meet the Droms!" she called.

They advanced on the town, Favew among them. This, too, was a message: he had found powerful friends.

They came to the wall. "Hail, Droms!" Nydia called. The translator reappeared in Vol's hands, making its flashes and sounds. The lenses of the Droms oriented on it, surprised. The weird aliens were speaking their language! "We are visitors from another galaxy. We have special powers, as you have seen. We mean you no harm. We just want to talk with you. We are on a mission that could save much mischief for both our galaxy and yours. Will you invite us in?"

The guards looked at each other with their forming lenses. Then an evident leader appeared, flashing a light. "We will converse with you," the translator agreed.

"That is the conservative leader," Favew flashed quietly.

Soon they were in a central court, facing out toward the massed Droms. "Who are you and what is your mission?" the leader asked via the translator.

Now was the essence. They wanted the cooperation of the natives, and that should be decided within the hour. "I am Nydia, a woman of the human persuasion in the galaxy we call the Milky Way. These are my companions in the Quest. The elements of Fire, Water, Air, Earth, and the Void are being disturbed, causing much mischief. The agent of that disturbance seems to be here in the Andromeda Galaxy, so we have come here to try to deal with it. We note that the Element of Fire is causing similar mischief here, so if we stop it in the Milky Way, it should also stop here. Are you with us in this objective?"

"No," the leader flashed.

Nydia had opened her mouth to continue, but got caught in a surprising pause. She forced it away. "No? Why?"

"Because you have to be fakes, wasting our attention."

A spot of annoyance hovered near. Nydia brushed it aside as nonproductive. She needed to steer a steady course, governed not by emotion but by her mission. "Why do you suppose we are false?"

"Because there is no sapient life in the foreign galaxy."

"Steady," Anthem said, playing calming music. "They banned Favew because he said there could be such life."

Ah, yes. They were flashing nonsense, but she had to meet it with sense. "And what evidence do you have to that effect?"

"We don't need evidence. Everyone knows there is none there."

"They are locked in," Anthem said. "They don't want to believe."

Nydia saw it. The Droms were in denial, not about to accept anything contrary to their mythology. They were wrong, but refused to see it. How could she fight that?

Rob caught her eye, mentally. She tuned in on his telepathy. "Oakley says there is one tangible difference they can't refute, obviously. Gender."

The Droms were unisexual. The members of the Quest, and indeed most others of their galaxy, were two-sexed. That was indeed a difference.

Nydia plunged in. "We are sapient, obviously. We come from the other galaxy. We have one quality you lack that can't be faked. We are dual-sexed. That is, we have two distinct sexes."

"So you say," the leader flashed. "But saying is not proving."

He was determined to deny it. She would have to plunge in completely. "I am female. My partner is male. This we can demonstrate."

"By pretending your body designs differ? So do ours, superficially. Not persuasive."

"No pretense. I am a woman. My companion is a man. This is not superficial." She was referring to their physical bodies, not their mental ones. She was actually a nymph, he an Element.

The leader was dismissive. "Prove it."

Nydia had spent her time since escaping the Retreat crafting herself into a woman. A significant aspect of that was modesty. Not flaunting her feminine assets publicly, merely offering hints around the edges, such as cleavage and brief panty glimpses. She had made significant progress in decency. Was she to throw that away?

Rob connected her mind to Ecstasy. "Yes, in this circumstance," the woman said. "Part of being a woman is to do what a woman has to do, and do it well, regardless of its nature. This can on occasion be a challenge."

So be it. Nydia nerved herself, then flung off her clothing and stood naked in her nymphly splendor. She saw some males in their party narrowing their gazes so as to avoid freaking out. She did have the body. Vol also stripped beside her. He, as an Element, lacked the social fear, and could follow her lead without difficulty. "Come inspect us," she said as evenly as she could manage. "You have nothing like it here."

Lenses formed and focused. Tendrils reached out to touch their skin. Nydia tried to keep her flesh from recoiling. She had to let them verify the reality. There were fundamental distinctions between the sexes, and these were not imaginary.

The leader still held out. "You could be crafted to make a false case. A special exhibit."

Now Noletta spoke. "We are all male and female." She flung off her own clothing, surely with less concern than Nydia, and Flame did the same. Ecstasy followed suit, and Oakley joined her. Then Santo and Noe.

Soon there were seven naked couples on exhibit, half of the participants male, half female. Only the children and Lilith remained apart, and of course Anthem Ant. There could be no further doubt.

"And there are the tunnels," Rob thought. "They can bleeping well use them to verify our origin for themselves."

Why hadn't she thought of that before? They could have spared themselves this embarrassment. "We came here by tunnel," Nydia said to the Droms. "One leads to the edge of your galaxy. The other leads to our own galaxy. Any of you can pass through them and see for yourselves what is beyond them." She glanced about, spying the nonparticipants. "Lilith will show them to you."

The demoness gestured. "This way."

The Droms actually did it. Volunteers flashed. Several of their number went to join Lilith. Rob followed the party telepathically, relaying news of its progress. They found the tunnels and entered them. They visited Xanth and were amazed not just about the presence of two sexes. Soon their report was in: affirmative.

There was a quick vote. Suddenly not only was Favew vindicated, he was the leader of Politan.

"Now we shall have a civil dialog with our neighbors from the other galaxy," he said with abiding satisfaction. "First, we need to provide them with a suitable residence during their stay here."

They set about it, the Droms now as dedicated to welcoming the visitors as they had been against it before. The politics had changed.

Soon the members of the Quest were ensconced in a multiple suite approximately similar to the one they had had in the Queendom of Thanx. Details differed, such as toilet accommodations, as the Droms did not eliminate in the same way, but overall it would do.

The evening meal was something else. The Droms sucked in nutritive mist, while the Questers settled for local berries and water. The point was not the food but the occasion.

Then came a serious session. Nydia clarified their mission, concluding, "So we need to reach the Demoness Andromeda and find out why she is messing up the Elements, and persuade her to stop. This may be a doomed operation, but we have to try."

"We are suffering too," Favew flashed. "Our land is being ravaged by fire, and we know the other lands are suffering from other elements. Other planets here as well. It is not just your galaxy. We don't believe it is the Demoness. She is helpless."

"A capital D Demoness can't be helpless!"

"Unless constrained by a Demon bet or the equivalent."

Oh. Nydia paused, assimilating this. "We know Demons make bets with each other for status, using mortals to help decide issues. It is like wagering that an ant will turn one way or the other. But this is way beyond that."

"Way beyond," Favew agreed. "Perhaps our mythology will clarify it."

"Ants do make turns," Anthem murmured. "In reality as well as mythology."

"Mythology!" Nydia exclaimed. Was he joking?

"Steady," Rob cautioned mentally. "I am unable to follow Drom thoughts well, but this is serious and probably relevant."

So it seemed. She needed to maintain an open mind, even for the unlikely. "Perhaps we should learn this mythology."

"Maybe we can experience it, in our fashion," Ecstasy said. "Let Rob unify us mentally, putting us in the scene the way I gather Anthem did when you explored Nerine's past. It may be the best way to learn the whole story efficiently. Nuances can count."

This method could perhaps pick up the feel of it, as well as the narrative. Nydia did appreciate Nerine's story better because of experiencing it herself, as it were. She looked around. "Shall we try?"

There was general agreement. The others might be as uncertain about mythology as Nydia was, but the Quest was in largely uncharted territory and could not afford to dismiss anything.

Nydia closed her eyes as the scene took hold, so that it seemed she had them open in a new venue, in the manner of a dream. As a nymph she had not dreamed, but as a woman she did. Now she was a Demon girl, secretly listening as her parents talked in the next chamber. She knew Demons were timeless and had no families as such, and Droms had no girls as such, but this was also a story of human-seeming folk. Demons might have no gender either, being creatures of the underlying forces of the universe, but for this purpose they did, and it was convenient to experience this as a girl. Others could fit into their roles as was comfortable for them.

"It's bad," her father Cepheus was saying. He was the king of the country, so his alarm meant that something really serious was afoot. Nydia recognized the voice of Oakley playing this role. "Poseidon, god of the sea, is really angry."

"All because I compared myself to his daughters, the Nereids, in beauty?" her mother Cassiopeia asked. That was the voice of Ecstasy, who, as the loveliest member of the Quest, was obviously suited to this role. "That was figurative, actually a compliment, because the truth is that I am lovelier than those sea spawn are."

"But he is a god. Gods don't like being compared to mortals, except to show how superior they are to them. His pride is pricked, and now he seeks revenge."

"So he is throwing a fit," she said derisively. "Like a balked child. What can he do, since we are not creatures of the sea?"

"He has caused floods to harm our land and a sea monster to ravage our coast. The damage is horrendous. Our people are suffering. We cannot oppose him. We have to appease him somehow."

Cassiopeia began to be concerned. "Appease him? How?"

"The word from the Oracle is that only the sacrifice of our most beautiful woman to the sea monster will suffice."

Cassiopeia froze. "But that means—"

Cepheus nodded. "He wants revenge on you for supposedly insulting his daughters. He is going to keep on harassing us until he gets it."

She sighed. "If that is the way it must be, I am ready."

Cepheus/Oakley was horrified. "But you're my wife and the woman I love!"

"I may nevertheless have overstepped in this case. I do not want our kingdom to suffer grievously because of a stupid god's misinterpretation."

He put on a canny look. "There may be a loophole. You are not specifically named, only the most beautiful woman. There just might be a prettier girl somewhere in the kingdom."

"Doubtful," she said seriously. "You married me because I was the prettiest."

"I did indeed, and so you were, and so you are today. But that was twenty years ago, and though you have kept your beauty, popular fancy has it that youth is a significant aspect of it. There just might possibly be a girl who did not exist then, who is now as lovely as you were, as well as being young. She just might do for the sacrifice."

Cassiopeia/Ecstasy considered, moved by the distant chance of survival. "We must hold a beauty contest of all the girls in the kingdom. Maybe a candidate is there."

"That was my thought."

Andromeda/Nydia turned away, covering the knothole that was her listening post. She had heard enough. Her mother was undeniably beautiful, but tended to speak too freely, and on occasion there were consequences. This was such an occasion. Now it was going to lead to the horrible death of some innocent girl. But what could she do? She was only a princess without power. She merely officiated at royal events, more show than substance. That would change when she became queen, but that could be a long time hence.

They announced the contest without revealing its ultimate purpose. The girls of the kingdom flocked to it, each hoping to be crowned the loveliest. Andromeda saw to the arrangements as the girls were systematically sorted, winnowing out the losers who were not as beautiful as they had believed or hoped. If only they knew that the ultimate loser would be the winner.

At last there were six finalists: interpreted as Noletta, Nerine, Anthem Ant in human illusion, Wanda Wand, Noe, and Lilith. All lustrous maidens. Nydia herded them to the judges' stand, where Flame, Flood, and Moonroe sat. "But it is traditional to have seven competitors for the final ballot," Moonroe protested.

Oops. One of the finalists had been disqualified for suspicion of irrelevance, and in the press of arrangements, Nydia had not thought to get a replacement.

"No problem," Flame said. "Andromeda, kindly step into the lineup."

What? "But I'm the organizer, not a candidate," Nydia protested. "I'm not even garbed for show." Indeed, the contestants were in elaborate gowns, with lustrous tresses, while she was in utility clothing with her hair in a bedraggled bun.

"Your status has changed," Flood said. "We are capable of assessing beauty regardless of the garb."

Embarrassed by her error and dishabille, Nydia stepped into the lineup. Now it was complete.

The trio of judges questioned the maidens closely, including Andromeda, and had them assume particular poses. It seemed ludicrous to pose in work wear, though she did unbind her hair. She had to at least pretend to be a competitor. Then they decided.

"The winner is Princess Andromeda," Flame announced. "She far outshines the others and is indeed the loveliest maiden in the Kingdom."

What? Was he joking?

"No," Rob said in her mind. "True beauty makes even the most rudimentary clothing shine. Only so-so ladies need exterior enhancement. You certainly don't. They are correct."

There was applause. The throng of spectators agreed. She had the honor of representing the kingdom. She would save it from the dreadful ravaging. She was the heroine of the day.

Cassiopeia was in tears. Her slip of the tongue had doomed her daughter. But there was nothing she could do at this stage.

Nydia was duly feted, then quietly conducted to the shore and chained by an ankle to a massive rock at the edge of the sea. Her feet touched the surface of the deep water, for this was the channel the massive monster would use. All she had to do was wait for it to sniff out the bait. That would not take long, as such things went.

She was doomed.

They emerged from the mythology. Now they understood that Andromeda was the chained lady, set out as a sacrifice for the monster. She had been there for eons, but time was largely meaningless to Demons. It might as well have been yesterday or tomorrow.

Now they also understood that the agitation of the Elements was merely a peripheral effect of the larger situation. It was because the approach of the monster disturbed the fundamental nature of local reality. When the behemoth arrived and feasted, things would settle down.

Andromeda was less the cause than the effect. Once her mother had spoken carelessly, the end result was locked in. Similar problems would have resulted had any other maiden been sacrificed.

Would the mischief really stop when Andromeda died, or suffered whatever it was that happened when a Demon was sacrificed? And if it did, when would that be in mortal terms? A century hence? A thousand years? A million? Would there be anything left of the world as they knew it?

They had assembled a formidable team for any nearly normal purpose. Did it make any sense to disband it unused?

"The notion rankles," Anthem said with a somber note.

"It does indeed," Wanda said.

"I wish a thrust of my blade could destroy the idea," Knife Knight said. "But this is beyond my power."

She agreed with the three of them. Something needed to be done. But what?

"You're the protagonist," Anthem said with a more positive tone. "That means you are the one in a position to do something."

"If you can only figure out what it is," Wanda said.

Nydia formulated a conclusion. "We've got to save Andromeda. She is blameless here."

"Yet Andromeda is a Demoness," Ecstasy reminded her. "We are hardly even ants in comparison."

"Literally," Anthem said with an ironic pitch.

Ecstasy smiled, evidently picking up on the thought. "No offense intended. What can we do?"

"I have no idea," Nydia confessed. "But we have to try."

"Try what?"

"We have to get to Andromeda and ask her what we can do. She should know, if anyone does. She has surely thought about it and has motive."

"Surely so," Ecstasy agreed.

There seemed to be next to no point in further arguing the case. If they did nothing, the awful mischief would continue. The chance of an ant was better than no chance at all.

"Amen," Anthem agreed with a background of distant hopeful music.

Meanwhile they soon learned that mischief was striking home more immediately. A raging fire was sweeping down on the town, too fierce for any Droms to attempt to oppose.

"That, at least, we can abate," Noletta said. She glanced at Flame. "If you are quite through crowning Nydia the winning beauty instead of me, despite her not being dressed for it, and sending her to be consumed by a monster, how about dealing with that fire?"

Flame smiled, knowing she was teasing. "Immediately."

They marched out to meet the onrushing conflagration. Flame lifted a hand in a "halt" gesture. The fire froze in place. Then he waved it back, and the fire obediently retreated. Finally he made a gesture of dousing, and the fire fizzled out. Nothing was left but steaming sod.

The Droms focused their lenses on it, amazed.

"Now we can move on," Noletta said.

"But the fire will soon reanimate once you are gone," Favew flashed.

"True." She considered briefly. "Flame and I may simply have to stay here and stifle it. It will also give us more time alone together." She glanced meaningfully at Flame, then looked at Nydia. "Agreed?"

It did make sense. "You had better stay," Nydia agreed. "We can pick you up on our return trip once we have dealt with the monster." As if that were mere routine.

They hugged each other in parting while the Droms' flashing lenses showed they were amazed in another sense. These galactic visitors had strange customs.

"I believe I had better accompany you," Favew flashed. "The translator is not perfect, and I think I know you sufficiently now to help navigate confusions. The mission is also important enough to warrant my direct attention."

Nydia glanced at Vinia. "Green?"

"Bright green," the girl agreed. Beside her, Noe nodded. That was her impression too.

"We are glad to have you with us," Nydia said sincerely.

Then the rest of the Quest marched on toward the next section of the captive planet.

Chapter 11

CONTACTS

They came to the edge of a sea. The purple water rippled in the coastal breeze, with white specks reflecting the canopy of stars above. Beyond it, the far shore was visible, low near the water, with mountains behind. It could have passed for local Xanth scenery except—

"Purple?" Nerine asked, bemused. She was a creature of the water, now land-bound; she noticed.

"This is the color of open water," Favew flashed via the translator. "Is it not the same in your galaxy?"

"Only if there is blood in it," Nerine said with most of a wince.

Then they had to explain about blood because Droms did not have it. Favew was polite, but it was apparent that the concept vaguely repulsed him.

Nydia found herself gazing at the canopy. There was something about it, apart from its brightness. She was accustomed to having light from a single close star rather than a monstrous mat of them, but that wasn't it. Nor was it the lack of any proper night; she understood about that. Something else. But what? The answer danced just out of mental reach.

"It's that you can almost see the near stars moving faster than the far stars," Rob said, picking up on her thought. "The way leaves in the water of a whirlpool accelerate as they get closer to the center." He, as a creature normally close to the ground, was attuned to such effects.

"Yes, that's it," she said, relieved. She must have picked up on the slow internal shifting of the glowing mat without being conscious of it.

"So that's why I kept looking up," Noletta said. "I thought I was getting nutty in this unusual setting."

"Me too," Nerine agreed. "We're feeling the vortex."

"You three are the un-nuttiest nymphs I've met," Moonroe said.

"And how many have you met?" Oakley asked, with five-eights of a smile. The remaining three-eights brushed by the other members of the group, causing their lips to twitch just below visibility.

Enough of this. "Time for the carpet," Nydia said, bringing it out.

"Carpet?" Favew asked.

That, of course, led to another explanation and demonstration. Favew was evidently amazed; his culture lacked flying carpets, which was not surprising in a region largely devoid of magic. But he had a caution: it would be better to use the established boat system, as crossovers between sections were monitored and travelers duly checked in. The arrival of a flying carpetful of weird aliens could set off an ugly confrontation.

"Good point," Nydia agreed, appreciating again the advantage of having a native in their party. They wanted to appear as native as possible, at least in attitude.

They followed Favew to the established boat dock, where a Drom hailed them. He had gotten news about the visitors, so did not have a problem other than slight awe at their proximity, as his flickering lens hinted. They boarded the ferry, a broad, flat craft like a raft that was hauled smartly along by submerged cables. No need to wait on whimsical winds. Of course, Aery could have summoned some, but that would have further advertised her alien nature.

Something showed in the distant water, approaching rapidly. It looked like the head of a sea serpent, with a dangerous sucking snout. Did it see them as a plateful of snacks? Nydia suspected that they would not taste very good, being abundantly foreign, but didn't want to test the case.

"I will slice off its snoot if it comes within range," Knight Knife said.

"If it doesn't vacuum you up first," Wanda said. "Best to let the natives handle it."

The boat guide had an instrument on the prow. He flashed at it, and it responded by orienting on the serpent and emitting a dappled overripe beam. It splatted the monster on the snout, sending it into a paroxysm of apparent nausea. The creature quickly submerged and was not seen again.

"What a foul stench," Moonroe muttered with another fractional smile. "Worse than rotten cheese."

"A mottled green noise," Oakley agreed.

Nydia felt vaguely nauseous herself. Even the translator looked a bit ill. What a problem a direct strike by that beam must be!

"We do have our ways," Favew flashed.

They arrived safely at the dock. The two Droms aboard flashed explanations to the harbor guard, who flashed understanding. There was no trouble, and soon the party was on its way across this island or continent, guided by Vinia's invisible green path. No new Droms were with them; it seemed that travelers were generally left alone to fend for themselves if they did not cause mischief.

It was wet. The land was faintly purple with recent rain, and there were puddles, pools, and ponds in all the hollows. They had to navigate carefully to find a route between them, and their feet were sticky with mud. Purplish clouds hovered low, as if awaiting their chance to strike when least convenient. Nydia thought of Fracto, back in Xanth, who reveled in raining on parades. Could he have a cousin here?

"Uh-oh," Vinia said. "Mischief we can't avoid."

"We can't back off and take another route?" Nydia asked, dismayed.

"No. The paths are mixed, but there's one that can't be denied. We have to take it." She took a breath. "It's not dangerous to us, just complicated."

"We trust your paths," Noe said encouragingly.

Yes, they did. "We'll take it," Nydia said.

Ahead loomed a dense, deep purple storm. Nerine nudged her companion. "I can abate that," Flood said.

"No," Vinia said. "The green says we have to go into it."

Flood shrugged. He had offered.

They had no choice but to forge through it, getting soaked in rain that looked like fresh grape juice. Water coursed to either side, and they had to splash through shallow purple puddles. Fortunately, Vinia was able to keep them on a safe route. There were no hungry monsters. Maybe they didn't like to get wet.

There was a faint flash ahead. "That's a Drom," Favew flashed. "In trouble. It's a distress signal."

"That's where the path goes," Vinia said.

They came to a rushing river. It seemed to have two channels. A Drom was trapped on a kind of island between them. The water was eating away at the sand. Soon the Drom would be caught and washed away.

"A damsel in distress," Moonroe said with a faint echo of his former smile. The Droms were unisexual, but this did seem to fit the case.

Vinia glanced at Flood. "Now use your power."

"Gladly." He gestured and the storm froze between them and the trapped Drom. The river also halted as if abruptly frozen. They walked across, tramping on solidified warm water, Favew leading. He flashed to the other Drom. She flashed back. Nydia was glad yet again that a native was with them because otherwise the other Drom would have feared an alien invasion.

They reached the island. Favew had a flashing dialog with the other Drom, the translator picking up only fragments. Then he addressed the group. "This is Wavef. She studies the environment. Her town of Metro is threatened by flooding, so she went out to investigate, trying to determine what is causing the disruption. She got so absorbed in the study that she forgot to make sure she had a safe escape route, and got caught when the river sprouted a second channel behind her. She was afraid she was doomed until we came. She is amazed by the way you froze the water in place without it being cold; she knew then that you were no ordinary creatures. I explained that you are friends from another galaxy with peculiar powers. She is partly reassured."

Which made sense, Nydia realized. It was hardly possible to trust outright alien creatures at the outset. They could be anything from curious passersby to downright killers. How could she reassure this person?

Noe stepped up to join them. "Hello. I am Noe, a person of no account. I assure you that we mean you no harm, Wavef. We are up against the same problem you are in our galaxy, and came here in significant part to discover the cause and deal with it. We're really on the same team. We can certainly use your expertise, and hope you will agree to help us."

Nydia saw Santo faintly nodding, and Favew, too, in subdued flashing. Just as Noe had helped them relate to Favew, she was now helping them with Wavef. Noe's name might mean nothing, but that was deceptive. She was something. She was doing what Nydia herself should have done: establishing what they all had in common.

Meanwhile, Flood gestured at the storm surrounding their position, and it grudgingly faded out. The landscape remained soaked, but no more water was falling.

Soon Wavef was indeed merging with the group. Still, she stayed close to Favew, the one familiar person there, although they had no prior acquaintance. She had studied the larger situation and clarified it for them, approximately assisted by Rob's telepathy. "The planet of GEH has five main sections, each dominated by an Element. At one end it is Fire, followed by ours, Water, then Air, Earth, and Void. Hitherto we have coped with mainly background phenomena, but recently, they have magnified and are causing us real distress. We need to discover what is agitating them before they do us significant harm." Her flashes paused briefly. "This is true elsewhere in the galaxy too. We observe and are in touch with other planets, which are similarly changing. I believe that something is affecting the black hole that is the center of our galaxy, causing it to flicker. That effect may be minor for the black hole, but it is devastating to we folk on the fringe of it."

Now Nydia spoke. "I am Nydia Nymph, the leader of our Quest, oriented on the same purpose. Are you familiar with the Andromeda mythology?"

There was a dark flash. "I place no credence in mythology. It attempts to explain natural phenomena in a manner that appeals to the more ignorant among us, but I am a scientist."

Already Nydia liked this person better. "We agree, in general. But our home world is governed by magic rather than science, and it is possible that magic is significant in this galaxy of yours also. Mythology relates more closely to magic than to science. The story of Princess Andromeda chained as a sacrifice to a monster becomes more persuasive in this context. The approach of the monster might account for the fluxes in the black hole."

Wavef paused thoughtfully. "This is an alternate manner of thinking. If I assume that magic is like a different kind of science, I can begin to make sense of it. But what kind of monster could it be?"

"A giant black hole. Its approach could be disturbing the existing black holes in our vicinity, making them flicker."

"So it could," Wavef agreed in flashing wonder. "But it seems demented to think that such a phenomenon could be sent here because of personal spite. The universe is not a living thing."

"Can we be sure it's not? We know so little of what is beyond our immediate grasp, let alone beyond our world or galaxy."

There were more thoughtful flashes. "We do indeed! We cannot afford to be limited by our ignorance. Assuming for the sake of this dialog that this myth is the case, what possible way could there be to save Andromeda?"

Nydia saw the others staying out of it. It was up to her to suggest an answer, however far-fetched it might be. Fortunately, the effect of the elixir of the Ein Stein remained, keeping her smart. She was able to draw from her template, assembling incidental facts into a larger speculation whose complexities would have wiped out her belief had she paused for sensible consideration. So she didn't pause. "Five of the members of this Quest are personifications of Elements. One remained in this planet's fire section to control the fires there, saving the people. Another is Water, whose power you have witnessed. The chained maiden, Andromeda, is the personification of Change or Flux. She is outstandingly beautiful. The monster could even be the black hole from which the universe itself sprang long ago. Perhaps it is hungry for the kind of beauty it lacks. Maybe we need to persuade it not to consume, but instead to marry Andromeda, making that beauty its own. In the mythology, she married her rescuer, but we can try to make the monster her rescuer instead. Once it is satisfied, the local fluxes should stop, saving the rest of us."

"Marry?"

Uh-oh. "It is a long-term commitment our kind makes, wherein two people agree to associate closely and raise a family together."

"Oh, we do something similar. Because juveniles require protection and attention."

"Exactly. If the monster marries Andromeda, it won't consume her. Instead, it would become her protector."

"And you mentioned personifications of Elements. This does not make sense to me."

"I have a special wand that can conjure the essence or spirit of something into a selected body, providing it with intelligence and feeling. My companion Vol is the personification of the Void. Voids still exist, here and in our own galaxy, but lack that awareness."

Wavef's lens flickered briefly on Vol. "Perhaps it is best that those other Voids remain bodyless and unconscious."

"I agree. Vol is all I can handle."

Wavef's lens tilted slightly as she looked at Nydia, evidently an expression of marvel. "You interest me. You are making nonsense almost palatable."

Indeed. "Meanwhile, we have more immediate problems to handle. Such as seeing to the survival of your species and ours. Should we visit your town and see what we can do for your folk?"

"Maybe we should," Wavef flashed.

They set off for the town of Metro, Wavef and Favew leading the way with the agreement of Vinia's green paths. The route was devious because of the pools collected all around, but there was always a way through.

They came to a massive dam that was barely containing its brimming water. "This is the last of a series of dikes we use to shield our town," Wavef explained. "Recent heavy rains have filled the others to their bursting points, literally. When this one goes, there will be no further protection for Metro."

Flood stared at it. The water sank until the lakebed was empty. It did not drain, it simply faded. "That should help for a few days," he said.

"But what about thereafter? The rains have been almost continuous."

"What indeed," Nerine said thoughtfully

Nydia saw the way of it. Flood and Nerine would be staying here to protect the town while the others moved on.

They came to the settlement. The outer wall resembled the dam they had passed, massive and tight. There was no entrance gate, but rather an elevated track that rose up over the wall and on down inside. Water could not use that to get in. But if it ever did get in, perhaps by spilling over the lowest section, the town would become a vast bowl of purple soup.

Wavef and Favew ascended the track and met with the guards at the top. Then they flashed back to the Quest members. "Come on over!"

Yes, it was really good to have natives representing them.

There followed a meeting with the equivalent of the town elders, facilitated by the improving translator and Rob's telepathy. Wavef described Flood's magic with water, and Favew told of the visitors' origin in the other galaxy. Then Nydia described their mission to ease the fluxes in the black holes and make the survival of all creatures in both galaxies more likely. It was apparent that Wavef was held in high esteem, and her endorsement of the visitors was potent. But there were, of course, those who doubted, as their persistent flashes showed.

Then another storm surged toward the town, raining with such ferocity that water coursed everywhere inside and outside the wall. The indications were that it would continue indefinitely. Wavef was concerned. It was perfect timing for a demonstration.

Flood and Nerine walked out to the ramp and up to the top of the wall, shielded from the deluge by a seemingly invisible curtain of dryness that surrounded them. Then he raised his arms as if in prayer, and the torrent ceased. The cloud shrank like a punctured balloon and disappeared. The starshine of day resumed.

They returned to the meeting. Now Nerine spoke. "We realize that the rains will return when Flood departs. We love being part of the Quest, but as with Flame and Noletta, we are obliged to support it by making this sacrifice. So we are prepared to stay here with you, suppressing the weather, until the others succeed in eliminating the larger problem. Then we can return as a group to our home galaxy and world. Are you amenable?"

There was no hesitation, even from the prior naysayers. They wanted the protection that had been so dramatically demonstrated, and they would treat the couple like the honored guests they were.

Wavef elected to remain with the Quest, assisting with Drom contacts in the other sections. Nydia suspected she liked Favew, as well as the chance to do something positive about the weather.

They were given a suite similar to the one they had used in the prior town, and set about relaxing. Then Favew approached Nydia while the others were busy. She turned on the translator. "We have a private problem we do not wish to discuss in public," he flashed. "May we acquaint you with it and seek your input?"

"Of course," Nydia agreed, hoping it was not that he and Wavef had had second thoughts and decided to remain after all here in her home zone, deserting the Quest. Even in this brief acquaintance, she had come to know and like the Droms, and to value their assistance. But their participation in the Quest had to be voluntary. She braced herself to be accepting of their choice. "Come in."

Favew flashed backwards, and Wavef came forward to join him. They entered the apartment Nydia was sharing with Vol, who stood in the background observing. He was still learning the ways of human social interaction, much as the Droms were, and taking his cues from Nydia.

Now Wavef flashed. "First, background. As I understand it, our social conventions roughly parallel yours. We form couple bonds with those we find compatible and maintain them until the offspring we generate mature sufficiently to function independently. It is what you term romance; couples do enjoy the process of generating progeny. Other members of the community do not interfere with such commitments, lest they cause annoyance or a scandal. But those others do judge the likely viability of individual couples and treat them as they seem to deserve. Social approval is important."

"I understand," Nydia said. "The social aspect can be overwhelming." As with the general condemnation of nymphs as wantons good for Only One Thing. She still smarted from that former disapproval, though she had been unaware of it until she left the Retreat and learned of the larger realm. She did not like being a second-class citizen, even in retrospect.

"Normally, Droms remain with their peer groups until two are attracted to each other and become a couple. As a couple, they can travel from group to group, accepted. But two Droms who are not a couple do not associate closely outside the group. We both wish to travel with your unit, to assist in completing your Quest, as it affects all of us. This means we should become a couple to avoid social censure. But we hardly know each other, and prefer to remain apart until we understand each other well enough to decide on coupledom. We might discover differences that would negate a more personal relationship. We prefer to keep it a business association for the interim. This is a problem. We do not wish to have to choose between the mission and social acceptance."

Nydia realized that this would be like an unrelated human man and woman sharing a house without being married. They might have perfectly sensible reasons to do so. But that would be severely frowned on by the community, and the dread Adult Conspiracy, if the Droms had the equivalent, might strike in some awful way. It was a legitimate problem.

"We hope you can draw on your alien culture for some guidance," Wavef flashed. "You should be relatively objective, as we may not be."

Her supposed objectivity was turning out to be no help at all. Nydia simply had virtually no practical experience with social nuances, local or alien. Her commitment to Vol had been based on her need to recruit him as an Element and his need for supportive company. That had rapidly become love, but only because they were lucky. Luck was by definition chancy. These two needed more certainty, which they were sensible to seek. What to say to them?

"Clarify details," Anthem Ant suggested inaudibly. "Stall until something occurs." There was encouraging background music.

"Look for some new attack on the problem from an alternate direction, thus slaying it," Knight Knife said.

"Explore for something perhaps concealed by illusion," Wanda Wand said. "The problem itself may be illusory." She didn't think much of the Conspiracy, which she saw as a construct by folk who liked imposing their foibles on others.

Nydia considered their suggestions, which made sense according to their perspectives but not necessarily to hers, trying to meld them into a viable whole.

"Consider the larger picture," Vol said. "There may be special aspects that change its nature when considered." He had learned to pick up on her private companions, and got along with them. Anthem was reading his thoughts and presenting them as silent speech.

The larger picture included several couples, one of which was more apparent than real: Santo and Noe, and their social convenience. Where was there a useful analogy? Nydia was stumped.

Then the elements, as it were, connected. She knew what to say.

She said it. "On occasion, appearance may be more important than reality. For example, our culture's usual couples consist of one man and one woman. Remember, we have two sexes. But some relationships have two men or two women. Some folk condemn that, and that complicates general acceptance. So sometimes they, well, fake it. That is, they pretend. This is the case with Santo and Noe. Both of you know Noe, who is very accepting of unusual folk, as you are to us."

"Noe," the two flashed almost together. They liked her.

"We are all very much concerned with the salvation of our cultures and our worlds," Nydia continued. "If these are lost, the approval or disapproval of other members of our species will hardly matter. So the Quest really is more important. But appearances do count. So I recommend that you do as Santo and Noe do, and fake it until such time as you are able to make an informed couple decision. Even if you are not romantic in private, you both need understanding and support, and you can provide that for each other. Your relationship can be real, just not exactly what others assume it is."

The two focused their lenses on each other.

"Fake it," Favew flashed.

"Pretense," Wavef agreed.

Then both lenses oriented on Nydia. "This seems feasible," Favew flashed.

"Thank you," Wavef flashed.

The two departed. Nydia turned off the translator.

"Congratulations," Vol said, this time aloud. "You have empowered them much as you have me. You are a remarkable woman."

"Your advice helped," Nydia said, speaking to all of them. But her knees felt weak. It had been a close call. In the background—no, closer, the middle ground—was her private pleasure at being called a woman, not a nymph.

"Now kiss him," Wanda said. "His knees are strong."

Nydia had to laugh, internally. She went to Vol and soundly kissed him. That was just the beginning.

The boundary between the Water and Air sections of GEH was a brutal desert. Dry heat radiated from it. Windblown sand mercilessly pelted the barren landscape, and any dunes that might have considered forming had evidently been intimidated into nonexistence. The same was true of clouds; the sky was bare where it could be seen at all. There were no plants. There seemed to be no coherence. In fact, just venturing out into the desert could get their skins flayed by the flying sand. This was dangerous.

"Uh," Nydia said, but her thought, if she had one, was blown away before it could emerge.

"There is very little contact between our towns at present," Wavef flashed. "We get along with our Air Zone neighbors when we encounter them, but have to take advantage of random lulls in the action. There could be one in the next moment or the next eon."

"My turn," Aery said, her sky-blue hair and eyes firming.

"Ain't she something," Moonroe said admiringly.

"I haven't done anything yet," she snapped at him.

"I was referring to your appearance."

"That's the handiwork of Ecstasy. She made my body."

He took it in stride. "Nevertheless, your body reflects your spirit. I love it."

That stifled her retort. It was evident that he knew how to handle her.

Aery raised her arms in a "heed me" gesture. The wind abruptly halted. They would not be blown away as they crossed.

Except that it was still horrendously hot. Flame was no longer with them to cool it, nor was Flood. What were they to do?

"I am not finished," Aery said, answering Nydia's unspoken thought. "I have merely asserted control. Now I will use it to accomplish my purpose."

The others were silent and flashless, waiting to see what she had in mind.

Aery made complicated gestures, as if conducting a hidden orchestra, concluding with a whirl. The wind stirred, this time forming a circle. A sandy column formed as it accelerated. Was it a tornado? The column rose high into the sky, darkening. A spray of water flung out.

"Waterspout," Moonroe said. "I told you she had something cooking."

Indeed she did. Apparently the whirl was sucking moisture from the air above, as there was none below. The waterspout expanded, spraying droplets onto the ground. The sand hissed and steamed. And cooled. She had done it.

Nydia realized that the Elements were not entirely restricted to their own variants. A storm consisted of air and water, just as a fire needed air to breathe and a volcano needed fire to heat and move its rock.

The column moved across the desert, making a wet path. They stepped out on it. The sand was warm and wet, but not boiling. They could handle it.

They followed the waterspout across the desert. Along the way, Nydia saw monsters similar to the one Flame had driven off, pausing in place, as if uncertain what to make of this phenomenon. What indeed!

"What is that encumbrance on them?" Moonroe asked.

Now Nydia noticed. There was a sort of vine or rope attached to the solid portion of each monster, as if they had gotten tangled in something and been unable to shake it loose. Two of them, actually, with a smaller one above. That was curious, as the void suction head should have been able to eat it off.

"These are steeds," Wavef explained. "The Air Zone uses tamed monsters to navigate the desert, as they can handle it. The harness is embedded and can't be removed except by the use of specialized tools. It also can't be sucked, as it contains antimatter that will explode the creature's snout if there is direct contact. The steeds quickly learn to leave it alone. That is how the Air Zone citizens normally cross to contact us. But only in the lulls. Even so, the riders wear protective armor."

"Antimatter," Vol said, impressed. "They must have mastered the art of clothing it with neutral substance, which in turn would be clad with normal matter, so it can be safely handled."

"They have," Wavef agreed. "It's a process they reserve to themselves, trading clothed items to other zones for special items or favors."

"Favors?" Nydia asked.

"Some Droms are more physically appealing than others. They are able to put a price on breeding."

"Ah. We humans have similar variances. Ecstasy, for example, is extremely comely in our view."

"She obviously is," Oakley agreed. Ecstasy just smiled. She still enjoyed being stunning.

They moved on, leaving the steeds watching. In due course, they reached the far side of the desert, where mountain slopes led up to cooler air and vegetation. Now the alien ferns seemed comfortingly familiar. They paused to harvest some edible fruitcakes and waterballs, then moved on.

The wind had eased somewhat, but remained fairly stiff. The ferns grew braced against the constant air pressure. This was indeed the Air Zone.

Nydia noticed that Noe and Vinia were now walking together, being girls of similar age, while Lilith was beside Santo, in fairly constant dialog. Respect might actually be becoming friendship. Lilith's body might not fascinate him, but she had vast historical experience Santo could well find interesting. Woe Betide was back in her floating crib, tuning out the dull details of traveling. Apparently the two demonesses did not feel any special kinship. They had probably known each other, in one form or another, for eons, and needed no further interaction at the moment. The assorted members of the Quest were getting comfortable with one another.

They came to a more organized section where the ferns were planted in rows. A Drom was there. Favew and Wavef went ahead to meet him while the main group stayed back. There was no point in alarming an innocent local. There were flashes and sounds. To the farmer, it might be like two regular folk escorting a contingent of weird creatures. Well, that was close enough.

Favew turned his lens to Nydia to report. "He is a food farmer serving the local town. This path leads directly to it. He says there is some kind of disturbance or problem caused by the fluxes, so they are distracted, but will be courteous to polite visitors."

Nydia smiled. "We shall be polite." She hoped that the problem would not impede their progress across this zone.

Now the path descended into a mountain valley. When the massive town wall came into view, Favew and Wavef flashed it, and soon received responding flashes. By the time the group reached the wall, their nature and mission would be well understood.

It was. They were welcomed into the town. The wind stopped the moment they entered, cut off by the wall and solid stone barricades. The locals knew how to handle wind, at least in their solid enclosure.

The problem turned out to be a recent storm of unprecedented force that blew away the enclosures for the steeds used to cross the desert. The creatures were essentially wild because fully tame ones soon lost their capability to handle the desert effectively. So when the enclosures went, the steeds bolted. Now they were wary, avoiding any townsfolk who tried to approach them. They still wore their harnesses, but those were useless without riders. The steeds needed to be caught and corralled; then they would behave. In fact, the capture of one steed would do it: the leader. The others would follow him. The proprietors did not want to risk hurting him or any other steed because that would make them less useful. A trained steed was valuable.

"We should help them," Rob said telepathically. "It would make for excellent intergalactic relations."

"Surely so," Oakley agreed. "But this is obviously not our field of expertise."

"Unfortunately," Moonroe agreed.

"We remaining Elements have powers," Eartha said. "But taming alien steeds is not among them."

"It seems the answer is blowing in the wind," Aery said with a smile.

"We do have to be practical," Ecstasy said. "We can't do everything ourselves."

"I hate to pass up a chance to assist our friends," Noe said.

"You're dithering," Lilith said. "Sometimes you just have to accept your mortal or elemental limits." Santo, beside her, nodded.

Nydia wanted to help. But how? She knew nothing about riding any steed, let alone an alien monster with deadly suction. She doubted that any other member of the party did either. Their cautions were well taken.

Then her private companions spoke. "Surprise is the key," Knight Knife said. "For victory, do what they don't expect."

"Use a shield of illusion to get close," Wanda said. "Illusion can make a thing invisible as well as falsely visible."

"Then use my contact telepathy to pacify it," Anthem said. She played a chord. "Especially if it appreciates music."

Then the three looked at her expectantly, mentally.

"Me?" Nydia asked, aghast. "I'm almost as unlikely a hero as I am a rider."

"Exactly," Knight said. "Surprise."

"Attainment," Wanda said. "No illusion."

"I like the challenge," Anthem said, sounding another chord.

It seemed that Nydia had been nominated, at least by her private companions. She discovered that she didn't want to disappoint them any more than the Quest members. Was she a fool, or was there some other guidance? Did it matter? She took an unsteady breath, then spoke aloud. "I volunteer."

The others looked at her in unison, amazed.

"To do what?" Ecstasy asked.

"To catch and tame a steed. Probably the leader, so the others will fall in line. Then the town will be back in business."

"Nydia, you are the head of the Quest," Ecstasy said. "You must not put yourself at serious risk. It would leave the Quest leaderless."

She was making sense. She always did. But Nydia had already plunged into the fray. "If I perish, you must take over the Quest, Ecstasy, and see it through to completion. I'm sure Oakley will steer you on the obvious track."

"Well spoken," Moonroe said. "I'm sure we all will support Ecstasy."

Nydia didn't give them time to dither further. She marched to the town elder Drom. "I will try to catch and tame the leader steed. Do you have a replacement corral for it and the others?"

He oriented on her. "Those steeds are feral," he flashed. "Even if you could catch it, it would be dangerous for you."

"I know. But I have to try."

He paused, assessing her—which, of course, was not easy, considering their totally different types. "If you can do this, it would mark your person, your species, and your galaxy with favor here."

Perhaps for a while, she thought. "But mainly, it's that you need this done."

"Give us eight hours, and we shall make sufficient repairs," he flashed appreciatively.

"Time for us to rest and sleep," Vol said, taking Nydia's elbow.

They retired to their new chambers, where those who needed sleep took it.

"As I come to know you better," Vol murmured as he held her close, "I am increasingly glad that you are the one who tamed me. You are an excellent woman."

She didn't try to argue. She still basked in being considered a woman. Tomorrow, as it were, she would do or die. More likely the latter. So she relaxed in his embrace and slept. She had acted to ease his loneliness; he was doing as much for her by his support.

In the "morning," they gathered by the hastily repaired corral. Nydia wore heavy pants, shirt, gauntlets, and a helmet, all provided by Vol. Would they be enough? She was about to find out.

Ecstasy approached her. "If you fail, you are still evincing more sheer courage than anyone I have seen in decades. If you succeed, voila!" Then she hugged and kissed her. Nydia liked this endorsement too. It was actually nice being a woman.

The Droms flashed the feeding signal. The steeds came in, hungry but wary. If any Drom tried to approach them, they would scatter. They were much larger than Droms, but they had to be to serve as steeds. They were surely formidable, but not actually predatory monsters.

Nydia nerved herself and walked out toward them. The creatures lensed her uncertainly. She obviously was not a Drom, but what was she? They did not scatter, but they did avoid her.

Then she got an idea. "Make me look like a steed," she told Wanda.

"Illusion has power," the wand agreed.

She saw it herself: suddenly she looked like a steed, clothed in a cocoon of illusion. The steeds paused, then decided that the stranger was worth ignoring. They stopped avoiding her. It was working! It was incidentally interesting that the illusion evidently worked on these completely different creatures.

Nydia oriented on the lead steed, who was focusing on the proffered feed. She took hold of his harness. She held on to the upper band and put one leg through the lower one, then the other. This equipment had not been made for human use, but would serve as long as she was careful. She half sat on the upper portion of the lower band.

Now the steed realized that something had changed. Wanda let the illusion dissipate; it had served its purpose. Nydia was mounted, in her fashion.

The steed bolted as if it had discovered a bug on its back. Close enough. It lurched out of the pack and into the wind of the desert, shaking her violently. Nydia clung to the bands, knowing that if she lost her grip and fell off, all was lost, probably including her life. She was doubly glad for the armor that protected her skin from the sand blast, and especially for the gauntlets that clamped desperately tight. She couldn't have lasted even this long without them.

The steed danced on the dirt, not so much moving forward as, well, bucking like a nervous horse. Nydia's template memories made the analogy: it was trying to throw her off. It would have succeeded if she hadn't been clinging for dear life, anticipating this. Already her arms felt strained and her legs were chafing despite the armor. She couldn't hold on much longer.

"Don't give up," Knight said. "Victory is mostly grit."

"The illusion of defeat dooms many," Wanda said.

"My turn," Anthem said. "Put your bare finger on its hide so I can make contact. Then I can send pacifying thoughts."

Nydia discovered that the gauntlets actually left the tips of her fingers bare so she could touch things directly. She managed to angle one hand so that a forefinger poked the creature's hide. She felt a tingle.

"Oh my!" the ant exclaimed. "It's sapient!"

It took Nydia most of a moment to absorb this. She knew the word, but the context seemed wrong. "It's what?"

"Smart," Wanda clarified helpfully.

"But it's an animal!"

"It's an intelligent animal," Anthem said. "The same as you are."

"But Rob checked their minds when we passed. He would have told me if they had been other than simple animals."

"Indeed I would have," Rob said in her mind. "This is news to me too. But I see it via Anthem's contact. This creature is indeed sapient."

The bucking steed became aware of this other contact. He paused his violent motion. "What is this?" he demanded. "Make yourself known."

She understood him through Anthem's contact telepathy. His thoughts were coming to her mind and being translated to words without passing through the mechanical translator. Her thoughts were similarly going to him. This was a truly private dialog, limited to the two of them plus Rob, Anthem, Wanda, and Knight.

Nydia plunged in. "I am the alien creature who is riding you. Some of you saw us as we crossed the desert. My name is Nydia Nymph. What is yours?"

Surprise registered. "We did see you, Nydia. I am Seven Steed, leader of the pack. How did you abate the winds?"

"The personification of the Element of Air is a member of our group. She has power over moving air."

"Amazing. I would not believe it if I had not seen the wind mysteriously drop, and if this direct mind contact did not make you credible. But it does not feel perfect."

"It is facilitated by my associate Anthem Ant, who possesses the power of contact telepathy and a trace of larger awareness. Tell him, Anthem."

"It is true," the ant said. "Nydia lends me her powerful mind, for I am relatively tiny, without the substance for big thoughts. I lend her my telepathy. That makes us both smart and telepathic to a reasonable degree. We are of quite different species, but we work as a team. Somewhat the way you work with the Droms, each contributing expertise."

"I am impressed." He returned his focus to Nydia. "Your thoughts are honest. There is no deceit in telepathy. Why are you here?"

"We have a vital mission to accomplish if we can. We are making our way to the Void, where we believe the Demoness of Change resides, hoping to persuade her to stop these fluxes."

"And why are you riding me? I have had no contact with the Demoness of Change, though I know of her."

"The Droms need you back so they can navigate the desert and keep lines of communication and trade open. I volunteered to help. I did not know you were intelligent."

"You're not supposed to know. We mask our minds, pretending to be dumb animals. That enables us to get along with the Droms anonymously."

This was curious, quite apart from their fundamental differences. "Why?"

"If they knew we are as smart as they are, they might see us as dangerous enemies and try to eradicate us. That would be pointless war. It is better to get along and track their activities, especially in this time of flux."

Fascinating! "It is that flux that brought us to this galaxy and this planet. We are trying to find a way to ameliorate it, as I mentioned before."

"Then we are on the same side. We can handle wind, but recently it has become so extreme that we fear the progression."

"So do we. The mischief is not limited to this world or ours; it spans two galaxies. We fear doom for the entire region if we do not act soon to ease it."

"Then we want to help. What can we do?" He believed her because he was aware telepathy did not lie; she believed him similarly.

"For now, return to the Droms as animals. We will honor your secret. Two of our number will remain here for a time to control the wind. I will let them know, and they will contact you without telling the Droms your nature."

"This is not sufficient. What have we to gain apart from local convenience?"

"Respect," Knight Knife said. "That is what a warrior craves most."

"Who are you?" Seven demanded. That led to an explanation of the other two companions.

"I would like to have associates like you," Seven said. "So would the other steeds. It would enable us to establish relations with quite diverse creatures."

Nydia stepped in. "Wanda and Knight are unique entities, not available elsewhere. But I can make a plea to Anthem's home anthill to provide interested telepathic ants for such purpose. Some might agree."

That did it. "We will cooperate. I will signal my associates now." Seven raised his lens and flashed to the other steeds, who flashed back. They might not be telepathic, but they had ready means of communication with each other.

That reminded her. "You conceal your sapience from the Droms by acting like mere animals. But you also eluded Rob's mind check. He should have picked up on your intelligence when we passed you before. How did you hide it?"

"There are telepaths in the Earth Zone. We feared they would read our minds, even from a distance, and tell the Droms. So we practice constant mind shielding."

"Fascinating," Rob said. "We are going there next. We must shield our minds also. Will you teach us how?"

"For the sake of camaraderie, yes. It is simply a matter of creating an animal or otherwise ignorant persona, then normally residing in it. The key is to do it routinely because telepaths don't warn you they are coming. Their power becomes useless if you put on a shield. You will have to practice until it becomes your default state. You cannot afford to carelessly expose your true minds."

"We shall do so," Rob agreed. "I have not encountered mind shielding before, perhaps because others did not know it was possible, and I have had free rein in their minds. Some of their secrets are intriguing."

"Surely so," Seven agreed with an alien chuckle. "I would love to spy on the thoughts of lovers in action."

"It can be interesting," Rob agreed.

"But with shielding, the lovers could prevent your snooping. We ants do not get spied upon."

"How do you know?"

"Our specialty is contact telepathy, as we lack the minds to broadcast. But we are aware of external telepathic fields when they touch us."

"And a companion ant could do that for me? Warn me so I know to clamp down harder and hide?"

"Yes."

"This excites me. I thank you for that prospect."

"This intrigues me too," Rob said. "To spy without being spied on."

"You will want an ant, too, when we return home."

"I will indeed. Thank you, Anthem."

"And we thank you for your cooperation, Seven," Nydia said before anyone could think to explore her own secrets. "This may save our mission."

That was it. Nydia dismounted, and Seven did not attack her. They had become, if not friends, business associates. She walked back to the corral. "They will return," she called. Indeed, the steeds were already moving toward the corral.

The corral superintendent approached her. "What did you do?" he flashed.

"I was able to persuade him that the steeds were better off under your care. They like being fed and protected. It's better than being feral, especially in this bad wind. Treat them right, and they will behave. In fact, you will hardly need the corral."

His amazement was evident, but he could not argue with the result.

Nydia glanced at Aery. "Are you and Moonroe amenable to remaining here to pacify the desert winds until we complete our mission with the Demoness?"

"We figured on it," Moonroe said.

"Then I think we are ready to move on. You can be our liaison with this zone." She paused a fraction of a moment. "I will brief you on details before we depart." Nydia shared the specifics of the private deal with the steeds, and of mind shielding.

Chapter 12

MINDS

The boundary between the Wind Zone and the Earth Zone was formidable. Volcanoes lined it, viciously spewing sparks, smoke, ash, and lava. Clouds of burning gases drifted seemingly randomly. The ground shook constantly from minor, medium, and major quakes. There seemed to be no safe way through.

"My turn," Eartha said. "But there will need to be stages."

"Stages?" Nydia asked. "Can't you just make it stop in a channel across, as Aery did for the wind?"

"I can. But the terrain will be rough, and the ground will still be burning hot for days. Merely halting it will not suffice. My power is moving rock, not cooling it."

"And we don't have Aery or Flood here to summon water to cool it," Ecstasy said.

"Makes no matter," Eartha said confidently. "I will temporarily divert a river."

They watched, impressed, as Eartha signaled the terrain beside the boundary. The ground heaved and formed a massive channel leading to a nearby river. The water coursed into it thirstily, appreciating the new route. It seemed to have no loyalty to its old groove. It splashed with abandon down into the boundary region.

There it sizzled into a swirling cloud of droplets and steam. Ouch! Nydia wondered whether that was an analogy for the human condition, when those who paid no attention to the morrow or the consequences of their actions abruptly ran lethally afoul of unanticipated effects. Like the ogre who had thought to tease Noletta and had gotten his butt toasted.

"Good analogy," Rob said in her mind.

That caused another idea. "Have you been spying on all my thoughts?" she asked with dismay.

"Only the interesting or useful ones. Most thoughts are like chaff, merely cluttering the scene, of little use to anyone not in the host body."

She suppressed a surge of irritation at the notion of her thoughts being chaff. He was, after all, a handy member of the Quest. He would have to tune out the routine thoughts of a group of people, lest the mindscape be hopelessly cluttered. Still, she was concerned about her privacy, something she appreciated more as a woman than she had as a nymph. "Like what?"

"When I first nighted with Eartha, I wanted to be sure to do it correctly. I am not human, and neither is she, as you know, despite our borrowed human bodies. We have both observed human activities over the centuries, and knew the words and mechanics, but that's not the same as doing it ourselves. There are nuances. The figurines have reactions that can be evoked, but without practice they can be clumsy. She wanted to get it right too. So I read your memory of your first intimate encounter with a male, which I recovered from your buried experiences as a nymph, and used that as the template. It worked perfectly."

Nydia remembered the volcanoes erupting in unison and felt a certain envy again. It had indeed worked. Her annoyance at having her most intimate experiences spied on eased; he did have a point. How else were two completely nonhuman creatures to emulate that most personal interaction? "Point made."

"You also enabled me to have my first experience of love, reading your reactions with Vol. It's a glorious feeling. I may be a serpent and she an Element, but we have come to love each other in our fashions. Now I truly know what it is all about, thanks to you."

Surely a rare compliment. Her dawning ire drifted away like an untethered cloud. She had no case. They returned to watching the river action.

The water heedlessly kept flowing despite the fate awaiting it. One thing about a river was that there was always more liquid where the present fluid came from. The cloud of mist grew big and pulsed with annoyance, but the ground beneath it was reluctantly cooling, and puddles were beginning to form and hang on. The stream of fresh water was coursing farther before vaporizing. Meanwhile, Vol delved into his stores of lost items and produced pairs of heat-resistant open shoes for everyone so that they would not need to gamble on their footing.

Finally there was a damp corridor across the boundary area. They took it, walking in the wettest spots, because those were now beneath the boiling point. The shoes helped.

They came to a cave in the side of a coagulated lava flow. Vinia gazed into it. "Green," she said. "The path goes inside. The other paths are chancy to bad."

"There has to be a reason," Noe said.

"A reason to divert our route instead of getting the bleep across this dangerous terrain?" Oakley asked skeptically. "That is hardly obvious."

"We have learned to trust the green," Ecstasy reminded him. "Obviously."

The others looked at Nydia. It was her decision again. She hated that aspect of her position, but was as usual stuck with it. Leadership, it seemed, was all about decisions. Her nymphly past had been all about performance of One Thing, a much easier process. "We do trust the green. We will check this out and move on efficiently when we know the reason for the green."

Nobody argued. They trusted her leadership more than it perhaps deserved. Vinia led the way into the cave, Noe pacing beside her, and Nydia following. But she shared Oakley's doubt. Why delay their journey to inspect a temporary cave, surely empty, when they really needed to get quickly to the safety of the next zone?

Rob answered her mentally. "Because this cave is shielded against telepathy. We need to learn mental shielding, and we daren't do it openly. The green knows."

Another excellent point. Her mind, if not hurting, was suffering some stretching as she learned unobvious things. "Thank you for that clarification." She was trying not to be too grudging.

"I am still learning. What is the appropriate way to alleviate a human person's annoyance?"

She reminded herself that he was not human. He really didn't know the nuances. "Render an apology."

"I apologize for spying on your mind without your permission. I will try to avoid doing that in the future."

He did mean well. "No, keep doing it, because you will need to emulate being human, and won't be able to ask permission at every turn. You have to learn by observing inside and outside other minds."

"Thank you." His mental tone was contrite, and she knew it was not pretense.

"You are welcome," she said sincerely. She found she was liking him increasingly as another nonhuman person.

"And I like you, as a non-serpentine person."

The cave opened into a fair-sized chamber with room for them all. It was warm, but not hot; the river water had done its job as it evaporated. That was part of the magic of water: it cooled what it departed from. There was also some light leaking in from outside, so they could see each other.

Now was the time. "Your attention, please," Nydia said to the group. "We are here because we have a very private bleep to consider." She paused. "Adult Conspiracy, get the bleep out of my dialog! This is no business of yours." Lo, it retreated. It seemed that here in another galaxy, the Conspiracy had less power, and could be backed off when it was being even more foolish than usual. She took a breath and resumed. ". . . a very private matter to consider. We are about to enter a zone where there are telepaths—that is, mind readers. They may want to peer into our most secret thoughts, like how our natural functions are performing or what we simply prefer to keep private, like a passing unkind thought about a friend or the savor of our last kiss." She paused to give the assorted looks of dismay time to appear on stray faces. "Our mission is important. We don't want others messing with our minds and maybe fouling up the process. So we need to be able to maintain our privacy." She paused again to give the looks of agreement time to show themselves. "This cave is naturally shielded against stray telepathy, like a dam against water. So here, while we have intellectual privacy, we need to practice making personal shields against mental intrusion so that when we resume our journey, the alien telepaths will not be able to sneak into our minds. The secret is this: to assume roles we choose and play them so well that no outsiders will even suspect that we are not what we seem to be." One more pause to give the thoughtful expressions time. "Are there any questions?"

Vinia had one. "What about us juveniles?"

Nydia smiled. "That should be easy. You must become so clearly a child, mentally, that there cannot be even the hint of a suspicion that maybe you know or suspect anything a child should not know. That you have no idea at all what fauns and nymphs do so gleefully in the Retreat or how baby orders are sent to the storks or what bleeps mean literally. That you are not even curious about such dull things. That all you care about is getting home so you can guzzle tsoda pop and boot rear and eat fresh cookies all day and never get sick or even full." Then she thought of something else. "Your colored paths, especially, should be completely hidden. Only your talent of telekinesis should exist."

Vinia's smile became inscrutable, then jumped to Woe Betide. "Got it. Just be completely ourselves." Bits of the smile touched several of the adults before fading out. The Conspiracy might bleep, but it could not erase fundamental understanding.

Now Moonroe had a question. "How do we practice mind control? We need more than just trying to be the popular notion of ourselves. We've been doing that all along, unguardedly."

Nydia glanced at Rob. "You are our general telepath. Do you have advice?" She knew he would be ready because of their dialog with Seven Steed. Facilitating things for one's associates was another aspect of leadership she was cultivating.

He nodded. "I have been pondering the matter. I think that we should try a play with assigned or chosen roles. If we become so persuasive in roles that obviously are not authentic that we can fool others, then we will have the technique to play the roles of ourselves well enough to deceive the alien telepaths. We shall be consummate actors, believing that we are what we seem to be. What we need is a challenging play with many distinct characters to practice on."

"You are already playing the role of a human man," Eartha said.

"But could I fool you if you did not know my nature? I need practice myself if I want to fool another telepath. Minds don't deceive each other."

"The play's the thing," she agreed.

"That seems apt," Nydia said. "Does anyone have such a play in mind?"

A silence swept in and took over. No one had such a play in or out of mind.

It was time for more leadership. What a multifaceted thing it was! Nydia looked at the demoness. "Lilith, you have been active in the affairs of the human kind since the dawn of history. You have seen things the rest of us have no inkling of. Do you have memories that can be adapted?"

The demoness looked startled. She, for once, had been caught off guard. "Um, let me think." In three-quarters of a moment, she nodded to herself. "Maybe Gilgamesh." She looked around as a wave of blankness crossed most faces. "He was a Sumerian king with whom I had relations, back when there was more magic in Mundania. A good guy, but he got arrogant and arbitrary, and the people petitioned to the Lord of Heaven for relief from his tyranny. That was a wakeup call for him. Then his life became complicated." She continued with details, describing a complex network of interactions involving a number of people and creatures.

"This will do for our purpose," Nydia decided. "We shall now all choose characters in this history to emulate—first come, first served. Do not announce your choices; merely think them, and Rob will let you know if someone else got there first. We have to trust him to keep our secrets as he has been doing all along. Your purpose is to emulate your chosen character so perfectly that no outsider will realize that it is an act, and no insider—that is, the rest of us—will know who is animating it. At the end, when the play has run its course, we will present a list of all the characters and try to guess who played which role. The winners will be the ones who fool everyone; the losers will be those who fool no one. Most of us will probably be in between, neither complete winners nor losers but imperfect to varying extents. Then the winners will coach the losers until they can do it too. We all need to be winners in the end; our mission and our lives may just depend on it."

This time, the look that passed among them was serious and somewhat nervous. This might seem like a game, but aspects were deadly.

Woe Betide had a question. "Can we children play grownup parts?"

Nydia smiled. "If you believe you can fool adults about your true identities, you're welcome to try. But you may wind up as losers because of your ignorance of what the Adult Conspiracy has hidden from you."

"Blip!" the child swore. She, like all children, resented the Conspiracy and wanted to sneak around it.

"However," Rob said, "you are not restricted to human child roles. You can probably play an animal or a monster, where the Conspiracy doesn't apply. As an animal myself, I can tell you that it is a considerable challenge to emulate an adult human man. Without my telepathy and Eartha's support, I'd have been lost."

"Fortunately, you do have that," Eartha said. "We Elements face similar challenges. Human adults are deviously complicated creatures."

"As another Element, I agree," Vol said. "But it can be well worth the effort." He glanced at Nydia. "I was perhaps the loneliest entity extant, despite my riches, but Nydia rescued me and taught me love. I really like emulating a man when I'm with her."

Nydia, the one caught by surprise this time, found herself blushing furiously. The others laughed, not at her, but at the situation. They understood about special relationships becoming real.

She fought for a grip and managed to get her fingertips on her composure. "Thank you, Vol," she said, faking normalcy. "The feeling is mutual. Now for the selection of parts. Each of you focus on yours. When we all are committed, Rob will project the background scene to all of us, and the show will be on. Remember, we are not alone; we are in, well, a historical or mythical play, interacting with others."

"I will need your help, Lilith, to get it right," Rob said. "Will you lend me your memory?"

"Of course. Come into my mind, you intriguing serpent."

Eartha frowned but did not protest. Lilith surely knew more about human secrets than most humans did, and this was their only source of detail about the epic. Rob had to go to her as the source to share the information with each participant.

They were all silent as they focused on their chosen roles in the Gilgamesh epic. Nydia cast about for hers. Who could she pretend to be that would fool others who had come to know her almost too well? She could surely emulate a woman in a leadership position, like a princess or queen, but that was exactly what others would know to look for. She needed someone unexpected.

Also her three close physical companions, Anthem Ant, Wanda Wand, and Knight Knife: "Are you taking roles too?" she asked them.

"We are," Anthem responded.

"Then we must separate mentally, if not physically, so as not to give away our parts to one another."

"We shall do that," the ant agreed. The three faded out, leaving Nydia by herself. It was an odd feeling. They remained with her physically, but had become like mindless objects.

Back to her choice. What truly surprising character could she play? Then it came to her. Gilgamesh! The male leader. Could she do it? A gender change? It would certainly be a challenge. She couldn't dither long because one of the males could take it. It was now or never. Make it now.

"Gilgamesh," she told Rob mentally, trusting that she was in time to get it.

"Got it." There was a tinge of surprise, which was actually a good sign. He forwarded Lilith's memory of Gilgamesh to her. She had not been fooling about having relations with him; she had been one of his royal mistresses for a time. Nydia received a jolt of the male experience of intimate contact, as understood by his companion. It was an education. It seemed that men really were into it for itself, not just for stork signals or social relations. She would have to school herself into being into it similarly. Her experience as a nymph gave her a thorough notion of the mechanics, but it had been more of a game, fun but not really serious. Now she understood that it was more serious for the male. She would have to eye every appealing female with a view toward seducing her if the occasion were conducive.

In due course—she wasn't sure how long that was, having been preoccupied, as the others probably were too—all the parts in the play were taken. The background scene formed. It was like stepping into another world. She was in a business chamber of the palace, facing an anonymous official. There was no hint who might be playing the role of the official or whether it was merely a programmed background character.

And lo, there was a script of sorts. She knew what to say. The challenge was to say it the way Gilgamesh would have said it so that no one would catch on that this was not only a fake, but not a king or even a man. She had to tune out her breasts and tune in a male crotch. And lower her natural tone of voice.

"They did what?" Nydia/Gilgamesh demanded, outraged.

"The populace petitioned the Lord of Heaven for relief from your tyranny," the official repeated. "He took pity on them and ordered the goddess Aruru to mold out of clay a wild man named Enkidu."

The goddess Aruru. Nydia had to take a moment to zero in on her. She was the Earth Goddess, who had assisted in making the first human people. Making people was her specialty. That was why the Lord of Heaven had gone to her.

And without even seeing her, Nydia knew who would choose that role. Eartha, the Element of Earth. She could play that part perfectly. Too perfectly; her identity would soon be known. But there was another aspect: what did she look like in this framework? The Earth Mother, of course. But Gilgamesh would see her as a sex object. Not that he would ever get close to a goddess in that manner.

Or would he? The ancient gods and goddesses had evidently had time on their hands, and liked to mess with mortals whose relative innocence was fun to tweak. So that was it: Aruru was powerful, but also a sex object.

But the official was still talking. She had better pay attention. "Right now Enkidu is learning the ways of existence, a monstrous creature who lives and eats with the beasts he saves from the snares of hunters. When you go to stop him, as no other man can do, he will fight you and kill you."

Which would end her role as the king. She couldn't afford that. "So it's a trap. I won't spring it."

"But he is tearing up the landscape. The farmers and hunters demand action," the official argued. "You'll be mocked as a weakling if you don't deal with him promptly, and there could be a revolution."

So there could indeed be. "Hades!" she swore, trying to be manlike in language. "Damned if I do and if I don't."

"That is the nature of the trap," the official agreed seriously.

Gilgamesh pondered half a moment. Nydia was rapidly coming to appreciate the negative side of kingship. It wasn't all feasts and fancy. There were responsibilities, and if they weren't met, it would demonstrate that no real man was playing the role.

Real man. There was an answer. The wild man would be a sucker for a female body. "Send our sexiest harem beauty to seduce him. Then the animals will know that he is not one of them and have no more to do with him. He will lose his place among them and will have to go away."

"Done," the official agreed, and departed to see to it.

The king had finessed the trap. But it didn't work out as it was supposed to. Gilgamesh had a magic mirror that would tune in on any scene he wished. He oriented it on the harem beauty as she arrived at the field the wild man was presently tearing up. She flashed her formidable attributes, getting his attention as she was so well equipped to do, then slowly walked to him, every step enhancing her bosom and pelvis. Nydia, getting into the role, licked the king's lips. How could any male resist that allure?

But when she was close, it was apparent that Enkidu did not know exactly what to do with her. He was interested, to be sure, but did not understand exactly what went where in what order. He really was wild, with no relevant experience.

The girl saw this and avoided her own disaster, which would be to fail her mission. "Enkidu, we must talk," she said, her tone enticing. "I will teach you what you need to know. Come lie on the turf with me, and I will guide your hands and whatever else so you know what to do."

How could he refuse? She was temptation incarnate.

"Why?" he asked. "What does a fabulous creature like you want with an ignorant lout like me?" At least he was not stupid.

She sighed impressively. "Some background, then. King Gilgamesh sent me to seduce you so that the animals will have no more to do with you and you will go away." It seemed she wasn't into lying.

"Why? What does he care about me and the animals?"

"You are a disruptive influence here. Farmers and villagers are suffering. If he does not get rid of you, the people may have a pretext to throw him out."

"So as it is with me and the animals, so it is with Gilgamesh and the people? Forms that must be followed?"

Not stupid at all! "I think I like you," she said, sitting up. Some beauties had no minds to speak of; this one was different. "Therefore, I will not seduce you after all."

Uh-oh. There was evidently a danger in smartness and in conscience. She was not supposed to make her own decision.

"If this king is so bad," the wild man said, "he needs to be removed. I think I have to challenge his power."

"Maybe you do," she agreed.

Nydia turned away from the mirror. This was bad. Instead of ruining the wild man with the animals, the woman was changing sides. Trouble indeed. Had the Quest member animating this part changed the course of the story? That could be a giveaway.

Gilgamesh was the strongest warrior in the kingdom. That was why he was king. He would have to tackle this personally after all. Nydia was aware that she was increasingly thinking like a man, which was the point.

Time passed in an instant. They met at the New Year's festival. It was a wrestling match with established rules and a huge audience. It would be fair; it could not be otherwise, as it was a public spectacle. Enkidu was huge and muscular, but Gilgamesh was highly skilled.

Except that this was not the original, but a reenactment. Could Nydia actually wrestle a man effectively? Her natural inclination would be not to oppose him, but to embrace him. Even if she had real muscles to do it, she, unlike the real Gilgamesh, lacked the skill to use them in combat. At any rate, she would have to try.

They wrestled, but Nydia, distracted by more than the combat challenge, could not quite summon all the necessary skill, and lost the match by a close margin. Well, she would have to play it as if the loss was legitimate.

There was also something else. When straining against the man, torso to torso, something had unnerved her, weakening her. What was it?

Then she got it. Enkidu was being played by Vol! She knew that presence up close in ways no other person did.

Still, on with the show. Gilgamesh stood, bowed to his opponent, and spoke. "You fought fair and won," he said. "Congratulations."

Enkidu seemed surprised. "You are not having me killed for embarrassing you?"

"Of course not. As I said, it was a honest match."

"Then I like you. I want to be your friend."

Gilgamesh was surprised. "I like you too. I thought we were enemies, but maybe we should be friends instead."

The two men hugged. They were now friends. And during that embrace, Enkidu whispered in her ear: "I know you, Ny, and am amazed. Well played!"

So he had suffered the same realization she had. "Keep the secret, Vol," she whispered back.

"Oh, yes!"

The story continued. Enkidu became Gilgamesh's constant companion, learning civilized ways. The maids of the palace liked him, but were wary of his original harem companion who now guarded his social life jealously.

There was a fire-breathing monster called Humbaba who lived in a cedar forest. It had one eye that could turn men to stone. It had stayed out of trouble in the past, but now was emerging to raid the neighboring farms. The creature had to be stopped. It might not be possible to slay it, but they could drive it away by cutting down the cedars, which was unfortunate, as they were sacred trees. But the kingdom needed to be rid of the monster, and it was not safe to fight it directly. Not with that deadly eye!

They took axes and marched to the grove. They tackled the first tree together, chopping at its stout trunk from either side. Gilgamesh liked working with Enkidu, just as Nydia liked being with Vol, and was sure the feeling was mutual.

The tree fell with a crash. The monster heard the sound of it and came roaring in to the attack, belching fire and casting its deadly gaze about. They could not escape it, as they were caught in a gully that gave the creature free access to them. Its fire could reach well beyond their swords, and they could not close their eyes to avoid its gaze because then they would be unable to see it to strike any blows or avoid its fire. Nydia realized that they should have prepared for this, maybe wearing armor and heat-reflective shields. Evidently, the original legend had not considered such details. Too late now; they were doomed.

Except that there was a nuance in the script. Nydia became aware of it as it happened. Gilgamesh's mother, the goddess Ninsun, intervened with the sun god to blind the monster with burning hot winds. That gave them the advantage, and they charged it and chopped at it with their axes, and managed to behead the creature. But it had been a close call. And it meant that Gilgamesh did have some godly blood from his mother.

Nydia wondered who had played the monster Humbaba. But, of course, its death would only boot that player out of the game, not actually kill him.

They stopped at a roadside traveler's cabin on the way back, not being up to the full trek home. It had been a tiring fight.

But the day was not yet done. As Gilgamesh made ready to sleep, a dramatically female figure walked up the path and accosted him. "I am Ishtar," she said as she opened her robe to display a phenomenal body. Nydia, being a nymph, was not ordinarily turned on by other women, but this was so potent she couldn't help feeling a tinge of desire. "Goddess of love and fertility. I saw how you defeated the monster. I want to have your baby." She took a deep breath that freaked out Enkidu so that he froze in place. No man could withstand that vision, and not every woman. And who was playing her? Surely Lilith herself; this was her ideal role.

Oops! Was Nydia now obliged to spend the night with Ishtar as a man, to protect her real identity? Suddenly her tinge of desire converted to a punishing turnoff. But as the story background played in her head, she realized she had an out. "I know you," Gilgamesh told her, squinting as if to shut out enough of her glory to enable him to talk. "You treated your lover Tammuz the shepherd god so insensitively that he died and went to Hell. I don't plan to go there myself."

"But I repented and went to Hell myself to rescue him," she replied. "So the seasons of the year returned, and no permanent damage was done."

"He was not the only one," Gilgamesh said grimly. "It is dangerous to be your lover. Some of them got turned into beasts. Get away from me, you harlot!"

Ishtar's amazement at this reaction from what should have been an easy conquest soon metamorphosed to rage. Her eyes turned fiery and sparks radiated from her hair. "You dare to turn me down, you incredible imbecile?" she demanded. "Have you no respect for the surpassing magnitude of my offer? Armies have been routed for less! I will have your ungrateful hide!"

"Welcome to it, strumpet," he retorted. "You shall not have my heart or my seed." For more than one reason.

She stormed off, jags of lightning shooting from the angry cloud over her head. Trust the demoness to get the special effects right!

"Well played again," Enkidu murmured. "I am glad it's only a script."

But the goddess's threats were not entirely empty. She so belabored the Lord of Heaven with threats that, to get rid of her, he sent the Storm Bull of Heaven, a formidable beast, and it stampeded down to gore them. But this time they were ready, and it was not a true predator. There was no fire, no lethal stare, only the formidable horns. First they blinded it with arrows to the eyes, then charged in and sliced its throat with their swords before it could orient on them by nose and ears. The Bull fell with a mighty crash, and they cut out its heart and proffered it to the sun god. That put them on the side of the gods, a tactical ploy, so that the gods would not agree to smite the two.

But Ishtar was not done yet. *Never underestimate the wrath of a scorned woman*, Nydia thought. The goddess arranged to send Enkidu a series of dreams revealing to him that the gods, outraged by the slaughter of the Bull, had decreed the wild man's death. Gilgamesh realized that Ishtar, having failed to move Gilgamesh, who was protected by his mother, had struck at an alternate target that lacked such protection. Enkidu, brawny as he was, was nevertheless a weak spot. Maybe they should have been more polite to her.

Gilgamesh tried to tell Enkidu that it was just Ishtar sending the dreams, pretending that the gods had done something. That he didn't really have to die. But Enkidu believed the dream and lay on his bed, gradually growing weaker.

Finally he died. Gilgamesh was grief-stricken. They had become such good friends, and now that was gone.

Unless.

Gilgamesh remembered how Ishtar herself had gone to Hell to rescue Tammuz. Death was not necessarily permanent in legends. Maybe he could do the same!

But the prospect of invading Hell made him pause. He was, after all, mortal, unlike Ishtar, and could find himself over-matched. Was there an alternative? Something that could be done in the living realm?

The thought sponsored the action. Gilgamesh girded his loin, put a suitable official in temporary charge of the kingdom, and set out to find the sage Utnapishtim, the only mortal ever to have escaped death. He would know the secret of immortality, and maybe Gilgamesh could use that to rescue his friend from death. It was certainly worth a try.

There were trials and warnings along the way, but he dealt with them almost incidentally, brooking no interference with his mission to save his friend. He backed off the warriors, slew the monsters, and disdained the seductive women, though he did make some mental notes on which of them might be prospects for later inclusion in his harem. Nydia was getting better at thinking like Gilgamesh. Women were objects to be acquired and used as was convenient, the young ones for romance, the older ones as servants. When they were no longer useful, they were promptly retired. A small part of her was annoyed, but she suppressed it as not fitting the role.

The route was plainly marked, though for some reason, few if any other folk seemed to have gotten far along it. In due course, he reached the Ocean of Death, a formidable barrier. The stink of decay hung over the Ocean. No animals drank from it; the bones of the few that had tried were lying along its bank. No fish swam in it; their skeletons lay on the bottom. No birds flew over it. The message was reasonably clear: this was not a safe place for ordinary living folk to be. But the sage was reputed to live on an island in the Ocean where he would not be bothered by passing petitioners.

Gilgamesh knew what to do. He walked beside the gloomy water until he came to the ferry station. There was the ferryman Urshanabi, snoozing in his boat. And who was playing him?

Gilgamesh produced a gold coin from his purse. Nydia suspected this was before coins of any kind existed, but never mind. "Up, man, and row me across." He held the coin up to the sunlight so that it flashed. "There'll be another on my return."

That was persuasive. Gold was a power metal anywhere in reality or fantasy. The ferryman snapped awake and rowed him smartly across the dark liquid to the island.

The sage was actually friendly, especially when Gilgamesh produced another gold coin. He had nowhere to spend it, but valued it for itself. That was part of the magic of this metal: folk were attracted to it without reason. Utnapishtim was married, but maybe he was a tinge lonely after having had no visitors for a few decades. "What is it you desire of me, Sumerian king?" The sage was old, but not ancient, with only a little gray in his hair and not many wrinkles in his skin. Since he was reputed to be centuries old, the preservative process was obviously working. He must have been locked into the age he had been when he achieved immortality.

"The secret of eternal life. It is for a good purpose. I want to save my dear friend Enkidu, who died recently. An elixir or spell might still revive him. You have escaped death. Tell me how you did it."

"Ah, that. I fear it will not do you much good."

Gilgamesh was impatient. "Tell me anyway. I will be the judge of what is good for me."

"As you wish. In the early days of the earth, a great flood destroyed the men and works of the kingdom I lived in. I had done a favor for Ea, the God of Wisdom, putting him onto some passing foolishness that amused him, and he warned me of its coming. I tried to tell others, but they chose to believe that if no flood had come yesterday, none would come tomorrow. So I organized my sons and we built an ark big enough for our families, stocking it with goods and food and recreational games to last at least a week, all while the neighbors laughed at us, thinking us fools. When the rains came, we battened down within it and waited as the water rose and floated it free of the city. The neighbors had to flee, at last knowing themselves for the fools. We lived there as the ark drifted, seeing the land we had known and loved submerged. We endured for seven days and nights, drifting we knew not where, until the ark grounded on a mountain. But there was no viable land in sight; the mountain was a bare peak. So we sent out three birds of our collection: a dove, a swallow, and a raven. The first two returned, having found nothing elsewhere to perch on, but when the third did not return, we knew the raven had landed. We gave sincere thanks to the gods for our safety. We managed to dislodge the ship and float free, and were guided to an island at the end of the earth where my wife and I now live, and have become immortal. Our sons and their families took the ark and sailed it elsewhere; we have not heard from them for some time, but they surely found suitable places to live as the flood waters slowly receded." He paused for a breath. "So I do not know the secret; it was a gift from the gods. Perhaps it is a quality of this island."

Hades! So there was no answer here. Gilgamesh ground his teeth so hard they turned red with heat.

"Still, there just might be a way," the sage said helpfully. "An herb grows at the bottom of the sea that will restore youth. Possibly it could youthen your friend to the point before his death, and thus renew him."

Well now. Gilgamesh thanked the man and went into action. He tied stones to his feet to weigh himself down, held his breath, waded into the

water, and searched out the herb deep under the sea. He harvested it and
waded back out, removing the stones. He would need to take it to where
Enkidu lay.

He paid the waiting ferryman another coin and was conveyed back to
the mainland. He marched toward home. When he passed a fresh spring,
he paused to drink and bathe, laying the plant on the ground. A snake
appeared from hiding and made off with the herb. Gilgamesh grabbed
for it, but all he got was the snake's old skin as it turned young again and
slithered happily into a thicket where it disappeared. The herb was lost.

Gilgamesh wept. Now he understood that there was no salvation for
his friend or himself. All he could do was return to his kingdom and exist
there until he, too, inevitably died.

Nydia emerged from the story in unmanly tears. But she had perhaps
accomplished her purpose, so thoroughly submerging herself in the role
that no telepath would have been able to tell that she was actually another
person. She liked Gilgamesh, despite his attitude toward women, but he
was not her reality.

"That was something!" Wanda said. "What part were you?"

She didn't know? That was an excellent sign. "I was Gilgamesh."

Wanda was amazed. "No wonder I missed you! I was checking only
females."

"And what were you?"

"An anonymous nymph who tried to tempt Gilgamesh on the way to
the sage. But he—you—brushed me off with hardly even a glance. I was
humiliated."

"Don't be. He—I—marked you as a harem prospect. I just couldn't
afford to dally at that stage. If a man had played that part, you surely
would have seduced him. I did not recognize you."

"I'm flattered."

"And you, Knight—what was your role?"

"I was the Storm Bull of Heaven. You slew me."

Nydia laughed. "I did not recognize you either. I might not have been
able to slay you if I had." She focused on the ant. "And you, Anthem—who
were you?"

"An outraged god. I did not know it was you I was condemning."

"You are forgiven." Nydia looked around at the others as they emerged from the story, opening their eyes and blinking. "It is time to determine how well we masked ourselves. Oakley, please go through our number and have the others identify which parts they played, if they can. The story was fun in its fashion, but we don't know what the aliens might do to us if they have full access to our minds. We need to know we can hide from telepaths."

"Yes, we do," Rob said. "I played the Lord of Heaven part, having little direct contact with other players except for Ishtar, whom I recognized, as I imagine others did too." There was a general murmur of agreement as they looked at Lilith. "So I walked to the cave entrance and cautiously extended my awareness, masking myself as a passing serpent of no account. I got it. The telepaths like to play games with folk, projecting thoughts into their minds that they think are their own, then watching as they act on them. Like impromptu couples making illicit love, or strangers fighting for no seeming reason. They think that's funny."

"We are not amused," Nydia said, speaking for all of them. "Playing roles in mythology is one thing; doing it for real is another." There was another murmur of agreement, this one angry.

"Neither are the normal Droms here. That's why they practice mind shielding. But sometimes they are caught with their guards down, as when distracted or sleeping, and there can be real mischief. Once a leader swallowed the tail of his partner. So they are tolerant about social blunders, knowing their origin."

"A traveling party of innocents could be a huge target," Nydia said. "We will try to protect ourselves. Oakley?"

"Lilith, you played Ishtar," Oakley said. "Obviously. You will need to tone down your enthusiasm for seductive behavior, lest the telepaths pounce."

"I shall," the demoness agreed contritely. "Ishtar was fun, but I will try to be completely boring hereafter."

"Who did Nydia play?"

There were a few guesses of female parts. They were amazed when Nydia identified herself as Gilgamesh. She had obviously passed the challenge.

"Ecstasy?"

Again the guesses were females. She actually turned out to be the sage, another gender crossover. Nydia had certainly been fooled.

So it went. Eartha was the Goddess Aruru, which several people did get. Oakley himself was the ferryman. Vinia was the sage's anonymous wife; she had managed it because no one questioned her knowledge of the Adult Conspiracy. Woe Betide was a subject who prayed for relief from Gilgamesh's early tyranny. Santo was Tammuz, who had to be rescued from Hell. Noe was the snake who stole the youthening herb. Favew was an anonymous warrior who opposed Gilgamesh on the way to the sage. Wavef was the harem girl sent to seduce Enkidu. The others applauded that performance, as no one had suspected she was not human.

Overall, they had done well. Few had given themselves away. They exchanged advice about masking themselves more effectively. They were ready to go.

"Now we must play roles of ourselves," Nydia said, "only dull, with no thoughts of another galaxy or a larger mission. We are just tourists seeing the sights, guided by two locals. Curious because our bodies are so different from the norm, but nothing of intellectual interest. Like animals in a Mundane zoo."

The others nodded. Their mental and emotional health, perhaps even their lives, depended on being so stupid that they simply were not worth a telepath's while.

The animals departed the cave and resumed their trek across the boundary section. But when they reached the other side, there wasn't much of a change; the land was still quaking and volcanoes were erupting.

Eartha lifted her hands, and the quakes and eruptions stopped. Nydia realized that they were about to lose another couple to keep this section secure for their return.

"Bogey," Anthem said with a sinister chord.

So now the telepaths were checking out the visitors. Nydia focused on being a largely empty-headed creature and knew the others were similarly dull. Feast on that, telepaths.

They came to a settlement. Favew and Wavef went ahead to introduce the party, and explained their ability to quell the disturbance of the earth as thanks to the help of a cooperative earth spirit. The Droms welcomed them, truly appreciating the geologic peace they brought. The telepaths among them did not manifest; they were not popular because of their mischief. All the same, the visitors kept their shields clamped down tight.

They spent the "night," and moved on in the "morning," leaving Rob and Eartha. It was almost anticlimactic after their session in the cave. But it could all too readily have been otherwise. Their homework was paying off.

The fifth and last section was the Void. Even the natives did not know much about it; its residents kept largely to themselves and did not socialize with the other sections. Visiting it was not encouraged; those who had tried were too apt to disappear. Nydia knew how that was. This Void, too, was one-way.

But they would have to go there regardless. That was where the Demoness Andromeda was. Vinia's green path led straight there.

Nydia paused to address the remaining Questers. "I have to go, and Vol with me. But any of the rest of you who would rather wait here . . ."

Her ellipsis was wasted. "We're staying with you," Ecstasy said firmly. "We're all in this together." The others nodded, even the two Droms.

Nydia felt herself tearing up, a liability she had acquired since turning woman. "Thank you." She faced the boundary and willed herself forward.

Chapter 13

BANG

The boundary was deceptively placid. Its hills were gently rolling, its plants were ordinary, the starscape shone above, and a streamlet ran calmly through it. There were even paths winding about, seeking level turf.

Nydia trusted none of this. She glanced at Vinia. "Where is the green?"

"This is weird," the girl said. "It keeps shifting."

"Can you track the shifts? So that we can switch to new paths as warranted?"

"I think so. But we'd better keep Lilith and Vol close, in case a shift puts us inside a void depression."

"Got it," the demoness agreed.

"I am here," Vol said. "I can nullify any void we step into."

Nydia was satisfied for the moment. "Then lead the way, Vinia. I will follow, and Vol and Lilith will follow me."

"I could make a tunnel through it," Santo said. "But I am concerned that a change might redirect it, leading us astray." He didn't add that such an error could be lethal.

"Yes," Noe agreed. "Best to save your tunnel for getting out of mischief if we blunder into it."

He squeezed her hand. "My thought too." She smiled and squeezed back.

It occurred to Nydia that though typical love might not be feasible for this couple, they had the equivalent. Friendship and mutual respect. And, of course, Noe could turn male if she needed to.

Vinia selected a path and pursued it. Nydia followed.

Almost immediately, the girl halted. "It's changing."

"Let me investigate," Lilith said. She faded out.

In half a moment, she was back. "You're right, Vin. It's weird. Not a void, not dangerous, exactly, but subtly different."

"Could there be illusion?" Oakley asked. "My sense of the obvious is not registering."

"We are going toward the Demoness of Change," Ecstasy said. "Of course things are changing."

"Obviously," Oakley agreed, chagrined. "You caught what I missed."

"We are associating closely, dear," she said. "I am picking up on your ability."

"You are indeed." He patted her svelte behind, and she smiled.

There was another couple that worked. But that was incidental to the mission. "So let's proceed," Nydia said.

They moved forward again. The scenery did change around them, but now they understood why. It was not a threat so much as change for the sake of change.

Until Vinia stopped again. "Uh-oh. Green just turned to red. I think the boundary shifted to put us inside a void."

"My turn," Vol said. He gestured. Nothing changed, seemingly, but Vinia visibly relaxed. He had simply shifted the boundary back. Green had been restored.

"You got the best possible man for this mission," Anthem said appreciatively, playing a resonant chord.

"I did," Nydia agreed. "I was lucky." She squeezed Vol's hand. "In more than one respect."

"Not as lucky as me," Vol said. They paused for a kiss.

The others smiled, understanding perfectly.

Soon they came to the other side of the boundary region. The landscape seemed to stabilize. But Nydia remained uneasy. Change was not necessarily limited to scenery.

"Perhaps we should check out the natives," Lilith suggested. "They have surely had experience with this sort of thing."

Excellent point. "Do it," Nydia agreed.

The demoness popped out. Soon she was back. "I checked a town. It turned out to be illusion, streets, houses, natives, and all. There is nothing solid there."

Favew and Wavef exchanged a lensed glance. "That perhaps explains our lack of contact with these Droms," Wavef flashed. "They don't exist."

"Curious," Oakley said. "Maybe the constant change unnerved the natives and they departed."

"That explains much," Favew flashed.

"It does indeed," Wavef agreed.

Another couple that seemed to be working out.

"So no sheltered suite tonight," Ecstasy said. "Can we find a cave?"

Vinia considered. "There does seem to be a path to one. But it's a fair distance."

"So we walk," Nydia said. "Through the changes, holding firmly to our reality. Lead on."

"It's fun," Woe Betide said from her floating crib.

"Would Metria think so?" Lilith asked.

"Maybe not. But Mentia would love it. She's halfway crazy."

"Craziness may be an asset here," Oakley said, laughing.

"An asset," Ecstasy said, emphasizing the first syllable as she squeezed his rear.

"Oooo, that's a naughty pun," Woe said. "It's a good thing I don't understand it."

"Neither do I," Vinia said. Clearly they both did, but were avoiding a nasty backlash from the Conspiracy.

Now the laughter was general. Nydia hoped it was relieving the background tension of the situation. They really did not know what they were getting into.

There turned out to be no wildlife either. This section had only plants.

In due course, they came to the cave. It was fair-sized, and edible plants grew nearby. It would do.

Vol produced rods and curtains from his endless stores so that they could have compartments providing a semblance of privacy for the "night." He came up with glowing stones to provide light in the darkness of the cave. Also assorted fresh pies and bottles of boot rear, so they did not have to forage outside. Nydia realized that it was probably better to use their own equipment and food than to risk the transforming plants outside. They had not encountered anything poisonous, but that could change.

Then her drink swapped from boot rear to toot rear. She spat out her mouthful before it could take effect. Since turning woman, she was conscious of social nuances. Women did not toot. Soon it changed again to moot. That would do. But it was clear that the changes were not limited to native products.

"We are nearing the conclusion of our mission, one way or another," Vol said in the privacy of their compartment. "Thereafter, the members of the Quest will return to their own lives. What then of us?"

What was on his mind? "Is there a problem?"

"Will I return to being just an Element, and you to your Faun & Nymph Retreat?"

She picked up on the tension. "Oh, Vol, no, no, no! When I committed to you, I meant forever, or at least as long as I live. I will join you in the Void, if you wish, or you can join me at the Queendom of Thanx, or wherever else we decide to stay. We're a couple."

He relaxed. "I am glad of that. I do not want to be alone again."

"You thought I would leave you once the Quest was done? Never!" She felt her tears flowing. "I'm not a nymph anymore. I love you!"

"And I love you," he said.

Then they kissed, and the night dissolved into rapture.

In the morning, they organized and resumed their travel. The scene outside the cave was now a chill snowscape, but Vol had warm overcoats for any who needed them. Soon the land became a hot jungle and the coats were returned to the Void.

The changes got worse. Savage storms alternated with burning dry deserts, and the land shifted without notice from plains to ragged mountains to deep seas. They were getting close. Could they hang on if reality itself changed in the presence of the Demoness?

"Nydia," Rob's mental voice came. "The perturbations are worsening. What are you up to?"

"I think we're approaching Demoness Andromeda."

"Can you hurry it up? The shifts are getting dangerous."

"We'll try," Nydia promised. "But how can you be ranging here mentally when the native telepaths can intercept you?"

"Eartha and I made a deal with them: help us save the galaxies and we'll all benefit. We are on the same side. They are buttressing me."

Oh. That did make sense. She looked around the group. "It's not just us. Rob says everything's getting worse. We may need to change our plan."

"And give up the mission?" Santo asked. "That's not smart."

"I don't know what to do," Nydia confessed. She was clearly in over her head, and pushing further forward might be really chancy.

"I thunk of something," Woe Betide said. "It's getting pretty wild here in reality. Why don't we just skip reality and make it a dream?"

At this point Nydia was ready to consider anything. They could get feedback from the sensible members of the Quest. "Tell us more, please."

"With Gilgamesh, we got into mythology, each with a part. We did what we wanted, as long as it was still the story. Can we do it again, with a scene we choose instead of all this chaos?"

"Child, you're making sense," Oakley said. "We can make our own reality within the broad limits of the play."

"Gee," she said, flattered by his acceptance.

Nydia glanced at Vinia. "Where's the green?"

"Woe's in a ball of green."

"Then let's do it," Ecstasy said. "Rob is with us to unify us telepathically, as before, and now he doesn't have to hide from the local telepaths. They want to survive too. But the details will count."

"I am thinking of a play of ourselves, a communal dream," Oakley said. "That is, we each play ourselves, as we learned to do in the mind-shielded cave. And we define the scene to our liking so that we can manage reasonably well. We are going to meet Andromeda, the chained lady who is, on another level, also the Demoness of Change. She will be a lovely maiden in our play, and we will talk to her and try to come to a mutual understanding. With luck and grit, we may be able to save the galaxies from further mischief."

"We'll be playing by our rules, not hers," Ecstasy said. "That could make a significant difference."

"It could indeed," Oakley concurred.

Nydia looked around. "Agreed?"

"Do it," Lilith said, and the others nodded.

Nydia looked at the two Droms. "What's your opinion? This is your galaxy."

"We agree," Favew flashed, and Wavef's flash echoed his. "This is all our universe."

"Then let's get to it," Nydia said. She looked at Vinia. "Is there a safe place we can camp physically while we organize our mental realm?"

Vinia focused. "This way."

The changing path took them to a roiling lake that shifted in size and color as they looked at it, but seemed essentially stable, with an island in the center on which grew a ring of local trees. Vol produced a boat that they poled across the colored water to the island. Inside the ring of trees was a glade that seemed relatively immune to the changes. Perhaps the trees, in proximity to the Demoness, had evolved to be resistant to such effects. This would do.

They settled down in the tree circle. "Now the scene," Nydia said. "Remember, Rob will put us in it, so we will be able to interact telepathically. The point this time is not to hide our identities, but to establish our setting and bring Andromeda into it if she is amenable. Then we can interact with her on a vaguely even basis. Remember, she may appear ordinary, but she is a capital D Demoness, like a galaxy to us grains of sand. Maybe we can make our point and stop the carnage. If not, well, we tried our best." She took a breath. "Who has a suitable scene in mind?"

"What about this one?" Ecstasy said. "This island ring of trees. Expanded to include Andromeda, who can't be far distant, spatially."

"I like it," Oakley said. "Expand this little lake to the big sea where she awaits the monster."

"As with the legend we saw before," Noe said.

There was a murmur of agreement.

"Good enough," Nydia concurred. "Only this time, we're ourselves, bringing her into our framework. It's not exactly the same story, remember, just a setting we have in common."

"And this is our castle," Woe said, "from which we can see her, chained by the water."

"We're ready, Rob," Nydia said physically and mentally. "Make the scene."

For an answer, the turf on which they sat slowly transformed to stone tiles, and the ring of trees became a surrounding wooden wall complete with turrets. Rob had clearly seen many castles in his day, and knew their nature.

"Now picture yourselves in this scene," Nydia said. "Occupants of the castle, suitably garbed. Yourselves as you would be if you really lived here."

The members of the Quest grew clothing, medieval armor for the males, appealing gowns for the females, and fancy juvenile outfits for the children. The two Droms were included, becoming human figures. Their experiences in the Gilgamesh epic surely helped, because Favew looked like a battle-hardened warrior, while Wavef was a seductive maiden.

Lilith peered over a battlement. "I see her," she called. "The chained lady!"

The others went to join her, ascending the steps to the top of the wall. There below was the maiden, shackled at the edge of the turbulent sea, getting splashed. Her gown was wet and clinging to her shapely body, and her elegant hairdo was sodden. She looked like lovely misery incarnate.

And in the distance, something immense was in the sea, swimming toward them. That would be the monster.

It was just the scene they had crafted, and the Demoness might reject it, but Nydia felt for her. She had once played that role herself. "I must go to her," she said tersely.

"I will be your handmaid," Lilith said, assuming the garb of a servant. "I will bring you back if you faint."

"Uh, thank you." She had no intention of fainting, but this was uncharted territory.

"And the rest of us are at your beck," Ecstasy added.

Oakley nodded. He was letting her do her thing, available for whatever she might need of him. "Thank you—again," Nydia said to them all. It might be meaningless on the larger scale, but she appreciated all the support she could get. She was conscious that of the three nymphs who had started this adventure, she was the only one remaining in the scene. She was waaay out of her milieu. She was hardly lonely or frightened, but loneliness and fright were like that sea monster, stalking her, ready to pounce the moment she lost her mental footing.

But first she had galaxies to save. She had to act.

Nydia walked out of the castle and carefully navigated the devious path to the shore where the chained lady stood. Lilith followed. Flecks of spume from the heaving sea spattered against her, soon reducing Nydia to a similar state of dis-dress as Andromeda. Lilith was unaffected, not playing the game to that extent. "Hello, Princess!" Nydia called. "May we talk?"

The princess turned to her. "You do know there's a monster coming?" she called back. "He can swallow two or three maidens as readily as one."

So she was accepting the crafted scene. That was gratifying. "Yes. But we have a little time."

"A minute or an eon," Andromeda agreed. "Who are you?" She knew, of course, but was playing the game. That was an excellent sign. From a distance she had looked lovely. Up close, she was scintillating, her aspect constantly changing but always outstandingly beautiful.

"In this setting, I am the mistress of yonder castle," Nydia said. She gestured back at the circular wooden turrets. "In my real life, I am Nydia Nymph, created out of incidental material two years ago, who more or less blundered into a Quest to save our magical Land of Xanth and its larger framework from the vagaries of out-of-control Elements. They are being stirred by change, which is becoming too extreme to handle. Hence my visit here."

"I am the Mistress of Change," Andromeda agreed. "But I have a problem."

"Yes. In our mythology, your mother bragged so incessantly of her beauty that the god of the sea was annoyed and demanded your sacrifice. But that's just a story. What is it in reality?"

"It is Big Bang, the spirit of the origin of the universe, who learned of my nature and fears I represent a challenge in his dominance. This was not my intention, but he means to make sure by destroying me. He is the most powerful of all the Demons, and the others can't stand against him. So they determined that I must be sacrificed to appease him. They confined me here in the Void section of GEH to await his displeasure." She glanced at the monster, who was now significantly closer. "Time is largely irrelevant. I may be destroyed in an instant or in ten billion years, but my fate is sealed."

So the Demons interacted much like mortals. They craved power and acted to secure it when it was threatened. "The other Demons did this to you? That is not fair."

Andromeda smiled thinly. "Fair is a matter of opinion, and power determines its application. Bang has the ultimate power. I must be sacrificed. I do confess my regret."

"I must do something about this," Nydia said, discovering that she liked the Demoness. Nydia might be no more than a grain of sand before a galaxy, but for the moment, they were like equals. "I don't want to live in an unfair universe. I must talk to Bang and acquaint him with the error of his outlook."

Andromeda smiled the smile of one who must educate a small child about reality. "Bang brought the universe into existence thirteen or fourteen billion years ago by exploding equal masses of positive and negative substance that repelled each other, tearing the structure of nothingness asunder. It is still expanding. He means to see that this does not change. As he sees it, I represent a threat to his creation. Your commentary on fairness will not have the impact of a grain of sand against the universe, by definition. All you can do is go home and hope that Bang does not destroy me during your lifetime. If you annoy him now, he may act immediately. For your own sake, give this up."

"No," Nydia said firmly. "I did not come all the way here to throw away my mission." She turned to face the water. "Bang!" she called. "You big blob of nothing! Come here and assume mortal man–form so I can tell you why you're an idiot!"

Lilith started to dissolve into smoke, and even the Demoness seemed taken aback. Who in her right mind, or any mind at all, dared insult the ultimate power of the universe?

There was an angry roar. The monster had heard and understood her. He blasted fire from his nostrils and fairly flew across the sea toward them. The water boiled and steamed, and the seabed beneath it quaked. He was huge, the size of a bloated whale, all maw and teeth, and roiling storm clouds trailed him, emitting jags of lightning. If this manifestation was intended to be scary, it was succeeding.

Just as he was about to crash onto the beach, there was a clap of thunder that shook the scene, and he changed, becoming a handsome human man in a tuxedo. He ignored Andromeda and oriented on Nydia. "Speak your piece, nymph," he said with deceptive calm as he stepped across the surface of the surging wave. The very air around him quivered with the power of his being, and the scenery around him was wavering. Both Andromeda and Lilith stood as if about to be blown away.

Nydia knew this was make-or-break time for her. If she failed, the galaxies would suffer. If she succeeded, she could save Andromeda—and the order of existence as they knew it. So she plowed on, inspired by the way the alien girl Squid had persuaded the Demon Chaos to cease his war with the other Demons. "You are an idiot because you have got the situation exactly wrong. The Demoness of Change is not your destruction, she is your salvation. Change is the reality of existence itself. Without change, there is nothing worth having. The cessation of change is death. You started the universe by changing nothingness to positive and negative energy, and those energies are still expanding into the original emptiness. That's continuous change, the very fabric of reality. If you stop change, reality will collapse, and your own existence with it. Are you fool enough to do that?"

Bang stared at her, the churning clouds fading to wisps of vapor. "You speck of annoyance, you are actually making sense," he said, amazed. "I got it backwards."

"You bet you did! Fortunately, you can save the situation. Consider Andromeda, the Demoness of Change. There is nothing in your universe so lovely as Change. Do not reject her. Embrace her. Make her part of your reality so that the present order of flux will be maintained." She paused for breath as she turned to face the Demoness. "Look at her, you exploding conception! Can you even imagine more beauty?"

Indeed, Andromeda was shimmering with inherent change, radiating the shifting joy of her nature. It was phenomenal.

"No," Bang whispered in wonder. It seemed that he had picked up the suite of human emotions along with the appearance.

"So embrace her and kiss her to show your commitment to her. Do I have to tell you how to do that?"

"Yes," he breathed, his gaze fixed on the scintillating beauty before him.

This was actually Nydia's area of nymphly expertise. She seized it. "Step up to her." He did. "Put your arms about her gently." He did. The Demoness stood still in her aura of perpetual motion, not resisting. "Purse your lips." Again he obeyed. "Touch them to hers lightly. Make a little sucking motion." He did. "Feel her response. When the feeling is mutual, little hearts or the equivalent will fly out." This was all a mere simulation, but it was the focus of their interaction. It counted.

Suddenly there was a burst of mini explosions radiating out, each a forming universe. The manacle on the princess's ankle blew asunder. The two figures in the center detonation changed forms, still linked by the kiss, becoming different males and females, but always lovely and handsome and devoted to each other.

"You did it," Lilith murmured, awed.

"I had to." Nydia knew she would suffer her own noodle-kneed reaction later. Right now, she had to maintain a tight grip on the scene. It was figuratively everything or nothing. But in the background, she felt the Elements relaxing. The disturbance of Bang's explosive presence was fading.

"Better move it on," Lilith said, "lest they kiss for centuries, literally."

She was right. "And that's how you do it," Nydia concluded. "Now end the kiss and come join our group so we can teach you how to be routinely social when you're not on duty maintaining reality."

The kiss broke. The mini universes sailed off to colonize virgin emptiness. The two Demons turned to her, obeying her guidance. "Lead on," Andromeda murmured. She knew Nydia had just saved her and the universe.

"This way." Nydia turned and walked back up the path to the castle. The two Demons meekly followed, with Lilith trailing.

They entered the castle. The members of the Quest were there, standing at silent attention. They knew what had happened—indeed they had seen it happening—and were waiting on Nydia. She was, after all, the leader.

Onward. "Oakley, Ecstasy, take this newly formed couple and explain what follows kissing. Demonstrate if you need to. They must be fully informed."

Ecstasy took it in stride. "This way, please," she said, and led the way into their chamber. The door closed behind them.

When the rest of them were alone, as it were, Nydia explained her plan. "This is all a mere inset story, but the emotions can be real. Treat Bang and Andromeda like the honored guests they are. When they are satisfied, we shall wend our way home." She glanced at the children. "You have no idea what Oakley and Ecstasy are telling the visitors."

"None," Vinia and Woe Betide solemnly agreed almost together.

"I knew you could do it," Vol said. "You know how to handle lonely entities."

"It was mostly sheer luck and grit."

"And womanly intuition," Noe said. "And phenomenal nerve."

"I'm not sure who else could have done it," Lilith said.

"Oh, surely others could have—"

"Stop trying to fend off their compliments," Anthem said with an emphatic chord.

"She's right," Rob said mentally. "You really did save the universe. Accept it."

"It's true," Favew flashed. "This goes well beyond locale or species."

Nydia shut up.

In due course, Bang and Andromeda emerged, looking more than satisfied. "Thank you," the Demoness said, and hugged Nydia. She felt herself changing through multiple phases without losing her identity. It was the effect of the continual changes wrought by the Demoness.

Then Bang shook her hand, and Nydia felt the metaphoric impact of the expanding universe. "Thank you. You opened my eyes to a new reality."

"You're welcome," Nydia said weakly.

Then the two Demons held hands and quietly vanished. They surely had business on other levels of reality. The local play was done.

The return trip back through the five sections was relatively simple. There were no disturbances or threats, and they made good progress. The violence of the Elements had indeed subsided, and the natives were delighted. They picked up the couples they had left along the way and returned at last to the tunnel leading from GEH.

Nydia turned to their Drom friends, but before she could speak, Wavef flashed. "This is not parting. We are coming with you. We consider it to be our honeymoon."

So they had become a couple. "Congratulations," Nydia said.

"It's the least we could do to appreciate the universe you saved."

They entered the tunnel as a group, and in hardly a moment and a half were back at the outlying planetoid. The Elements provided air, water, and a comfortable temperature. Then they took the longer tunnel to the home galaxy and Xanth.

Where there was a welcoming party awaiting them.

Demoness Demesne appeared. "We knew you were coming," she said. "We felt the land relax, and the rogue elements settled down. That meant you had succeeded. We are vastly relieved, and you are certainly welcome at the Queendom of Thanx, all of you. We have prepared a suitable suite."

They walked toward the Queendom. The path wound past a pasture. There was a small, friendly bull. "You may come pet me," he said. "My name is Adora."

Nydia did so. "Isn't that a female name?"

"I am female, in a male body. I refuse to be cowed, so I focus on being nice."

Now she got it. *Adorable!* They were back in the land of puns. "At least you're not a loud audi bull."

"These are my friends," Adora said, indicating several sheep grazing nearby. "Thank Ewes. They are very grateful to be here."

Nydia groaned. It was good to be home!

Favew and Wavef flashed perplexity. "The Land of Xanth is largely made of puns," Nydia explained. "It's part of the magic."

It took a while to clarify the concept of puns. The two Droms were amazed. Noletta spied a bottle of shampoo. "I haven't washed my hair in ages!" she exclaimed.

"Don't," Demesne warned. "That's fake. It will poop your hair horribly." She took the bottle and opened it. A foul brown odor poured out. "Sham Poo."

"Oh," Noletta said, chagrined. "I've been away too long!"

Nerine spotted bean plants beside the path. "Coffee beans!" she exclaimed. "I'll harvest some for my next cup."

"They're black," Vinia said. "Caughee beans. They give perfect recollection, but with uncontrollable coughing."

"Bleep! I should have known. Good thing they're not invisibili tea plants."

They walked on. They came to a collection of pretty cushions laid out appealingly. "Oh, I'd like to sit down and rest my feet," Moonroe said.

Demesne laughed. "Don't. Those are reper cushions, comfortable to sit on, but uncomfortable when you get up."

He laughed ruefully. "Now I get it. Repercussions."

They rounded a curve. Suddenly there was music, and what appeared to be small loaves of bread sprouted little arms and legs and moved around in patterns. They paused, watching, mystified. What was it?

Anthem Ant laughed. "I recognize the music. That's abundance."

"That's what?" Nydia asked.

"Those are bread rolls. Buns, actually. It's a bun dance."

Nydia winced, suppressing a groan.

"Oh, look, what a nice coat," Noletta said.

"Don't touch it," Demesne warned. "That's a yellow jacket. Try to wear it and it will sting you like a nest of wasps."

Noletta frowned. "Oops!"

The path veered around what appeared to be an enormous heavy envelope. "I recognize that," Oakley said. "You push it to accomplish something."

There was a collective groan.

Nydia shook her head. They were definitely back in the land of puns.

The grand entrance to the Queendom came into view.

Then, to Nydia's amazement, Bang and Andromeda appeared, formally but not excessively dressed. "Introduce us, please," the Demoness said to Nydia. "We have a favor to ask."

What was going on? Nydia stifled her curiosity and did the job. "Demesne, this is Andromeda, the Demoness of Change, recently freed from confinement in the other galaxy. With her is Bang, Demon of Detonation, who is responsible for the explosion that started the universe." She turned to the couple. "This is Demesne Demoness, Queen of the Queendom of Thanx." Then back to Demesne. "They have a favor to ask of you."

Demesne was clearly taken half a step aback. But she had encountered Demons before, including Demon Chaos, so handled it with grace. "Any friend of Nydia's is a friend of ours. She saved Thanx from an uncomfortable squeeze. We will accommodate you if it is within our power to do so. What is your request?"

"We understand that you hold weddings here."

"We do, when our citizens want them."

"The two of us desire to get married. This is largely symbolic, as Demon affairs differ somewhat from mortal ones, but we plan on interacting further with mortals and will honor their conventions when associating with mortals. Can you provide the ceremony?"

"We shall be happy to. My husband Grossclout will officiate if you wish."

"Thank you." Andromeda glanced at Nydia. "I will need a Maid of Honor for the occasion. I hope you will agree to serve."

"Me?!" Nydia exclaimed, achieving two punctuation marks again. This was completely unexpected. "But I'm just a—"

"A friend who saved my existence."

Oh. She managed to jam the overwhelm mostly back into its mental compartment. "Yes, I will be honored to serve." She realized belatedly that Ecstasy had really educated the couple on social nuances.

The Demoness glanced back at the demoness. "My partner also has a request."

Demesne looked at Bang. "Yes?"

"Please set up an enclave where mortals, Elements, demons, and Demons can comfortably interact. That way we shall be able to visit without arousing uncomfortable repercussions. We will not stray from the enclave unless invited. It can be a place where beings who are not ordinarily part of the human community can relax and learn the ways of mortals."

Demesne nodded. "Like a Mundane fan convention, where fans, authors, and publishers interact on an equal basis. We shall be glad to do that. Access will have to be limited to prevent awkward intrusions, but visitors who qualify will be welcome. We'll call it Element Enclave."

"That will do." He took Andromeda's hand.

"Bye for now," the Demoness said, flipping Nydia a kiss with her free hand. They vanished.

Nydia relaxed. And fainted.

She woke lying on a bed where Vol had just set her down. "I'm so sorry," she said. "I thought I had it under control. So much happened so fast! I didn't mean to embarrass you. I'm sorry I messed up. I just—"

He shut her up by kissing her. That covered it. He had picked up pretty well on social conventions himself.

She sat up on the bed. And saw something. A flicker in the air, akin to the spirits of the Elements before they were conjured into the ectoplasm figurines. Was it a ghost? What would a ghost be doing here?

"Uh—"

He looked. "A female spirit. Some get lost in the Void."

Nydia went back into Decision Mode. "We'd better check this out.

Maybe there's a contingent of lady ghosts in Thanx, but if so, they should have their own residence. Something's wrong."

They checked with Vinia. "Let me see it," the girl said. "We do have ghosts here, but they're friendly and don't try to spook folks. This may be a newcomer."

Back at the room, the flicker remained. "It's green," Vinia said. "It does seem to be unfamiliar."

They checked out the other rooms of the suite, Vinia zeroing in with her paths focused on ghosts. There turned out to be six ghosts, and they did not belong to the local ghost contingent. They were strangers, and they had appeared just a few days ago. No one had died recently in the Queendom, so it was a mystery.

Vol produced a spirit translator. It was amazing, the variety of lost things that existed in his domain. He set it up in their room and turned it on. "Now talk to her," he told Nydia.

"Hello, lady ghost," Nydia said. It wasn't as if she had never talked to a spirit before. "I am Nydia. Who are you and why are you here?"

The ghost was startled. "You're talking to me!"

"Yes. This is a translator. We were assigned this room to stay the night, but it seems you're already here. Why?"

"I am LeeAnne. I was leading a tourist group through the wilderness when a rogue dragon pounced and ate all six of us before we could pro-test. We are not used to being dead, so we made our way to the closest community, which is this one. We're hesitant to contact the local ghosts, who might think we're intruding on their territory. So we're just sort of in limbo here, not knowing what to do."

"The dragon!" Nydia echoed. Suddenly her outfit became that of a warrior woman, and her sword was in her hand. Wanda Wand and Knight Knife had heard the word. Then they realized it was a false alarm and faded. "That must be the one we avoided when we visited the Queendom before."

"It must be," LeeAnne agreed.

"Let me consult." Nydia raised her voice to ceiling height. "Oakley! I think I need your advice."

In barely two moments, Oakley and Ecstasy arrived. "We have six ghosts," Nydia said. "Victims of the dragon we three original nymphs avoided. They don't know what to do, and neither do we. Is there an obvious answer we are missing?"

"Obviously," he agreed. "Did the Good Magician not promise you nymphs souls upon the completion of your mission, so you could be complete people? Ghosts are the manifestation of lost souls. Why wait on the Magician when you have perfectly good souls here for the taking? They should be happy to have lives again."

Amazed, Nydia looked at LeeAnne. "How do you feel about this?"

"He's right," the ghost said. "We'd love to live again."

"But our lives are surely different from the ones you had before. We have other relationships, other passions, other memories. It would be a whole new framework for you."

LeeAnne floated closer. "Any lives would be better than being dead! I would merge with you now and live your life with you if you were willing. So would my companions."

Nydia glanced at Vol. "Would you still want me if I had a soul?"

"I would want you if you had ten souls, as long as you remained you."

Someone had to be the first to try this out. To determine via experience whether this was viable. To take the enormous risk of a mistake. That, it seemed, was her role as the leader. "Then join me, LeeAnne, if you want to."

The ghost floated up to her and surrounded her. Then it sank into her, and she felt the sheer exhilaration of completeness. For the first time in Nydia's existence, she was whole. She remembered from the template some of the Good Magician's words. "Only those with souls care about them." Now she cared.

Nydia turned to Vol and kissed him. She felt his body transform as her new soul lapped over him. Her emotion magnified immensely. Her love for him had been like a nova. Now it was a supernova.

Glorious! LeeAnne thought. Nydia sensed LeeAnne's exhilaration as she felt physical limbs and body processes again after losing them. Breathing and heartbeat. Physical sight and sound, and touch on skin. Smell. Taste. Pressure of natural functions in process. As a ghost, she had felt nothing physical, only the vast bleak loss of life.

And now the appeal of the appreciation of a man. LeeAnne had missed that most of all.

"Glorious," Anthem Ant echoed with a resonant twang. "Now you are Woman Prime."

Nydia broke the kiss. "And now we must see to the others."

They saw to the others. Soon Noletta joined with a fiery-tempered soul, and Nerine took one who was familiar with the sea. Three down.

But three ghosts remained. What of them?

"Have you two Droms considered taking on souls?" Oakley asked.

The two deliberated, then decided to gamble. Favew took the male, and Wavef took the female. It was clearly a revelation for both, and for the souls, but a joyous one.

And the child. "I'll take her," Woe Betide said.

"But you're a demon," Nydia reminded her. "Demons don't have souls."

But the child was already merging with the willing spirit. "So I am the very first demon with a soul," Woe said, satisfied. She seemed very human.

So all the ghosts were gone. All were now alive again, and more than satisfied to be so.

Demesne appeared at the door. "I am embarrassed," she said. "Our staff got the wrong suite for you. This one is haunted."

Nydia gazed at her with the full authority of a souled woman. "Not anymore."

Author's Note

Each novel I write is its own adventure, personally as well as fictively. Two novels ago, Carol, my wife of sixty-three years, died, and I distracted myself from my grief to an extent by burying myself in Xanth. One novel ago I remarried, knowing I couldn't bear to live alone. Thus came MaryLee. I am old, close to eighty-eight as I write this, and thought I was in good shape. This novel, well, I completed the first draft. Next day I suffered violent shakes as my fever rocketed to 102 degrees Fahrenheit. Yes, it was the Virus, COVID-19, surely the latest variant at the time, BA.5. I had had my preventive shots, and we wore masks religiously when leaving the house and practiced social distancing. But the Virus has become more cunning as it goes, finding new avenues to score. It doesn't help that other folk, tired of restrictions, preferred to pretend the pandemic was over. Ninety percent of those we encountered were maskless while the carnage continued. The Florida government was no help; rather than enforce sensible precautions, it tried to hide the figures, and actively discouraged schools from protecting their students. Amazing folly! When it comes to craziness, Florida yields to no other state.

For the past seventy years I have lived a healthy vegetarian lifestyle, eating well, taking supplements, staying lean, and seriously exercising. But fate got at me anyway. During this novel, I came down with a heart condition. It seemed that the timing of my heartbeats went askew, so that the upper chamber did not completely clear the blood passing through. The risk there was that some of the delayed blood could stagnate and form a clot. If that clot then got out, it could land somewhere dangerous, such as the brain, causing a stroke. There was also a flutter, rapid pulse, and high pressure. Mischief indeed! Suddenly I was put on $600-a-month medication to regularize the beat, reduce the pressure, eliminate the flutter, and thin the blood to prevent that threatened clot. It reminds me of the old "shut up" jokes, one of which was "Mommy, mommy, what's a vampire?" "Shut up, kid, and eat your soup before it clots." The medication seems to be taking effect; my pressure is down, my beat is normal, my blood oxygen level is very good, and I'm hoping that no clot is forming.

Not that all is otherwise well. I have on occasion remarked on how I have zero belief in the supernatural, though I earn my living from it. That is, I write fantasy, this novel being an example. That disbelief annoys the supernatural, so it does its best to get back at me in little ways, especially now. Bright blood appeared in my right eyeball, slowly spreading. No pain—just, well, an eyesore. After a few days, it faded. My nose dripped constantly, not badly, just enough to annoy. I developed incontinence. I had an intermittent sore throat, making swallowing painful. I felt either too hot or too cold, having to constantly remove or add clothing. I slept and slept, day and night. I suffered bad fits of coughing. I had wild dreams that made no sense when I woke. One was of the writer Herman Wouk. (What did Herman do after he fell asleep? Herman Wouk.) One of our air conditioners developed drips, chronically flooding the floor, and several times a day, I had to sponge up small buckets full of water and dump them down the toilet. We lock up the house each night; one day the key worked, but then would not release—it refused to leave the lock. I tried it every day, and after a week, suddenly it let go. No explanation. My main computer has a useful feature, "recent documents," one of the options I use each morning to load my working files for the day. One day it refused to give me that menu. Everything else was there, just not that. I had to struggle to work around it so that I could get my work done. After a few days, it was back. MaryLee is not strong physically; normally we grocery shop together, and I push her around on "the contraption," a wheeled seat attached to a shopping basket so she can shop without dropping. When the Virus made me stay home, she had to shop alone. Normally there are personnel to help out. But this time there was nothing; it was as though she had become invisible. She had to bag the groceries herself, load them in the basket, trundle them out to the car, load them into it, and drive home, worn out. It took her days to recover. I was not amused by her treatment. Fate likes to toy with me, but I still refuse to believe in the supernatural, so the war continues.

And of course, it wasn't better on the global scene. During my writing of this novel, Russia invaded Ukraine, committing savage atrocities and threatening those who disapproved. Any claim Russia has to being a civilized nation is now moot. The US Supreme Court overthrew Roe v. Wade, allowing states to outlaw abortion, and other long-term precedents are following. Real mischief is brewing as democracy as we know it is compromised. I am reminded of the Chinese curse "May you live in interesting times." These are indeed interesting times.

I normally include pages of reader suggestions and puns in each Xanth novel, but this time I lacked the gumption to do more than a few. Heart complications and the Virus depressed me. Sorry about that. A fair number needed more play than could be accommodated in this novel, so have to wait for the next, #49, whose title seems to be *Knickelpede Knight*, featuring a scholarly nickelpede who sets out to map the Land of Xanth—you know, all the nickelpede mounds, ant hills, dragon dens, mermaid pools, centaur stables, elf elms, and oh, yes, human towns—before things complicate. It'll be wild, even for Xanth. Yes, some of the present characters will be involved, like Anthem Ant and Noe Human and maybe a couple of newly married Demons.

And the assorted credits for reader suggestions.

Credits:
Gas cap, Abundance—Cal Humrich
Ein Stein, Push the Envelope—Jim Loy
nickelpedes have five scents—David Seltzer
Com Pewter's Smart Phone makes smart remarks—Robert Blaut
book blank except for last chapter—Jack Goldstein
Pat, Colleen, Quintessa—Kate Brooks
The Game—Amanda Plageman
Poplar and unpoplar trees; necromance—Richard van Fossan
Orchard Mantis—Benjamin Talon Diegmann
Foot of the bed—Mary Rashford
Sun gets a corona virus; thank ewes—Tim Bruening
Corona injection, cow jumped over the moon, the elemental Droms—MaryLee Jacob
Udder failure—Stephen Hendry

Moonshine, Sunshine, Earthshine—James Blakeney
Abacuss—George Pope
Character with autism—Kimberly Johnson
Encyclonepedia—Nora Cook
Air Show, Peep Show, Road Show—Pasquale Lerro
Have a cow on the moon, for all the cheese—Emily Mateka
Shampoo—Julie Brady
Reper Cushions—Douglas Brown
Caughee Bean—Andra Genius
Invisibili-tea—Thomas Pfarrer
Yellow Jacket—Guinevere Stoops

And my credit to my proofreaders, Scott M. Ryan, Doug Harter, and Avi Ornstein. Errors seem to grow on the page after my editing, but my proofers catch them.

If you enjoyed this novel and want to know more of me, you can check my website at www.HiPiers.com, where I have news of my career, a character database, do a monthly blog-type column, and maintain an ongoing survey of electronic publishers and related services for the benefit of aspiring writers. I do try to help others in my fashion.

Until we meet again, next novel . . .

About the Author

Piers Anthony is one of the world's most popular fantasy writers, and a *New York Times*-bestselling author twenty-one times over. His Xanth novels have been read and loved by millions of readers around the world, and he daily receives letters from his devoted fans. In addition to the Xanth series, Anthony is the author of many other bestselling works. He lives in Inverness, Florida.

THE XANTH NOVELS

FROM OPEN ROAD MEDIA

OPEN ROAD

INTEGRATED MEDIA

INTEGRATED MEDIA